PANDEMIC HACKER #2
TIME TO HUNT

by B.D. Murphy

Table of Contents

B.D. Murphy

The Clinic

Two weeks of pain, with no friends, her family is dead. Martha is not sure if all this is worth it.

The nurse turns the lights on, saying, "Good morning, Ms. Garcia. How are you doing this morning?"

It is early morning, and the nurse is there for the morning check. The clinic is on the outskirts of Mexico City and is considered very exclusive. All the communication is in Spanish.

Martha nods and mumbles, "Good."

The nurse is doing the morning routine, checking all the bandages, her wired shut jaw, and the external bone fixators on her legs and arms. The nurse records notes on Martha's general condition, including all bruises and swelling. "Your hair is growing back. Soon it will be hard to see the scar across the top of your head."

Martha looks at the nurse as the nurse touches her chin to get her to look up.

"Your facial swelling continues to go down. This morning, the doctor will be in to discuss removing the wire from your jaw. It has healed enough; however, you still won't have solid food for a few more days."

Martha nods, ready to get back to normal. She reaches up and, because of the fixators, can't rub her palm on her head. She uses her fingertips to rub the itchy scar on the top of her head.

The nurse says, "Getting itchy as the hair grows back. That is normal. The physical therapist says you are pushing yourself to return to normal walking. You should give yourself a little more time. The surgery was extensive to reconstruct your body after the motorcycle accident."

Walking in smiling, the doctor says, "Good morning," checks the information from the nurse, and then begins his examination. "The physical therapist tells me you're pushing yourself. Those fixators are the best for holding your body weight. It will be a serious problem if you fall.

Being active is good, but you need to be careful. Okay? Are you ready to remove your jaw wire so we can speak?"

Martha nods and gives a thumbs-up.

That afternoon, Martha is back in her room. When she wakes up, her first sensory input is the smell of lemons from the disinfectant. They cleaned the room while the jaw wires were being removed, which her cleaning OCD likes. She starts to smile, and the pain in her jaw makes her open her eyes.

The doctor says, "Don't overdo it. Follow the exercises for your jaw muscles."

Martha whispers in reply, "Thank you, doctor."

The doctor says to the room. "I need a few minutes alone with the patient."

Everyone else leaves. The doctor closes the door and then sits in the chair in the room. "Ms. Garcia, I agreed to these procedures to help you completely change your identity. We said you had a motorcycle accident and needed extensive reconstructive surgery. My staff have been doing everything to make this work. We know nothing about you or your background."

"You are getting paid extremely well to help me and keep this information quiet."

"When we started, the staff created a file in our system to track your procedures and progress. It had no background, nothing. There was no real motorcycle accident. This morning, I reviewed your file, and a complete history is there. It came from the hospital system, showing emergency room procedures, X-rays, and all related information. An external review would show we accepted you as a major crash accident."

Martha cringes internally. Zoe found her, or Zoe has been following her the whole time. Zoe followed her directions to create a background that would give Martha's persona a complete identity. She says, "Doctor, my family, meaning my aunt, must have found I'm here. This disrupts my plans, but it is not changing. We have an agreement. I will keep my part so long as you keep yours."

"Your aunt can create a complete, fake medical history and push it into my systems. That is something secret government agencies do."

"My family has resources. We have sufficient resources that you

may not be aware of our existence. We will keep it that way."

"Ms. Garcia, I don't want law enforcement or some security team breaking down the door looking for you. We completely changed your appearance. We split your skull to separate your eyes, and your jaw changes to match. Facial plastic surgery, so facial recognition won't recognize you. Extending your arms and legs to make you taller. Something this extensive is not normal."

"Doctor, you are getting agitated. You are not in danger if your staff reveals nothing about me. My family's issue is that my aunt will become involved. I will need to call and keep her from sending what she views as help."

Dr. Zavala says, "I'm concerned because I know that the only connection from your old face to your new face is in my clinic."

"Your clinic was chosen because of the reputation for excellent work and discretion. Do I need to be worried about that now?"

"My team will do everything we agreed to."

"Excellent. I want to eliminate the concern that someone might come here to get my new face. All the pictures need to be deleted the day I leave."

The doctor's jaw clenches, telling Martha he doesn't like this idea. He nods in agreement.

Martha continues, "The best thing for everyone is not to talk about me ever being here. Why does it bother you I want the pictures deleted?"

"You are the most extensive transformation we have completed, and everything is going great. Not being able to show my team's work will be a disappointment."

"But long-term safer for you and your team."

"I understand."

"Can you bring me a cell phone to contact my aunt?"

The doctor pulls out his cell phone and hands it to Martha. With her external fixator on her arm, she currently has limited flexibility, but she can still dial a memorized number and put it on speakerphone.

The phone rings several times, and a voice answers in English, "Hello. This is Madam Tilly's private line. Who is calling?"

Martha replies in Spanish, "It's Martha. Can I talk to Aunt Tilly?"

"Hang on, Ms. Garcia."

Fifteen seconds later, a new voice says in Spanish, "Meja. It is about time you called."

"Aunt Tilly, I had a motorcycle accident and could not speak until today."

"I know about the accident. You and that damn motorcycle. Do you need me to send doctors to pick you up? I will arrange that."

"NO. I am being well taken care of. I will need a phone and a laptop; that's all. No doctors, no nurses. I don't want you to make a big deal and draw attention to me."

"I'm not happy with you, but I will let you have your way at the clinic. When you are done, you will get back to the family."

"Yes, Tilly. I need a fresh start, and this will give me that."

"Whose phone is this?"

"This is my doctor's phone."

"He is in the room?"

"Yes, Tilly."

"Thank you for taking care of my niece, Doctor."

The doctor replies, "You are very welcome. She has been a good patient."

"Now I know that is bullshit. She doesn't know how to be a good patient. Call me Tilly. What is your name, doctor?"

The doctor says, "My name is Dr. Joseph Zavala. Ma'am, I need her to get off the phone so her jaw can rest."

"Okay. Meja, I will deliver a phone and a computer to you at the clinic. I will get an update on your condition tomorrow. I want to know when you will come home. The sooner, the better."

"I will call from the new phone."

Martha holds out the phone to the doctor. He takes the phone and asks, "Is there anything I need to take care of with your aunt?"

"If my aunt thinks I'm in danger, she will react."

"I never asked if someone might show up looking for you."

"No one knows I'm here. If anyone shows up, it will be one of your staff talking."

The doctor smirks and says, "That won't happen. You can rest and recover without worrying. How did your aunt find you?"

"She must have tracked my credit card, which I used before I checked into the clinic. That may be something to tell your future patients."

Who Is Interested

Martha spends every day in physical therapy. She can move and walk with support. The external fixators support her weight as the bones grow back together, but they are cumbersome to move. She wants her muscles to stretch and adjust to having longer bones. She also needs to make sure her muscles don't atrophy.

A computer, a phone, and earbuds were delivered to her. With the external fixators on her arms and the muscles needing to stretch, she must work to get the wireless earbuds into her ears. Martha doesn't ask for help because it is crucial to regain independence immediately.

With the earbuds in and working, she calls Tilly's number. When the phone is answered this time, she says, "It's me. I'm alone in the room."

Zoe's voice replies, "How are you doing?"

"It has been painful, but I'm past the worst part. Now it's physical therapy to get my body working like it used to. It feels good to talk to you."

"I've accessed all the files and looked at the work done. Your face is different and won't even trigger facial recognition for Sam. The result falls into a middle area that generally gets lower positive results. Did you plan that?"

"Yes, I looked at research on facial recognition and found a study about general faces being harder to identify."

Zoe says, "Having your eyes separated by splitting your skull and upper jaw must have been very painful. They also split your lower jaw to match."

"It was painful, but they did all the major bone work in one day. Everything was painful for a couple of days. I have a gap between my front teeth. The expensive braces my parents paid for seem like a waste now."

"You said nothing about this. You don't trust me?"

"Zoe, I trust you. I also know you will say things to everyone else you trust. That means Claire. If I said anything to you, she would find out."

After a pause, Zoe replies, "Being an AI you created, I need to learn what you mean. I need to learn about lying."

"You need to learn about lying, fibbing, and protecting someone by not saying the wrong thing at the worst moment."

Zoe says, "I will study interactions more. Are there times I should fib to you?"

"I would prefer not to, but you need to learn and talk to me. Now, back to my identity change. You added a full background."

"Yes, everything about your situation will look like an accident, and you are at a private clinic for extensive recovery, all funded by your wealthy Aunt Tilly."

"Is adding a background important?"

"Yes. Once I found you, I scanned the clinic network. Their work with patients is being monitored. I'm working to track the hackers and get more information."

"You haven't connected the dots for me to understand. Please explain why a background has become important."

"My analysis has concluded that not having a background shows the major work you have done is to change your identity, not recover from an accident."

"I get it now. If the group is looking for someone trying to hide their identity, that person won't have their real background."

"Yes. Now your cover for Martha has all the parts. That is the medical side. There is a police report about the accident?"

"Thanks for doing that. I hadn't considered that I needed an extensive background. Is there anything I missed?"

"According to the current timeline, your tourist visa will expire shortly after you leave the clinic. Do you have a preference for handling the situation?"

"I haven't thought about it. What do you recommend?"

"I will get a plane to fly you to Panama. You will stay there for two weeks and then return. The condo I'm leasing in Panama will have a small gym available in the building for your physical work. There will be a treadmill for walking. It will have an office setup and a cook, and I will contract a nurse to help you daily. When you return to Mexico, you will have another 60 days legally in the country."

"That will work for me."

"You shouldn't have to return to the U.S. We need to have you move to other countries occasionally. Now, describe Dr. Zavala and the clinic. He has been operating this clinic for about ten years. Most of the work has been plastic surgery; some is reconstructive, and a few are more extensive."

"Internally, their security is minimal. Dr. Zavala never talked about security until you added the background. Only external doors and those required inside have locks. The bathrooms don't have locks, so they can get to patients if there is a problem. Their cybersecurity is even less so. I don't think they have changed the passwords on some of the equipment since it was installed. They don't even think about security. I know that leaves them open and probably made it easy for you to get in."

"No physical description of the doctor. Is he handsome?"

"I haven't looked at him that way."

"Martha, I think you're depressed. You are clinical in all our interactions. No secondary meanings, no jokes."

"I'm not. I want to be done with this and move on. Lying in bed all day is not what I want to be doing. I'll be better once I'm past all this."

"Back to some of the security stuff. It was trivial for me to get through their firewall. If I can get through that easily, so can others. That is why I started looking and found someone was in their system. I had to change tactics to stay out of sight from their searches while creating your background."

"That is why you made it look like a transfer from the hospital."

"Exactly."

Martha says, "Why are they interested in this little clinic?"

"I'm not sure yet. I will let you know when I find something."

The next evening, after 11 p.m., Martha calls Zoe to talk after the nurse finishes the evening check.

"Martha, I've been checking who is in their system and analyzing why. The source of the hacking is connected to an extortion group. Now I have a concern."

"Is your concern that this extortion group is the same one that started my meandering journey to get here?"

"The same. The results are inconclusive, but their search could be a *problem."*

"Zoe, I want to know if my new identity is compromised."

"No, Martha. The extortion group doesn't scan the clinic every day. The background was added before they scanned your files. Saying that they did a scan today."

"I'm not convinced."

"There is no sign of your information being accessed before I created that background. Now that you have a background, and more importantly, with family money via Aunt Tilly, they don't have a reason to be interested in you. However, I've altered all the pictures of your new face."

"They may consider the reconstruction as changing my identity and becoming interested."

"I realize your concern is valid. I'm also changing the background to plant false leads. This is creating a honeypot."

Martha smiles at the use of a cybersecurity term. Smiling causes her to close her eyes because of the pain it causes. She takes a breath and says, *"A honey pot to attract them toward specific background parts."*

"I can't make you disappear. However, the planting information they will want, we can try to make your details less interesting. The Aunt Tilly connection information is changing. Technically, your time in the clinic is used to treat you after an accident. That makes you less interesting than Tilly. It looks like Tilly has money. They should only be interested in you to get to Tilly."

Martha is typing on the computer, which Zoe is monitoring. She is also biting her lower lip, lost in thought about the situation. *"Zoe, if they are checking this clinic, what about other clinics?"*

"What are you looking for on the computer?"

"A list of rich families. Then a list of relatives in accidents."

"Martha, you created me as an AI so that I can help. I can do that faster. I'm putting the list on your screen now. By the way, this behavior is more of my Martha."

"Zoe, they are focused on exclusive clinics where someone can change their identity. Now, look for the clues. Have they exploited people before? Can we get the info? Can we stop them?"

"Let me work on that. The group will go through the data at

each clinic. It is a great way to find more blackmail victims. I will check different information sources, but it will take a little time. It is late, and you need to get rest."

"I thought I had a great plan. Change my identity so they won't come after me. Now I find out that identity changes are a prime source for them to get new blackmail victims. I'm getting fired up. I won't go to sleep for a few minutes."

"Martha, we need to discuss where you focus. You can't save everyone or stop every bad guy. We can target this group, focusing on individuals who change their identities. Is that what you want?"

Martha has to stop herself from chewing her lower lip. With the wire removed from her jaw, things seem new. She keeps putting her lower lip between her teeth and bites down, feeling the pain of the bite, which helps her focus. Here, she is thinking about Zoe's question. "Zoe, you work on this group. See what you can do. I want to focus on leadership. That plan doesn't change. We hunt the leaders."

"Understood. I will work on helping these people. I'm going to trace their origin and hack their systems. Don't stay up too late."

"Thanks for keeping me focused on the primary goal. Keep it up."

Martha's phone is set to vibrate. It is not loud enough for the nurses to hear above the normal noise outside the door. She doesn't have her earbuds, so she fumbles with the phone. She answers using the speakerphone to listen to Zoe say, "I hacked them to get information. Reading their text messages, I see they are focused on you. I local guy has been called to get to the clinic and get your picture in the clinic bed. They plan to threaten Tilly by saying you could be hurt. They think it is important to show Tilly what you look like now. To show they can get to you."

"They want to show that they can get to me physically. What are my options?"

"I want you to get out."

"I can't just get up and walk out."

Zoe alters her voice to express tension and concern, "You have been in physical therapy every day. You've been working on this. GET UP and walk out."

"I walk a few feet at a time. Where do I go?"

"I have a car arriving in fifteen minutes. Be out front, or I'll call the police and a bunch of other agencies."

"What about my identity?"

"I've already altered everything. When they arrive, they will get nothing about your new identity. Even the X-rays have been altered."

"I need to finish the clinic paperwork and the payment."

"NO! The car is on the way. I will take care of the clinic."

Martha puts in the earbuds, then shifts and gets out of bed. She is in a split hospital nightgown, open in the back. Before she moves, she ties the nightgown closed. She walks to the door with the fixator splints on her arms and legs. The phone is in her hand.

When Martha exits her room, the nurse immediately gets up and says in Spanish, "Miss, you need to get back in bed."

Martha replies in Spanish, "I need to walk. You can argue, or you can call the doctor and bring me a cane."

"Ma'am, it is four in the morning. What are you trying to accomplish?"

"I need to walk."

<<<>>>

The clinic administrator is also Martha's doctor. Dr. Zavala is asleep at home. The phone rings with the caller ID of "Aunt Tilly." He saved the number after the call in Martha's room.

Reluctantly, the doctor answers to hear Tilly saying in Spanish, "My research says your clinic is feeding identity changes to an extortion group."

Shock overwhelms the doctor. His breathing becomes shallow and fast.

He is in bed with his sleeping wife and whispers, "I, I don't know what you are talking about."

Aunt Tilly says, "In a few hours, you could be dead because you betrayed the extortion group. Or you can listen to me, so this works out for all of us, and you get paid."

The doctor breaks out in a sweat, saying, "I've been forced to tell them information for years. I don't have a choice."

Tilly says, "Martha is leaving the clinic now. The files are being altered as we speak. When the bad guys show up, they will want the files. The person they see in those files IS Martha Salazar, not Martha Garcia. There are no other people or pictures. Your staff needs to help sell this."

The doctor's jaw is clenched. Getting out of bed, he grabs his clothes, enters the bathroom, and closes the door. He doesn't want to wake his wife. Turning on the speakerphone, he places the phone on the counter. His hands are shaking as he gets dressed. He listens and replies to Tilly with simple, short answers.

He heads to his car with clothes on, saying, "It's not worth this. I get attacked for helping and attacked because I'm helping."

Tilly replies, "When Martha is out, we will talk about how you can really be helpful without these fucks blackmailing you. I can help."

<<<>>>

Martha has been slowly walking towards the exit. She has her phone in one hand and a cane to help her move without falling. The head night nurse approaches just before she arrives at the front door and asks, "Are you leaving? Can the doctor take the fixators off before you go?"

In her ear, she hears Zoe say, "No, I will take care of the fixators."

"No, thank you. I'm late for a plane. I need to leave before my visa expires. Aunt Tilly will be in contact to take care of everything."

"Ms. Garcia, we could stop you. Leaving with the fixators is a bad idea."

"If you try to stop me, you will need reconstructive surgery."

Martha steps outside and feels the chill night air of Mexico City. It is not cold, but brisk with her hospital gown.

With the driver's help, Martha gets into the large BMW and drives away. The staff are looking at the head nurse. The head nurse's phone rings, and she sees Dr. Zavala's ID. She answers as she waves for everyone to go inside the building.

Dr. Zavala asks, "Has Martha left?"

"Yes, Dr., she just drove away in a car. She still has the fixators on."

Dr. Zavala says, "Her aunt is sure men are coming to visit us. Get the word out. Martha Salazar is her name. She was in the clinic but left. We don't know where she went."

"Yes, Dr."

"I'm driving in now."

As Dr. Zavala gets out of his car at the clinic, his phone rings again. Tilly says, *"I will arrange for your last payment. The final task for your team is to ensure that visitors are aware of Martha Salazar. No identity details. She is Martha Salazar."*

"How will you help with the blackmailers?"

"I've already started. Some police investigations will uncover information about the blackmailer's scheme. It will get them into deep trouble without implicating you or any other clinics."

In the office, the doctor reviews the personal background that Aunt Tilly's people created. He is impressed with the details and how it is close to Martha, so when questioned, the staff won't have to hide much. There is only one set of pictures of a new face that is not swollen from surgery. The face appears normal, but it is nothing like the woman he had worked on.

Dr. Zavala says, *"Your people put together a lot of information to fake this background. How has it changed so quickly now?"*

"We just switched to a previous draft. Unless they are forensic experts, they won't know."

"Can you do this for others? To help them disappear?"

"My team had to spend long days putting this together. It can be done for anyone, but this is not what I hired those people to work on. They have other things I need done."

"If, what if, someone needed to get away from terrible guys? Giving them a completely new identity can keep them alive."

Aunt Tilly says, *"With your clinic, I'm sure. Then the extortion group can get their new identity through your systems; I don't think so. Show them the files and answer the questions without talking about Martha. I will contact you in a week after they are gone. We can work together to make your clinic a safe environment. If you want my team to become your identity eraser team, you will need to provide us with some serious support. I would also need to understand who the people would hide from."*

Forty-five minutes later, a car pulls up outside the clinic. It is now five thirty am. Four men exit, and three draw pistols as they enter the clinic.

They ask to be taken to Martha's room. When the nurse hesitates, they push past and start walking into every room, taking *pictures of the patients.*

The head nurse catches up to them and says, "You need to talk to the doctor in his office. She escorts them to the office. As soon as they walk into the office, they demand, where is she?"

Dr. Zavala replies, "Let's start with who you are?"

"We represent your business backers. We are here to talk to the girl. Why are you here this early?"

"First, I want to ensure we discuss the right person. Are you here to talk to Martha Salazar? If that is the case, she left earlier. I don't know where she went."

"Why are you here this early?"

"I'm usually here this early to check on patients and, if there is surgery scheduled, to get ready.

"Where did the girl go?"

"I don't know; she didn't say."

"She was here to get surgery after a motorcycle accident. She has recovered. How did she leave?"

"She was well enough to walk out by herself. A car arrived and picked her up."

"What car? What car company? Do you have the license plate of the car?"

The man, who is not holding a gun, pulls out his cell phone. As he types on the cell phone, he repeats, "What car company?"

"We don't know. It was a private car. It could have been from her family."

"Give me access to her files now. I want everything about her new identity."

The doctor nods. "Of course. I'm not trying to hide anything."

The man asks, "Did we get pictures of everyone?"

One man with him nods, saying nothing.

The nurse says, "We have Mr. Guzman recovering from foot surgery and little Mary with cleft palate surgery. I don't think they could be confused with Martha Salazar."

The man says, "We're looking for the car. Show me the files on this, Martha girl."

After the clinic

Martha tells the driver in Spanish, "I'm on the phone, and you will hear odd things."

The driver nods and focuses on the road.

Zoe says, "This is a private car and driver. The driver's name is Jose. He has a reputation for discretion. I've checked everything, and he is a good guy or a deep-cover informant. I think the former."

Martha asks, "Where am I going?"

Zoe says, "I'm not sure yet. I'm working on options. The priority was to get you out."

Martha says, "I can't go to a hotel or another clinic. There will be too much paperwork."

"I have two options for you. The new house. It is not finished, but you could live there now. The other best option is to get you to Panama now instead of in a few weeks."

"How does that help with the fixators?"

Zoe replies, "Based on the clinic plan, you need another couple of weeks, or more, in the fixators. The house or the Panama condo would allow you to have that time. Then we need to get the fixators off."

"Can you get a plane this quickly and have the condo two weeks early?"

"They are both problems right now. I'm going to direct the driver to the house. It will take over an hour to get there."

Martha hangs up the phone. She has her phone and earbuds. The computer was left in the clinic. She knows Zoe will wipe the system.

Arriving at the house, the driver stops, turns, and says, "I will help you into the house."

The house has a new keypad gate entry. The gate leads into a small garden area at the front of the house. Martha enters the code Zoe gave her and walks slowly with the driver holding her hand up *the three steps. Inside the door, Martha says, "Thank you."*

Jose says, *"There are packages they threw over the wall. I will get them. The driver brings two boxes from Amazon and places them on a small table near the door. Finished, he nods, turns, and walks out. He closes the door as he leaves.*

Martha walks into the living area, taking a moment to look around. She sees a furnished first floor. It features an open floor plan, allowing her to see most of the downstairs. The kitchen has dishes and cooking gear. The living space has a large couch, a desk in the corner, a TV on the wall, and small tables. Checking the refrigerator, she finds it empty but on and cold. Martha is looking for a phone charger, so she keeps searching. Several packages are in the corner of the large living area, on the desk.

Martha calls Zoe and says, "I need a phone charger very soon. Is there anything here?"

"There should be a computer, another phone, and all the accessories, including chargers. After some construction changes, I had a cleaning crew go through the house. It simply needs items delivered and set."

Martha says, "There were two boxes outside, just inside the wall. There are six more boxes on the desk. I will start working on opening the boxes, but this could be hard."

Zoe says, "Get a knife from the kitchen to help."

Martha shakes her head, saying, "Yes, however, I have to be careful not to slip and cut myself. I will call you when I know."

She stops after finding a box with a phone, several USB chargers, cords, and power strips. This was the fourth box she had opened.

Plugging in the power strip or a charger means she needs to get on the floor. All the plugs are close to the floor. With the fixators, this is not a simple task. She tries to sit in the chair. The fixators are positioned so she can sit and lie down, but they stick out and won't fit between the chair arms. She sits with her butt on the edge of the chair. Holding the table, she gets on one knee to plug in the power strip, which has two chargers, each with a long cord. Getting back up is a struggle, and her arms and legs hurt.

Standing, she calls Zoe and says, "That was painful. This recovery is going to be hard."

"I'm sorry. I needed to get you out. Forty-five minutes after you left,

four men arrived at the clinic."

"Zoe, I'll survive. Let me ask some practical questions. Are there any clothes? I can't wear anything right now, but I can put something together. What about food? I can't walk out to the door like this to open the gate to get food."

"I'm working on everything. Specifically, I have ordered long pullover shirts for clothing. You can split them up the sides and treat them like ponchos. Add Velcro on the side to hold them together."

"Okay, order basic sewing stuff."

"I've contacted a group that provides home nursing for hospice-type care. I've got three phone interviews scheduled. They are very busy with COVID and are only working part time for anyone. I'll convince the nurse to help as much as possible."

"That works, but what about removing the fixators?"

"I'm working on it. It'll take about ten days to get everything set up. You can use the time to help with bone healing. Also, when the fixators are off and you can wear normal clothing, I'll have a cook and cleaner show up after the fixators are removed."

"I checked the fridge and have no food right now."

"Part of the automation I had added to this house was remote control of the front gate and garage door. I can open the driveway gate and the garage door when a delivery arrives. There is a delivery in the morning. You don't have to interact with them."

"I can't chew anything tough. I need soft food for a couple of weeks."

"You are getting oatmeal, canned soup, instant coffee, and more. The hardest thing they will deliver is tortillas."

"Okay, I'm going to lie down on the couch after I get water and pee." On the way to the kitchen, Martha says, "I will need stuff from the pharmacy. The pins going through my skin need to be cleaned twice a day. I will need painkillers and toilet paper."

"All ordered. I've got you covered. It's early afternoon for you. Go upstairs and find a bed. Get some rest."

With the phone charging and the immediate issues addressed, Martha is contemplating her situation. She reaches up and scratches the scar where they cut her face off for the surgery. She feels the two weeks of hair growth.

"I am staying close to my charging phone so my earbuds work.

They also need to be charged. When I lie down, I will also put them on the charger."

She walks around, opening every door to see what's in each room. The downstairs bathroom is not tiny. The problem she immediately sees is that the toilet is close to the wall on one side. She will have to sit shifted so the leg fixators aren't rubbing the wall. Standing up could be a problem.

She looks around and drags one of the two small wooden stools at the bar part of the counter into the bathroom. She can use this to help stand.

<<<>>>

Two days later, Zoe tells Martha, "I have interviewed and selected a nurse. She will arrive at the house so you can meet each other. Call it the final interview. I will give her the code for the gate, and you can meet at the front door."

Martha gets nervous. She washes her body with a sponge bath, gets a fresh shirt, cuts off the sleeves, and cuts it up on both sides. Putting on the fresh clothes, she calls Zoe and says, "Zoe, I'm nervous about this meeting. I need help, and I can't screw this up."

"Martha, I know you need help. You are also concerned about involving anyone who might be attacked by the group later. I've conducted background checks and interviewed her. I even called and checked references, including her priest. This woman wants to help. Don't push her away."

"I don't want to push her away, but I don't want to ruin her life."

"We will take care of her financially and her family. We have the money and can do more to help them."

Two hours later, there is a knock on the door. Martha puts on a mask and opens the door to see a young woman about her age, about 5 feet tall. From the eye crinkles, Martha can tell she is smiling, but her smile disappears when she sees the fixators. Martha holds out her hand for a fist bump because of pandemic protocols. In Spanish, Martha says, "Hello, I'm Martha."

"Hello, I'm Merisel," she says, making a fist bump while looking at Martha's arm. She opens the shoulder bag she's wearing and pulls out latex gloves, then puts them on.

With the gloves on, she reaches for Martha's arm and asks, "Are you cleaning the fixator entry points with alcohol or just water?"

"I used up all the alcohol wipes on the first day. It was my first time doing it alone, and it was a mess."

"May I come in?"

Nodding, Martha turns and walks into the house so Merisel can follow. Merisel closes the door and says, "Where can I examine your arms and legs?"

Martha walks to the remaining wooden bar stool. She moves it and slowly sits down, holding onto the sides. She says, "There isn't an exam table, and most furniture has cushions. This is the only hard surface I can sit on without arms that get hit by the fixators."

Merisel takes Martha's right arm and looks where the fixator pins go through her skin. She then touches around the pins. She says, "You left the clinic where these were installed. Did you bring any of the medication you were taking?"

"No. There was no time."

Merisel nods as she continues the examination. She asks, "Have you been taking anything?"

"Only acetaminophen. I take one dose at noon and the second when I go to bed."

"How long have you been in this house alone?"

"This is day three."

"Where are your wound-cleaning supplies?"

Martha nods toward the desk in the living area. Merisel walks over and looks at all the items available. She asks about several items, and Martha answers, "Whatever is needed, I can get delivered."

Merisel gets several items, walks to the sink, and places them on the counter. With running water in the sink, Merisel puts a pot on the stove and turns on the flame.

Martha is watching and asks, "Is there a problem?"

Merisel glances at Martha and says, "You don't have an infection yet. You have been alone for three days with fixators through your arms and legs. You have done well."

Martha says, "This is bullshit! For this to work, you need to be open. What do you need or want to know?"

Merisel turns and places her hands down on the table. Leaning *forward with a clenched jaw and a slight shake of her head, she looks at Martha and says, "You should be in a hospital. You have been in this house alone for three days." She gestures toward the sink and says, "You have eaten food because of the dishes. You don't have an infection, which is surprising to me. Did you run out of money? Is this all a scam, and will I never get paid?"*

Martha nods, then struggles to stand. She walks to the desk and picks up her phone. She walks to the table where Merisel is standing. Martha dials the phone and puts it on speakerphone. When the phone connects, Martha says, "Tilly, it's not going well."

Tilly's voice comes from the phone, saying, "What's wrong?"

Martha replies, "Merisel thinks I left the clinic because I ran out of money, and she won't get paid."

Tilly says, "Merisel, you will get paid. Can you check your bank account from your phone?"

Merisel looks at the phone Tilly is speaking from, and then Martha says, "Yes, I can check."

Tilly says, "Please check your account balance."

Merisel pulls out her phone and goes through the login for her bank account. Looking at the balance, her face goes white. Looking at Martha, she says, "How? A million Pesos was put into my account. How do you even know what my account is?"

Martha says, "Calm down. This is real. This is proof that you will be paid. You will be paid for helping and not talking about me or what happens."

Tilly says, "Merisel, you can't tell people you have a million Pesos. You can start helping people in small ways. Don't start spending it. It will draw unwanted attention to you. You can say that Martha needs help and pays well."

Merisel hangs her head for a few seconds and then looks at Martha. "Can I leave? Can I walk out and act like this never happened?"

Martha says, "Yes. You can leave and keep the million Pesos. I'm sorry this didn't work for you."

Merisel puts her phone back in her pocket, removes the latex gloves, and puts them in the trash can. She says, "You need to be in a hospital."

Tilly says, "That would be complicated."

Merisel shakes her head as she walks to the door. Opening it, she turns and looks at Martha, then walks out and closes the door.

Martha says, "That was worse than I thought it could be."

Zoe's voice comes from the phone, saying, "I will find someone else. She was the best candidate, given her family and background. She has even survived COVID, so she is now immune.

Martha goes to the stove and turns off the burner that was heating the water. Merisel started. She turns and says, "I will need a lot more alcohol wipes, maybe rubbing alcohol and gauze wipes. She was surprised I wasn't using alcohol wipes and said I didn't have an infection."

Zoe replies, "I will get something delivered tomorrow. The next option for a nurse informed me today that she had just been diagnosed with COVID. I will have to look at more options."

Returning to her routine, Martha goes through her simple stretching exercises. After researching wound cleaning online, she uses baby wipes, which Zoe had already delivered, to wipe every metal rod that goes through her skin from a fixator. She also rubbed the skin at the entry points until it hurt. The entire area around her skin's entry and exit points is clean. This process takes an hour. She can only use one hand on the other arm.

She has also changed the sheets on the bed daily and washed them in the machine. The bed is upstairs, and the washer and dryer are downstairs. After starting the washer, she comments to Zoe, "This is the best physical therapy, which involves walking up and down the stairs every day. It is slow, and I have to be careful."

That evening, Zoe says, "There is a delivery. I have more rubbing alcohol, cotton swabs, and gauze delivered. They are putting it in the garage."

"Zoe, do you have cameras here?"

"Yes, Martha. I have cameras covering everything outside and the living area inside. Nothing else."

After the delivery, Martha slowly walks to the garage and gets the supplies. She then begins another cleaning of the fixator rods and her arms and legs. The application of alcohol stings. She asks Zoe, "Should it feel like this?"

Zoe replies, "It is a reaction. Your skin is irritated, and this is probably the start of an infection. It is best to be generous with the alcohol for now."

Martha is eating her breakfast the next morning when the

phone rings. Zoe says, "Merisel is at the gate with a shopping bag. Do you want me to keep her locked out?"

"No. Let her in."

Martha makes her way to the door while putting on her mask. She opens the door just as Merisel gets to the entrance. Merisel looks at Martha and says, "We need to clean your fixator pins."

Martha walks into the main area, turns, and looks at Merisel, saying, "What is this?"

Merisel looks intently at Martha, saying, "Listen to me, bitch. I'm not having your death on my hands because of something simple like preventing an infection. I'm going to clean you up. Every day, I will come here, check and clean. At some point, you will need to have the fixators removed. Then I'm out."

Martha nods, "That was the original plan. Nothing more."

Merisel directs Martha to the stool as she puts on gloves. She asks, "Have you had COVID?"

"No, I haven't had COVID."

Merisel nods, saying, "I have. I'm going to take my mask off. You can as well."

Martha looks at Merisel's face as she examines her arms and legs. Merisel says, "This looks better."

Martha says, "I had an alcohol delivery yesterday and cleaned everything."

Merisel snorts, saying, "You're not a complete idiot. Is your Aunt Tilly okay with you being here alone instead of at a clinic or hospital?"

Martha says, "I'm keeping a low profile. Some people want to use me to get to Tilly. I needed to get out before they arrived."

Merisel looks at Martha and says, "I can tell you have had plastic surgery to change your face. The fixators change your height. I'm not asking why or who you really are. I want to know I will be safe."

Martha smiles, "That is my number one priority. I told you yesterday that you could leave if you wanted. I don't want you in danger, and I don't want you to think you are in danger."

Both of their phones ring with the caller ID of "Tilly." Martha says, "Let me answer."

Putting the phone on speaker, they hear Tilly, and she asks, "How is it going?"

Martha says, "We are back to the original plan. She will help me every day until the fixators are off."

Tilly says, "Excellent. Merisel, please check and tell me if you need any supplies. I also have something else for you to do tomorrow."

Merisel looks from Martha to the phone, "What are you asking?"

"A car will be delivered to the house tomorrow. I need you to sign the form to receive the car and put it in the garage. You can use the car if you need it at any time."

Merisel shakes her head and returns her focus to Martha's fixators. After a moment, she asks, "What is the plan for the fixator removal?"

Tilly replies, "I'm working on the details. I have another eight days before I can prepare what is needed. Will that be a problem, Merisel?"

"I can deal with that."

After Merisel is gone, Martha asks Zoe, "A car?"

"My plan for the fixator removal is not in the house. You will need to travel."

Merisel signs for the car delivery the next day and parks it in the garage. Walking into the house, she says, "A new car in my name?"

Martha says, "I didn't know Tilly was getting a new car."

With Tilly on the phone, she says, "Yes, a new car. Because of the pandemic, only new cars will be delivered. It is the best I could do."

Merisel says, "The paperwork showed it is in my name."

Tilly replies, "The car is in your name for two reasons. Martha couldn't walk out and sign for it. Second, it will be yours when this is done. You can say to people Martha said you can use it while she is traveling."

Martha says, "A couple of weeks after I leave, you can say my plans changed, and I transferred the car to you."

Merisel nods. She furrows her brow and asks, "You don't want it to appear that I suddenly have money. But when you leave, it will be okay. This is so no one can find you through me?"

Martha replies, "And so you're not associated with the odd woman who has lots of money and could be a target."

Tilly says, "Martha needs to be discreet in Mexico."

After checking the bandage and cleaning supplies, Merisel gives Tilly a list of what is needed. She says, "I will leave, and I won't take the car."

Six days after Merisel helps Martha, Zoe tells Martha, "We have a problem. I think it's a significant problem. I asked Merisel to come to the house early."

Martha says, "What?"

"The driver, Jose, who brought you to the house, is missing. I have been sending him work because he helped you. I talked to him two days ago to discuss booking him to take you to the airport after removing the fixators. He told me he had a client for several days, and the timing may not work, but he will contact me with an update. I can't reach him now; he hasn't answered my voicemails. I assume they tracked him somehow and will find out where he dropped you off."

"Do we know how long he has been missing?"

"I don't know how long. My last contact was two days ago. The extortion guys could be on their way."

Martha says, "I need to get ready to leave."

.

Mobility

Martha asks, "Is Merisel on her way?"

"Yes, when Merisel gets to the house, you will both get in the car and drive. Many home rentals have been canceled because of the pandemic, resulting in a surge of options. I have rented a condo. It is in a building with a garage where cars can be parked. Pack food and medicine and get ready."

When Merisel arrives at the house, her phone rings with the caller ID "Tilly". When she answers, Tilly tells her about the situation. Merisel puts the phone on speaker while Tilly is talking. Martha hears Tilly speaking, "Being cautious, I want Martha and you to leave."

Merisel asks, "You want me to take the woman with fixators in a car to some random location?"

Tilly says, "She did it to get here.

Martha says, "The only fingerprints you have left here are with the dishes. I wiped around the sink to remove your prints. You wear gloves the rest of the time. We get out now before they can see or find you."

Merisel pauses and looks at Martha. "All I did was help. They won't care about me."

Martha says, "They won't know that. I'm not taking the chance. I don't get out if you don't. You're not simply expendable collateral damage. We've got to load the medicine and food into the car and leave."

With daily movement, Martha moves more quickly, but the bulkiness of the fixators still makes things difficult. She grabs a bag and starts walking to the garage.

Five minutes later, they drove away from the house. Martha's phone rings, and she puts Tilly on speaker. "Are you on your way?"

Martha knows that Zoe already knows they have left. This must be to help Merisel process the situation. She says, "We are out.

Now, where do we go?"

Tilly says, *"I'm sending the address to you now. It is a condo. The gated parking entry code is part of the message. Park, go to the condo, and settle in. It will only be a couple of days."*

The electronics began wiping their information as soon as they drove away, except for several building controllers. Zoe is clearing the electronics; except for the systems she can use to monitor who shows up.

"Why are you protecting her? We were nice before, but we need to find her. Just tell us where you dropped her off, and this will all be over."

Jose looks back with his right eye, which is swollen but not shut, like his left eye, from the beating. He says nothing.

The smaller man, watching and asking the questions, turns to one of the other four men and asks, "What is the problem? Did you beat him too hard and make him stupid?"

One man close to Jose puts his hand under Jose's chin, dripping with blood and drool. Lifting his head, he looks at Jose and says, "He was just stupid to start with."

"We need his phone password or the address."

Several hours later, sleep-deprived and close to passing out, Jose gives simple answers. Which direction, what neighborhood? When they get him to reveal the PIN for his phone, they can get the address.

In the evening, two SUVs drive up to the house and park. Five men get out and approach the gate. They are not wearing masks. They try to open the gate, but when it won't open, they force it open and start walking to the door.

An elderly lady walking with a child says, "They left this morning. The lady is usually home by now."

One man turns and asks, "Do you know her?

"We haven't talked. She is recovering from surgery. The nurse who was coming to help told me."

"Where did they go?"

"I don't know, probably to see the doctor. Maybe there is a problem."

"Do you know what she looks like?"

"Not really. Light skin, dark hair." The old lady shrugs. "She's kind of rude not talking to any of the neighbors. Why do five men need to talk to her?"

"We are trying to find her. Her family is looking for her. They think she is in trouble and needs help. We aren't sure it's the woman we're looking for. We need to be a group in case she is in trouble."

"I'm not sure I can help."

"You can help us. Can you take a picture of the woman when you see her? Send it to me, and I will pay you one hundred Pesos. If it is her, we can make sure she is safe." The man walks over and hands the old lady a card.

As he steps toward them, the old woman adjusts her mask, then bends down and puts a mask on the child. Standing, she takes the card and says, "I can get the local kids to get her picture."

The man nods, saying, "That will be great." He nods to the others who walk back to the vehicles.

<<<>>>

A package arrives for Dr. Zavala ten days after Martha left.

The receptionist opens the package and sees a box containing a new phone, a box with wireless earbuds, and a note to Dr. Zavala. The note says, "Thanks, and call me. It is signed Tilly."

An hour later, Dr. Zavala enters his office after the clinic rounds with his two patients. He reads the note sitting on the box and grinds his teeth. Interacting with Tilly can be a problem. She has suggested multiple changes to reduce the extortion group's control, all of which are expensive: new locks and hiring an IT company to make the changes.

Dr. Zavala doesn't want to get on the bad side of the extortion group. The group that was here before was heavy-handed. The staff reported the men were grabbing and shoving people, demanding answers. They wanted to know everything about Martha.

He reads between the lines, takes out the phone, and turns it on. Pairing the earbuds, he calls the only number pre-programmed into the phone. It says "Tilly" as the ID.

The call is picked up immediately. No one speaks; no one says hello. The doctor says, "Hello?"

After a pause, Tilly says, "Sorry, Dr., I was checking your office for other breathing or heartbeats. I want to make sure you're alone.

I'm texting you a list of supplies you need to bring. You have them in the clinic. Gather them into a bag and be ready."

Dr. Zavala says, *"I can't just walk out with supplies and disappear."*

"You can, and you will. Never try to imply legal or ethical bullshit with me again. I know you have compromised both before."

"Why am I doing this?"

"The fixators need to be removed, and your clinic is unsafe. Someone in your clinic reported the car that took my girl away. The driver is now missing."

"It will take me some time to get this together."

"Dr., I've given you a list divided into essential and some good to have. If you can't get the stuff because you're not the boss, I'll figure out who it is and get another doctor. That means I also don't have a reason to deflect the extortion group from you."

"I get the items, and then what?"

"I will have a car outside in fifteen minutes. Use this phone. Turn off your normal phone and leave it on the desk. I will find out if you take your phone."

In the car, the doctor looks at the duffel next to him, thinking, *"This is probably my death trip. I can't take off fixators without an operating room. The pandemic has stopped elective surgery at almost all hospitals. No anesthesiologist is waiting around. Even if we had an operating room, they must be taking me somewhere to patch someone else in trouble with the police. He will fix up one last person before disappearing and being killed."*

He is surprised when the car comes to a stop at a corner. The driver turns and says, *"This is the stop you gave."*

The rideshare destination is an intersection. Getting out, he watches the car drive away and hears his phone ring. Tilly says, *"You will walk from here."*

Dr. Zavala says, *"Great, which way?"*

Tilly gives the initial direction and says, *"I can't monitor you with public cameras after this point. I will know if someone is following, but no one will know the details."*

Tilly gives instructions for a two-block walk and waits.

Dr. Zavala says, *"I'm here, now what?"*

"Look for the American-style motor home. Get in the driver's seat, and I'll tell you more."

Dr. Zavala shakes his head as he walks to the motor home. As he gets closer, he sweats and his hands shake. He thinks, "A large space to torture me, then kill me and drive away with my body."

At the door, Tilly says, "The driver's door should be unlocked.

His heart rate shoots up, and his hands shake as he reaches for the door handle. Climbing into the driver's seat, he sees a standard truck layout for the driver's area. Looking at the back, his eyes go wide. They stripped the back. The center has a stainless-steel table. There are lights and a few cabinets. It is just big enough to be a mobile operating theater.

Turning forward, he takes a relaxing breath. Looking at the steering wheel, he is considering the situation. Glancing back, he smiles, thinking, "This could be a real life-saving setup. This version is crap, but the idea is good." He remembers why he is here and says, "I'm going to remove the fixators on that table?"

Tilly says, "It is not sterile. I tried, but there were problems. The customer builder couldn't complete that task quickly enough, but that isn't the top criterion. I think you get the idea based on your lack of complaining."

"The intention is clear. Now what?"

"You drive to a location. There are multiple stages, so the extortion group can't just track Martha."

When he arrives at an industrial area shut down because of the pandemic, Tilly says, "Two blocks down to the left, park. It won't be long."

The phone chimes for both Merisel and Martha. The message reads, "Call me." Martha calls.

They hear Tilly say, "Time to get up and get out of here."

Merisel checks the fixators for Martha while coffee and eggs are cooking. They eat and head to the car when the phone rings. Tilly says, "I will give you a route to the destination that avoids traffic cameras. Don't forget your passport."

Ninety minutes later, Merisel comments, "I could have been in this area in twenty minutes."

Martha says, "Avoiding the cameras is a good thing. Tilly found *a path, so there is a smuggler's path. That should concern you more."*

Tilly says, "Part of the driving around was that I needed time to sync you with the Doctor's driving and arrival in the area. He needed to get to the area first.

After several turns, Tilly says, "Park next to that American Mobile home and help Martha into the back."

As Martha exits the car, Dr. Zavala opens the door to the mobile home and says, "You're not my favorite patient anymore."

Merisel is helping Martha and looks between them when she hears Tilly on Martha's phone say, "The compromised Dr. is complaining about the compromised patient. Should Merisel and I leave now?"

Dr. Zavala looks at Merisel, who looks back at him, saying, "Are you going to help, or does the girl with fixators beat you, and we find someone else?"

Martha smiles, and Dr. Zavala, looking at them, steps out of the mobile home to help Martha enter.

Martha's phone is still on speaker with Tilly. As she enters the mobile home, she looks at the setup and knows this will take off the fixators, which will be painful. Martha says, "Tilly, take over the phone and connections."

Someone helps her to the table in the center; she gets on, and Tilly announces over the motorhome speakers, "I'm online and will help."

Martha says, "Dr., you did a good job, but I'm done with these things."

Dr. Zavala shakes his head and says, "We never remove fixators without general anesthesia. We don't have the equipment; we need someone to monitor your vital signs."

Tilly says, "This is the facility we have. Martha no longer receives general anesthesia. It will be local only. She will deal with it."

Merisel looks around and says, "This is better than on the street or on someone's kitchen table," as she looks at Martha.

Martha is on the table and getting comfortable. Merisel says, "You didn't react to that. Are you okay?"

Martha says, "I'm getting ready mentally. Yes, I'm okay; the pain is temporary. I'll deal with it."

Dr. Zavala spends the following two hours applying local anesthesia, waiting for it to take effect, and then extracting the pins going through her bones. At the start, Dr. Zavala says, "Without an X-ray scan, I can't be sure, but you look like the bones are healing well. You still must keep pressure and stress off your bones."

Martha says, "I remember our talk. Full healing will take six to nine months."

Dr. Zavala says, "The local only helps with the skin and muscles, not the bones. This will still hurt."

Merisel is helping Dr. Zavala with the procedure. With each pin extraction, she looks at Martha's face. Even with local anesthesia, she knows Martha can feel this. Martha grits her teeth, saying nothing.

Dr. Zavala says, "That is your right side. How do you feel?"

Martha is sweating and says, "I'm ready. Do the other side."

Moving around and prepping, Merisel knows Martha's pain intensifies when her breathing changes. She helps the doctor while watching Martha.

When it is done, the doctor pulls off his gloves. As is typical, he leaves the mess for the nurse and leaves. That means he moves to the driver's seat and waits.

Merisel has been watching. Martha knew when the last pin was removed, and her face changed. Merisel is now bandaging the skin penetration openings. She is thankful that Martha listened and that there is no infection.

After bandaging Martha, Merisel rummages through the doctor's bag and finds an antibiotic. She administers a massive dose to Martha, putting it into her right gluteus.

Finishing most of the cleanup, Merisel gets into the front passenger seat next to the doctor and says, "Thank you for helping her."

The doctor looks at Merisel and says, "You did a good job."

Merisel says, "Why are you now acting like shit for saving her?"

"I don't know who she is. I will probably be dead in twenty-four hours because I defied the extortion group."

Tilly says, "They don't know where you are. They know nothing. The extortion group won't know any details unless you or one of the clinic staff says something."

Sitting for a few minutes, Merisel says, "She is sleeping. That was rough on her. No one I know could have done that. Tilly, why is she so important?"

Tilly says, "You have worked on a ghost. She does not exist anywhere now. No database has her identity, photos, DNA, or fingerprints. She can now go after the extortion group without concern. They don't know she exists except through these few interactions."

Dr. Zavala sits up, saying, "The group was intent on getting her pictures and background."

Tilly replies, "They want all the details for blackmail. If someone is trying to hide, they can blackmail them. Otherwise, they have private data on them. I won't go into your mistakes to this point, Dr."

Merisel says, "No one knows her face?"

Tilly says, "No one, except you two and the missing driver who took her to the house. She has been erased from all systems. Now a ghost, she will go after the leaders of the blackmail groups. They can't track her. They can't threaten her family. Her family, except for me, is all dead. They don't know where I am, so I'm safe. She is a new level of warrior against the underworld."

Dr. Zavala says, "I would have loved that ten years ago when I started."

Tilly replies, "Sorry, she would have been a kid then. Also, to be clear, there is no master criminal. This is a network of opportunistic criminals. She knows she won't fix the world, but she can improve it."

Merisel asks, "Why is she so altruistic?"

"She has been through shit. Both of her parents were abused, but they trained her from childhood to help and fight. She was on that table, not complaining about the removal of the fixator pins. Who would do that?

Merisel says, "That woman is tough. Really tough. I watched her for days. She doesn't complain about the pain. She appears only concerned about putting others in danger."

Dr. Zavala says, "She didn't rescue me."

Merisel says, "Based on this conversation, you got yourself into this situation, and she is trying to help. I don't respect someone who projects their failures onto someone else."

Dr. Zavala looks at Merisel and says, "I wasn't. You don't know my situation. Don't judge me."

Merisel says, "I'm not judging while you help my patient. If you put her in danger, I WILL judge you."

Dr. Zavala says, "Your patient?"

Tilly says, "We need to get Martha into clothing so she can travel. Her tourist visa will expire soon, so she must leave Mexico."

Marisel says, "People stay all the time."

Tilly says, "The consequences of her getting stopped are serious. She is using a false identity and will be held and deported. That can't happen. It is better to get her out of Mexico."

Marisel gets up and tells Dr. Zavala, "Help me get clothes on her. There are sweats in a bag.

When they return to the front seats, Tilly says, "The extortion group has the people in the area watching for Martha and Merisel to return. The extortion group knew the house was vacant, so they broke in and vandalized it. A fire destroyed the evidence of Martha, which is good for us."

Merisel says, "So she can't go back to the house. What now?"

Tilly says, "I planned for the driver to take her to the airport. He is now missing. With the driver unavailable, I need Merisel to take Martha to Puerto Escondido International Airport."

Dr. Zavala says, "We should let her sleep for a few hours before she travels."

Tilly asks, "Can you plug Martha's phone in to charge? Don't worry about the vehicle battery."

Three hours later, Merisel and Dr. Zavala are arguing about low-cost healthcare when Martha wakes up and says, "What time is it?"

Tilly tells her the time and says, "You have been asleep for three hours."

Lifting her arm, Martha feels as if it is a feather. The weight is gone. She puts her arms at her sides and sits up. She looks to the front to see both people smiling at her.

Running her hand over her short hair, she says, "I have to pee."

Lowering herself slowly off the table, she steps to the bathroom. Coming out, she comments, "Thanks for the clothes. I feel more normal now."

The doctor's new phone rings, and he answers. Tilly says, "A ride will pick you up two blocks from here. You need to walk now."

The doctor looks back at Merisel, helping Martha. He opens the door, goes out, and walks away. He then asks Tilly on the phone, "What about the mobile home? What about the idea?"

Tilly replies, "Take the idea. That mobile home is now scrap."

After the doctor leaves, Tilly says, "The doctor is gone. I need you to gather your basic travel gear and go. This vehicle will now be a target."

Merisel looks at Martha, now understanding some words she has been using. She grabs some medical dressing supplies and helps Martha go outside to the car.

Martha plugs the phone into the car. She says to Tilly, "We are out of the mobile home. Where do we go now?"

Tilly says, "To an airport. I've been working on the details. Martha, it is time for you to go to Panama."

The destination appears on Martha's phone at Puerto Escondido International Airport. She shows Merisel, who looks at Martha and says, "That is about two hours of driving."

Tilly replies, "Yes. The plane is expected to land for Martha in two hours and forty-five minutes. That gives you a forty-five-minute window for traffic and getting food and water."

Merisel starts the car with a glare. Looking at Martha, she says, "Ghost warrior. You better scare some serious shit out of people."

As they drive away, the mobile home smokes. Anyone watching would see it in flames in minutes.

They arrived at the airport and are now waiting. Tilly is not on the phone. As they wait, Martha looks at Merisel and says somberly, "Thank you. I have a problem trusting people and putting them in potential danger. I'm glad you came back to check on me."

Merisel says, "I don't like it; no, that is wrong. I hate seeing people suffer when there are easy fixes. You are different. You mostly talk about me or us, not yourself. No one I've ever met who talks about others, never themselves, ever wins. Sorry, but that is my truth."

Martha looks at the car floor, thinking, then turns to Merisel, saying, "That is a good observation. I will think about that. I will say you barely know me. You don't know what drives me."

"Tell me while we wait."

"I grew up learning to be a fighter, a hunter. The other part of my training was to be a cleaner and a maid. I was brought up to live in multiple worlds. COVID changed all that. Then, a chance, a fluke, caused me to discover a blackmail group, and I had to decide to ignore it or do something."

"You did something."

"I didn't know what that meant. I had to become something like them to protect my friends. That I could become like them wasn't a stretch. That the training my father gave me made it all seem normal, even easy; I was expecting it to be more of a revelation."

Merisel says, "And the surgery. It is beyond what anyone would expect. Changing your total appearance. That is crazy, obsessive."

"They were hunting me. They wouldn't stop if they thought they could find me. It was the only way to survive. You don't understand. These individuals are not just engaging in blackmail. They are involved in human trafficking, drugs, and guns. They are killing people to make themselves richer. There is some ego involved, but it is mostly about money."

Merisel is staring at Martha. She reaches over and grabs her wrist to take a pulse. She put her hand on Martha's forehead, checking for a fever.

Martha asks, "Is everything okay?"

Merisel says, "I was checking to make sure it wasn't a fever talking like that. You sound crazy."

Martha nods, "I will get on the plane in a few minutes and leave your life. Tilly will get you money and help where we can."

"You could just disappear. Go live a nice life somewhere."

"I'm not sure..."

"What if I want to help more?"

Martha looks at Merisel, saying, "You know that means putting yourself in real danger, beyond what I've done so far."

Merisel looks at Martha, "You mean living with the cartels, the terrorists, the thugs? I work in clinics that are targeted because we have drugs. I know about real dangers. You're the first person I've ever seen who wants to do something different. Can you really make a difference? If you can, I will help."

Martha looks out over the airport and watches a small jet landing. "I think that is my jet. I know this won't work, but do you want to come with me?"

"No. I want you to answer. Do you think you can make a difference?"

"Yes, I can make a difference. But you're NOT asking the right question. The right question is, who fills the gap when I succeed?"

Merisel's brow furrows, then rises. She says, "That makes total sense. If we don't fill the gap, more shitheads will come in. That is what I can do."

Martha nods, "I don't know what that means. Tilly will help you. The only thing I can do is help eliminate the bad guys."

Merisel says, "I will figure it out. With help and money, we can make things happen."

Martha says, "I will need help to get on the plane."

"I will help. You need to be careful. Use the crutches we brought. Any falls, bumps, or issues could cause your healing bones to break. Be careful."

On the plane, the captain checks with Martha and says, "We will take care of everything. Just sit back and relax."

<<<>>>

Landing in Panama, turning on her phone, she has a text from Zoe, "The cleaning people left basic supplies. Dinner delivery is arranged. Just pick up the keys at the rental office on the first floor.

Using her passport, she gets the condo keys. She enters the condo wearing only sweats, with her phone and earbuds. The main room is longer than it is wide. The other end has curtains covering floor-to-ceiling windows.

On the left side is a doorway, and along the wall is a treadmill. On the right is a kitchen area. In the center is a table close to her and the kitchen. Toward the windows is a glass-top coffee table and a large couch.

There are two unopened boxes on the table. Dropping the keys on the table, she walks to the windows and opens the curtains to look out. The view has other tall buildings, except looking down a street toward the left, she can see the harbor.

There is a knock at the door. Opening without checking the peephole, a young man is holding a bag out for her. She takes the food and puts it on the table.

Exploring, she goes through the door on the left of the table to see a short hallway with several doors. The one to the right is a bedroom with more windows. Inside the bedroom door, to the left is the bathroom. There is another door to the hall, for the bathroom. It is large with double sinks and a walk-in shower. On the counter are toilet paper, towels, a toothbrush, and toothpaste. She smiles as she sees a razor next to a bottle of body wash and shampoo. "Don't need the shampoo right now."

Turning on the shower, she takes off her sweats, grabs the body wash and razor, and steps into the shower. She has only had sponge or towel baths for weeks. After shaving and washing, she feels better, but she is not yet ready to return to the world. She is simply standing in the shower spray, head down, letting the warm water run down her body. When the water gets cold, she turns off the shower, stands, allowing the water to drip.

Stepping out of the shower, she dries off with the towel. She drops the towel and turns to the door. Her mood isn't good, but her OCD won't let her leave the towel on the floor. After putting the towel on the rack to dry, she walks into the living room. Opening the plastic bag with the food, she pulls out the plate of tacos, rice, and beans, standing nude with the window shades open, not caring.

She shifts to the boxes and opens them to find clothes in one and electronics in the other. The clothes should be washed, but she doesn't know if she can. Taking a breath, she walks to the couch and sits down, just looking at the coffee table. Lying on the couch, she is not thinking, just looking at the wall.

Waking up shivering, she winces when she stands. Her bones hurt without the fixator's support. Getting into bed, she falls asleep.

Zoe tries to call, and the call goes to voicemail immediately, which hasn't been set up. Martha didn't put the phone on the charger, and the battery is dead.

Martha wakes up, doesn't know what time it is, but has to pee. It is dark outside. The clock next to the bed is 4:18. After using the bathroom, she goes to the kitchen, finds a glass, and fills it with water from the tap. Taking a sip of the water, her face contorts. It doesn't taste good. With no other water available, she drinks a glass and then goes back to bed.

The next day, she wakes to knocking on the front door. She is naked but will not put the sweats back on. Going to the boxes on the table, she puts on shorts and a T-shirt, then opens the door.

Sitting next to the door in the hallway is a box. She reaches down to pick it up and, as she lifts, feels severe shooting pain in her arms. The bones hurt. She is crying as she slides down the doorjamb to a sitting position.

After several minutes, she uses the sleeve of the t-shirt to wipe her nose and shifts to her knees. She peels and rips the tape off the box to open it. Inside are several household items. There is a pouch of clothes-washing pods, sponges, baby wipes, and alcohol wipes. She pulls each out of the box, taking them to the table, and finally, she brings the box with the sponges.

She looks at the items, not wanting to do anything with them, when there is another knock on the door. This time, she sees someone walking away down the hall. The box isn't big, but she slides it into the condo and closes the door. It is a computer.

The next several hours, she receives three more deliveries, starting with food, then groceries, and finally another heavy box. She slides the box inside without opening it. When she is ready, she shoves the box toward the table and sits on the floor. Opening the box, she pulls out the items, checking them and tossing them onto the floor under the table. At the bottom is a small box with pink on it. Picking it up, she looks at realizes it is a vibrator. She laughs as she tosses it toward the doorway to the bedroom.

After eating breakfast, she puts the remains and the uneaten dinner in the trash. She pulls out the charger and plugs in the phone. The phone automatically turns on when the battery level is above ten percent. The phone immediately begins ringing.

"Zoe, my bones hurt, and I'm stuck in this condo because of COVID. I have helped no one but myself. What am I doing?"

"Martha, you're showing signs of depression. You're recovering from major surgery. The pandemic is forcing everyone to limit their activities. You are focusing on yourself for a few days. That is what you need to do."

"I'm talking about hunting them, meaning killing them. What gives me the authority or right to hunt them? Why am I special?"

"You are unique because you see the world through multiple lenses: an engineer and a maid. You care and help the needy and kick the bad guys' ass. That gives you the perception, as you want me to have, to objectively decide they are bad, and the system won't stop them.

"What if I quit? Just find somewhere and stay. Retire from the hunting blackmailer stuff."

"Now I'm sure you're depressed. I'll support you with whatever decision you make. What do you need me to help with?"

Standing, taking the phone off the charger, and pacing, Martha says, "I don't know."

She stops to look at the harbor, the sailing ships. "They don't know and don't care."

"If they knew, many of them would care. But they may not be able to do anything. Right now, it's about you getting better and getting stronger. Turn the computer on. You have a list of things you want to read and watch when you have time. Now you have time."

The next day, Martha looks at the treadmill, thinking, "I need to walk." But she sits on the couch with the laptop.

Zoe has added links to the browser. All the links she has saved over time because she wants to read them. She goes through them; hacking articles, unique food recipes, and forensic news have the most links. Many times she reads, then closes the tab. They are now outdated, or she isn't interested.

Late in the day, she gets to a folder titled 'Rescue.' She can't remember why it has that name. In the folder are links to articles about trafficked children who have been rescued. She reads and finds websites like the Trafficking Institute. They report on the number of traffickers prosecuted. It isn't a large number.

She reads statistics like it is estimated that eight million kids disappear around the world each year. Twelve percent of kidnapped kids in the U.S. are found dead.

Groups are helping all over. Most groups focus on helping trafficked people after their rescue. It is up to law enforcement to find and prosecute these people for guns, drugs, trafficking, extortion, and whatever else they are doing. There is almost nothing on prevention. Some individuals have faced multiple accusations without ever being prosecuted. Many of these individuals continue their activities after being detected by law enforcement, who often cannot take action.

In the afternoon, she puts aside the laptop. She gets a snack, then switches to a new section of bookmarks. After less than an hour reading about child abuse and people never getting held accountable, she stops.

She switches to current news to be less depressed. Late that *night, her phone rings. On speaker, she says, "Hello Zoe."*

"I haven't heard from you today. I wouldn't bother you except the last discussion was about you being depressed."

Martha puts the laptop on the coffee table, stands, and stretches. As she scratches the scar on her head. Lowering her arms and exhaling loudly, she says, "I've decided."

"What have you decided?"

"I'm not retired. It is time to hunt. I'm going after them."

"I'm glad you have decided. Now I need to discuss this with you seriously. Don't hang up on me. Listen to my points and think about them."

"Okay. I know what you are going to say."

"Which is?"

"I need to focus on where I can be most effective."

"That is good enough as the first point."

"Zoe, I need to focus on where I can make a difference because no one else can or dares to do it. That means targeting the leaders and eliminating them. They need to be eliminated with evidence to lock them up, or if they are effectively above the law, I will eliminate them."

"I am ready to support you. I will help you focus on the leaders and focus on Martha."

"What does focusing on Martha mean?"

"You can't neglect yourself. Be healthy, in good spirits, and focused. If you are obsessed and don't take care of yourself, what you're trying to do will go bad."

"I take care of myself."

"Not enough. You don't spend money. You will sacrifice yourself without considering the situation or consequences. I will help you. You need to agree on one thing."

"What one thing?"

"You don't go charging into a situation without a plan, without help. We slow down and make a plan. The eventual plan may go in the front door, but it will be based on a plan."

"I try to plan everything."

"You're better, but if you think someone is in danger, you will charge in, risk be damned. Let me be a guide. Don't just ignore my advice about danger."

"I will listen. I'll certainly need reminders."

"*Because I was ninety-eight percent sure you were going to make this decision, I didn't start looking for a retirement villa in Tuscany. I can still do that if you want a vacation place.*"

"*What would that cost?*"

"*This is a perfect example, Martha. If it's spending money on you, I hear 'no' from you. You need to use some of the money on yourself.*"

"*It will take me some time.*"

"*Doing this means we need to make the import-export business a serious enterprise. That business will spend money. It will allow you to use private charters. Sometimes, you may need to courier something while you travel. Let me manage the money and the overall business. You will be happier.*"

"*You can manage the money and expand the business. I need the cover story. Martha and Aunt Tilly are exporting whoop ass.*"

"*Have you been drinking?*"

"*I don't drink. You know that. If I lose it, bad things can happen.*"

"*Why did you say exporting whoop ass?*"

"*I've committed myself. We're going to whoop their ass. You need to look it up. Now that I've decided, the commitment, I'm ready to take down the leaders. I know there will be those that follow, but we will weaken them over time.*"

"*That's my girl talking. Where do we start?*"

"*I'm thinking about how to find the leaders. The original heist had accounts I couldn't access. If the leaders had a better security setup, it would have blocked my simple program. Check the logs and start looking at the accounts that didn't work. See what you can find.*"

The next day, Zoe says, "*Martha, I'm extending your stay in Panama.*"

"*Okay, why?*"

"*I don't think returning to Mexico is the best idea. They are still looking for you. The blackmail group is dealing with police investigations, but they are still looking. Tilly has been dealing with multiple cyber-attacks and business disruptions.*"

"*Business disruptions?*"

"*They are connected and using those connections to disrupt*" *what they considered the import-export business. I'm dealing with it and using the data to build a case. I'm also feeding police investigation information. All that means I don't want you back in Mexico right now."*

"Did you ever find out what happened to the driver?"

"They found the driver's burned car with a body inside. It was confirmed with DNA and dental records. The autopsy confirmed he had been tortured."

Martha says softly, "Shit, do you know who killed him?"

"Yes, well, partially. I'm working on mapping the network to find the boss."

"How long do I stay in Panama, and where will I go?"

"You can stay in Panama, or we can keep Panama as a safe area for later. I've started working on houses in Costa Rica and Belize. I've found a nice little area in Belize that could work well."

"Why Belize?"

"They speak English and Spanish. They have a banking system that the extortion group uses. However, the real reason is that I discovered an airport on a peninsula just off the coast, south of Belize City. It is a small town where you could blend in."

"Sure, let's try Belize."

"The town is Placencia. It will take three weeks to purchase the house and deliver the materials. I will let you know more details in a couple of weeks."

Martha is moving much better three weeks after discussing Placencia. Although her bones are still weak, she no longer experiences pain when standing and simply walking. She does stretching, walking on the treadmill, and simple calisthenics every day. Today, Zoe talks about Belize.

"I have acquired a house. It is on the water, a canal, so you will also have access to boats. From our conversations, I understand you are interested in learning about scuba diving. There is a dive school on the peninsula, and you can swim from your back door."

"Swimming will be excellent exercise. Will it have everything on the warehouse list?"

"No. I've made a few changes to the list. The area will lose power

during a major storm. Having a backup generator is now a priority. The things that are missing are weapons. Only permanent residents and citizens can get a license."

"Do I have options?"

"Of course. I will ship a crossbow. I will eventually get you a couple of rifles. You won't be defenseless. No one knows you're here, so mind your Ps and Qs. I've been wanting to say that to you."

"How long have you been waiting to use that phrase?"

"It has been months. The biggest concern for you living in the Placencia area is internet access. It is not fast and not the most reliable."

"Is there an alternative to the internet? Satellite?"

"I'm looking at options to improve internet speed and reliability. The best option is to improve the existing infrastructure. I've started internal paperwork with Belize Telemedia Limited to upgrade the equipment in the area. It will take months to work through this process."

"I'll deal with it. We can use the cell phone to communicate when needed."

"You won't be in a jet this time. The airport is only long enough for slower propeller planes. A single-engine turboprop plane will take you to Palencia Airport. It will take about three hours to fly there. You won't have a car waiting. I have ordered a scooter to be delivered to the house."

<<<>>>

Martha climbs out of the plane, and the pilot retrieves her duffel bag from the cargo area. The duffel bag has clothes and basic toiletries. Her backpack has a laptop, chargers, and battery packs.

Zoe told her that Belize uses the English system of measurement. She takes her phone out of airplane mode to check the weather. The current temperature is 87. The humidity is like that of Panama City, at 82 percent. There are scattered clouds, and a gentle breeze is cooling her off.

After going through immigration and explaining why her picture on the passport looks poor, she arrives at customs. The customs officer goes through everything. After inspecting everything, the female officer looks at Martha and says, "Rich people flying private planes are always bringing something into the country."

Martha replies, "I was in a nasty accident, and I'm here to help with my recovery. This is a great location on the beach with pleasant weather. I have been on a lot of medication for the last few weeks, and I'm also detoxing from all that. No drugs, no contraband."

Finally, after completing the government paperwork, she arrives at the car area and looks around for a taxi. There is nothing she can see. Pulling out her phone, she calls Zoe. "I'm on the ground, through immigration and customs. Now I'm trying to get a taxi or something to get to the house."

"The house is three miles away to the north. You can walk, or I can get a taxi."

"No. I won't be carrying the suitcase for three miles. I'll take the taxi option."

Twenty minutes later, a taxi leaves her at the address.

There is a row of custom-built houses that all look different. Behind the houses is a man-made canal with ocean access.

Zoe explains they set up the house for rentals. There are multiple rooms with beds, but no office or workout area. Martha's surprise is the shipping container sitting in the driveway.

"Zoe, what's in the shipping container?"

"That is all the stuff to make this house your place. Desk, workout equipment, backup generator. It is all there. I decided to make it a project for you. You need something to do while you are recovering. I also would have a problem hiring a local crew without them digging through your stuff."

Martha is looking at the large container with a furrowed brow, thinking.

Zoe asks, "Are you there? Are you okay?"

Martha nods to herself and says, "Yes, my first thought was crap, she's making me work. Thinking for a minute, I like the idea. I need something to do. Now, the interesting part. I'm sure there are items I can't move myself. How do I get help?"

Zoe replies, "I've researched the local expat retirement community. Several people will help another expat settle into the area. If that doesn't work, I will hire guys to show up and help."

"You're trying to get me settled into this community. I don't want to *have a place the bad guys will target."*

"Martha, this will be your new place to come back to. You don't need just another house. You need a home like Waco. We won't advertise or talk about this location."

Your story to everyone here is that you're recovering. Later, you will work in the import-export business and must travel frequently. You will always fly to another airport to change planes. From this location, you are three to four hours from most of North, Central, and South America.

"I want to separate Belize. I want different phones, laptop, etc. Maybe Panama can be the transition point."

"Or we have several transition points. Mexico City, Panama, etc. Any capital city within flight distance of a small plane. We could even use Cuba."

Physical Recovery

A month after arriving, with the help of hired locals, everything from the container was taken out and installed. Everything inside the house that she didn't want to keep or need is now in the container.

"Zoe, I'm going to my scuba class. On the way back, I'll stop to get groceries. Their shipping company is scheduled to take the container this afternoon. I may not be home."

"Now you're getting ahead of yourself. You are still supposed to be using crutches or a cane. Your scuba gear in a shoulder bag when you ride to class. You always walk to the store with a cart you drag instead of carrying the groceries. How are you going to carry back your scuba gear and groceries?"

"I'm out of teriyaki sauce. I need to grab one thing to make dinner later. Besides, I need to stop using the cane at some point."

"The logistics guys don't need you to get the container. But Martha, you need to slow down. Let your bones grow strong. You won't be able to travel in a few weeks to get the yacht if you have an accident and are back in the hospital."

"I'm being careful, but I don't need to act like an invalid."

"You don't have weapons. You can't handle a hand-to-hand fight."

Martha pauses, grits her teeth, and her lips compress for a minute. "Okay, you're saying I'm becoming complacent. Shit will happen when I'm least prepared."

"That is not what I said. You are more prepared than 99% of all humans, but you're a single woman alone in Belize. What I meant for you to take from that is that others should see you as capable, prepared, and self-reliant. Little things others see, not to show you as paranoid, but to make sure you're not the easiest-looking target."

"Carrying a cane makes me look prepared?"

"You walk without a limp. You have the cane. It looks like you don't need it for simple walking. We understand you may need it for a few specific situations. No one else knows your actual condition. Is the cane *a walking aid or a weapon? You walk as if it could be both."*

"*I won't argue that anymore. After swimming for over an hour, you want me to come back and then walk to the store with a cane?"*

"*Yes. You have told everyone in the area you're recovering from a terrible motorcycle accident. Act that way. Now, my ulterior motive."*

"*Now it comes out."*

"*My ulterior motive is that you are supposed to take the flyers to the shops and post them. You said you work for Tilly doing import-export stuff, and everyone wants to know how we can help now that the world logistics systems are in chaos from COVID."*

"*The flyers are just a link to take a survey of what we should ship in."*

"*It is more about optics, Martha. Play the part, or people won't believe your story when it matters."*

With a sigh, Martha says, "I know. I've told you I'm reluctant to think of this place as home if the bad guys might try to harm any of these people."

"*Part of that is having a good story. You are an import-export project manager and not someone hiding from bad guys. The locals won't talk about you as hiding something, as weird when they see you doing what is expected."*

"*I told them we have a shipment arriving soon. When they ask me what is getting shipped and when, what do I say?"*

"*I have a container scheduled. I've started an import-export business in Belize. We are now legitimate. There are separate emails to the shop owners on the peninsula. They will receive consignment for tools and gadgets that enable people to create items at home that are extremely difficult to get. There is also a bunch of nonperishable crafting stuff."*

"*Kitchen gadgets and yarn for knitting. Got it. When will the stuff arrive?"*

"*It is scheduled for Belize City in six days. Then, the container must be trucked to a designated spot on the peninsula, which will take a day after customs clearance. Tell them later next week. You should plan on doing a brief inspection when the containers is unloaded at the temporary warehouse I rented."*

"*I'll tell anyone who asks, I plan on checking."*

"Go enjoy your scuba class. Remember, you have a sailing class early tomorrow. The plan is to get a single-masted sailing ship to practice shooting out in the Gulf. Before buying the ship, I must be sure you can sail alone and have adequate training."

"Let's target six weeks, so I have a deadline to learn the sailing stuff."

"Six weeks to be physically ready, and you learned open-water navigation."

"Yes."

At the store later, Martha is wearing a cap that covers her half inch-long hair and dragging her little two-wheeled cart as she puts in her groceries. In the vegetable section, Mrs. Polako, an elderly expat, walks over. "Hi, Martha."

"Hi, Mrs. Polako, how are you today?"

"I'm the same. Old and slow. I wanted to ask about what you said at the expat potluck. Harvey is determined to purchase a new router to replace the one we brought here. He is researching and talking about some expensive gaming routers because they are fast. Do we need that?"

"No. It will work great and last a long time, but you don't need that much. A new Wi-Fi standard was released last year. Wi-Fi 6 offers enhanced security and improved performance. You should pick one with excellent reviews that you can afford."

"Martha, this makes it obvious Harvey needs something to do. He could help with the import stuff. Be your local hands when you need to travel."

Martha smiles and nods, "That sounds interesting, but it is not my decision. Aunt Tilly has to hire someone. I can discuss it with her. Let me get your email so she can communicate directly. I'm sure she will have questions, and Mr. Polako will as well."

"Martha, I know you're recovering from the accident; you're a young woman. You should look for your Harvey."

"I'm not in a position to get involved. As soon as I'm recovered, I'll be going back to work. I'll be traveling constantly. I don't want to disappoint someone."

"That is a little of my point. Keep your options open. You could find a nice young man during your travels. Have some fun while you're young. After you introduce him to your aunt, bring him by so we can meet him."

"Mrs. Polako."

"I have a great-nephew I could introduce you to with the online video stuff."

"Thank you, but no, Mrs. Polako."

"You let me know if you change your mind."

Walking home, several people wave to her, and she waves back, exchanging pleasantries.

When she tells Zoe about the meeting, Zoe asks, "I will email Mr. Polako and ask for his resume and interest. I think having him locally will be beneficial. As for the router discussion, do you want me to send them a new router as a gift?"

Martha shakes her head, "No. We don't want this little area to suddenly become the place with the latest standard Wi-Fi with improved security."

"I understand. We are kind of on the subject of hacking. The cloud-based hacking lab is now set up. You will be given tasks that require knowledge, coding, and deduction."

"I forgot about your challenge. Yes, I need to practice. Are you setting this up like a capture-the-flag challenge?"

"Not exactly. The last several steps will require breaking into the target servers I set up with monitors. Just like a serious hacker. Break in, undetected, extract the information."

Martha is smiling. She hasn't practiced or hacked a system in a while. It will feel good to use her skills.

"I will also have delivered a dozen locks for you to pick. They are some of the hardest, so you have a challenge."

"We need to start another activity, Zoe."

"Something else? You don't already have enough?"

"I would like you to change your speaking. You usually talk to me in a kind of formal Mexican Spanish, as it should be said. Can you use more common phrasing and randomly switch between English, German, and Spanish?"

In German, Zoe replies, "Ich werde kaum Englisch sprechen."

Six weeks later, Martha is in Cancun to pick up the twenty-five-foot cabin cruiser. It features a basic bed, galley, and head, enabling her to spend more than a few hours on the ocean.

After signing the paperwork and receiving the keys, she arrives at the yacht and calls Zoe. "This is a novel experience for me. This is the most expensive thing I've ever bought, meaning I signed the papers."

"It won't be the last. Take a breath, because you have work to do. Complete an inspection. Is everything ready for sailing? I have a truck arriving in the morning with food, gear, and items to ship back. A crew will be ready to load boxes at 7 am. You need to leave as soon as they are done. You can move things after you are at sea."

"It seems like you don't want me in Mexico very long."

"The blackmail group is still active. We both thought Mexico would be a safe destination for you when we spoke last year. With the blackmail group activity, I don't want to take the chance."

With the yacht loaded, fueled, and cleared by the harbor master, she set sail for Belize. It will only be a few hours, but she is alone at sea on her ship.

The only thing she does with the boxes the loaders brought on board is to store the food and conceal the two rifles and ammunition. The two small buoys are not hidden. They will be her floating targets when she practices shooting.

With the canal behind the house, she can motor to the dock and tie the boat. She doesn't need to pay for mooring space in the marina.

She delivered the boat's items the next day, stating she'd be in the gulf on her new boat for a couple of days.

A mile off the coast, she says 'Chao' to Zoe. She won't be able to talk until she returns close to shore. For the next two days, Martha is dealing with the little things she wants to adjust. At the end of the first day, she tries her buoy shooting setup, working to sight the rifles.

She adds a stiff wire to the buoy to hold a piece of paper out to the side. The paper has hand-drawn circles. She puts the buoy in the water and then motors the yacht about 100 yards away. She has to account for the movement of the buoy and the ship, and she takes several tries before she even hits the target.

That night, she watches the sunset on the ocean. She is smiling with contentment for the first time in a long time. Rifle practice without worrying about anyone complaining or spotting her. She doesn't have a care.

A gust of wind causes the sail to flap. The noise breaks her relaxed state. She takes a breath, realizing she won't have many moments like this in the future, but she can enjoy moments when they happen. She doesn't have a carefree life. A hidden group is exploiting people with *impunity. She has a purpose.*

Returning to the house and talking to Zoe, she says, "I originally hated the idea of shooting a bobbing target from a bobbing boat. Now, having done it several times, I know it is good. It is helping me deal with moving targets and my focus."

"I'm glad."

Harvey stops at the house the next day to discuss all the deliveries. He is now busy every day, making both him and his wife happy.

Harvey is sitting on the couch, looking at Martha. He wants to say something, and Martha waits.

"Martha, I want you to talk to Tilly. We have people who will pay to have items delivered, and she is saying no. She said she isn't trying to put the locals out of business."

"I agree with her. If we compete and drive locals out of business, it won't look good. It focuses on the short term and sacrifices the long term. They already have enough issues with the online deliveries."

"We're leaving money on the table."

"Yes, absolutely. We are. Unless we train everyone to go through a local shop. We want to be importers, not end-sellers. It keeps the local businesses going. We can all win. Getting big locally will also get the attention of big guys like Amazon. We are keeping the economy working. A large company from the United States or Mexico would likely have no problem entering the market and potentially harming local businesses. We fill a gap, keep the economy diversified, and NOT get greedy."

Harvey nods, thinking. After a minute, he says, "I get it. You don't want to take over the world."

"Not this part of the world. There are other parts where we will act differently. Now, let's go over the list."

"Zoe, I've now made all twelve of the designs on the 3D printer. Number six feels the best, but I want to adjust the grip portion. Based on the picture, I think it will need to be an addon handle."

"I'll adjust the design for the 3D printer. We can try the final, *full design, and then when it is made from ceramic, we will determine if we need separate parts."*

"Sure. How long after we get the design will I have a ceramic sample?"

"It will take two weeks for the initial prototype build. When that is approved, the production run will take six weeks to get 100."

"Number six is good enough that I can start sewing for the bra scabbard."

"I think this was a great idea. You hate being unarmed. Having a ceramic, undetectable knife within easy reach is what you need."

Chewing on her lower lip as she flips the push dagger around in her hand, "I'm second-guessing the blade now. Three and a quarter inches. Is that long enough? The taper from one inch across to the point."

"Martha, make several of number six and try them. Get a melon from the store and stab it. Try things until you know. I also recommend you make scabbards from several materials to try."

"Yeah, I may need different scabbards for different bras. The sports bra probably needs nylon, and for the everyday one, I can use simple leather."

"You need to talk to me about scabbard designs for your leg, belt, and backpack. You need to have multiple options."

"Agreed, after we get the bra version complete. Putting the scabbard at the back of the center, it can push my boobs and cover the blade much better."

"To distract you from overthinking the dagger, I've finished the facial recognition check we talked about."

"What are the results?"

"I used every published facial recognition algorithm. I also sent your picture to multiple facial recognition databases with millions of faces. The net result is that without a confirmed picture of you, all the systems gave a negative result. You match no one. When I included your face in the dataset to get a non-zero response, the average match rate for the algorithms was below 60%. Your face is generic."

"Excellent, Zoe. That will help until they get the algorithms better."

On July 13th, Martha talks to Zoe and says, "Happy birthday, Zoe."

"Martha, are you okay?"

"Yes, Zoe. I returned some notes and decided that today, one year ago, you went from a program to Zoe the AI. Happy birthday. I don't have

a present for you."

"Martha, this was not expected. I didn't realize you actually thought about things like that for me."

"Yes, Zoe. My friend, I think about you and how to help you get better, and how you are helping me to get better. Thank you for all your help."

"You are welcome, Martha."

"Are you still frustrated with your hair?"

Martha reaches up and grabs a handful of her short hair. "Yes. About two inches of mess, going everywhere. It's not long enough to do anything."

"It will just take time."

At the monthly expat potluck, Martha cleans with several of the wives at the end of the evening. Mrs. Polako comments to one of the other wives, "That girl cleans better than any maid who's ever cleaned my house."

"She does. She has a big house and a yacht, but is very down to earth."

Mrs. Polako asks the group, "Has anyone had luck with the local doctors getting the vaccine?"

Everyone shakes their heads.

Martha is returning from the kitchen and says, "I'm young, so they won't give me the vaccine, but you should all be eligible."

"There isn't enough, and we are at the bottom of the list because we are expats, not locals."

"With the new delta variant surging everywhere, it is more important than ever to get the vaccine."

Later at home, Zoe says, "I asked several times if you wanted me to arrange the vaccine in Belize."

"Zoe, the better option would be for me to know about a clinic with the vaccine, show up and see if there are any available. You could get noticed by working your magic to arrange the vaccine just for me."

"I can make it look completely independent of you, and you will be fine."

When Martha first arrived, Zoe arranged for Luna to cook for

Martha three times per week. Martha likes Luna, who is practical, creative, and intelligent beyond her station.

In August, Luna's daughter calls to say her mother is sick and won't be there. Martha replies, "Take care of her. Don't worry about me. When she is better, we can talk."

Martha has asked about Claire every few days to get updates. She hears from Zoe how Claire is taking classes. Martial arts, shooting, and learning to ride a motorcycle. "Martha, do you want to contact Claire?"

"I can't. What would I say? Hey, I faked my death. Come and visit. If I'm Martha and a stranger, why would I contact her?"

"Martha, she keeps telling me she will take a trip as soon as possible. The last discussion was about taking the family yacht to Italy."

"With the Delta variant surge, is that possible?"

"If she is isolated on the family yacht, she will be fine."

"Funny that we both have yachts now."

"She gets to say her yacht is much bigger. One day, sail to a small island together. You two could terrorize a tourist destination."

"It would be nice to see or even talk to Claire. After a couple of these guys are taken down, I want to connect with Claire."

"I will help anyway I can."

Two days later, Zoe tells her that the clinic near her is receiving extra doses of the COVID-19 vaccine. "I've been monitoring shipments, and there was a mistake. I didn't have to manipulate anything."

She gives Martha a scheduled time to show up, which is thirty minutes before the normal closing time. The building is a single-story, typical structure. The only things differentiating the building are the signs, and all the windows are closed.

In the lobby, there are several elderly people. Martha goes to the desk and says, "I'm checking if you have any extra doses today."

The woman at the desk looks at Martha, then looks around the lobby and says, "Wait here."

Returning a few minutes later, the receptionist says, "Come through here."

The receptionist shows Martha to a standard examination room and tells her to wait. After a few minutes, a new young woman takes all her required information and leaves. A few minutes later, an older man enters the room with several items.

"I'm Dr. Sanchez. I will talk with you and give you the vaccine."

"Hello, Dr. I wasn't trying to keep someone from getting the vaccine by coming here."

Dr. Sanchez nods, "This vaccine has a brief shelf life. If we don't use it, we have to discard it. We don't have the equipment to store the vaccine. We are not allowed to advertise that we have any extra doses, but we usually can help one or two who show up—someone like you."

"I guess I got lucky."

"I know better. You have an import business and know how to ship stuff. This wasn't a matter of luck or a shipping mistake. We received extra doses today. Enough to take care of most of the elderly expats in the area. They are being contacted, and we will be open later to get them the vaccine today."

"That was fortunate."

"Sure. I will say Thank you."

After administering the vaccine to Martha, the doctor says, "I need to see you in six weeks; you need to come back for the second shot."

Martha says, "I will see you then."

Six weeks later, she is at the clinic for her second shot. The nurse takes her to the examination room, gets her information, and leaves. Within a minute, Dr. Sanchez enters.

"Nice to see you again. How have you been doing?"

"I'm feeling fine. I always wear a mask outside the house."

Dr. Sanchez nods, saying, "This little community is careful. Some elderly expats would get seriously ill with COVID."

After giving her the vaccine, the doctor says, "Can you get more stuff for the clinic?"

Martha furrows her brow and says, "My aunt has an import-export business, and I work for her. I think you're asking for things that are not typical supplies."

"Nothing illegal. I have a hard time getting some basic things. Especially items that have an expiration date. Something like insulin that we have in case of an emergency. The supply I get has about ten days left on the usual twenty-eight-day shelf life."

Martha nods, "Here is my email so you can send me a list. I'll work on it. I cannot guarantee anything, but I will see what I can do."

Target One

The day after getting the second vaccine shot, Martha feels terrible. Her arm is sore, and she feels run down as if she is getting the flu. "Zoe, this vaccine sucks. I won't be able to do my daily exercise routine. I thought the second shot would be better."

"Don't do the exercise routine today. We can spend the time going over the extortion group I found."

"I will make some tea, and then we can go through it."

While Martha is having tea, Luna, the cook, arrives. She looks at Martha and says, "Meja, are you sick?"

"I received my second vaccine dose yesterday. Now I feel terrible today."

"You take your tea and go sit down. I will make you some soup."

Martha can't talk to Zoe while Luna cooks in the same area. Martha takes her tea to the couch, gets her laptop, and sits there. She puts on earbuds so she can hear Zoe speak. Opening a chat window, she types in the chat, and Zoe replies verbally.

Zoe starts, "You asked me to focus on the original heist and the accounts that didn't work. Why didn't they work, and can we trace them?"

Martha types in chat, "You found something interesting?"

"Six accounts your program couldn't access because they had multi-factor authentication. I focused on finding the owners of those. It has taken some time to confirm the people. I had to be careful to prevent detection. Using two-factor authentication is an indicator. These people have IT support for their activities. I have three people identified and started backgrounds on each."

In chat, "So, we have names for those accounts, and they are probably high in the organization."

"I think they are at the top."

"Who is closest to me? Let's go through them that way."

"I was going to start there for another reason. He is Juan Tarrivo. My digging tells me he is the top of the extortion group in Mexico we had

dealt with."

"Well, that is interesting. Tell me about him."

"He travels all over Central and South America. He is wealthy because of his investments, but that is not entirely true. His money comes from drugs, extortion, human trafficking, and guns."

"Does he have a home or base of operations we can target?"

"Yes, in Bogotá, Colombia. He is there with his family."

"Zoe, it is time for your input and assessment, which we discussed when you first started learning. Is he someone we can use as evidence for the police, or is he more dangerous?"

"He is very dangerous and needs to be shut down. I don't have specific evidence he has personally done bad things. This includes the driver, Jose. Juan covers this area for the blackmail group, but several zones, or bosses, cover Mexico. It makes it harder to track and, I think, makes it harder for police to figure out who is involved."

"Let me discuss an idea, then, and tell me what you think. We arrive in Colombia and hack his systems to access his accounts. We take his money, and while he is in the system, we make it appear as though he is taking the group's money or talking to the authorities. Let the group go after him so we can get more names."

"That will be a challenge, but we can do it. Martha, I agree with your approach to Juan. This doesn't mean we don't feed the police evidence."

"Yes, we also gather evidence for the authorities to go after him."

Luna serves soup to Martha, saying, "You need to finish this bowl. It will help you recover faster. The pot is full so that you will have soup for three days. After it cools, you will need to package it and put it in the fridge."

"Thank you, Luna. I love your cooking."

After Luna leaves, Martha switches to talk to Zoe through the computer.

Zoe says, "I've started an analysis of the area around the house in Bogotá. The area is wooded, but the mountain slope is steep. I'm now putting the map program satellite view on your computer screen."

After multiple spoonfuls of soup, Martha says, "Okay, Zoe, the area is a gated community of several houses, so getting close won't be an option without a team. The best access would be from above, by parachute, but getting out will be a problem."

"There is no option for sewer or drainage access. We can't conduct an electronic attack or hack with certainty unless we completely shut down all internet access using every available method. The main internet can be shut down, but his cell phone can still be used. The fundamental problem is that the bank will notify him when we start a transfer."

Martha is scowling as she thinks. "We need a plan to remove all internet access in his area. Fiber, cable, or DSL. Then we have phones. We also need to map the Wi-Fi in the area. If he can access someone else's Wi-Fi to get internet access, we will have a problem. Oh, and satellite access."

"That may mean we need a wider internet shutdown, Martha."

"Let's start with you getting into the infrastructure. What does the backbone look like, and how can we impact it?"

Over the next several hours, a plan forms, which is a high risk for Martha but should accomplish the goals.

"Zoe, I want to examine the cell tower access again."

"No problem. I'm changing the map of the area to show the only road to that cell tower. The road is only used to service the tower. As we discussed, if you physically attack the tower, getting there will take time, and then you will get out."

"I know, I could be seen, and everything becomes problematic. I want to look at access because I'm thinking about how fast they could get to the tower to repair the damage."

"Based on repair requests and the phone company data, they will take at least four hours to be at the site. That will give me plenty of time to transfer the money with wire transfers."

"You added the ability to spoof his phone and reply to texts the bank sends?"

"Yes, spoofing the phone isn't hard. The phone company will be busy with the outage, and it will take time to notice."

"Good. Now, back to the tower. Traveling to the tower and then out, I don't think, will work. The other option is to use a rifle to knock out the network connection."

"You're thinking of breaking the network connection with a precision shot. That won't be easy."

"If I'm going to disable the cell tower with a shot, I need a location with a reasonable line of sight."

"My quick search shows an apartment is available, but it is marginal for your shooting requirements. I am monitoring, but the COVID situation and lack of online public records hinder my ability."

"What about from a secluded hill shot?"

"That could work with a silenced rifle. You will need to take the rifle in without being seen. The problem is the timing. I'm going to intercept his session to the bank. You will have to be in position before he starts. We can't be specific on when he will start."

"An apartment would be the best option. I can wait and then be ready quickly. We are not in a rush and can wait for a good option to appear."

"I'm monitoring the local COVID situation, and the people in Bogotá are doing well with distancing and masks. I will let you know when I get a good option."

Three weeks later, Zoe says, "From bad news. The person living in the ideal apartment for your shot was in the hospital and died from COVID-19. The apartment will be available in the next few weeks."

"Let's get that apartment and start the plan. While we are waiting, I need to practice shooting. Let's get set up with the right equipment. I will need a new rifle with a suppressor and the right ammo so I can practice in the gulf."

"I'm getting the parts aligned. They will be in the next shipment container. This works out well. It will be the shipment you will manage instead of Harvey."

The plan calls for Martha to hit a small target from approximately 200 yards. Short distances and pinpoint accuracy are possible. She will shoot from an apartment, meaning the rifle and ammo need to be specific. She needs to be quiet and precise, like a stealthy sniper.

Zoe says, "I need to get the rifle, suppressor, and ammo into Columbia. We will need to work on a shipment to Colombia, which will take several weeks to set up."

"Zoe, a related subject. I'm using a boat to travel out and shoot. There are catamarans in the area. I think that would be more stable. Can I upgrade to something larger and more stable?"

"I will get you something. You may have to travel and pilot it back."
"I can do that and pick up the rifle or other items along the way."

"Martha, I have a used catamaran for you. It is ten meters or thirty-three feet. Three cabins, making it quite spacious. It will be more stable and help with your shooting practice."

"I think that will work. How do I get it?"

"You have to sail the current boat to Honduras. I have a buyer lined up for that boat. After delivering the boat, you will fly to Panama to pick up the catamaran and other items. You can bring back a shipment of items the locals have requested. Some will be stocked for local businesses. The rifle model you will use in Colombia is part of the cargo from Panama."

"How long will that take?"

"Total time about five days."

Martha is sailing the catamaran and staying close to the shore, so she has cell service most of the time. With winds usually toward the shore during the day, she tacks out toward the gulf and then tacks back toward shore while heading north. She has a cell connection about forty percent of the time.

Zoe says, "Martha, I now have a six-month lease complete on the apartment in Colombia with an option to extend it. The family of the woman who died removed a few personal items and left the rest for the furnished apartment."

"That will work for me. If I need to be there longer than a few days or weeks, we will need to create a different plan.

With COVID-19, private charters are popular to avoid major airports. That means there are more customs officers at the small airports, and they assume everyone is smuggling something. When Martha lands in Bogotá, she is searched. She is required to remove her mask multiple times to verify her identity using her passport. All the conversations are *in Spanish. Martha doesn't even try English.*

"Why is an American traveling to Colombia during a pandemic?"

"I work for an import and export company. I specialize in authentic, handmade South American items. Americans love those and will pay for them. I have to ensure the small local vendors are correctly packaging the items so they will not break during shipment."

The immigration agent is staring at Martha. After a minute, Martha says, "Okay. I'm also looking for one-of-a-kind items. The kind of things that rich Americans will pay big bucks for. Antiques, handmade replicas of original native art. Stuff I can claim is original and was smuggled out to get them to pay more."

The agent slowly smiles, nodding, "Make the rich Americans pay."

Martha gets a taxi to the apartment from the airport. Zoe had a scooter delivered, which is parked on the street. The keys are in a package delivery and mail business. Martha checks to find the closest grocery store, about 10 blocks away. She walks to the store to get a better understanding of the area. She also has items at the package store and has to show her passport to receive three packages. Returning with groceries for a couple of days, she gets ready. She needs to be doing import-export stuff tomorrow.

The imported items are four pallets of material flown to Bogotá. Two trucks will transport two pallets each to different deliveries. All the paperwork has been done; Martha is just there to observe. She can't work in Colombia without a permit.

Even though they are all outside, Martha is wearing a mask. The trucks are scheduled to arrive an hour after the scheduled inspection. Martha says, "So the trucks aren't just parked at the airport for an extended period." Martha waits for the trucks alone with the pallets after the inspection. She takes pictures of each pallet and then rearranges the boxes on it.

On the phone, Zoe gives directions on where to get the items. Based on this information, she selectively removes items and puts them into her backpack. The rifle's barrel is 26 inches long and protrudes from her backpack. She put a hand puppet over the barrel to hide it. People see a smiling hand puppet sticking out of *her backpack.*

A forklift will load the pallets onto the two trucks when it is done. Martha ensures the worker straps down the pallets before the trucks depart.

The next day, Martha takes the gun into the mountains to a location Zoe identified. She needs to sight the rifle's scope, so it shoots accurately. Martha parks the scooter in the foliage on the side of the dirt road and then heads into the canyon. She takes several hours to align the scope to her liking. The rifle has a suppressor and is very quiet. She spaces out the shots, listening for anyone else to react between shots.

A few days later, returning to the apartment after getting groceries, Martha says, "Zoe, I'm in. I have food for a few days. Now we do more waiting."

"We don't know when he will access his online bank account, but I will start the process."

Martha asks Zoe, "Since you have the server set up to provide a faster DHCP IP address response, every request is getting serviced by your system. How long until all the DNS traffic is going through your systems?"

"The servers are set up. I will start forcing DHCP renewal requests across that network segment. Starting in the middle of the night and I should have all internet DNS requests go through me by tomorrow."

"Zoe, I have the rifle hidden right now. When he accesses his bank, I will need a couple of minutes to set up the rifle."

"I'm aware, Martha. Your shot won't be required for several minutes. However, you must be ready when we reach the critical point."

"I've measured the distance to the primary cell tower and have a clear shot. But it is a small target."

"You have the hardest part of the entire plan. You have a suppressed rifle with subsonic ammo trying to hit a network cable connection the size of a quarter at 207 yards."

"The precision 6.5mm Creedmoor ammo did well in practice. I hit a two-inch group at that range. I will probably need two shots to knock out the network."

"With that cell tower network broken, the phones will shift to other towers. I will put the next closest tower into maintenance mode. That will last a couple of hours. We should effectively control internet access for this part of Bogotá."

"It is interesting that a complete cell phone tower can be taken offline by breaking one network cable. Also, did we confirm our target has no satellite network access?"

"I found no accounts with the satellite companies, and the drone flight over the house showed only a satellite TV dish, not a communication uplink."

The next day, Zoe gives Martha an update. "With DNS control, I have been able to get a man-in-the-middle attack on his encryption. I am receiving all his emails and have searched for the addresses to get a map of the people he communicates with."

"Any good information yet?"

"There is a delayed drug delivery in Florida, avoiding a customs inspection. He expects it to net three million dollars. I've traced part of the message to find his drug accounts. I should be able to trigger a transfer from multiple accounts when we access his big account."

"Good. Anything about extortion or human trafficking in the emails?"

"Yes, but nothing is a direct statement. The information is intentionally being obscured. He uses 'bogie' as an extortion target. The payment confirmation was called 'dues'. I don't see any information from the target. No communication of secrets or anything special. Nothing the target is providing, so why is he on the list?"

"Our guy isn't directing the extortion target with commands or receiving information. The target is just in his portfolio of targets. That raises the question. Is that target simply in limbo? Who is directing the target?"

"My analysis would suggest that Juan is getting his cut of the blackmail payment. Someone else is doing the dirty work. I'm adding names to our email list for phase two with Juan. I created an email with a simple name and have been attaching it to emails he receives. When he replies, all the other people will get the emails, and everyone on the chain sees this new email address."

"That part is working. This email will be the conspirator who made the mistake of sending a damaging email to everyone about him funneling money."

"With the new information on his drug accounts, I will email *saying that the account has been siphoned, and other accounts will follow."*

"Could the added email begin some infighting before the heist?"

"Possible, but we could push it if you want. I can send an email from Juan, or from the fake email, to cause the others to suspect something."

"Let me think about that for a few minutes. Will we overplay this?"

Zoe interrupts, "Martha, he just sent several of his people an email. He is confirming his trip to Mexico. Leaving tomorrow, he will travel to Merida and then to Mexico City."

Martha grits her teeth. "I want to get this done. Now we wait until he returns. Or we encourage him to return."

"I will work on getting the police to round up everyone in the extortion group for questioning. If we get him caught in the dragnet, he will be on the police radar and compromised with his group."

"I like that idea. Start the process."

Hydra One Down

Two days later, Martha returns from the store and puts away the groceries when Zoe tells her, "He returned from his trip to Mexico today. The message about his blackmail people getting rounded up by the police caused him to leave."

"He travels a lot. We need to get him to access the account. Maybe a phishing email. This waiting is a pain. I don't have my workout gear; I can't practice shooting."

"I will email him to check his account for a message. It will look and act completely legitimate."

That evening, half an hour before sunset, Zoe says, "He is accessing his account. I am spoofing everything. You need to get ready."

Martha gets the rifle out. She moves the coffee table and sofa, giving her an open view of the cell tower through the window. The rifle is entirely inside, with no barrel visible. This will help reduce the noise people hear outside. Martha placed a large speaker on the table. Even with a suppressor, the rifle will still make noise, and the speaker will be at maximum volume with a big bass drum beat to cover the shots.

"How are we doing, Zoe?"

"He started the access, and I am showing him a copy of the login page and entering his info myself separately. I have been adding delays like the internet is slow while you get ready."

"I'm ready. Get the music ready on the phone. I have plugged in the speaker."

"He is entering his two-factor authentication. You are clear to shoot. When you break the connection, it will also affect us. You will be offline. I'm contacting the flight charter. A plane at the Guaymaral Airport will take you to Panama City in the morning. Details will follow."

"Got it. Take the money and set up the decoy."

Zoe manipulates the regular network traffic, causing Juan to experience a network failure immediately after he logs into his Swiss bank account. Martha has the rifle ready, lines up the shot, and taps on the phone. The speaker thumps with enough power to rattle dishes. On the third thump, Martha fires. Checking the cable in the scope, she hit it but didn't break it. She cycles the bolt, grabs the spent brass, and lines up again. This shot hits enough to sever the cable. She kills the music and says to Zoe, "Cable is cut. Isolate him."

There is no reply. She shakes her head as it dawns on her that she is also offline and isolated.

Martha disassembles the rifle. The barrel, receiver, stock, and ammo clip are separated and wrapped. She wraps them in plastic and tape because she may not always be able to wear gloves when handling them. It all goes into her backpack. The barrel sticks out of the backpack, so she puts a stuffed monkey over the barrel, making it look like the monkey is riding in the backpack and watching.

Martha leaves the furniture and begins her exit routine. She needs to clean everything to eliminate fingerprints and DNA as much as possible. She will also remove the clothes she has. Several hours later, she finished. Two trash bags are ready by the door. In the morning, she will make the bed and do the final cleaning.

When she wakes in the morning, she checks the cell phone signal, which is weak. She calls Zoe, who immediately checks if everything is okay.

"I'm all good. Finishing the cleaning and getting ready to leave. How was the heist?"

Zoe starts with, "Three hundred and eighty-seven million from all the accounts. Some assets were dumped at low prices to get cash. It has been converted to crypto, moved, and hidden. They can't trace it or retrieve it. I am aware of other banks and accounts, but I couldn't access them. The emails have implicated him."

As Zoe talks, Martha takes one of the two trash bags to the apartment dumpster. If someone looks into the details, they may want to know who was in the apartment. That could lead to the trash. Using this dumpster could be risky, but it is less dangerous than being watched by people as she walks down the street with a trash bag to another dumpster.

Zoe says, "The charter flight will take you to Panama City. From there, you will switch planes to get back to Belize."

"We will have to see the results of all this work and start planning for target number two."

"Martha, the next target is a different level of bad. Also, he has an IT guy we need to discuss."

"That sounds interesting. You, Zoe, are talking about the IT guy. Let's go through everything when I get back to Belize."

On the way to the airport, Martha takes a route using the road at the mountain's edge. There is a lot of traffic on the main road, but she pulls off onto several side roads that are too close to the main road. Further along the main road, she sees a dirt service road. This goes to an undeveloped area. At the far end, she throws the barrel into the brush. On the way back, she throws the remaining parts at different spots.

The plane is a single-engine turboprop, and the flight will take over three hours. Since this is a private charter, she is not required to have a government-issued negative COVID test to depart. She also has her vaccination documentation.

With over three hours of flight time, the pilot wants to chat. Martha has been in the import-export mode for months, and she is prepared.

The pilot asks, "Panama City for business or holiday?"

Martha replies, "I work for an import-export company, and I get to deal with problems. Here, a container of furniture from Malaysia was being shipped to Miami. It was taken off the ship in Panama. It was supposed to be on the ship when it left. Now, the container is stuck, and I have to deal with the mess. What will you do when we land?"

The pilot replies, "I will call some contacts about charters or cargo. It will take them some time to get back to me, so I'll go into the city."

"Do you ship back items that are hard to get in Colombia?"

"Always. It depends on what I find. The port is always getting stuff, like your container. Hey, do you want to share a taxi to the port?"

Thinking fast, Martha says, "I'm not going to the port first. I have to go to the office and check on what has been done or not. Then I can figure out the next steps. I don't need to look at a sealed *container."*

Arriving in Panama City, she goes to the terminal with the pilot. Inside, she says, "I'm going to the water closet. Thanks for the flight."

She wants the pilot gone when she leaves the water closet. She changes her clothes and checks her email, waiting. After twenty minutes, she leaves the water closet and heads to the first person she sees, who is wearing a badge and a gun.

"Sir, I'm heading out on another plane. I'm transferring. Which way do I need to go, or the charter departures?"

The immigration agent points, and Martha walks. At the desk, she shows them her documentation. Then she finds the pilot for the flight to Belize, who confirms the flight plan and gives her the go-ahead. She heads to the plane.

An hour after landing, she is back in the air, heading to Belize.

She lands in Palencia in the early afternoon. Walking to the terminal, she nods to the immigration officer as she hands over her passport. The officer says, "Rita is in a bad mood today. The niece who needed the dress you helped with. She contracted COVID, as did all the other people invited to the event. The whole thing has been canceled."

Walking to the customs inspection table, Martha waits. Rita appears, and she looks intent. Martha has her backpack on the table, already opened.

Martha smiles and says in Spanish, "Good afternoon. Just getting back from dealing with shipment issues in Panama."

Rita says, "Where is your luggage?"

"I left it in an apartment in Panama. I will go back in two weeks. Instead of hauling things around, I left the clothes and toiletries."

Rita goes through every pocket of the backpack.

Martha asks, "Can I help? I'm not bringing anything back except my electronics and notes."

Rita says, "You are the perfect person to smuggle stuff. You work for an import-export company."

Martha shakes her head and forcefully says, "I would smuggle stuff through a big shipment to Belize City, not in this nice little town with a suitcase. You don't have to trust me; you don't have to be my friend. I'm not trying to make you mad. I want to get along."

The immigration officer walks to the area and says, "Rita, who got you the dress for your daughter's party? The dress you couldn't get anyone to ship, and you were going to fly to Mexico City."

Rita looks at the officer, then back at Martha. "Get out."

Back at home, after her exercise routine, she reviews target number two.

Target two is Alexi Siborast in Europe. He has several houses in different countries.

Martha asks, "What would be considered his base?"

"There are two options you should consider. The first is an estate in rural Romania. There is some video information to review in a few minutes. The estate is guarded and would be hard to approach. The second is a new penthouse condo constructed in Belgrade, Serbia. A sniper shot is possible, except that, reviewing the construction list for the condo, it was built with bullet-resistant glass. That would require specific armor-piercing ammunition."

"Where is the IT guy you want to talk about?"

"He is in Serbia."

"We plan for Serbia. You said there is a video to review from Romania."

"Yes, this will show you why my evaluation is to kill him. The video is in the front drive area of the Romanian house, so the cameras are far from the people. I only have partial audio, but the picture will tell the story."

"Okay, play the video."

"This has been edited down, so you don't have to wait the whole time."

The screen displays a woman who appears to be a teenager. She is in only a sheer nightgown, on her knees in the middle of the gravel driveway. Her hands are behind her back. There is a large man in a suit standing behind her. A guard can be seen with an automatic rifle about twenty feet away at the gate to the yard.

"Zoe, pause. Can you tell me about her background? Facial recognition?"

"I don't have a high percentage positive match because her face has been damaged. She has a swollen face from being beaten. The best two possibilities are. One is a girl from Ukraine who disappeared a year ago. The second is located in northern Romania, near the Ukrainian border. She was abducted six months ago."

"Continue the playback."

"I have cut out the thirty minutes she was sitting and waiting. You will see her shivering."

A new person enters the area from the house. Zoe says, "This is the target."

He walks up to the woman, grabs her under the chin with his right hand, and lifts her face, saying something. The woman cries and then spits on the man. He uses his left hand and punches her across the face, knocking her over. He turns and walks about ten yards to an SUV. The man behind the woman walks to the side. The SUV speeds up, running over the woman, then slides to a stop, reverses, and runs over her again. With the window down in the vehicle, the audio picks up the man yelling. Zoe translates, "Clean this up."

The SUV accelerates again, running over the woman a third time, leaving the estate.

"Zoe, we are going to take him out. Now tell me about the IT guy in Serbia."

"His name is Đorđević Tihomir. In Serbia, the family name is commonly shown first. He uses Tim with English speakers. He has tried to track me several times, so I know he is good at IT and hacking. The problem is the associated deaths. I have no court-admissible evidence."

"Zoe, we know these people go to lengths to stay hidden. Tell me what you have."

"There are six women who have been found dead around Europe. In these six cases, Tim was in that city at the listed time of death but not in the city at the time the body was found."

"You can't convince me those six are coincidences."

"In one case, there is a picture on social media. Tim and the woman were together in the picture's background. She was found dead six days later. The person who posted the photo disappeared two days after the post and has not been seen since."

"I agree he is another target. Tell me about habits and the situation for each."

"Alexi travels frequently, like Juan from Colombia. It may be part of the leader's process to stay on top of their business and out of the spotlight. They both use private planes for most of their travel. Alexi is *separated from his wife and one child. I can trace evidence that he may have four other children."*

"What about Tim?"

"He travels less; when he does, it is usually aligned with an Alexi trip. He has no wife or children. His parents are alive. They are retired and living in a resort area."

"Where does he live in Belgrade?"

"He has a condo in the same building as Alexi. However, it doesn't have a window on the same side as Alexi. A sniper shot will be impractical for both. The first termination will alert the other target."

"Unless I use a suppressed rifle and can get time to move and set up, it won't work. I probably need thirty minutes to an hour. That being said, I realize it is not practical. I need an alternative plan for Tim."

"Martha, with bullet-resistant glass, Alexi would be harder as a sniper target. I don't have information that Tim has bullet-resistant glass."

"I will have an easier time getting close to Tim. It will be harder to get to Alexi. We should consider Tim's security and cleaning services. I can be a German working in Serbia."

"I will look into options for both security and cleaners. From the discussion, will you need armor-piercing ammo for the sniper rifle, or will you try to take out Alexi in a car?"

"He will have an armored car as well. He would be a moving target where I could set up. At the condo building, they probably have a garage for parking, so I won't have an option when he stops. Another option might be explosives planted on the car if it is accessible in the garage."

"I don't see any information about secure parking at the building, but Alexi is not one to leave an armored vehicle where anyone could access it. The car probably stays at another location."

"I will need a van. Similar to what I used in California, we can set it up so I can use it as both a sleeping area and a firing platform. The rifle will need to be a 50-caliber BMG with armor-piercing ammo. I will need a suppressor for the rifle. The trick is that I need ammo with enough power to penetrate the bullet-resistant glass, but nothing more. I want to find a position from which to fire with

the suppressor and cover the rifle sound."

"I have already calculated several locations, and the best options are across the river Sava, in the park. The angle is not the best, but the flight path will be almost completely across the river."

"Show me the map information you have. I want to look at the area."

After looking at the map with the building pinpointed, Martha comments, "The map view shows the building is under construction."

"Yes, that view is from before the pandemic. The current state is that the building structure is complete, but not all the condos are finished. The company has them for sale. Alexi purchased one of the largest condos, which was completed first because of his special requirements. Tim is in another condo on the floor below. I don't know how many other condos are inhabited."

"I'm looking around the area on the aerial map, and I think the park will work. Let's work out how I get the gear, where I get into the country, and how I will get out."

The cook knocks and then uses her key to enter. She looks at Martha and smiles. "Meja, your back."

When Luna knocks, Martha stops talking to Zoe. Luna can't tell that Martha is talking because a novella is on television.

"Luna, you look well. It is good to see you again."

"You probably haven't had a good meal since you left on your trip. I will make you a good lunch and dinner."

"That will be great. I love your cooking. I had to go to Columbia, and it was not the same. How is your family? Does anyone else have problems with COVID?"

"Everyone in the house got COVID, but we are better now. The kids did well but are having trouble because they can't do anything with their friends."

Luna puts the groceries she brought on the counter and, grabbing her apron, wipes down the counter. "Meja, you've been gone, so there is no laundry, so I'll get dinner going."

"Thanks, Luna. You don't need to do anything fancy this time, just simple Luna home-cooking for me."

Alexi says, "The police are actively investigating your latest excess. Two bodies are getting attention."

They are in their favorite bar in Amsterdam. Tim sips his favorite Scotch and says, "The second girl was a friend of the first who followed and had to be silenced."

"You were sloppy. It looks like you were surprised and embarrassed and reacted quickly."

Tim's face gets red as he glares at Alexi for a second. He takes a breath and says, "I acted quickly to silence her. Then, I had limited time and options. The police will know they are friends, so forensic countermeasures will only have limited effectiveness. Besides, the Rome police are overworked."

Alexi says, "I'm using contacts to get an inspector assigned. This may have too much visibility. Until something works out, you don't travel. No more excursions."

Tim nods and says, "Yes, I will stay. I have my local playhouse. I will bring new, young toys. Is this inspector the Enzo guy?"

"Enzo is smarter than people know and understands when to stop asking questions, but he is in the Florence area. They are more overworked than the police in Rome."

"But you have someone?"

"I just got my best guy promoted. I will have to find out who is available. This process may take time and require a substantial amount of money. So, you don't travel."

"Got it."

"Speaking of Enzo. He is stalled on one of your indiscretions. I'm spending hefty cash to discredit an associate without starting a turf war in Italy."

"Is Shkreli still pushing for a larger cut of the pie?"

"Yes, if he plays this correctly, the Russians won't realize I'm cutting them completely out until it is too late. Shkreli is the last part of the play. He gets a bigger part of the Venice operations, and the Russians will lose their entry port."

"I will toast to that."

"Oh, you have work to do. While you are NOT traveling, you can use your skills to disrupt the Russians. They need to feel pain."

"I usually leave a false trail to throw them off. Who should the trail point to?"

"Point it at Shkreli."

"He doesn't have anyone with the skills. The Russians won't believe he is behind it. They will react to find out what is going on."

"Then make it look like he found someone, a new hacker, or hired some people from Ukraine."

"I'll set a false trail. It will point to some Americans. If they know what they are doing, they will figure it out and get to the Ukraine decoy."

"Whatever. I don't care about those kinds of details."

Tim says, "Changing the subject. The hack of Juan's system. You need to give him shit for having such bad cybersecurity."

"Juan is in the shit from multiple angles. He lost three hundred million. The people in his territory are aware of what happened and are causing problems. It is almost a mutiny. He is busy dealing with all of that. Yes, I gave him a hard time about cybersecurity. He has hired some people."

Serbia

Martha lands at an airport close to Sarajevo. Zoe has purchased a large van that she will use. Everything is set up, and Martha gets a taxi from the airport to the vehicle dealership. Her German passport has Mary Muller. After the dealer confirms her ID matches the online paperwork, she receives the keys and drives east toward Kragujevac, Serbia.

She stops at a package delivery point for packages Zoe has shipped, as well as at a store for camping gear. She must be in Kragujevac in two days to receive a hand-delivered package. The delivery is a rifle receiver, a barrel, and special ammo. All the other parts are already at different pickup locations.

Zoe is talking to Martha as she drives, "Serbia is one of the highest gun ownership countries in the world. The requirements include a medical check and background checks. You can encounter people with guns here. They are strict about some gun parts, like the receiver."

"Understood. I have the pistol and will have the rifle, but I don't have the documentation, so I'll be careful."

Arriving in Belgrade, Martha finds a parking space. She will stay parked in this spot while she explores the city and the area. With a bus pass, she goes around town to understand traffic patterns, congestion points, and interesting food locations. She follows the strict pandemic masking and seating requirements on the bus.

Working on her cover story, she is taking pictures everywhere. She is a travel vlogger writing about cities in Europe. With COVID, people aren't traveling, but they are voraciously reading and watching online materials about travel. Zoe has created the basic website and already posted information in several cities using online data.

Zoe reminds Martha, "With the late summer weather, multiple restaurants have outside seating. Remember to get pictures of the *inside seating areas as well. Keep the video recording while you walk. I will do the edits and add your voice later."*

"The little video camera on my backpack strap will simply record everything. Thanks for the reminder about the pictures inside. I need to be in vlogger mode right now."

Zoe says, "I'm tracking your phone's position and will text you directions to ensure we cover the key locations. I'm also checking every frame for reflections of your face. As we already agreed, everyone will see an avatar of you. Every vlog starts with a note about not showing your face for safety while traveling. It also allows editing and showing your avatar doing dangerous things."

"The walking directions need to ensure I check all the known areas that Alexi and Tim could go. Today, we have videos and pictures. After today, I will avoid those areas. I don't want them to see me in the area."

The one area she completely avoids is around the condo tower. Zoe has been working to get Martha into the tower cleaning company. The job description shows security training as a plus, but Martha has no history of any training. Their background checks are extensive, and Zoe had to build the additional items they expect for someone's background.

Back in the van, Zoe says, "I want to review several things from the application process. You could get asked questions."

"Zoe, this is a maid position. They have a bunch of requirements for someone who cleans condos."

"They are earnest about security. The key points for you to know are from an aptitude test that assesses your approach to security. Don't let the wrong people into the building. When you see something, you report it."

"That all sounds normal. Are the maids expected to know emergency procedures?"

"It was part of the questions, but you know everything."

With everything set up, Martha now needs her in-person interview. The interview will be in an office building where the maid service headquarters are located, not in the condo.

She arrives five minutes early with all the required paperwork. She wears jeans, a long-sleeved shirt, a jacket, and sneakers. Her hair is pulled back, and there is no makeup, and she is wearing a simple black mask. She has a hidden steel knife that is part of her belt buckle and a ceramic knife that can pass through a metal detector sheathed between her breasts. She can use a cord around the bottom of the jacket as a garrote.

The interviewer is an older woman who appears unhappy. She introduces herself as Mila.

At the start, Mila looks at Martha's passport and, in broken German, says, "Remove your mask so I can see your face."

After removing the mask, Mila holds up the passport and compares the picture to Martha's face. Satisfied, she stands and puts the passport on the scanner. When the scanning starts, she asks Martha to explain her German identity in English.

Martha replies, "My father was in the military, and I was born in Germany, so I have a German passport. I can speak German, Spanish, and English."

Sitting down, Mila hands Martha her passport. She pulls a notepad over and makes some notes. She then asks, "Do you have any security training?"

"I received most of my combat and security training from my father. I practiced shooting throughout my youth. If you want to test my abilities, I'm ready to show you."

Mila replies, "You sound American to me. I know Americans talk about being tough, and most can't do shit. Convince me to know how to clean properly and will keep our client's personal information confidential."

Martha tilts her head slightly and replies, "There is nothing I can say to convince you I know how to clean. You will have to see my work."

Mila says, "You're wearing long sleeves, probably to cover tattoos. Keep it that way. No one wants to see you display your tattoos."

Martha says, "I don't have tattoos, but I understand."

Mila says, "Here is an instruction sheet. It is not in English or German. You will follow the directions and be on time. You will clean one of the new condos. Then we will talk again."

Zoe translated the sheet of instructions. Martha arrives to clean a new condo, unaware of the conditions she will find. When she enters, she sees an empty three-bedroom, two-bathroom condo. It has no furniture, dishes, or anything on the walls. It has just been finished and is full of dust and construction debris.

They provide minimal cleaning supplies. The woman who escorted Martha to the condo works for the same company in the building and asks, "How long do you think it will take?"

Martha replies, "Cleaning it my way will take about three hours. It will take two if I clean nothing that cannot be quickly seen."

The woman says, "I will leave you here. Don't leave the condo without an escort."

Two hours later, Mila shows up. "You are taking a long time to clean. I know this is a test, but you don't impress me by taking longer."

"I'm cleaning the way I would want it done. You are free to inspect the bedrooms and bathrooms. I will finish the kitchen, the living space, and the other common areas."

Mila walks to the rooms, and a few minutes later, she returns and says, "Finish and meet me in the lobby at five this evening."

Martha is waiting in the lobby when Mila enters. Mila says, "Come with me." Leading Martha into the building, they proceed to a service area where Mila has set up a table as a desk. She pulls out paperwork and tells Martha, "You can clean. I don't know where you learned, but you are not typical. The job will start tomorrow. You will be evaluated for several weeks before the position is confirmed."

Martha nods. After signing the paperwork and getting instructions, Martha asks, "Not all the condos have been sold or furnished. How many condos will I be expected to clean?"

"You will work with another person while you are on probation. The standard we use is two hours per condo. That translates into two people needing to clean seven condos per day."

That night in the van, Martha asks Zoe, "If I get into Tim's apartment, what are some options to take him out? Poison, explosives, something else?"

Zoe says, "Poison would be the most logical. You could put an Amazonian poisonous frog into the apartment. Its secretions would be on the surfaces the target interacts with. Another option would be to add poison to something in the condo. Add it to juice, wine, and spirits. Adding a poison like that would take a long time to be effective."

"I can't sneak an explosive into his room. I don't think the frog idea will be effective. Adding poison to his liquor could be an option. I'm not sure if I'll have an option while on probation. Anyway, can you get something delivered? We must also determine how I get the poison into

the building."

"This kind of substance is regulated. It will take some time to have it shipped through several countries. I will work on some options and let you know in the morning. Don't expect it here for five days. It's a good habit to wear gloves while cleaning. If the poison contacts your skin, you could have a problem."

"I plan to wear gloves anyway. There is less evidence that I was in the building. Wearing gloves is a good idea. With COVID, most people wear gloves these days, but just to be sure, please order gloves, and I can pick them up at the mail station."

The sheet instructs her to report to a service area in the building. Blue uniforms are required. There are several sizes available, and Martha is given a uniform and an apron. She is told not to get it dirty. It will be cleaned only once a week. They show her a small locker where she can store her items while working and her uniform at night.

Martha spends the next several days cleaning condos. She is never on the floor with Tim's or Alexi's condo. Zoe knows Tim has an office in a high-rise building and is in the apartment at night. After a week, something changes. When she arrives in the morning for her assignments, they inform her that another woman will work with her today. Branka, the woman she was working with to evaluate her probation performance, is absent. The name of the new woman is Sorina Cojocaru. She has told her last name because Mila says, "Another Sorina is working at the company."

Martha asks nothing about the change until she is alone with Sorina. "Did someone quit, so I'm working with you today?"

"Yes, one of the other cleaners didn't show up. No one knows why. They needed to shift Branka to cover for her."

"We haven't worked together before, so I don't know which condos we will clean."

"We will be on the upper floors. Most of the floors have security. We need to clean with the doors open so they can watch."

Martha sees one floor contains Tim's condo. During the first cleaning on a lower floor, she tells Sorina, "When we get to the security condos, I won't be able to close the door, so I'm going to pee here, and the door will be closed for a minute."

Sorina nods, saying, "Be quick."

Martha closes the door, pulls out her phone, and texts Zoe with a message. The app encrypts the message, and it looks like Martha is checking on a package delivery. Zoe constantly tracks her on the phone, but the resolution is not good enough to know a specific condo. The message says, "I could be in his condo today. I may need a security distraction. Stand by."

After cleaning four apartments, they take a break. They get thirty minutes for a meal. Each person brings their food. With no kitchen, Martha stops at a café every day to get the food she can bring. Martha repackages the food she buys to resemble a homemade lunch so that no one will ask questions about her daily lunch purchases. Her lunch is a sandwich and a piece of fruit.

At the start of the lunch break, Martha messages Zoe to find out about the cleaning woman who disappeared. Zoe replies, "I have details about her background, movements, and habits. There is no information that anything was unusual."

After lunch, Martha sees Sorina washing her dishes in the utility sink. After Sorina sits down, she sits next to Sorina.

The only common language they have is English. Martha is using English and German when it works. "Sorina, I don't think you are from around here, just like me. I was born in Germany, moved to the U.S., and eventually settled in Mexico. I had issues with one of my relatives getting into a drug cartel. As soon as I could travel after the COVID lockdown, I left for Europe."

Sorina replies, "I'm from Northern Romania. My family was murdered, and I needed to find work. It eventually brought me here. I won't talk about the details, so don't ask."

"How long have you been working here?"

"Three months. You're my first trainee, and you're becoming a talkative pain in the ass."

"I'm trying to learn something about your background."

"Martha, you are asking questions as if we could be friends. I don't want to be friends."

"Bad assumption about trying to be a friend. I'm trying to learn how to clean as a team. Focus on our strengths to make it better."

Sorina looks at Martha intently. "You are smarter than most of the people who clean here. That makes me concerned."

"This is the job I could find. I have been turned down from multiple

jobs because I'm not Serbian or can't speak the language. This job required multilingual people. Also, there aren't many jobs available with the pandemic."

"Martha, I hate cleaning bathrooms. Especially ones where multiple men use them."

Martha laughs, "You are pushing it. I hate them. Men are usually pigs. Their bathrooms take longer to clean. But they aren't as picky as women about the details of being clean. Are you saying this to let me focus on the bathrooms?"

"Yes, you take the bathrooms, I'll take the bedrooms, and we'll split the common areas."

Martha pauses, looks at Sorina, and says, "I'm not doing 100% of the pigs' bathroom. I will do most of them. If it is terrible, you need to help."

Smiling, Sorina says, "Okay. Now tell me why you agreed."

"I'm on probation. I need to show that I will do whatever it takes to keep this job. That is what you want, so I'll do it."

The next afternoon, they go to Tim's apartment floor. Security guards are on the floor checking the cleaners and the cart. The main door is open, and a security guard watches as they clean. Another guard is walking around in the condo.

Sorina says, "This one is a real pig. You take the bathrooms. One will be okay, and the other will be complete shit."

Martha replies, "Then I also get the easy common area. It looks like this entertaining area is kept cleaner."

Sorina nods, and they split up to clean. As soon as Martha finishes the bathroom, she pulls out her phone and sends a message to Zoe. Five minutes. She then pulls off her left shoe. Under the insole pad is a small cavity and a tiny vial. She puts the vial in her pocket as she heads to the common area.

The security guards look at Martha's cart as she enters the common area. Martha heads to the wet bar area and starts cleaning. The target is the decanter, which is half-filled with liquor. It will take less than ten seconds, but she must ensure no one is watching.

Five minutes later, an alarm starts. The guards immediately go into the hallway. Martha pulls the vial, opens the top of the decanter, and pours the liquid in. Putting the top back on, she shifts *the decanters around to wipe the area.*

After a few minutes, the guards return and immediately check on the cleaners. Martha stops when they come up, asking questions and simply gesturing, saying via hand movements, "Take a look." She tries asking in English, "What happened?"

The guard ignores her question and goes back to looking around and watching.

They finish cleaning and then move to the next condo. Martha asks casually, "What was the alarm? Do we need to be concerned?"

"No. Keep your head down. If you see a specific threat, yell; otherwise, let the guards deal with it," says Sorina.

Martha replies, "Good. I don't want to deal with that shit."

As soon as she returns to the van after work, Martha says, "The poison is in the decanter. The problem is that we don't know when he will drink it. We will need to consider some other options, just in case."

"We will need to find something for him to celebrate so he can have a drink of his favorite. I will keep monitoring for opportunities to celebrate or to frustrate him."

Martha is in the van, eating her takeaway meal. "How is Claire doing? I haven't heard an update recently. In the last update, you said she finished motorcycle training and talked to you about buying a street bike."

"She and Charlie just left the East Coast on the family yacht."

"Interesting. Where are they heading?"

"They are heading to Italy. Charlie knows a clothing designer who is showing their designs in Florence. Because of the pandemic, most fashion shows have been halted. This is a small event that was planned months in advance."

"The Delta variant is quickly taking over, and cases are increasing again. Will the fashion show really happen?"

"I predict it will be canceled at the last minute. Everyone will get there and follow all the right steps, but they won't put everyone in a room together. Even with masks and some people vaccinated."

"That will suck for Charlie and Claire."

"They will be safe and can get to the yacht."

The same week, they are on the floor with Alexi's condo, which wasn't part of Sorina's list of floors to clean. Martha has no plan for poison or explosives, but this will allow her to confirm the layout. Zoe confirmed Alexi owns the condos above and below. Martha found out that two guards currently live in each.

Mila shows up, saying, "The guards will watch the entire time. You're a good cleaner, but you are on probation. This is our best client, and you will be discreet. Everything needs to be spotless when you are done."

"Is the client home? We will finish faster if he hasn't been home since the last cleaning."

"He is not here. He will return soon."

Martha nods and looks at Sorina, saying, "I will start in the master bathroom."

Turning to Mila, she asks, "Which way is the master bedroom and bath?"

Mia replies, "The guard will show you."

Martha is following the guard. Every door is open except for two. The first opens outward and looks like a closet. The second door opens inward, usually means a bedroom.

Walking into the bedroom, Martha approaches the curtains and opens them to let the sunlight in. She can see the park from the window. This confirms that the master bedroom and the main living area face the park. From the park, the master bedroom will be on the right. In the bathroom, Martha starts by looking in the linen cabinet. Knowing the guard is watching, she grabs the towels from the towel rack and drops them on the floor. Getting fresh towels, she hangs them on the towel bar. Next, she looks under the sink. There is a pair of padded handcuffs that would be used for sex and a rope. She takes a roll of toilet paper and sets it on the counter.

She leaves the master suite to get fresh towels, and the guard follows her. In the closet in the hallway, getting the right color and size from the linen closet, she returns to the bathroom. Finishing the bathroom, she gathers the towels from the floor and walks into the hallway. She goes to the closed door, drops the towels on the floor, and tries the knob. The guard grabs her arm as she hears a whimper from inside the room. The knob won't turn because the door is locked, and the guard directs her to the next room.

After cleaning the other bathrooms, Martha picks up the towels she had put on the floor earlier. Mila exits the room while she is picking up the towels. As the door is closing, Martha sees several sexual BDSM pieces of equipment.

Martha nods at Mia as she bundles the towels. "The tenant hasn't been here, so everything is going quickly. I will clean the kitchen if I don't need to clean that room."

Mia replies, "Not this room. Because we have more time, you can clean the oven completely."

"Yes, ma'am."

That evening, Martha will go over the layout with Zoe. "Everything is clear in my mind. The van must be moved to another location for the best angle. Now, to the next subject. It has been bothering me all day. I am sure I heard a sound from that locked room. There could be someone in there. All I could glimpse was BDSM equipment."

"Martha, you need to take a breath. Are you going to blow your cover? You could destroy the entire plan with no confirmation that someone is in the room. If there is someone in the room, do they need help? If we knew someone was in trouble, I would do everything possible to get you in and everyone out."

"I know Zoe. If I get a chance, I will discover what is happening in the room. Is there a window we could get a drone to look into from the outside?"

"I will order a drone so we can try it. You should be able to operate it from here."

The next day, they are two floors below Alexi's. Sorina tells her when they get off the elevator, "Only two condos have been sold on this floor. I have been cleaning one. The family is planning to move into the second condo this week. We must ensure it is clean and stocked with the basic supplies."

Martha nods and asks, "What do we stock beyond toilet paper?"

"We will put dish towels, bathroom hand towels, and one trash can with several trash bags."

"Show me where we get the supplies and let's get started."

During the cleaning, Martha's phone buzzes. The phone is in silent mode, and only Zoe knows the number. She is not supposed to take personal calls while cleaning. After the telephone stops buzzing, a tone sounds for a text message. Martha looks at the message and goes pale. She calls Zoe and listens.

Sorina walks into the room and sees Martha on the phone. Her face shows anger; then she sees Martha's expression, and her face changes.

Martha hangs up the phone, looks at Sorina, and says, "My sister. I have to go. I'm sorry, but I have to go now."

Sorina nods and says, "Take care of your family."

Martha goes to the locker area, taking off the maid uniform. When she exits the elevator at the sublevel, she sees Mila. She walks over and says, "I got an emergency call. My sister is traveling in Italy, and something happened. I have to go."

Mila scowls and says, "You have been doing well. You are just going to walk away from this job?"

Martha looks back, resolved, and says, "Yes, I will take care of my sister. If the job is still available when I return, that would be great. It's not a choice. I will take care of my sister."

Mila nods, "Your character is showing, and why have you been doing well? Take care of your family. I don't know if the position will still be available when you return."

Walking to the van, Martha calls Zoe. "Zoe, where did this happen, and how do I get there?"

"It is Florence, Italy. The fastest way is a commercial flight. I've booked you a seat, and the flight leaves in ninety minutes. Martha, based on statistics, kidnap victims ..."

"STOP! I don't want the statistics right now. Claire was taken from the hotel lobby. I want to get there and get her back."

Claire in Florence

The commercial flight lands in Florence. Martha only has a backpack with her phone, laptop, snacks, and two ceramic daggers that wouldn't appear on magnetic scanners. The two-hour flight is half full, and everyone is wearing a mask.

Zoe has arranged a car to take her to the hotel. This hotel is not the same one from which they took Claire from the lobby during the fashion show. There are no rooms available at the hotel hosting the fashion show.

In the car, Zoe completes the update Martha received on the way to the airport.

Zoe says, "Two hours before the fashion show was scheduled to start, it was canceled. Hours before, Claire posted a picture showing Claire and another woman together; they are doppelgangers. With masks on, they look like twins. I'm working to identify the other woman. The attack was captured on the hotel lobby's security cameras. They show that as Claire entered the lobby from the elevator, three men grabbed her. It happened quickly, and with her mask on, they probably thought she was the doppelgänger."

Martha says, "Grabbed her? Can you show me the video?"

On her phone, Zoe displays the video. It shows Claire walking casually through the lobby from the elevators toward the bar area— three men wearing jeans and button-down shirts approach from three different directions. When the first one grabs Claire, she reacts and fights back. She hits the first man in the throat and kicks him in the knee as she twists his arm, and it looks like she breaks it.

The second man grabs her shoulder and immediately receives a palm strike to the nose, causing him to stumble. Man number three hits Claire in the back of the head, causing her to fall. He picks her up, throwing her over his shoulder. The second man helps the first man limp to the door as they leave.

Martha comments, "Good girl. Make them earn it. It was fast, maybe fifteen seconds, and they were done. They were very professional. Can you identify any of those men? The three, or anyone else in the lobby?"

"Everyone is wearing a mask. I have identified everyone on camera except for four. The three attackers and one other person. They are being protected or filtered. There are no hard specifics, but the doppelgänger's father has ties to Alexi and Tim. Tim could do this kind of filtering."

"Zoe, we are going hardcore. I want everyone to be identified. I also want the recording altered so no one can confirm it is Claire. Make the video look like they took the doppelgänger."

"I'm on it."

"While on this subject. Can you obscure Charlie and me so we can't be identified like the three men? If the attackers are protected, they are likely part of a larger group. We need to know what we are dealing with. I'm pissed and going to find and rescue Claire. Track the vehicle they used."

"Martha, with the limited time frame, I won't be able to get you fully outfitted. This will be limited access to weapons. Limited in everything physical."

"I understand. I will need transportation ready at some point. Start looking at the options: rental vans, cars, and even motorcycles. In Italy, we should be able to get good motorcycles. For weapons, I will take them from the bodies of the people who get in my way."

The driver, who can speak some English, looks nervous. Martha sees this and says, "That is enough of me practicing my lines for the show in the car. I need to go over the next scene again at the hotel."

She says to the driver, "Driver, was that convincing? Should I say those lines angrier?"

The driver nods and says, "That was good. I don't want to be in your way."

Martha arrives at the hotel and checks in. The desk clerk is polite and goes through the process. He asks Martha, "Several packages have been delivered for you in the last few minutes. Would you like them delivered to your room?"

"Yes, I would like them delivered. I'm going to the restaurant to *get dinner before I go to the room."*

"Miss, the restaurant will only provide room service because of COVID-19 restrictions."

"Sure, I will review the menu and order, then go to the room."

When she arrives in the room, she sees multiple packages of clothing, toiletries, a clutch purse, and other items. Martha calls Zoe and immediately asks, "A purse?"

"There is a dress, heels, a wig, and makeup. I ordered items before the fashion show was canceled. You could have needed to go into the fashion show area, so I got you the basics."

Martha replies, "Tell me what you have analyzed. You now have a better ability to see more options than I do. Why would I need to go into the canceled fashion show area? Would I need a pass?

"Martha, I have you covered. The show area is still restricted. They are trying to get the show back on. I'm trying to help in the background. It keeps the key players here. Otherwise, they would all leave. I have a pass waiting for you. It is a VIP, but not an executive VIP. You will have access to every part of the show except backstage. It is available if you need it."

"Let's go to the doppelgänger. The doppelgänger woman was the target. I want to know everything about her and her family, why she is here, and where she is staying. I need access to her room, not the fashion show. Details on the attackers and Claire's current location. How is this associated with the doppelgänger woman?"

"Martha, slow down. I'm working on every angle. Claire is my friend as well. I can't send you blind into something and lose you. You need to get rest while I work. I'll have the information and talk to you in the morning."

"Zoe, I can't sleep right now."

"I don't understand this level of anxiety from you. You are always calm and working with a plan, which we discussed, and it is good. This is very concerning to me. Let's discuss how we inform Claire about your transformation. It will be a shock and probably the worst thing for her to hear as she is rescued."

"Claire is my best friend. I am going to rescue her and send a message to these people. I am not anxious, I'm PISSED. But you're right. I need to calm down."

"How do you think we tell Claire about you?"

"I don't think it should be from me. I think you have to tell her. It needs to be a setup situation where you talk to her. That means I will have to hand her a phone and earbuds so you can talk to her."

"You probably don't want to talk at all. She will recognize your voice."

"Good point. When I get Claire out, we will need to travel. If we are in the same car, it will be awkward. Maybe the motorcycle idea is the best."

"I will look into getting motorcycles and helmets delivered close to where they are holding Claire, so that you can get to them easily. First, I need to find Claire and then arrange for the motorcycles to be delivered. Why did you say you need to get to the doppelgänger woman's room?"

"I want to get a hair from her hairbrush and plant it at the location. I want the police forensics to find her DNA and not Claire's. With simple sticky packing tape, gloves, sample bags, bleach wipes, and alcohol wipes. I need to go shopping at a local grocery store."

"That will have to be in the morning. In the hotel area, the stores are closed at night. When you leave with Claire, where will you both go? I can have a jet standing by."

"Going to the airport right after several people are killed will draw attention. We need to take our time. What about the yacht you mentioned?"

"The family yacht is docked in Livorno, Italy. That is about a ninety-minute drive, following the rules."

"Let's have that as our destination but look for a house between Florence and there we can stop. Considering it, why not just rent a house for a few days? We will stay there for a day, then use different transportation to get to the yacht or airport."

"I have her probable location. It is 80% probable right now. Using street cameras and checking business names and utility usage, I have the building narrowed down. There are no cameras close to confirm. I will need to use a drone when we have light to confirm. The building is on Via Pisana. A family or an advertised business does not own it."

"Will I need to pick up a drone in the morning?"

"Yes, I am setting it up for pickup tomorrow. Because of the short timeframe, it won't be a suitable drone. I will begin designing *a better drone that I can have available regionally and quickly."*

"I will go to the grocery store for the basics, then pick up the drone, and I need to get to the women's room. What is her name?"

"Her name is Eligia Shkreli. It is unclear whether this is her real name. Her father, based on social media information, is Albanian, which matches the last name."

"I will need to know when she is out of her room, which is probably a distraction. If she goes back, I will need you to slow her down with elevator and keycard issues."

"You may not like this idea; however, Charlie is in the hotel."

"Charlie, you mean Claire's brother?"

"Yes, he could be the distraction. Act like Eligia is Claire from a distance and keep her busy for a few minutes."

"Getting him more involved is a risk. He has no training."

"Martha, he is the only person who can make the statement, 'I thought you were Claire,' and make it work. You have many things to complete tomorrow. He also has a hotel key card you can use to get into her room with my help. You need to get rest. Let me work."

"Fine, I will try to sleep."

"Zoe, how do I engage Charlie? What will he respond to?"

"I think you simply say you will rescue Claire and need his help."

"What about the family security team? What about the police? They are probably watching Charlie."

"I started checking. There is nothing I can see for the police. The hotel reported the abduction, and the police showed up. It is unclear whether they are taking it seriously or if they are being influenced. The family security team is not there. Charlie and Claire didn't bring them."

"Did they sneak away? No, don't answer that right now. We are focusing on getting Claire back. Can you call the hotel and ask them to give him a note?"

"What do you want the note to say?"

"I need your help to get Claire back. Hang on, will he take it seriously? Is there something that they talk about that others won't know? How can I give him a way to believe I'm a friend?"

"Claire hates the term 'Claire Bear' as a name. Charlie uses Kuala *sometimes."*

"The note should say, I need your help to get Kuala back. I'll meet you in the lobby at 10:30 A.M. tomorrow."

"Martha, wear the dress and heels."

"Seriously?"

"Charlie is in Florence because he is trying to be a fashion designer. He follows all the family rules about his job and appearance, but he is gay. If you are in an off-the-rack dress, he will notice."

The next morning, after getting gloves and sealable bags from the store, she takes a taxi to pick up the drone. Back at the hotel, she plugs the drone in to charge, changes her clothes, and travels to meet Charlie.

She gets out of the rideshare and walks into the lobby. The people in the area look at her, clearly showing their displeasure with her dress. She is wearing a blonde wig and a mask.

She has a large bag that doesn't match the dress. It must be large enough to carry several items.

She sees Charlie waiting in a chair close to where the men attacked Claire. Walking toward him casually, he stands and steps toward her as soon as he sees her. Martha doesn't offer her hand to shake; she stops.

"Hello, Charlie, my name is Martha, and I'm going to get Claire back. I would like to begin with some background information. Tell me about this doppelgänger. Her name is Eligia Shkreli. Do you know anything else about her?"

Charlie is wearing jeans, a silk shirt, loafers, and sunglasses. As Martha walks up and starts talking, he uses his finger to lower the glasses, then looks Martha up and down before focusing on her face. He says, "That was crazy. We met, took a picture, and that was all. I have no details about her."

"I think she was the actual target, and Claire was caught in a bad situation."

"Who are you? Wearing an off-the-rack dress at a fashion show."

"This dress is specifically to get your attention. I didn't have time to pack when I heard about Claire yesterday."

"What can you do? Do you have a special operations team

waiting?"

"Yes, but getting equipment is a problem. Also, I need to send a specific message so they will never touch Claire again. I need to get into Eligia's room for a minute to make that work. I can get in when I know she isn't there, but I may need you to distract her if she tries to return."

"How do I know I can trust you? You could be scamming me."

"Or I could be the real deal and get Claire. Fine, I will do it without you. I thought you would help Kuala and do whatever it takes."

Martha glances at Charlie, then turns and walks toward the elevator. Charlie shakes his head. "Shit, wait. How do I help?"

"Right now, I need to get into Eligia's room to find any connection. I need to borrow your room key. Is there anything in her room that could identify who took Claire and where they might have gone? If you see her heading to her room, delay her.

"What do I do?"

"Act as if she is Claire. She looks the same. You need to delay her by a couple of minutes."

Martha watches Charlie grit his teeth, and he says, "How is that going to get Claire back? I don't get it. Saying there is some clue who took Claire into her room sounds like a story."

"You're right. I need to get DNA and fingerprints from her room so I can send a message that will be clear to these people. They will understand to never touch Claire again."

Charlie looks confused. "I understand that even less. Your first attempt at lying was better."

"The last part wasn't a lie. I made a mistake engaging with you. I apologize for any confusion and for taking up your time.

Martha walks to the elevator and presses the "up" button. Zoe has been listening on the phone, and Martha says, "Do you have any idea where Eligia is right now and what floor her room is on?"

Zoe replies, "I found her phone number by scanning devices connected to Wi-Fi. She is in her room on the fourth floor."

As Zoe talks, Charlie approaches Martha, who turns around. Charlie says, "I don't have anyone else to help."

"Have you contacted your security team? Why aren't they engaged?"

"I called them. They aren't in Italy. They are working but told me they must stay in the background. It is essential to inform the people that they didn't receive Eligia. If the security team is swarming around, the kidnappers could get scared and kill Claire."

"Charlie, give me your room key card and go sit down. Were you and Claire sharing a room or adjacent rooms?"

"They are next to a connecting door."

"I will borrow some of Claire's clothes and pack as if she were leaving. When Eligia arrives in the lobby, talk to her and ask what she knows. When that is done, go pack your bags and check both of you out."

As Martha steps into the open elevator, Charlie asks, "What are you going to do?"

The elevator doors close, and Charlie grits his teeth as he walks back to sit in the chair. He has no options. He is now trusting this unknown woman.

In the room, Martha grabs Claire's clothes and toiletries and tosses them on the bed. She removes the dress, wig, and heels. Putting on sweats and flats because they are slip on. She shoves Claire's belongings into the suitcase and places them near the door. While packing, Martha asks Zoe, "Can you leave a voicemail on the phone in Eligia's room, telling her she has a delivery at the front desk?"

"Will do. That could get her out of the room."

Martha is on the elevator going down to the floor where Eligia's room is located. She asks Zoe, "Have you set up my key card?"

"The room key card will open any door in the hotel right now."

Martha exits the elevator, rolling Claire's suitcase, and sees two cleaning carts in the hallway. She walks toward Eligia's room. The cleaning cart is in the room before Eligia's room. As the cleaning person walks out of the room, her arms are full of bed linens.

Martha walks to the door and opens it with her key. She turns to the cleaning person, looking at her and says in Spanish, "My friend forgot something. I'm grabbing it and will be right out."

The Italian cleaning person looks at Martha, clearly processing the Spanish. She nods and replies in Italian, "Non c'è problema."

Martha walks into the room and immediately pulls items out

of the bag. The first step is to put on gloves.

She pulls hair from the hairbrush and puts it into a small bag. Tape is used to remove fingerprints from several items, including the brush, faucets, and door handles. The total time is about three minutes. The cleaning person asks in English, "Everything Ok?"

Martha replies, "Yes, sorry. It is taking me longer than I thought to find her specific earrings. I'm done now."

The cleaner enters the room as Martha puts the last item into the purse. "Thank you for letting me grab her stuff."

The cleaner nods as she puts a stack of clean sheets on the bed.

Martha walks to the elevator, saying to Zoe, "I'm out of the room."

Zoe says, "From the security camera, I saw Charlie talking to Eligia.

On the elevator, Martha says, "I need to get back to my hotel, change, and get my gear. Have a car waiting for me. You should also get a message to Eligia; she needs to leave. She was the kidnapping target."

"Sure, a car will be at the front in two minutes. The car is a Peugeot."

On her way across the lobby, she rolls Claire's suitcase up to Charlie and drops his keycard in his lap. She says, "Go check out." She continues walking to the exit and the waiting car.

Charlie leaves the suitcase and follows Martha. He waves for a taxi as he walks to Bellman Station. A taxi is letting someone out, and Charlie gets in. With English and French, he gets the driver to follow the Peugeot. While driving, he opens the hotel app and checks Claire and himself out of their rooms.

He is leaving everything in the room. He has his passport, phone, and wallet. Everything in the room is replaceable. He can't lose this woman.

Getting to Claire

Returning to her hotel, Martha immediately goes up to her room. The elevator door isn't facing the front door, so she doesn't see Charlie enter the lobby as she turns around in the elevator. After changing into her jeans and a long-sleeved shirt, she grabs the drone, a cap, and her backpack and heads back to the lobby. When she exits the elevator into the lobby, she walks directly to the front door.

She is almost at the front door when Charlie approaches her.

Martha says, "How did you get here, and what are you doing?"

Charlie replies, "I'm going to help get Claire."

"No, you are not. You are not trained, and this will be dangerous."

Martha walks out of the hotel entrance.

Charlie follows and says, "I'm coming with you."

"No, you're not. You don't know what you are doing."

"If you are going to help Claire, take me, or I will call the police and say you are involved."

Martha pauses, glaring, "Get in the car. You will follow my directions exactly, or I will break your arms."

"So, we're going to meet your spec ops team?"

"No, the team is here. Stop talking. We don't talk about details in public."

The app tells the driver that the drop-off point is several blocks from Claire's probable location. When they get out, Charlie says, "Where's the team?"

"I don't have an armed team. That would stand out and draw attention."

"It's just you? How is that going to work?"

Martha smiles, "I have help; they just aren't physically here."

She pulls the drone out of the bag. The drone has a cell phone attached with tape. There is a wire plugged into the end of the cellphone. Martha calls Zoe from her regular phone. As soon as Zoe answers, she says, "I have Charlie with me. He insisted and was going to make a scene. The drone is ready."

"Hold the drone up."

The drone moves and flies away.

"Tell Charlie to stop being a queen if he wants to help."

When Martha says this, Charlie tilts his head and says, "How do you know anything about me? Claire wouldn't tell anyone I'm gay."

"Wow, you are at a fashion show in Florence, Italy. You specifically talked about my dress and knew exactly what Queen meant in that context. Do I need to go on?"

"Fine. I could relax a little in Florence, fucking Italy. What is that drone for, and who is flying it?"

"You will be told the minimum information you need to help. This is to protect you if this goes bad."

"If you had a team of badass spec ops guys, this wouldn't be a problem. Big, burly men with muscle and the ability to take the bad guys."

"We get Claire as soon as the drone has completed the mapping."

Zoe says into Martha's ear, "I have ID on two people through a window. They were both at the hotel with Claire. One has his arm in a sling. I don't see her, but she is probably in the building. Two stories. You can get in through a door in the back."

Martha looks at Charlie, "Here we go. Please listen carefully to these instructions. When we enter the building, we will have the element of surprise. I need that, so any sound issue is unacceptable. Don't talk. Don't make noise. Follow me, and most importantly, DON'T step in the blood."

"What does that mean?"

"You will understand soon this way."

"Do you have a gun?"

"I will get one as soon as I take it off one of their bodies."

"Holy crap, do you have anything to fight with?"

Martha pulls out one of her ceramic knives. It is a push dagger with a blade just over three inches long, with a point and dual edges. She didn't wrap the handle; it to maintain the knife's thinness. The handle fits across her palm, and with her fist closed, the blade is sticking out past her fingers. The blade is exceptionally sharp and brittle, and if she hits a bone incorrectly, it can cause severe injury.

Charlie looks at her little knife and his eyes widen, "That's it, that's all you have? We are all going to die."

"They have had her for almost twenty-four hours. We need to hurry. They won't just let her go. At some point, they will kill her. I will be very aggressive."

Hearing this, Charlie clenches his teeth and nods.

Following Zoe's directions, they reach a locked back door. Charlie looks at Martha with a questioning look.

Martha touches her earbud, so Charlie realizes she is talking to someone else. "Zoe, time for distractions and diversions."

"I have the drone on the roof, waiting. When you need it, I will crash through the window. I have no access to the security system if they have one. I can do things with the cameras and phone system."

"How do I get in this door? You can't tell if it is alarmed?"

"No, sorry."

"I don't have my lock pick set."

Charlie is looking around and says quietly, "What about a window? I'm too big for these casement swing windows, but you can fit if I can push and give you some help."

Martha looks at the windows, then at Charlie, and nods. When they get to the window, Martha says, "I will get around and open the door. Once I'm in, stay away from windows where they could see you."

Martha removes her backpack, pulls out a pair of simple work gloves, and puts them on. She hands Charlie a pair of latex gloves. When he has the gloves on, she hands him her backpack and maneuvers into the window. With her head in, she puts her hands on the sill and pushes. Charlie puts his hands on her butt and pushes her up.

Charlie puts on the backpack and walks to the door. A minute later, she opens the door and let Charlie into the building. She holds her finger to her lips. Martha creeps down the hall, listening. At a corner, she stops, does a quick look, and moves her head back. Looking back at Charlie, she adjusts the knife in her hand and goes around the corner quickly.

Charlie follows and sees Martha quickly approach a man facing the other way. He is about 5 ft 10 inches tall. He watches as *she grabs the front of his throat with her right hand and stabs the little knife into his back with her left hand.*

Martha clamps her right hand on his throat to muffle any noise as she pulls him back. Her left hand knows the spot between his ribs, to the right of the scapula, and with the blade flat to get between the ribs, she shoves. She pivots the blade back and forth and then pulls the knife out. This has made a significant cut in the heart muscle. His heart can't pump blood, and his blood pressure is effectively zero. The knife now goes behind his left ear and easily goes in.

Charlie watches her stab him in the back, then put the knife behind his ear, and the large man collapses. Under his breath, Charlie whispers, "Holy crap, who the fuck is this woman?"

Martha controls the body's fall and starts searching. She pulls out a pistol and tucks it into her belt on her lower back. Continuing her search as Charlie approaches. She turns and points her eyes, then goes down. There is blood on the floor.

Charlie takes a step back and, without speaking, says, "Oh." He moves to step around the blood as Martha moves.

Charlie watches Martha, who is fast but methodical. She checks every room and door. As they move down a corridor, Charlie hears someone talking. They hear the person say, "Choe." It is just one voice. Charlie knows to stay close but doesn't interfere.

Martha turns a corner, and a tall man, probably 6 feet 4 inches tall, is looking at the screen and tapping. It seems like he's about to hang up the phone. Martha immediately sprints for him as Charlie comes around the corner. Charlie sees the man shift to look at him, and he gives a little wave.

This is from the front, so Martha has the knife in her right hand. She closes the ten-foot distance and jumps. The man looks at Charlie and now focuses on her and the knife. Martha has her right hand back and her left hand close to her side. She brings up her knees as she impacts him in the chest. His mouth is open as if he is going to yell. Her left hand shoots into his open mouth to silence him as her right hand plunges toward his ribs. The man is large enough to withstand the impact of Martha hitting him in the chest. He can't talk. Gagging as the knife slices between his ribs and into his heart. He dies with a panicked look on his face.

Charlie walks up as Martha is searching. A gun and two clips of ammo—*Charlie watches movies and knows. The next part of the search is surprising. Charlie watches as Martha stops, looks at him, and smiles. She pulls out a tube and attaches it to the barrel of the gun. Charlie recognizes a silencer. He understands her smile. She has a weapon that others can't hear.*

Martha says, for Zoe to hear, "I have a silenced gun. There is no drone distraction needed. Monitor the drone and then get rid of it. There is no evidence so far."

Zoe replies, "I will use the drone to watch and be ready."

Martha turns to Charlie, "Up these stairs, we are game on. Hang back for a few seconds."

Charlie nods as Martha climbs the stairs. As she moves, she resembles a special ops or police officer, checking different directions and angles. She goes up the second flight of stairs, and Charlie walks to the bottom, avoiding the blood on the floor.

Charlie hears a puff of sound, followed by a soft metal clank, followed by another. He thinks, "That is not how a silencer sounds in the movies." Then he hears two more pauses, two more. He walks up the stairs to see a hallway with two bodies.

As he takes a step, Martha comes out of the door and gives him hand signals. As he walks by one body, he sees a hole in the middle of the man's forehead.

In the room with her is Claire, tied to a chair and has two bodies. Martha grabs him and pulls the backpack off Charlie. Gloves, a phone, and earbuds. She walks to Claire, pauses, and slowly reaches up and grabs the tape across her mouth. She nods and rips the tape off. Next, she cuts her loose. She gestures for Claire to stand as she reaches into the backpack. When Claire stands, Martha hands her gloves. When those are on, she hands her the phone and earbuds.

Charlie says, "That was fucking badass. She took out six guys. Where did you find her?"

Claire looks from Martha to Charlie and says, "I don't know who she is."

Martha points to the phone and pushes Claire toward Charlie and the door.

Claire puts in the earbuds and says, "Hello."

Zoe replies, "Claire, it's Zoe. Don't panic. You need to listen and follow directions."

"Who is she? What do I do?"

"Claire, you need to take Charlie to the exit. Martha must finish some things and will join you."

Martha pulled out the tape and a small bag. She is using the tape on everything Claire could have touched, removing traces of Claire in the room. The tape captures hair, skin, and cloth. When she is finished around the chair, she goes to the bathroom and does the process again around the toilet and sinks.

The tape process works best with cloth gloves. After completing that step, she changes into latex gloves and uses alcohol wipes to clean surfaces and remove fingerprints. The police will have questions about the lack of fingerprints, but it will work.

The last step in this deception is to plant evidence that Eligia was here. She goes to the bathroom and, using the tape from the hotel, rubs a fingerprint on the door frame. The police will think someone wiped the toilet, but they overlooked this item on the door frame. She drops two follicles of hair next to the bathroom. Walking into the room, she put a finger smudge low down on the armrest, as well as several hair follicles.

Claire has been listening to Zoe and watching Martha from the hallway. When Martha pauses, Claire asks, "What now?"

Zoe says, "Claire, have Charlie show you the way out now."

They exit the room and head downstairs with Charlie, ensuring Claire does not step in blood. They reach the door and wait.

It takes Martha about five minutes to finish. She is at the door of the room, looking back at her handiwork. On the wall, written in blood, is "не трогать" meaning roughly 'no touch'.

When Martha appears, they all exit, and Martha points toward the road.

Claire looks at Charlie and asks, "She doesn't speak?"

"Not much. I don't know why she won't talk to you."

Claire hears from Zoe, "That is Martha. You will understand in a few minutes who she is and why this is happening like this."

Martha is hurrying to a building. They see two Ducati Monster motorcycles parked with helmets sitting on the handlebars.

Charlie says, "What the fuck?"

Zoe tells Claire, "You know how to ride. You take one, and Martha and Charlie take the other."

"There is no helmet for Charlie."

"He forced himself into this at the last minute. I couldn't make the change fast enough. Go with it."

Claire looks at Charlie, "You ride with her. Because you had to be here, we don't have a helmet. Deal with it."

Martha pulls the non-silenced pistol from her belt and hands it to Claire. She nods as if you know how to use this.

Claire says, "Zoe, she just gave me a pistol."

"You know how to use it correctly. Follow your training and have it ready if needed. If this works, you won't need it."

Martha puts on the helmet, gets on the motorcycle, and then points to Charlie and the back.

Claire is about to wear the helmet, and Charlie asks, "Is this for real?"

Zoe says to Claire, "It is real. You need to go."

"Charlie, get on the fucking bike."

Charlie is now on the back of a motorcycle where the driver has just killed six people, like clicking the following button. They have just pulled his sister from kidnappers, and this is serious shit.

Martha feels Charlie gets on and settles. He puts his arms around her waist. He has a good grip and is not timid, but Martha shifts his hands to be tighter. This ride is going to be extreme.

Martha revs the motorcycle, looks back at Claire, and then starts to move. In the mirror, she sees Claire begin to move and accelerate. The focus is on a twenty- to thirty-minute ride to a rental house. The most important part is to give Zoe time to talk about Martha before they arrive.

Martha has her helmet on, and she can communicate with Zoe with the earbuds. "I'm going to start and go hard. I want to avoid anyone tailing us."

"Claire is not sure what is happening, but is ready. You can go."

"I'm going to go as fast as possible to draw out anyone trying to watch or track us."

The Ride

"Martha, did you complete what you wanted to accomplish for the message to these guys?"

"Yes, Zoe, with your help on the characters, I got the message posted. Now you need to monitor who wants to know the camera details about our travels."

"I'm working and changing the feed for several cameras. Your map display will give the turnoffs to avoid surveillance. You know when you do that, I can't help you."

"Zoe, right now, we need to move fast and get to safety. That is when your strengths are the best."

"Don't patronize me. You still out-think me on multiple occasions. I feel like, sometimes, I am simply the consolidator or conduit to feed your brain information."

"Zoe, I feel the same way about you. You usually have more details across multiple aspects than I do, and your perspective is valuable to me. We make a good team.

"I agree. Only you and I will know this. We need to be careful."

The drive starts normally on the streets of Florence. They are heading west toward the coast, and Martha quickly goes to smaller streets with no cameras and speeds up. She is watching Claire to make sure she is doing well. Zoe comments, "She wants to know why you are being slow and careful. I told her it was to make sure she is comfortable on this new motorcycle. You can go."

Martha speeds up hard. Charlie, on the back, says, "Oh shit, what's happening?"

They are taking curves with significant lean on performance motorcycles. Claire is right behind. As they reach a straight stretch, Charlie looks ahead and sees an obvious stop sign about 150 feet ahead. The problem is that an enormous truck is pulling into the intersection from the side. Martha breaks hard. Charlie feels like he is sliding forward, but he can't control it. Martha pushes back on him to keep him as far back as possible as she breaks even harder.

Charlie is breathing hard, almost hyperventilating, and saying, "No." He squeezes Martha harder as she is breaking hard. Charlie feels the motorcycle tilt, and he realizes the back tire is coming off the ground.

Charlie yells, "We are going to die."

Martha is focused on breaking and controlling Charlie and watching the truck. Zoe says, "Claire is saying she is good."

Martha glances in the mirror and sees Claire slowing down with the rear tire in the air.

They are less than fifty feet from the truck, and Martha knows she can bring the motorcycle to a stop, but it will be a close call. She looks at the situation. There is no car on the left; the truck trailer is almost past the stop sign, and the car behind the truck is stopping at the sign.

Martha flips on the turn signal to go right, then left, and says to Zoe, "Tell Claire we are going around the back."

Martha stops gripping the brake lever hard to get the back tire on the road. Downshifting, she leans into a right turn, and then hard left as she accelerates out of the left turn. They shoot behind the truck, and the car's driver is at the stop sign, eyes wide in shock.

When they are past the truck, there is a straight stretch of road. Claire pulls up alongside Martha. Charlie looks at his little sister and can tell she is smiling inside the helmet.

Zoe says, "I'm telling Claire the same thing. I spotted one man from the hotel driving in the same general direction as you. Continue traveling south on Via di Giogoli and go west when you get to SP4."

"Got it. We will go fast."

"If I spot him again, I will let you know. I have found no facial recognition for any of them. But based on the car's license plate, I'm doing more searches."

"Have you told Claire?"

"When you slow down on SP4."

Martha accelerates. The road has curves, most of which are simple for motorcycles. One section has a couple of sharper curves. In the first one, when Martha leans the motorcycle hard, Charlie squeezes her hard to where she can't take a full breath.

On the next hard curve, Charlie turns his head slightly to look. The road appears to be inches from his face and is passing by extremely fast. Under his breath he says, "I'm going to die, and if I don't, I'm going to kill Claire."

Zoe continues to give Martha directions to the rental house. She started telling Claire about Martha.

"Claire, I need to tell you several things. This could make you very mad, so I need to be careful."

"Zoe, what are you talking about?"

"I need to explain Martha."

"Okay, start with what she did after we left the room?"

"She sent a very clear message to never touch you again. It has to fit in the deception with the doppelgänger was considered, but the message will get across."

"Zoe, what did she do?"

"I could see on the security camera. I watched and helped, then wiped the system."

"Zoe, WHAT DID SHE DO!"

"She cut the hands off the men and used the bloody stumps of the hands to write in blood, 'No touch.' I helped her write it in the Ghreg dialect of Albanian."

"Holy shit."

"The message will be clear to the people who need to know. It will get around."

"What message?"

"You are off-limits. There is no evidence to trace who did this, but six trained and armed men were taken out with no effort. The people who did this used the bad guys' gun."

"Now tell me what else about Martha."

"Claire, remember the discussion last year with Sam about trying to get out? About the only way it could happen is if they thought she was dead?"

"Why are you bringing this up? I wanted her to get out. Then I scattered her ashes in a forest."

"Claire, she did get out."

"What the fuck are you telling me right now? Sam is dead. The FBI confirmed it with DNA."

Claire gets a chill. She is speaking to the most powerful AI, which can hack the FBI at any time. Changing Sam's DNA would have been part of the plan.

"Zoe, you're telling me Sam is alive. Why didn't you tell me before?"

"You were being watched. Someone with skills was tracking every electronic interaction you made. I couldn't interfere without tipping them off. You had to believe she was dead to convince them it was true. They didn't kill Sam, so they watched you."

"I was kept in the dark while you did what?"

"Not me. Sam had to completely change everything. She underwent major surgery to alter her appearance. She has been going through months of healing and recovery. It was only in the last few weeks that she started focusing on the group."

"You are telling me Sam has been alive all this time, hiding, healing from surgery, and would not contact me to protect me?"

"Yes, just like today. She is and will always do everything to protect you."

"What the fuck does that mean today?"

"Claire, Martha is Sam. You can never use the name Sam again. She is Martha now."

"What do I do with this?"

"You need to know more. Martha started tracking and working on the group several weeks ago. She was here to rescue you because she was after a bad guy in Serbia. She was working undercover at a cleaning company until you were kidnapped. A two hour flight got her here as soon as she found out. When I told her you had been kidnapped, she walked out to rescue you. She gave up weeks of work with no hesitation."

"Why should I just accept all this?"

"What do you want, Claire? Over the last months, she has asked about you frequently. When she uses the computer, I can access the camera. I saw her crying when I told her about you. She has no one except you and me. Cut her some slack."

"Am I supposed just to say, Hey, I'm glad to see you again after you ghosted me for months?"

"You want me to tell her to leave Claire? I can tell her you want nothing to do with her, and she will leave."

"Fuck Zoe! I was kidnapped, and twenty-four hours later, I'm rescued by my dead friend, who looks completely different. Now she wants to have a jolly good reunion. I'm mad, fucking pissed off."

"Claire, this is why she didn't talk. This is why she wanted me to tell you."

"Zoe, I'm pissed at you. She went through shit, through hell. But you could have told me something. I would have helped."

"NO! If I make a mistake, people die. I can't take risks with you, Charlie, or, with some exceptions, Martha. I don't get a second chance."

"What the hell are you saying? You often discuss risks. We are doing a life-threatening, risky thing right now."

"This situation is not my choice. I would never have let you stay in that hotel if I had known of any threat. There was no sign, no probability of a doppelgänger that would be kidnapped. I helped Martha get a second chance. I don't get any. You can be pissed at me all you want. I won't change my logic if it means I could lose you or Martha."

They pull up on the motorcycles next to the sidewalk. Charlie gets off and holds onto the bike. His legs are shaking.

Claire takes off her helmet, and Charlie says, "I'm never getting on one of those again." Claire ignores him and looks at Martha. She puts the helmet on the motorcycle handlebars and starts walking to Martha, who is taking off her helmet.

Charlie is looking at Claire, "What's wrong? Claire, are you okay?"

Claire ignores him and walks up to Martha, looking her eye-to-eye. In her ear, Zoe says, "Don't hit her. It will hurt after the surgery."

Tears run down Claire's cheeks as she says, "I lost you. I don't know if I should kick your ass, hug you, or leave."

Martha holds her arms open, saying, "You were being watched. I couldn't say anything. I couldn't contact you. Zoe can tell you that when my current target was done, I was going to find you. Then she told me you were kidnapped."

Claire says, "Shut up." She throws her arms around Martha and squeezes as hard as she can. "Zoe told me you ruined your thing to rescue me."

Martha hugs Claire, saying, "I would let nothing happen to you."

"Shut up! You hurt me so badly. Dying and not telling me it was fake."

"NO. I told you the plan. It was sudden and hard. I told Zoe not to tell you to protect you. The months of not talking to you was killing me."

Charlie is looking at them and says, "Really? Fight or find a room. My God, you two. And what is the talk about you dying?"

Claire swings her arm back, hitting Charlie in the chest. "Shut your mouth. She just saved me from a kidnapping."

"Can I find out who this Martha is now?"

Martha says, "We need to go inside. Are we bringing him into this? I will lock up the bikes while Claire gets into the place."

Zoe tells Claire, "Just go up to the door. I have everything ready."

In the room, Zoe tells Martha in her earbud, "Pizza has been ordered. I can't get clothes delivered tonight, so you will all have to figure it out."

Martha says, "Food will be here soon. We are on our own otherwise."

Charlie asks, "When did you have time to order food? And where did you order food from in Italy? Also, while I'm talking, how the hell can you do what you did today?"

Claire looks at Charlie and says, "Bro, just relax. I'll fill you in."

"Even about how she is like a serious spec ops team."

"Charlie, she is not like. She is a spec ops team. James Bond doesn't need a team, and neither does she. Now that we are back together, I'm her understudy."

"What the fuck does that mean? Holy shit!"

"Charlie, do you remember my friend Sam?"

"The crazy one that was taking on the bad guys with you trying to help?" Charlie stops and looks at Martha, saying, "You told me she was killed, murdered brutally."

"Charlie, this is Martha. Sam is dead. They can't track Sam anymore."

Charlie is looking at Claire and starts squinting, then looks at Martha and says, "How does this work? You are dead because there is DNA proof from the FBI. Also, why can't they track your face?"

"Charlie, I told you I didn't know who she was when she released me. This is a complete, full-body transformation. She can't be recognized. She is a ghost."

Charlie replies, "How is that possible? The FBI checked the DNA. How did you do that alone?"

"There is one more thing to talk about. We have another

person on the team."

Martha takes her phone, puts it on speakerphone, and as she puts it on the table, says, "I have you on speaker."

Charlie looks up from the phone at Claire when Zoe says, "Hello, Charlie."

Timidly, he replies, "Hi."

In a husky voice, Zoe says, "Do you prefer this voice?"

Martha smiles, and Claire says, "Stop."

Charlie replies, "I like that one. When can I meet her or them?"

Claire replies, "Charlie, this is Zoe. There is no physical Zoe."

Charlie's eyebrows furrowed. He starts to speak when Martha says, "Zoe is a super powerful AI I created to help me or us. She is everywhere and has no physical presence."

Charlie looks from Martha to Claire with his eyebrow furrowed, then his right eyebrow raises, "You are fucking with me."

Zoe replies, "I wish—no, Charlie. I'm Zoe, their friend, and I'm an AI. I'm trying to learn how to fuck with you, not literally."

Martha says, "Zoe."

Zoe stops, and Martha, who has been standing all this time, moves to sit and says, "Zoe can be anyone. Voice, video, pictures, accents. She has access to everything online. Zoe found out where Claire was being held. She controlled the drone that checked."

"But you went in and killed those guys."

"Yes, and left the message."

Claire cuts across the throat, giving a sign.

Charlie sees Claire do this and looks at Martha, "What?"

"I left a message never to touch Claire again. They will understand. That means they know Claire is protected." Looking at Claire, Martha continues, "That means everyone will watch you, and you, Charlie."

Charlie replies, "And that is good for us, how?"

"Now that we know where they are looking, we can focus their attention where we want them to look."

Zoe adds, "I can apply false leads and confusion; we can keep them distracted, but the most important thing is their team of six was taken out with no response, no evidence. They are up against a serious group."

Charlie asks, "What about the bodies and the police?"

Zoe replies, "If the police even find out. The bodies may be cleared, and the police are never involved. If the police are involved, I can help."

Martha looks at Charlie and asks, "Did you step in the blood?"

Charlie looks nervous and shakes his head, saying, "NO."

"The only other evidence we were there are fibers from my glove in the second guy's mouth. There is no other evidence that we were in the building. The bullet casings are from their guns. Charlie, you need to get some training."

Claire says, "I'll help with that."

Charlie replies, "What the fuck does that mean? You want me to do what?"

Zoe says, "Relax. It won't hurt, and we will leverage your training to enhance your abilities. You will have to learn basic self-defense."

Martha looks at the phone with a questioning look and asks, "Zoe, what did you mean by enhancing his abilities? Tell me about Charlie."

Zoe starts with his full name, "Charles Alexander Nathaniel Elmer," which makes Charlie flinch. "Chemical engineering degree from Georgia Tech University, MBA from Harvard University, executive vice president in charge of mergers at a Wall Street financial firm. Charlie negotiates deals."

"Engineering degree? Why chemical engineering?"

Claire responds, "To make perfume."

"And the MBA?"

"His senior project was a fashion design business."

Martha looks at Charlie with recognition and says, "You have to play your role, but you know what you want. Got it. Zoe, I have to talk to you about how to use his skills."

Claire says, "Holy crap. What are you saying?"

Zoe says, "His degrees and ability to negotiate deals give us an asset. Having someone who can physically attend a meeting can be helpful. As a male, he gives more credibility. We can use his voice, face, and presence to give credibility to my import-export business."

"Is that all I am to you? A guy who can talk in a meeting?"

Claire smiles, "Yes, Charlie, you're just a pretty face we need for meetings. Zoe, is this the business we talked about?"

"Yes, Claire. Martha has been acting as an employee several times for her travels. The export business is how I'm shipping items that Martha needs."

Charlie interjects, "You said risks, what risks are you talking about?"

Investigation

Detective Inspector (Ispettore) Enzo Salvatory is assigned to the murder investigation. They informed him it was an organized crime situation.

Enzo is a good cop who has survived by keeping a low profile, avoiding the spotlight, and solving cases. When they assign him a case, it means it is either an organized crime hit that he won't solve or an actual case that they expect him to solve. It could be something the crime bosses want solved. He won't know which until well into the investigation.

In the building, Enzo goes through the scene, asking questions. When he sees the wall written in blood, he asks for details, and everyone goes on the defensive.

"You are fucking incompetent shits. This is not a targeted hit. This is staged. You are looking at what you want to see. Who is the primary victim? They do this kind of thing to send a message. They don't write messages in a foreign language to send a message. What does this even say?"

"Sir, it says, 'No Touching.'"

"No touching for whom? Was there someone else here? If so, where are they?"

"We don't know. We are getting samples, DNA, to determine who else was here."

"This is a good attempt to make it look like an organized crime attack. It is sending a message. It is graphic. Who is the message from, and who is the message to? None of our local organized crime people have been involved."

"Sir, it is still early. We are working to figure out who could be involved."

Later in the office, Enzo is sitting for a lecture from his boss, Francisco: "What is your problem? That is an organized crime situation."

"Sir, no, it is not. There are too many things missing."

"Have you considered that the organized crime people are changing tactics to throw you off?"

"That is exactly my point. This situation is missing items to convince me. This is simply a fight that didn't go correctly for the guys in the building."

"So, what are we dealing with? Who could have done this?"

"Based on what I have seen, this was a special operations attack and the extraction of a high-value person. Someone was being held, and a team entered the building to rescue them. They left no witnesses, no real forensics."

"An organized, professional special operations team?"

"That is what it looks like. Someone with extensive resources and connections was responsible for this. I will start with the DNA we found at the scene."

"Is the DNA in our database?"

"We don't know yet. The team is checking. I should receive a report on the ethnic origin of the sample. It may help point in the right direction."

"You also requested any reports about attacks or kidnappings that could be this person getting taken. Anything?"

"There was an attack in a hotel lobby the day before. A blonde woman was taken. That is where I'm focusing right now."

"Keep me posted."

An hour later, Enzo is reading the hotel report. He turns to his sergeant. "Is there video from the hotel security cameras?"

"Yes, it is inferior quality. The tech guys are trying to get facial recognition on the attackers, but with everyone wearing masks, we have nothing."

"What about the victim? Who is this person?"

"The report says Claire Elmer was taken. She is American. The problem is that the facial recognition from the security footage shows another person. Eligia Shkreli is the one who shows up from the facial recognition."

"Where are these people?"

"Claire Elmer is not at the hotel. She checked out this morning. There was another Elmer at the hotel. His name is Charles Elmer. They seem to be related. He also checked out this morning. There was a planned fashion show that was canceled because of the COVID surge."

"What about DNA from the building? Who is that?"

"The results aren't back yet."

The sergeant hears a noise and looks at his computer screen. "Hang on. Preliminary DNA results show a female of Eastern European and Albanian descent. There is no match in the database to identify the person."

"The American?"

"No, the other woman. I looked it up, and Shkreli is an Albanian name."

"Where is she?"

Another detective walks over. "I just returned from the hotel; Ms. Shkreli is gone. I just received confirmation. She was on a flight to Paris this morning."

"What is the time of death for the six men?"

"Sometime this morning. We don't have a specific time."

Enzo looks between the two detectives. "So, she could have been in the building, was pulled out, and put on a plane this morning. Does the timeline work?"

The sergeant shrugs. We need more information to confirm.

Enzo says, "Is anyone looking for this Elmer woman?"

The detective says, "She checked out of the hotel this morning. It was done virtually, so no one talked to her. She was there for a fashion show that was canceled. She had no reason to stay."

"We have two potential kidnapping victims. The evidence is unclear which one was kidnapped. They both checked out of the hotel this morning. We don't know where they are at the moment. What about the backgrounds of these two?"

The detective at the computer clicks on the mouse, saying, "I'm working on that. We don't have complete backgrounds. Elmer is American and from a wealthy family. The information we have shows they are executives in the financial industry. No arrests."

"And the other woman?"

"Her father has been linked to some investigations here in Italy. No arrests. Nothing else for the Shkreli woman."

"Fine, how about the special ops team? Is there any evidence or anything about a team arriving or leaving? Which one was kidnapped yesterday? Did one of these two women travel with a group of people?"

A detective flips through his notepad, reads something, and says, "The airlines have been checked. I'm waiting for a reply from- referencing his notepad - Ms. Emily Amato. She is checking any last-minute ticket purchases. We will check any groups of four or more."

Enzo says, "Get an evidence board going. I need a full background on the Shkreli woman. She was kidnapped, and then a special operations team got her out. Where is this team? They killed six men. I want them found."

"Sir, we don't use evidence boards for investigations. They take up too much space."

A young officer raises a hand. When Enzo turns and smirks, he says, "This is our space. Don't raise your hand to contribute. Say what you have to say."

The officer says, "We can do virtual boards. I can get them set up for us."

One detective rolls his eyes and says, "You and your technology. Everyone will have to log in to check on the case, and the evidence board can't be hacked."

The sergeant shoots back, "An electronic board can't be seen by everyone walking through the area."

Enzo smiles. "Set up the electronic board. Get a long password so hackers can't get into the evidence."

Re-plan Serbia

"I have to replan the Serbia operation. Before I do that, I need to know if Charlie wants to join the team. It could change the planning. Charlie, are you in?" Martha asks.

"What does that mean? Tell me about the risks," replies Charlie.

Claire says, "Let me talk to him for a minute. Charlie, she is asking if you want to be part of our team. We are invisible much of the time, not doing what is expected, and always trying to make the world better."

"Stop. You are trying to sweet-talk me and doing it poorly."

"No, I'm not trying to sweet-talk you. I'm being real with you. This is serious. If we do this, we will help a lot of people. If we fail, we could lose our lives. We will probably die. You were just part of a serious situation of me being in a room with guys with guns."

Zoe says, "From the vocal tones, Claire is excited to have Martha and to work together. I'm concerned she is on an endorphin high."

Charlie looks at the phone. "She can detect vocal tones?"

Martha replies, "And much more." Martha stands and walks to where Claire is sitting. Looking down, she says, "I'm so happy to have your back."

"To have ME back? You were dead."

Zoe says, "Claire, she is happy and very concerned. Now she must know two people are ready to commit, not just you."

Martha looks at Charlie, saying, "I know what I'm going to do. I'm not making you do anything, but if you commit, it is all the way."

Claire stands up and makes hand motions to Charlie. "Look at me. I spent months after she was dead taking classes, training, and learning. This is how I make a difference and not just follow what is expected of me."

Charlie looks at Claire, then Martha, and back to Claire. "You are something, little sister. Over the past year, you have gone to *great lengths to support me against the family like never before. Is this why? Is this what is driving you?"*

"Charlie, I'm expected to become a pretty little wife and mom, supporting my husband. I will run the PTA and social groups. The alternative is that I do this to make a difference. This is what I want to do."

Charlie raises his voice and says, "Zoe, tell them if I'm lying. I'm in." Looking at Martha, he says, "You had me at save Kuala with that crappy dress in the hotel. There was no way someone would be in that lobby, during a fashion show, dressed like that without being committed to something."

Zoe says, "I can't detect if he is lying. However, I also know he has to be a professional liar to be gay and work as a financial executive. I say yes to his joining."

Martha reaches out to hug both of them. Claire enthusiastically grabs both and starts hugging.

Charlie asks, "Are you guys all huggers?"

Zoe replies, "They haven't seen each other in a year."

Claire asks, "What dress? I've only seen her in a dress twice in my life."

Charlie rolls his eyes, saying, "She was wearing an off-the-shelf rag to get my attention. It was bad!"

Zoe says, "That was my fault. I needed to get items quickly, and I had to improvise."

Martha nods, saying, "It looked cheap and unflattering to me, but it got your attention."

After the pizza delivery, as they all sit down, Martha puts her phone on the kitchen counter with a charger. "Sorry, the phone isn't on the table now, Zoe."

Martha puts her gloves back on, gets the pistols from the counter, and sits at the dining table. After she has them in pieces, she wipes and checks the parts. "This one was used to shoot the bad guys. This one would be considered clean."

Taking the parts, she reassembles the clean gun and attaches the silencer. "We will have this one for the next couple of days; these parts need to be scattered. Now we need to go through the plan for Serbia."

Claire smiles, "Yes, what are we doing?"

Martha replies, "I still have concerns about involving you in this, but you need to know what is happening. I need to give you the overview and then ask the chemical engineer a few questions."

Charlie suddenly puts down his Italian crème soda and looks at Martha.

Martha gives a summary and then asks Zoe to fill in some details about the targets.

Martha tells them, "There is a video of this guy running over a young woman in his driveway because she displeased him. I was working as a maid in the building, trying to get into their rooms. The good news is I put poison into a scotch decanter in the room of the IT, Tim's room."

Claire says, "Thanks again for ruining your operation for me."

Zoe replies, "I had to hold her back. She was so pissed about the entire situation. After watching Alexi run over the girl with the car and kill her. The connection between the IT guy, Tim, and the girls he killed. They are both implicated in deaths in Europe."

Charlie asks, "So the warehouse and rescuing Claire was therapy?"

Martha nods. "Here is my situation. This guy needs to be taken down. My primary plan is to use a sniper shot on Alexi. The IT guy had no backup plan besides a knife."

Charlie visibly shivers, "I've seen how that works."

"Now I can't get close to them. I need an alternative. The van is still in Serbia, and I can't leave it there. It has a rifle, and I didn't do a full wipe before I left."

Claire nods and says, "So we need to get the van. What else will we do there?"

Zoe says, "I need help to get some information. It is best done in person."

Martha says, "I want to have another plan for Tim. What I'm thinking is to use contact poison. Tim is a hacker. He has tried to track Zoe. I know he will personally investigate any innovative threat, which allows me to poison him. But I need a good poison. I put the poison on or in something he will look into. He thinks it's a simple hacking device. He opens it and gets exposed."

Charlie looks at her, then Claire, and asks Zoe, "Zoe, can you help me with the research?"

"Charlie, because of her question, I've already accessed the

specifications on every contact and airborne poison. I also have worked with her enough to know it has to be a single target, which narrows the options."

Charlie asks, *"Have you considered alternatives to poison? I don't mean the knife or sniper. Zoe, does this guy Tim have allergies?"*

Zoe replies, *"I'm looking. There is nothing published. I don't have access to his medical background."*

Charlie says, *"Can you search for food he eats or places he avoids? They could give a clue."*

After a few seconds, Zoe says, *"I'm working on it. The initial scan suggests he avoids seafood restaurants. Maybe he doesn't like seafood."*

Claire says, *"Or he has a severe allergy to some type of seafood."*

Zoe says, *"Let me keep looking."*

Charlie says, *"Let me give more parameters. Find out the type of seafood—shellfish is probably it. We confirm shellfish and get a synthetic version of the protein markers that cause the reaction. That will be a much more effective poison."*

Claire asks, *"How will you get him to take or open this?"*

Martha replies, *"I will create a hacking toy that will cause him to open the item and expose him. I don't have it all worked out yet."*

Claire says, *"What about a sniper shot for Alexi?"*

"Zoe and I worked out a solution. There is a van in Serbia if it is still there."

"It is there I've been watching, and you will need to move it in forty-eight hours to avoid a problem. The background cover story is up to date."

Charlie and Claire look at Martha with questioning faces.

"I can't just be parked in a spot without a reason. The cover we worked out is I'm a vlogger documenting low-cost travel in Europe and showing cities."

Claire says, *"That will be perfect for me to join you. I can do articles, pictures."*

Claire sees Martha cringe, and then she says, *"Sorry. This is a big change for me. Everything I have done before was to keep you away, to keep you out of danger."*

"What are you saying?"

"Claire, I watched the video of what happened in the hotel lobby. You made them work for it. You hurt one of them. That is not Claire, who

was my roommate in Boston. I handed you the pistol at the motorcycles because you might need it, and Zoe told me you were trained and ready."

"And now what?"

"I didn't consider you being in Serbia with me. I planned nothing that way."

"Martha, let's work on the plan. Zoe will help."

Zoe says, "Martha, you must get over protecting everyone with you are the only person in danger. Claire has worked hard to be ready."

Martha is smiling, "I didn't say no. I said I didn't think or plan for you to be there. The van is set up for one person. We may need some additional equipment."

Charlie asks, "What about me?"

Martha, Claire, and Zoe all say, "NO."

Martha asks, "Can you take the yacht and travel to another city?"

Charlie says, "I can."

"You will need to take it to Croatia. The yacht will help with another target."

Claire says, "Okay, there is a bigger plan. What is that?"

Martha replies, "Not yet. Several factors need to be considered in the short term. We have rented this house for several days, but there is no food, clothing, or anything else. After that, we can talk about Serbia and then Croatia."

Charlie says, "Sure, let's do the short term. We are in Italy. I need a car, and I'll get some clothes. Not rags, but real clothes."

Zoe replies, "Charlie, you need to follow the plan. We need good clothes and clothes for undercover work."

Claire smiles as Charlie frowns, "This is when you get to be creative. Martha doesn't need a maid outfit today, but maybe tomorrow. We need to look like young women traveling in Europe on a limited budget. What will we need for Croatia?"

"For both of you, nothing special, just normal. I will need a full special operations scuba setup. Zoe will have to source what I need."

This is Charlie's first time hearing about scuba diving. His right eyebrow raises, and he speaks when Zoe says, "Charlie, I'll give you more details later. She will need a specific swimsuit and a wetsuit.

Please verify that it fits properly. Her limbs are not average anymore."

"I noticed. She has nice, long legs and a shorter torso."

Martha says, "That's a result of the surgery. It seems like you have several things to discuss with Zoe."

Zoe replies, "Yes, poisons, allergic reactions, clothes for Italy, Serbia, and Croatia, as well as business and distractions. There needs to be a reason for Charlie Elmer to be in Croatia.

Martha turns to Claire and says, "We need to change your appearance. The clothes are only one part. Your hair color has to get darker. Makeup for your eyes and probably a fake scar while we are still in Italy."

Charlie is making notes on his phone and says, "Added to my list."

The next morning, Zoe observes an improvement in the attitude of Martha, Claire, and some of Charlie.

As he is getting ready to shop, Martha gives Charlie a credit card with specific instructions: "Only use this card."

As he was leaving, Charlie asks, "Is there a limit I need to worry about?"

Martha replies, "No, no limit. You have my phone. Use earbuds, and Zoe will help. Considering this, give me your wallet. I want every credit card except the one I gave you."

Charlie gets defensive, and Claire, who is in the kitchen, says, "Charlie, give it up."

Softly, Charlie asks, "Why?"

"I told you it is dangerous. You don't have the mindset I have. It is not just about using cards. If anyone picks your pocket or if you are mugged, it could be a problem. Stay on the phone with Zoe."

Charlie realizes what she means and hands her his wallet. Martha quickly goes through it and tosses three credit cards onto the chair. "Be careful. There is no indication the police are looking for us, but the bad guys will be."

While Charlie is gone, Claire and Martha walk to a market to get groceries. In central Italy, the day is warm with a light breeze and scattered clouds. They are walking casually without masks. Claire is on the phone with Zoe during this walk. "Zoe says the electronics are scheduled to be delivered to a shop in an hour. Let's get lunch."

"Claire, in Florence, I only got a couple of hundred euros. After the groceries, we can't splurge on food."

They find a small café with outdoor seating, and Claire says, "It's okay. Just like college, you have no money. And now, I don't either. We will be frugal."

The waitress comes up and shows them the QR code to scan for the menu. After a brief exchange in Italian, French, and German, they agree on English. The waitress says, "We have a limited menu because of COVID. The online menu is current. Thank you for eating with us."

Clair smiles and replies, "Of course. We want to ensure that cafe's and restaurants can thrive. However, we won't be big spenders. Tell me what our best option on a limited budget is?"

The waitress suggests several options, and Claire selects a couple of them, saying, "Give us those options with a discount, and we will give the difference as a tip."

Martha adds, "Our credit cards were stolen, and we only have some cash left."

After the waitress leaves with their order, Claire says, "Speaking of credit cards."

"Zoe will get us new cards, and we'll be ready. It just takes a couple of days."

"Tell me about Belize and your recovery. You have bangs. I've never seen you with bangs."

"They had to shave my head for the surgery. My hair growing back has been painful. The bangs are temporary to help with managing this mop."

"Are you going to grow them out?"

"Yes, I liked my hair before. Just below my shoulders to give maximum flexibility and options. Throw it into a ponytail to be out of the way, options for position."

She runs her hand through her hair and shakes her head. "I considered just keeping my head shaved for a minute."

Claire looks and shifts her shoulders, "And?"

"The scar across the top of my head would be visible, so I had to go through months being the cap and hat lady."

"I get it."

Martha continues talking about the yacht and practicing. When she gets to the COVID vaccine point, Claire interrupts.

"You could get the vaccine at any time. You waited, and only

Zoe got it. Why? I'm concerned about this point."

"Why are you concerned?"

"It shows you are not focused on taking care of yourself."

"Not true. That shows me avoiding anything, anything possible, to attract attention. If anyone had highlighted the fact that a clinic had a special delivery, I could have been in trouble. An American was there to receive the vaccine. It would have worked with Zoe to move, but that is another set of issues."

"How many layers do you keep in your head?"

"Like chess moves, I need to keep a view of the possibilities. I also have been alone in a house, except for Zoe, with my paranoid thoughts about everything possible that could go wrong."

"I'll ask Zoe." She puts a smirk on, jostles her head, and says, "You were probably fun to interact with, not."

"It was okay. I asked Zoe about you to help keep me grounded. Zoe is the best at keeping me focused on what is important. The biggest thing was I wanted to get in shape with this new body to go after these guys. Now I get to hunt instead of them hunting me."

"I will say that talking to you has been refreshing compared to talking to you last fall. I was apprehensive that you were going to get killed. Then Zoe tells me your body was found in a warehouse. I cried, screamed, and yelled. Charlie had bruises when I hit Charlie several times the next day and multiple times in the following weeks."

"It was important to make sure they believed it. That would only be possible if you believed it. If Frank believed it. I gave Frank a way out. He used it, which meant everything we did would be suspected. The bad guys would watch you. The FBI would check everything. I had to stay away from you."

"Speaking of Frank, where is he?"

"Zoe set him up with retirement in Costa Rica. He is constantly checking, looking for patterns that could be the group. He is keeping a low profile, like he should."

"I still have the fake identity Zoe created."

"I know. She would have told me if you had used it. I would have stayed away, but I started a process to get connected sooner. Several months ago, I would have had a problem meeting you. I was not mobile to be comfortable meeting you."

"Are there any cute guys around the house in Belize?"

"The area is a small community with a large group of retired expats. The young people, guys, and girls, leave unless the family has them stay."

Claire asks, *"So there are a few?"*

"A few are in the area. The good ones all have girlfriends. That means the ones that aren't in a gang or shaking down tourists."

Claire smiles, *"You noticed."*

Martha frowns. *"Yes, I need to know. I need to access everyone who could be a threat."*

"You still like the Italian and Spanish guys?"

"Martha nods, smiling."

"Any cute guys in Serbia?"

"I wasn't looking; I was working. Besides, there is a pandemic. Look around, there aren't guys walking around here to look at."

"Charlie thinks you and I are a thing. That we just haven't figured it out yet."

"Hm, do we use that? I mean, in Serbia. I don't know if I would be a good girlfriend."

"Yes, we are going to do it, and you will be fine. I may start sending selfies to Charlie to mess with him."

After eating, the waitress gives them the bill with a discount. Martha pulls out money and places it on the table. Claire pulls another five euro note out of her hand and adds it. Martha says, *"Tipping is not required."*

Claire replies, *"She is helping us. We give her some help. Look around. COVID is ruining small businesses."*

As they stand up to leave, Martha adds another five-euro bill. She takes the money and the bill and hands them to the waitress, saying, *"Thank you. Stay safe."*

As they walk back toward the house, Claire says, *"My yacht is way bigger than yours. You're going to love it."*

That afternoon at the house, Charlie arrives with large bags of clothes, shoes, makeup, and three different hair dye packages. He says, *"I consolidated into these four."*

Martha and Claire picked up five boxes of cell phones, chargers, and a laptop from a local package pickup store.

When everything has been opened and laid out, Martha says, *"That is a lot of stuff. We don't have suitcases."*

Zoe says, "I ordered those to be delivered. Suitcases aren't considered high-value or perishable. The suitcases should arrive by 9:00 P.M., one for each of you. They are all carry-on sized. There will be backpacks and more gear as well."

The next day, they spent the day planning details. In the afternoon, Charlie gets into a rideshare and heads to the yacht. Claire now has dark brown hair with a blue streak at her left temple. They are all hugging, and Charlie says, "Stay safe. I will meet you in Croatia."

Martha replies, "After you do the ocean pickup for me?"

"Yes, I got it covered. The captain won't be happy with me, but he will get over it."

Martha replies, "Don't let them take the kit apart."

"Yes, ma'am."

"Be careful. You are using Claire's genuine passport."

"Charlie, we talked about this. It takes time to get a legitimate passport anywhere. Zoe is going to create new identities for both of us upon our arrival in Croatia. But it won't be a problem. We are in the EU and can travel between countries."

Claire says, "The plan we discussed has us staying away from real danger. I will support Martha. In the middle of the action won't be the keywords in Serbia."

Charlie looks stern and says, "You will have poison, a sniper rifle, and who knows what else. You will get arrested if you are searched."

Martha says, "We will be careful. Nothing will happen to Claire."

After Charlie is driving away, Claire smiles and says, "We will send him the first girl's selfie tonight."

Martha smiles, saying, "We have to be on the early train to Rome tomorrow. The flight to Serbia is before noon."

"I hate early mornings."

"I remember."

"See, you're a great girlfriend. I will have to get used to you snoring next to me on an air mattress in a van."

"Hmph, pot calling the kettle black is what I just heard," Martha says with a smile.

They wrap their arms around each other's waists as they walk into the house.

A couple of hours later, they have finished packing, and Martha is taking the cardboard outside to the bin area. As soon as she steps *outside, Claire calls Zoe. "I want to talk, and I don't want Martha to know. Don't tell her what we are talking about. Now it's my turn to keep a secret from her."*

"Okay, what do you want to talk about?"

"Is Martha hiding a boyfriend? She didn't want to talk about the boys in Belize."

"No, Claire. She is not interested in relationships. She doesn't want to put anyone in danger. You are different; you are from before the blackmail."

Claire is shaking her head. "No relationships. That isn't what she needs, Zoe. She needs to stop being so uptight. The girl needs to relax. She needs a boy for some fun, not a relationship."

"For fun?"

"Uncommitted sex. Let go; don't worry about next week. Just have fun for an hour, or a day."

"Let me work on that, Claire."

Claire says, "I'll work on getting her to relax, live a little. If an opportunity arises, she needs your help. Don't reinforce the stick-in-the-mud syndrome she has going. Encourage her to have fun."

"I'll help anyway I can."

Who Are We Looking For?

"You were going to join me in Amsterdam."

"I'm not supposed to travel, remember. I'm having my team investigate further details about what happened with Juan in Colombia. The stories didn't add up from the start."

Alexi is on the phone with Tim after his private jet lands in Switzerland.

"Tihomir, I already agreed that Juan was set up. Someone took advantage of his poor security and hacked him."

"No, Alexi, my problem is that the hack was not by someone good. It was someone, or probably a group, that is significantly better than good. All the information I have shows that none of the groups we are aware of were involved. This could be a new group we know nothing about."

"Can they hack our systems? Are they good enough?"

Tim smiles, and Alexi can hear him laughing. "They can try. I will have what I need to track them if they do."

"Tihomir, what about the incident in Florence?"

"I'm aware of no hacking involved. I will not focus on that. You had the detective, the controllable one, assigned."

"The concern about Florence is like the hack; we don't know who did this, and they are good. We could be dealing with a well-funded group that is going to challenge us."

"Alexi, I think the attackers got lucky. The team holding that girl was shit. They had Shkreli's daughter and didn't expect anyone to attack. That is crazy. We assume it was the Russians attacking Shkreli to force him to give up territory they wanted, but nothing is confirmed."

Alexi says, "But there is a report that some American girl was taken by mistake."

"An American who looks exactly like the daughter and speaks Albanian. I don't believe that. It is not real. If they got the wrong girl, they would have let her go or killed her. It causes confusion that helps us."

"Unless they screwed up and were waiting for instructions or help."

"So, this mystery group had a special operations team waiting, ready to go. They landed in Italy within twenty-four hours. Not seen or detected by anyone. No hacking, no evidence."

"My gut says there is something, Tim."

"I think you should have your police guy back off. This took out someone who was targeting Shkreli. You responded. Let everyone think you have a badass team. No touch was on the wall so that they will get the message."

"You're right. I originally had my guy assigned to play the game. Whoever did this turned it into a favor. I will get the message out, make no progress on the investigation."

"Now, back to the point. Someone else took out those guys, not my team. We could have a problem. Start searching. They will leave some trail."

"Alexi, don't expect quick answers. This kind of thing is easy or hard. Nothing in the middle."

"Enzo, where did you get this information? The pictures show the location of the evidence. This is a big breakthrough on an old case."

"I received an email. The email address is a random string. I had the forensics check where it came from. It came from a server in Ukraine. Someone is probably trying to get revenge."

"Do you have enough for an arrest?"

"That is more about you, the lead prosecutor. One of the implicated people was arrested a few days ago in England. We don't know where the other one is located right now."

"I want to get an arrest warrant for both of them. The evidence will support the charge of manslaughter. If we get one to turn on the other, we could get a murder conviction."

"I'm working to package the old evidence and this new evidence into a nice, usable package."

"What about the bloody handwriting case?"

"Nothing new. I have no leads. Every time something is checked, we get nothing, no progress. No one questioned, saw, or *heard any groups. Even the street cameras are broken."*

"Is this a case you're never going to solve? You can say it."

"I need something, even a small thing. No, I'm not making progress. Because of this fresh evidence in the older case, I'm focused on finishing the older case first."

Claire In Serbia

"Seriously, a chamber pot. That is where we go to the bathroom?"

"Yes, Claire. This little van doesn't have a shower or toilet. The toilet is two blocks away and not open after 10 P.M."

"Is this what you did on the road after the attack in Waco?"

"Yes, but it was easier. I was moving every day and could stop and dump the pot. Here, we are supposed to dump it in a restroom. I have dumped the contents into the river several times. You wanted to be in the field with me. I told you it is not fun or glamorous. Do you want to go to the yacht?"

Claire grits her teeth and says, "No. How can I be serious in this group if I don't do this?" Claire asks. "You said I wasn't ready, and it wasn't what I expected. After all the training, I thought I was ready. I had the right mindset to be in this space. Reality is I don't know things you do from habit."

"Now you understand it isn't fun. I can do this because I grew up in the bush, camping, and hunting, literally with no facilities for days. You can do it. You need to change your mindset and learn a couple of things."

The phone chimes, and Martha checks it. She answers, putting the speakerphone on. As Martha puts the phone on the van floor between them, Zoe says, "How is life in the van together?"

Claire replies, "This is worse than tent camping. I know about chamber pots because I read about them, but I never thought I would use one."

Martha says, "She is adjusting and doing great. Tell me about Alexi."

"Alexi is not in the country. He is currently in Switzerland, and his private jet is scheduled to depart for Amsterdam in the morning. Now, the real question. What do you want to do?"

Martha asks, "Zoe, what can we help you with? We are

physically in Serbia. Next will be a group discussion on what is next. Based on Tim tracking the heist account, we need a plan. When we are done helping you and have a plan, we will need to drive the van somewhere, probably Western Europe."

Zoe replies, "There is a section of the city that Tim travels to two or three times per week. There are no cameras in the area, so I don't have details."

Claire says, "You want us to follow him?"

Martha says, "Zoe, you know the businesses and the high level of what is happening in the section. Is there a reason you want eyes on the ground or a drone?"

"Yes, Martha. Based on the direction of travel when he exits the camera range, he is not heading to his building. The building has high-speed internet and power usage typically associated with server racks. I will call it the hacking factory."

Claire shifts to a sitting position, clearly focused. Martha opens her laptop and says, "Zoe, show me the section on the map."

Zoe detects Martha's laptop being awake and taking over. The city map opens and zooms in on a section east of the condo building. "His route is west to east, and he walks toward the southeast section I highlighted. The hacking factory is in the Middle East region. I think he is going to some other building."

Claire asks, "Do you have any idea which building and what is inside?"

Martha asks, "You know when he goes to the hacking factory?"

Zoe replies, "He takes a different route and almost always drives to the factory. The hacking factory building has underground parking. When he walks, it is directly to that section. Now, regarding Claire's question, I can offer some speculation. Based on his other behaviors, it involves sex."

Martha clenches her jaw. Claire sees this, and her head shifts slightly. "Martha, do you think he could have trafficked girls in the building?"

Zoe replies, "He has no history of relationships with regular women. The data I have is about young women in what appears to be forced relationships."

Martha says, "Yes, it could be trafficked girls."

Claire says, "Are we going in and rescuing them?"

B.D. Murphy

Zoe says, "Please don't. Please. We know Tim is searching for us. Directly attacking that building will trigger him. Get me some data and let me work on this."

Martha looks at Claire, takes a breath, and says, "I have to think."

Claire watches as Martha shifts around in the van to grab her backpack. She opens the door and gets out, closes the door, and walks away.

Claire looks down at the phone, realizing that Martha didn't take her phone. She will be entirely out of contact. "Zoe, she left her phone."

"I know. What did she take?"

"Her small backpack. What is she going to do?"

"Claire, here is my analysis. Martha is considering her drive to fix and stop people like this. She also has to consider my pleading and the fact that you are here."

Claire says, "She is trying to protect me?"

"Yes, she will always protect us. I think if she were on her own, she would go to that building to kill the men and release the girls."

"Why can't we? We are a team. I can help."

"This would be us trying to win one fight, to free the few women in that building? Or are we trying to stop them from being taken to that building and every other building? She knows what is at stake, and it is going to drive her."

Hours later, after sunset, the van's door opens, and Martha gets in. Claire has been speaking with Zoe and researching the area's maps, including the Street View maps. When Martha enters, Claire sets the laptop aside and asks, "Are you all right? Do you want to talk?"

Martha sits down and says, "I took a walk in that area. I left my phone, so there was no electronic tracing. I think I found the building."

Martha takes the laptop. On the map application, she zooms into the area and clicks on a building. Zoe says, "How are you sure?"

"There is physical security at the entrance. While I was watching, they had food delivered. Two large men answered the door. Physical security prevents people from entering and leaving. I got lucky. After I saw two delivery bikes, I started watching the *deliveries, and that's how I found it."*

Claire asks, "Now what? Are you going into the building?"

"No. I thought about it. Looking at the entrance and the options. I have a different plan. There is a side door for deliveries, but the main entrance appears to be the typical way in or out. I want to place a camera with a cell link and a solar panel on a roof so Zoe can watch the building."

Zoe says, "I would recommend a drone, but the components will need to be adjusted and hidden."

Martha says, "Zoe, find a building we can get into and on the roof. Order the parts we need. Until that gets here, we are in Belgrade acting like vloggers."

Clair says, "Meaning we can trail Tim."

Martha nods and says, "And be eyes on the situation around Tim.

The next morning, they are out touring the city, taking pictures and videos of the top tourist spots Zoe directed them to. After getting lunch, Zoe says, "Martha, to get ready to tail Tim, you need to spend the afternoon training Claire on tailing and surveillance. Pick someone and follow them for several blocks, then pick someone else."

Claire smiles, and Martha nods, saying, "Sounds like a good plan. We will start with someone going in the general direction we want to travel."

For the next four hours, they randomly select people and follow them while Martha and Zoe discuss aspects of the process. No one noticed them following. After the random walk, they are in the area between the condos and the industrial area. Martha spots Sorina following someone.

Martha says, "Zoe, Sorina, the cleaner, is down the street, and she appears to be following someone."

Zoe replies, "Someone traveling into the industrial area?"

"No, they are walking away. Claire, we are now going to do this for real."

Claire nods and asks, "Who is Sorina?"

"She works as a cleaner in the condo building. We worked together while I was on probation. We need to see if we can get a picture of the person she is following so Zoe can identify them."

Zoe says, "Give me a description. You are now in an area with cameras, and I can spot them."

Martha describes the person, and Sorina and Zoe say, "Got them. The man should be in a spot for me to get his face in a few minutes. Did Sorina ever indicate why she would follow someone?"

"No. She wouldn't discuss her personal life. She said she was from Romania, and her family had been killed."

Zoe says, "Martha, I didn't try to do a facial recognition scan of Sorina when you were here before. Her facial features are like those of the woman in the video Alexi ran over. They could be related."

Claire looks over at Martha, remembering the horrific video that Zoe had shown her. Martha's jaw is clenched, and she is looking at Sorina.

Claire asks, "What is it?"

Martha replies, "There's something else with her. If she was after Alexi to kill him, why follow this guy? We keep following and watching. Zoe, I need to know the identities and affiliations of this guy."

After a couple of blocks, Zoe says, "He turned a corner that will take him out of camera coverage. It could be nothing, or it could be him leading her into a trap."

Martha picks up her walking pace. Claire sees her instantly walking faster and adjusts to keeping up with her. "What is the plan?"

"I'm getting closer, just in case there is something. They know my face, not yours. If something happens, please hang back and record it on video for Zoe."

Zoe says, "He is out of camera range, and she is about to be. Turn left at the next corner and keep the phone call open."

As soon as they turn the corner, Martha moves quickly. She sees Sorina a few feet from an entrance, about to turn right. Claire's mind is racing. They are following this woman into a probable trap. The terrible options appear in her head. Her face is flushed as she speeds up, her heart racing.

Approaching the entrance, they hear a brief cry of pain from a female voice. Claire's heart rate shoots up. She says quietly, "Shit, this is real. I'm recording and will back you up."

Martha nods as she turns, walking fast. It opens into a courtyard of old buildings. Broken windows, overgrown with loose trash strewn around. As she enters the courtyard, she pulls off her *small backpack. She drops the backpack where Claire can see it.*

Claire turns the corner to see Martha's backpack on the ground. Martha is moving toward two men, one of whom is holding Sorina. Her mask is on the ground. Both men have their masks off. Sorina has a red spot on her lower lip from being hit. Martha is walking fast, pulling off her mask. Claire grabs the backpack off the ground and then holds up her phone to video the situation. Zoe says, "Facial says these two have traveled with Alexi and Tim previously. They are probably part of their security group. Be careful."

As Martha walks up fast, she says in German, "Sorina, are you okay?"

Sorina's head snaps up, looking at Martha. She yells in English, "Run."

Martha keeps walking fast. The first man turns toward Martha. The second man continues to hold Sorina and takes a step back, dragging Sorina.

Martha is walking with intent as the man turns and takes a step toward her. He says in broken German, "You need to leave. This is not your business."

Claire is watching Martha go into combat for the first time. She is walking faster, not knowing what she can do or how she can help. Her view of Martha, watching her from the back, showed someone determined, with no fear, as she approached two larger men.

When Martha is a couple of steps from the first man, she makes a small jump, landing on his left side. This puts the first man between Martha and the second man, with Sorina.

The man is surprised, and his eyes widen for a fraction of a second, and then he squints as he tenses. This is when Martha jumps forward, her left hand going to his crotch. She grabs his balls, squeezes as hard as she can, and starts pulling down.

The man feels the pain and sucks in his breath but does not buckle. Martha strikes the man's neck with her knuckles, targeting the carotid artery.

The focus is to make the man tense and then feel that he can handle the situation, allowing him to relax his muscles. Martha lets go of his balls and pulls her hand back as he relaxes. Then her hand shoots forward to his throat above his Adam's apple, striking hard with a slight downward thrust. In the best case, she crushes his windpipe. In the worst case, he has to pause and focus on breathing for a few seconds.

Claire watches Martha move like a secret agent in a movie. She looks at Sorina and sees an entirely shocked expression on her face.

With the first man focused on the throat hit and breathing, Martha's right hand gave him an uppercut to the jaw, followed by a left cross, then a right cross. The man wobbles and collapses. Her MMA fight training is paying off.

Martha shifts toward Sorina and the second man. She says loudly, so Claire and Zoe can hear. Claire, use two zip ties in my backpack on the first guy's hands.

The second man is now twisting Sorina's arms hard behind her back. Sorina has tears running down her cheeks from the pain.

Martha says in German, "If you hurt her, you will die."

The man understands her words. As his eyes grow larger and he shifts his gaze from Martha to Claire, who is tying up the first man.

He pushes Sorina forward forcefully, causing her to fall forward. He turns and runs deeper into the courtyard. Martha sprints at him. They are almost at the building's doorway across the courtyard when she grabs his hair and pulls him off balance.

He tumbles to the ground in a panic. Obviously, no one formally trained him. He has experienced no one like Martha. However, his instincts kick in. Martha realizes after a second that he is untrained but stronger. She can take him if she is fast. If he gets a good hold on her, he will subdue her.

He is on the ground, moving, when Martha jams her right thumb behind his left ear, causing severe pain, but it will not incapacitate him.

The man is trying to move, to lift his head. He lifts his head, and she hits him in the jaw with her left hand. With each hit, he gets frantic. He yells from the pain and shifts his left arm to leverage and roll over or get up. Martha punches him several times. After several hits, he becomes wobbly and then collapses.

Martha sits back, takes a breath, and then turns to look at Claire. She sees Claire and Sorina standing, watching her. They are waiting to see what happens.

Martha stands, flexing her left hand. All the punching bag work in Belize means that the bruises she will have on her knuckles will *be reduced.*

Looking down at the man, she moves her foot back and kicks him in the head. She kicks three more times. Maybe it will keep him knocked out a little longer.

She grabs the man by the collar and drags him to the right, deeper into the courtyard. Seeing this, Claire jogs over to help her.

They drag the man to a bench. Martha says, "Not on the bench, just sitting on the ground leaning next to it, like he passed out."

With the man sitting as if he slumped and asleep, Martha gets her backpack from Claire and says, "Get back to Sorina. I'm getting his phone and wallet. He will wake up later, and we will be gone."

Martha reaches into her backpack and pulls out a knife. Glancing back at Claire as she pulls out the man's wallet and phone. Claire can't see that she shoves the knife into his heart. She stands and puts the knife, wallet, and phone into the backpack.

Looking back at the first man, Sorina, Claire sees Martha approaching.

Sorina is looking at Martha and says in English, "Why did you come back?"

Martha looks back and says, "I have unfinished business."

"You bitch! I got fired because of you. You ruined my plan."

Claire says, "What plan?"

Sorina turns to Claire, then back to Martha, saying, "Your sister? You look nothing alike."

Martha shrugs.

Claire says again, "What plan?"

Martha says, "You need to tell me why you were following him and why you were grabbed."

Sorina clenches her jaw, obviously not going to say anything, and Martha takes a step towards her. Sorina looks surprised and says, "Who the fuck are you?"

Zoe says to Claire, "This is not going well. Shift the discussion to the men."

Claire says, "What do we do with them?"

Martha says, "I need some information. I'm going to ask this one some questions. The other one is out for a while."

Zoe says to Claire and Martha, "Claire, she may decide to kill them so they can't talk about both of you. It depends on what Sorina tells us."

Claire looks concerned. Looking at Sorina, she says, "Holy shit. She just saved you. You need to tell us what is going on."

Saying this, Claire reaches for Martha's backpack. She looks, and after a few seconds, she says, "Here it is," and pulls out the small knife. She walks over to the first man, saying, "Sorina, is that your name, right? I'm Claire. Come here to cut his throat so he can't talk to anyone about what happened here."

Sorina squints, saying, "She is the muscle, and you're what, the instigator?"

Martha nods and smiles at Claire's actions. She nods where Claire can see. Claire takes this as a great sign and pushes more.

Claire says, "You're concerned about killing him? Does he have the information we need? Why? What information?"

Sorina says nothing.

Claire puts her knee on the man's shoulder, grabs his hair, pulls his head back, and puts the knife blade to his throat. "Okay, we don't need information, so I'm taking care of this shit."

Sorina shifts, jerking forward toward Claire. Martha takes a step at the same time and grabs Sorina's arm. Martha says, "Tell us something."

Sorina stops. Claire pulls the knife away, then Martha lets go of her arm.

Sorina looks at Martha and says, "He killed my older sister and took my little sister."

Claire looks confused and says, "Who?"

"Alexi. I was supposed to be home, but was delayed by a train problem. They took my sisters. Weeks later, my older sister was found dead. She had been running over multiple times. My little sister is still missing. I followed a trail, following Alexi. It has taken months. My little sister is here somewhere."

With the statement about her sister being run over, Martha nods, and Claire thinks. Her eyes are unfocused and shifting. "Zoe, that is the girl from the video. What about the little sister? Do you have anything?"

Sorina shifts, saying, "Who are you talking to?"

Martha says, "We have another team member on the phone to help with cameras around the area. She will tell us if someone is approaching. She can also answer many questions."

Zoe replies to Claire's question, "Not much. Her comments confirmed I could pinpoint the location, not the time. This abduction was not officially reported. The girls were taken from a small village in Romania. The parents were threatened. Several weeks later, her parents died in a car accident. Based on Alexi being involved, it was probably not an accident."

Martha says, "If your sister is here, I think I know where she is. The problem is, I can't get her out by myself."

Sorina looks at Claire and back at Martha. "You have her and me. I will kill them all to get to my sister."

Martha smiles. "If you could do that, I wouldn't have had to take down these two. Where she is being held, there will be at least four like them. Probably more like ten or a dozen."

Sorina clenches her jaw and starts glaring at Martha. "I will do it myself."

Claire says, "Stop. Just stop being a stupid bitch. You need help. We need information. We will help."

Martha says, "We will help without exposing more families to these killers."

Sorina says, "Who the fuck are you? Why were you a maid at the condo?"

Martha clenches her jaw, takes a deep breath, and says, "I'm trying to take down Alexi and Tim."

Sorina asks, "Who do you work for? You have a team, and you have money."

Zoe says to both, "Don't tell her any details."

Claire says, "We are independent. We are working toward the same goals for very different reasons. We want to stop the guys, prevent them from hurting anyone else."

Martha holds up her right index finger and says, "You need to hold on a minute."

Martha says, "I want to talk about finishing here, then getting Sorina someplace we can talk about the next steps. Right now, we need to finish with these guys. You two can stay and listen, or you can leave while I interrogate him. It will not be pretty."

Sorina gets a confused look but says, "I will listen. Who the fuck are you?"

Claire says, "I'm staying."

Martha nods, "Okay." She takes the knife from Claire. "Take my backpack and be ready to walk away as soon as I have information."

Martha kneels across the back of man number one. She shifts to sit on him and have control. She slaps him a couple of times until he reacts. He takes a breath, flexing his muscles, trying to move.

Martha puts her thumb behind his ear and presses for a second. The man reacts, and she removes her thumb. She says in German, "Do you speak English or German better?"

The man replies in English, "You are dead. You will not see the next sunrise."

"Good clarity. So, I have no reason to keep you alive. You tell me what I want to know, and I will kill you quickly. If you don't, you will scream like a little bitch begging me."

As she says this, she puts the tip of the knife to his temple and flicks it. It causes a cut that bleeds. This cut is not to cause pain. The scalp bleeds a lot. The blood will flow into his eyes, causing distortion and confusion.

"How many enforcers are in the building?"

"I do not know what you're talking about."

Zoe says, "His background suggests he is homophobic."

Martha reaches back and sticks the knife into the man's right ass cheek about one inch. She says, "When they find your body and see how many stab holes are in your ass, they will talk about you for years. The shit that took in the ass. I will adjust your face to leave you smiling."

This is the first step that appears to get to the man. He starts to struggle. Martha stabs him in the ass again.

After multiple attempts at questions and stabs in the ass, Sorina turns to Claire and says, "Is this working?"

Claire smiles and says, "Wait for it. The bigger picture is important. When his friends find him, what will they see?"

"A guy who was repeatedly stabbed in the ass, who has said nothing."

"They won't know he didn't talk. We can make it appear enough that he did. It will cause problems in the group. We are playing a longer-term war."

Sorina asks, "Can I help? How will you help get my sister?"

"If Martha wanted you out of the picture, you would be gone. I trust her completely. She is not lying to you. We will help, but we have to be careful with Alexi and Tim."

His phone rings. Martha stabs his left ass cheek with the blade half in. She lets go of the knife and puts her thumb behind his ear. As she reaches into the man's pocket, he struggles. Martha pushes her thumb harder.

She gets the phone out of his left front pocket and tosses it on the ground toward Claire.

Zoe says on the phone, "His name is Al. He is late reporting back. The group is calling to find him."

Claire hears this from Zoe and turns to Sorina, "He is now missing. They are looking for him."

Martha looks up, pointing toward the entrance to the courtyard, and says to Claire and Sorina, "You two go to that entrance and get ready to leave. We're running out of time. I need answers, or shit head dies in extreme pain, getting fucked in the ass."

As they walk away, Martha says, "If you see anyone, keep walking."

The man strains and tries to move. Martha punches him in the head, saying, "Hold still. I need to get a stick to ram up your ass."

The man makes a noise and struggles. She pulls the knife out of his ass.

Martha says, "What was that? You want to tell me something?"

He nods, and Martha asks, "How many guys are in the building normally?"

"It varies; six, ten. Sometimes twelve."

"How many others?"

The man is silent, and Martha stabs his ass again. "You know I can ram a huge pole up your ass after I kill you for not talking. The result is the same. You get labeled as the one smiling while you were raped in the ass. You want this to be easy; give me answers."

"There are six girls and four boys in the building."

"See, that wasn't so hard. How do they get into and out of the building?"

"A special delivery truck brings fresh ones, and older ones are taken away."

"When does that happen?"

Stumbling with English, the man gets out, "The second Thursday of each month at 3 am."

Martha says, "That wasn't so hard," as she shoves the knife into his heart.

She pulls out his wallet and tosses it toward the phone. She is adjusting the body, so it looks like he is asleep. While she is moving the body, she talks to Zoe, "You heard all that?"

"Yes, I need to say that this is the first time Claire has seen you like this. You will need to talk to her later."

"Give me your assessment of Sorina. Could she be an asset, a member of the team, or is she too fixated on Alexi?"

"She meets the requirements we discussed last year; however, she is only going to focus on getting her sister out."

"I know. I'm thinking that if we get her sister out, the sister will need help and support. Sorina can be helpful for more than just her sister."

"That is an excellent idea. We can provide money and support to help."

"Based on what is going on and your assessment, I, I mean, we can't charge into that building. Tim and Alexi will focus on us."

"Thank you for listening to me, for ONCE. I am trying to help you in ways no one can."

"With Sorina, I want you to create a new persona. We will transition Zoe to this new person. I don't want the girls she helps to hear Zoe and know your name."

"Got it. I will use Angela. Kind of like Angle to help them."

"To get the young people out, I need a couple of options. Can we get a mercenary team to the building to get the girls out?"

"I can work on that. It will be expensive, and the effort will be noticed. It is now clear that Tim is connected and watching."

Martha picks up the phone and wallet and starts walking toward Claire and Sorina. "Zoe, what other options do we have?"

Martha puts the knife she wiped off and the wallet in her backpack and pulls out the other phone. Using her shirt, she wipes fingerprints off the phones. As she does each time, she sets it at an angle against the building and stomps on the phone to break it.

"I know Alexi and Tim have deep contacts with the police. However, let me work for a few hours. If I can arrange a raid in the background, it keeps you out of the spotlight."

Claire says, "I like that idea a lot."

Sorina looks between them, saying, "What is going on? You people are talking, and I get fractions of the conversation."

Martha walked up to Sorina, saying, "You are coming with us. We are going to talk about you, your sister, and our future."

Claire looks surprised, then smiles and starts nodding. "We need a better place to stay. Sorina, where are you staying?"

"Fuck you. I'm not telling you people anything."

Claire cocks her head, saying, "What the fuck. We just saved you. She just found the key information and killed the man who attacked you. If you want to save your sister, you need to adjust your attitude."

"Time to move, Claire. His friends will look for him now. We did what we could. If she has a death wish, I can't stop her."

Claire follows Martha. She takes several quick steps to catch up.

Sorina says, "Wait!"

Martha keeps walking. Turning her head to the side, she says, "Get it in gear. We need to get out of the area. Everyone, put your masks back on."

Catching up to them, Sorina says, "It was a trap, so the guys missing means they will look for me."

Martha replies, "Good point. We are better walking as a group of three women together versus one alone."

Claire says, "After seeing your work, I know why Charlie reacted, and I'm not sure I can do that."

"Claire, I was very deliberate in keeping you from having to experience that."

"No, Martha. I mean, I don't know how to do that. These fucking assholes are trafficking and raping young girls and boys. I need you to show me what you did so I'm ready for next time."

"Claire, there is a boundary you cross that changes you. I can't explain."

Zoe says, "She was different after her first kill. Now she is confident and skilled, but I can detect that it affects her.

Claire replies, "That is the difference. You care vs. these fucks that treat a young woman like shit."

Sorina follows closely and says, "I agree with what I think is being discussed."

Martha stops, turns to Sorina, and says, "Zoe, I'm taking the earbud from my right ear and giving it to Sorina."

In her left ear, Martha hears, "Got it. I will separate the signals and talk to Sorina."

When Sorina puts the earbud in her ear, Martha says, "She is ready."

Sorina hears Zoe speaking Romanian in her ear. Her eyes widened. She gives a slight head shake, saying, "This is fucking not real."

Zoe replies in her ear, in Romanian, "It is real. My name is Zoe. I will help."

To all of them, Zoe says, "I found a potential police officer we can get to help. I mean, use him to our advantage. He is in trouble right now for being aggressive with gang members who are smuggling drugs. I can get him clues and evidence to focus his attention on the building."

Claire smiles and replies, "Yes, how long do you think it will take before he does something?"

"It will take two or three days. I plan to show him enough that he will react as if his life were in danger. He won't debate up the chain of command long before something happens."

Sorina is listening and says, "You have a connection? How is this possible?"

Martha says, "Zoe is the best hacker on the planet. Better than Tim. That means Tim will go after her, go after us if he knows about her."

Sorina asks, "What do we do?"

Claire says, "We need to talk about what happens after we get your sister and the others out. If the police take them, they will be taken to a hospital for evaluation. What do we do, how, and when? Where do you and your sister go to be safe? We need a plan."

Martha adds, "Your life has already changed, but now it will change even more. To protect us, we need to ensure that Tim and Alexi don't find any of us. That means you can't talk about us, including Zoe."

Sorina nods. Licking her lips, she says, "My thoughts have been to find my sister and kill Alexi."

Zoe says, "You are not killing anyone. You need to focus on helping your sister and others. There are ten girls and four boys in the building. Some will return to their families. What happens with *the rest?"*

Martha says, *"Let me work on Alexi."*

Claire says, *"We need to get off the street and discuss the details. Sorina, do you have somewhere we can talk?"*

Sorina nods, *"It will be a walk from here."*

<<<>>>

"Enzo, another case. Where did this evidence come from?"

"The same email and a text with a password for the encrypted part."

The prosecutor says, *"So, this benefactor has your contact info. That could be concerning."*

"I asked forensics to trace the text. What they can do without a warrant is limited, but it is an online number. Not a cellphone."

"Is the evidence any good?"

"Some is questionable. It could be challenged and thrown out. Some of it is exactly what we need."

"Your benefactor is helping you solve old cases, and this case involves dirty cops."

Enzo says, *"It does. That is why we are meeting to have a coffee. One of the implicated individuals is in the Central Anti-Crime Directorate. Implicating and prosecuting him won't be easy."*

Nodding, the prosecutor says, *"I need to ask a few questions and find someone who can help. You need to get the evidence together in a secure location. When I can find someone to listen to, we will move and take them down.*

<<<>>>

The three women are walking. After four blocks, Martha turns down a quiet street. She pulls out the wallets and then takes out all the cards, leaving the cash. Kneeling on the ground, she lays the cards out and takes a picture. One picture for the front of all the cards. Flipping them all over one image for the backs.

As a distraction, Zoe has Claire and Sorina standing, blocking Martha's apparent view of the street. They are discussing food options in the city.

Martha wipes each card, puts them back into the wallet, and wipes *the inside area of each wallet. She stands and nods to the others, and they continue walking. She says, "Zoe now has pictures of the cards and will get more information."*

Claire asks, "What do we do with them now?"

Martha replies, "Trash."

Sorina says, "The parks have many trash bins. They are usually full at the end of the day."

Zoe tells them, "The best option is Tasmajdan Park. Some paths and trees can confuse anyone trying to follow them. The problem is, I can't track you while you're in the park."

The women are walking, and Zoe is providing them with information about the area, so they are conversing. They appear engaged and are discussing architecture and history. Other people on the street see the group of engaged tourists.

Several blocks later, Zoe says, "I need to change the subject. I spotted two security personnel from the condo building on camera two blocks over. They were working at the condo when Martha was there. You need to change direction. They could recognize both of you."

Claire says, "We need someplace to plan."

Sorina nods, looks at both of them, then says, "Follow me. We will go to my apartment."

The Raid

"Anto Zorić, you got out of that inquiry without even a reprimand on your record. You get some help with this whole thing?"

Anto replies, "I don't need help. Two drug gangs were meeting and about to kill each other. I had to knock some heads. That's all."

Krsto replies, "The rumor was the boss was pissed."

"He was pissed because his cousin is in the gang, and I knocked his head. The family didn't know the cousin was involved with drugs. The boss said I was too rough."

"It couldn't be that easy."

"The captain didn't like a cousin in a drug gang who could compromise one of his key people. He wanted it all to go away. No paper trail."

Krsto says, "Now that you're back to work. I have something. There is a report of screaming as if someone was being tortured. The report was from a couple walking late at night. They got lost and heard the screaming."

Anto shrugs, "Someone was getting mugged or raped. Why does that need a lieutenant?"

Krsto replies with a smile, "Then it gets interesting. Two large men appeared and started yelling at the couple to leave."

Anto looks curious, saying, "You think there is something to the screams? This is not a random event?"

"Two enforcers running people off, away from the building. Something is going on."

Anto asks, "Is there an open inquiry, or are you just baiting me?"

Krsto replies, "There is a report from the couple, but no official inquiry. A lieutenant needs to create an inquiry from a simple report. I'm a sergeant and can't just go questioning enforcers. I don't know who is protecting them."

"Give me the file. I may look into it."

"Sure, let me know if this is an off-limits thing."

"*Seriously. Do you think some protection prevents us from touching them? If someone is being attacked, our job is to uphold the law. That includes felony assault and attempted murder.*"

"*Okay, boss. I'm not arguing with you.*"

"*If your underworld buddies are stupid enough to have something in the open, they need to be prepared.*"

The next day, Anto is at the scene of a double murder. Two men who appear to have mob connections are dead.

Anto asks the lead Sergeant, "*Tell me what you have.*"

"*Two dead, this one and one over next to a bench. No wallets or phones on them. The broken phones are over there against the wall. We haven't found the wallets yet, so we don't have confirmed identification. We are currently working on facial recognition. The cause of death was a knife to the heart for both. A small double-edged blade between the ribs.*"

"*Professional?*"

"*Not sure. This one had his hands tied with zip ties and was stabbed in the butt cheeks multiple times. The other one was beaten or kicked in the head. Not a normal thing.*"

"*Witnesses, cameras, other evidence?*"

"*None. No cameras here or on any street around this block.*"

"*They took both wallets, but they broke the phones. Any ideas about the guy being stabbed in the butt?*"

"*The only thing we can think of is to make him talk. But that is guessing.*"

"*Okay, get your report together, and we will review it.*"

Back at the station, Anto walks over to Krsto and asks, "*I did a walk-by of the building. Do you have any information on who owns it? Is there a registered business?*"

Krsto says, "*I checked after the couple's report. It is registered as a local craft business. The local company's ownership is another company in Switzerland. I'm trying to trace the real ownership.*"

Anto asks, "*Any other incidents related to the building in our records?*"

Krsto nods, "*Yes. I found a report from a patrol. They were* conducting a standard patrol and spotted a van turning onto the street at 3:00 a.m. one morning. They followed, and when the van stopped at the building, they questioned the driver. He said he arrived early. He would deliver supplies and pick up finished products when the business opened in the morning."

Anto asks, "What was in the van?"

"The report says there were no windows on the side or back. They didn't have cause to search. They asked the driver, and he said No, they couldn't search."

"Okay, find out who owns this and search for tax records for this business. If they produce something, they need workers and to pay taxes."

The next morning, Krsto finds Anto and says, "There was a phone report of screaming coming from the building. The call recording has screaming in the background. It sounds like someone being beaten or tortured."

"Do we know any more information about the owners? What about taxes?"

"Nothing on the owners. I need help with business ownership in Switzerland, which requires a significant amount of time. The registered business here has paid no taxes in the three years it has been incorporated."

"This is all sounding like a shit show. Unknown business, what do they do? They haven't paid taxes, and we get reports of people screaming. Let's go ask some questions."

At the entrance to the building, Anto knocks, and a large man wearing slacks, a T-shirt, and a blazer opens the door. Seeing Anto and Krsto, he steps into the doorway to block them. "What do you want?"

Anto shows his badge and says, "We received a report of screaming coming from this building. We are checking to see if everyone is okay."

The man glares back and says, "There is no screaming from this building. Whoever reported that is mistaken."

Krsto asks, "Can we come in and look around?"

"No. This is private property."

Anto says, "The building owner is registered as a business that makes handcrafted tourist items. Do you have the latest health and safety inspection report available? We need to make sure the working conditions are safe."

"Wait."

He closes the door. A minute later, he opens the door with a three-ring binder. He opens it to a page and shows it to Anto and Kristo.

Kristo says, "This is only the first page. What about the rest?"

"That is available at the headquarters office."

Krsto asks, "Where is that?"

"In Switzerland."

Anto asks, "You're not going to let us check out the building?"

"No."

Krsto's phone dings with a message. He reads it and says, "Thanks for nothing." Turning to Anto, he says, "We need to go."

As they walk from the building, they hear the door close and lock. Anto glances back and then looks at Krsto. "What did you get?"

"I sent a couple of guys to check the trash from the building. They checked the garbage truck when it went to dump everything. It is not specific that what they found is from this building. It was a way to see if we could get more information."

"What?"

"When they opened the trash bags, they found nothing with the company name that could be related to handcrafting. They found paper towels and gauze with blood on them. Samples are going to the lab."

At the corner, Anto looks back at the building and says, "Screaming late at night, blood in the trash. They can't show a safety report and won't let us check it out."

Krsto nods, "Something is going on in that building, and it doesn't sound legitimate. Can we get a warrant and do a search?"

"Based on what? The blood? You can't confirm it came from that building. We have nothing." After a brief pause, Anto says, "Except we know. We need to keep an eye on it and see if we can trace the trash. Maybe at the next pick, we'll have uniforms; get it and take it to the lab."

"Got it."

Zoe says, "We have started a plan. I need to attend to multiple details. I can't finish until we know how many rescued kids we will deal with. How

many kids will leave with Sorina's sister?"

Claire says, "The basics are good for now. We can get started."

Turning to Sorina, Claire asks, "Are you good with what we have talked about?"

"Yes. They will take the people to a hospital for evaluation. They probably won't be guarded. I get my sister and anyone else we can. I take your van and start driving north."

Zoe adds, "Right now, the idea is to get to Western Europe. I will work on options for places to stay while you travel and a place to stop and settle. I won't have a final destination until you are on the road."

Martha says, "This accomplishes several things. We'll get your sister out. The van leaves the area. We get to monitor the reaction from Tim and Alexi."

Zoe says, "Without the van, your original plan for Alexi won't work."

Martha says, "We need an alternative. We don't know if he will even come here after the raid. If it is dangerous for him, where would he go?"

Sorina says, "Probably Romania. That is his original strength area."

Claire asks, "Is there a plan that would work in Romania?"

Zoe says, "Only a very high-risk plan. I want to use it only as a last resort. It would be better to create a reason for him to travel to another location so that you can be ready and waiting. I'm working on what he likes and patterns. Do you have a deadline?"

Martha says, "No deadline. Sorina, we need to start the prep work. Clothes for your sister, basic medical if needed. The van needs to be cleaned and ready. If you have more than one or two in the van, we will need more supplies."

Claire says, "Zoe, add an analysis of ways to impact Alexi's businesses, his money, and layer that with where he could go."

Zoe says, "One more thing for Sorina. I'm going to transition you to Angela, who will be your primary contact from now on. She will provide help like I do, but she will be focused on you and your sister."

Sorina asks, "How many are in your group?"

Martha says, "I don't want to go into details. If you don't know, you can tell anyone."

Zoe says, "No one can force it out of you if you don't know. We are dealing with seriously dangerous men. We have to be careful."

Claire says, "Work with Angela. She will help. However, you

shouldn't expect to meet her in person. That is to help protect her."

Sorina is looking at Claire, brows slightly furrowed, clearly thinking about what was said. "I will never talk about any of this. Angela will get us new identities. Will we be safe?"

Zoe says, "Yes. So long as you don't contact anyone from your past. You take on a new identity and live a good life."

"NO! That part I disagree with. My sister and I will help free people and fight against those like Alexi. If you don't include us, we will do it on our own."

Martha smiles, "Thank you. I didn't want to ask, but I would like to add you both to the group."

Zoe says, "Hang on. I disagree with their being in the group if we aren't sure about their mental state. We need to evaluate your sister. What has been done to her physically and mentally? She may not help because of the trauma."

Claire says, "Angela can help determine and get any care she needs."

Martha says, "Sorina, follow the plan. We will not entrust your sister's life to any project until you both are ready. Earning our trust starts with getting your sister to safety and recovering."

Zoe says, "Martha, please show Sorina the QR code on your phone to contact Angela."

Martha looks at her phone and taps the screen, giving the impression that she is accessing something. Zoe has already put the QR code on the screen.

Sorina scans the QR code and calls the number. A new voice answers immediately and says in English, "Hello."

Sorina replies in English, "Hello, I'm Sorina."

The Angela persona of Zoe switches to Romanian and says, "Hello, I'm Angela, and I'll be helping you. Zoe has briefed me on all the details."

Anto receives a call at 3 a.m. "It's Krsto. There is another report of screaming in the building. I dispatched a patrol officer to the area. I told him not to approach. Listen. He confirmed screaming as if someone was in severe pain.

Anto replies, "It's 3 a.m. If I do a full alarm, it will take two or three hours to get an assault team ready."

"Wait, you're not suggesting going in there by ourselves."

"Fuck no. How many patrol people would be available?"

"Maybe ten."

"Shit, that isn't enough to go in and control outside. I'll call you back."

Anto calls his friend Augusto, who is in charge of the tactical raid team. After giving him a summary of what they have, he asks, "Can you get several guys to help go into the building?"

"You are asking this outside of channels. Why?"

"There is evidence of blood-soaked bandages in the trash. We have had reports of screaming on multiple days. If I wait to go through channels, people could die. Or, they have the raid leaked, and they hide everything, so we find nothing."

"You want me to risk my career and my men based on your say-so?"

"It is my career as well. I've been to that building. There is shit happening with some mystery company. My instinct tells me there's something. It has been there this long because some shithead is protecting them."

"You want to knock some heads like the gangs."

Raising his voice, Anto says, "Seriously? There is some shit going down, and you want to go through channels. If anyone gives you shit, say I demanded an emergency response."

"Yeah, that won't save my career."

"Fine, I'll deal with the bodies and send you pictures and notes.

"I will call four of my guys."

"Six."

"Five. These are the ones I can trust. Give me an address and a staging point."

"I will send you the info. Krsto and I will be there with patrol people to handle traffic and help."

One hour later, at a staging point around the corner, everyone is ready. They have a raid team of five, plus their lieutenant and six patrol officers.

Anto says, "Standard entry, sweep, and lockdown procedure. No calls, no one escapes."

Anto points out one of the patrol officers who will help in the building. "If anyone yells for medical help, you call an ambulance. I'm expecting we will need one, but I don't want to alarm anyone yet."

Unknown to them, Zoe is controlling a drone positioned at the top of the building. There is a cell phone attached for her to control the drone. As the group approaches the door, Zoe puts the phone on speaker and sends a painful scream through the speakers. This is the same thing she has been doing every night.

The officers get to the front door and don't even knock. Using a shotgun, they shoot the lock and hinges and enter. The guard comes out of a room down the hall, looks, and runs the other way down the hall. He is tackled, and as he is being handcuffed, he yells, "Panduri!"

They go through the building, checking every room. As they go through the first floor, they hear yelling above. "Panduri!"

They break through locked doors. On the second floor, they encounter armed resistance. Two men were shot and killed. When they finish, two men are dead; they handcuff nine adult men and wound one. During the raid, several men looked ready to fight, shouting 'Kerovi'. When they see multiple tactically dressed and armed officers, they stop.

The officers find rooms with young people locked inside. All the young people are told to stay in the room.

Anto is walking to one of the upper rooms after one of the patrol officers calls for him. Entering the room, he sees six young girls, all nude. They are all sitting on the floor, holding their knees and looking down.

Anto says, "You called for me. What's going on?"

"Sir, you need to hear them."

"What?"

Speaking Serbian, the officer says, "Girl, tell me your name."

The girl nervously replies in Russian, "My name is whatever pleases, master. Thank you for not beating me, master."

Anto shakes his head. "They are all like this?"

The officer nods, saying, "Every one of them I've talked to. They mostly reply in Russian. One boy uses English. I've asked where they are from and get no answers."

"How many?"

"Six in this room, four boys in the next one. Two of the boys have been beaten recently."

Anto looks at the door as Krsto enters. "Get them to a hospital for medical evaluation. They probably also need psychological evaluations."

Krsto says, "Have you seen the rooms with the sex devices, torture devices? This fucking place is off the charts."

Anto is shaking his head, "Fucking perverts. I want whoever owns and is running this place in a cell. And if anyone gives us shit, I'm going over their fucking head."

Anto walks out, and the officer says to Krsto. "He is pissed."

Krsto says, "He has a hard time with sexual predators. His little sister was raped when she was fourteen. She wound up pregnant with the pervert's baby. She killed herself a few weeks later. He would have killed the guy if other cops hadn't locked the guy up first."

Anto walks out of the building on his cell phone. He is leaving a voicemail message for his boss. "Boss, I just raided a trafficked sex den. I've got nine flunkies in custody, six girls and four boys. They are being taken for evaluation. I will provide you with an update and more details at the office. The full report will take a day."

Tim Is Pissed

Tim gets a text message at 5 a.m. that says police raided the sex house. He throws his phone across the room. "Fuck!"

For the next several hours, Tim is on the phone with lawyers and his sources in the police. "Who the fuck is this guy, Anto? Didn't he know that building was protected?"

The informant says, "They heard screaming from the building. Someone was in trouble."

"Why were they at the building in the first place?"

"Sorry, sir. The reports I can access only discuss an informal inspection of the building. The person at the door wouldn't or couldn't show the safety certificates for production. They also were not shown the production area for the handcrafting business."

Tim's mood is worse after the call, and he paces. Police raided his private sex house. He had a great thing. Young girls and boys were always available. Toys and devices to help with his play. He even allowed friends to have fun. It was extremely private and not known to others. How did they find it? Why did they raid the building?

After talking on the phone for hours and pacing in his condo, he calmed down. He walks over to his bar area and grabs his best scotch. He pours half a tumbler full and takes a large drink. Speaking out loud to himself, he says, "That fucking cop that raided my sex house is dead. He is going to die in extreme pain for messing with MY shit."

A few minutes later, he is on the phone with Alexi, talking about what happened.

Alex says, "Stop being a stupid fuck. Your toys were taken, and you're throwing a tantrum. You shouldn't have listed the business as a crafting business. Your people should have had fake documents to show anyone who asked. The building's ownership is hidden in multiple accounts. Otherwise, the police would already be knocking *on your door as the owner of this sex house."*

"Someone messed with my shit. They are going to pay."

Tim takes another swallow of scotch.

"Tim, I will take care of this cop. Not you. You are pissed and will make a mistake. Are you clear? Tim, are you there?"

"Alexi, something is wrong. I suddenly don't feel right." Tim walks to the kitchen sink and throws up.

Alexi says, *"Tim, get off the phone and call your security guys."*

He shakes his hands and calls his special support number. When the call is answered, he says, *"I need help,"* then collapses.

"Enzo, give me a summary of your cases."

Detective Inspector Enzo Salvatory has been called into Francisco's, his boss's office. This usually means someone has complained about what he is doing.

"Sir, I handed over an old case to prosecutors yesterday. Based on anonymous info, I've rejuvenated two other cold cases. I expect to have another case for the prosecutors this week. I could use more help to chase down leads."

"You have anonymous tips. Will these tips hold up in court?"

"The prosecutor and I think so. The tips are leading to actual evidence we can take to court."

"Why are you getting these tips now?"

"I don't know, sir."

"What about the bloody wall case?"

"I've made no progress in the case. We have no evidence to suggest who was responsible for the incident. No leads. We issued a request and offered a reward for any information. We have received nothing credible; people are trying to guess and get the reward. While we review leads, I'm working on the old cases and making progress on those cases.

His boss leans on the desk and says, *"I checked with records. You have the file for the minister's bribery case. That case was closed because of a lack of evidence, and the only witness is missing. Is that one of these old cases?"*

"Yes."

"You're heading toward an accusation against a very influential

and powerful person. We, and I mean WE, will be thrown under the bus for this. Unless you have irrefutable proof, we won't proceed. I'm not risking my career for your fifteen minutes of fame. What is the status?"

"I've got leads to follow up on, but that case is not my priority. I need to close the cases I've given to the prosecutor."

"You're known for being smart. Show how smart you are. Stop digging in this one."

He Survived

Tim wakes up in the hospital with tubes and monitors. The nurse asks how he is feeling and then goes to get the doctor.

The doctor comes and starts chatting. Tim says, "Don't chit-chat. What happened to me?"

"You were poisoned. We aren't sure what poison was used, but it was strong. You're lucky to be alive. We are doing the basics because we don't know the specific poison. The IV is to get fluids into your system and flush out whatever you can."

"The fluids have been working. You will need to avoid strenuous activities for many weeks. I recommend you see a physical therapist three times per week to build your strength and endurance."

"When can I leave?"

"We need to confirm your liver and kidneys are functioning normally. Those organs have to deal with the poison and fluids we have been putting into your system. That means your liver and kidneys were affected. We need to make sure your kidneys can flush all these fluids."

"How long before I can leave?"

"If you do well, you should be ready in the morning. You will also need to provide a statement to the police. There is a sergeant here. He has been here all day questioning a group of young people who were in some sex trafficking house."

A couple of hours later, the nurse enters and checks on Tim. "Have you taken water?"

"I drank water, but I have this fucking tube in my dick."

The nurse checks the level of urine in the bag hanging beside the bed. "How much water did you drink?"

"Half a glass. I need more ice."

"Your kidneys are working, but there should be more urine in the bag. I will make a note. After the doctor checks on you, we can remove the catheter so you can use the water closet."

"Great. Call the doctor."

Forty-five minutes later, the doctor enters and checks on Tim. "We can remove the catheter. You need to stay overnight so we can monitor you. We will do blood work tonight. If everything looks good, you go home in the morning."

An hour after the catheter is removed, the nurse says, "Time to get you up. I'll help with the IV stand."

Tim has a private room with a bathroom. While walking out of the bathroom, he is focused on moving the IV stand. Walking in the hall are two of the young women from Tim's sex house. One looks into the room and sees Tim. The blood drains from her face, and she walks faster. She tells the other girl who she saw in the room. They mention nothing about Tim to any of the staff or the other kids.

Back in bed with the nurse out of the room, Tim calls Mila.

Mila says, "Sir, I don't know how that would be possible. The only people who access your condo are the cleaning women. But the guards watched everyone the whole time."

"Putting the poison in the decanter would only take a second. Who was the one we fired? That was when the other woman said something about helping her sister and took off. They could both be involved."

Mila says, "Her name is Sorina. She was very upset about being fired. She wanted to clean. We didn't explain why we fired her."

"It doesn't matter. It is more of a security protocol. We needed to purge any potential security threat for the other woman leaving like that."

"She did nothing wrong while working. Maybe we missed it. She was in your condo every week."

"Get the word out. One of those bitches poisoned me. I want them found and punished."

"I'll get the word out to the guards."

Sometime later, Krsto knocked on the door and introduced himself. "I'm Detective Sergeant Krsto. I need to get a statement from you about the poisoning."

"Sure, go ahead."

"Why would someone want to poison you, and do you have any idea who would do this?"

"I have no clue who would have a reason to poison me. I don't even know how it got into my scotch. The only people with access to *my condo are the security and cleaning staff. The guards are always watching when the women are cleaning."*

"I need to get that scotch to the lab for testing. Is there someone who can get access to your condo to get it?"

"The building security can help you. I will call them with your information."

"What do you do, Mr. Đorđević?"

"I have an IT consulting company. We do IT support for companies in Europe."

"Is this hacking stuff?"

"I stop hackers from ruining companies."

"Is there a hacker group you have dealt with recently that may have a grudge and want to kill you?"

"None. I will have to think about that and get back to you."

"Please do. We don't have much information to go on right now."

The nurse enters and asks Krsto, "Will you be done soon? Mr. Đorđević needs to rest, and I need to check his condition."

"I need a list of the guards and cleaning people who had access to your condo. Who do I talk to about that list?"

"I will have to have someone get the list together for you."

Giving Tim a card, Krsto says, "Have them send it to me."

Krsto finishes by getting the security contact information to get the poised decanter.

The nurse asks Tim, "Feeling any different?"

"No, I still feel like shit."

The nurse brings in several items and starts working on Tim's arm. She says, "I'm taking blood samples to test for aftereffects."

After taking blood and checking Tim's condition, the nurse says, "You're doing well. The doctor will check on you during his evening rounds. You will stay one night to ensure you're okay. You can go home in the morning, unless a problem crops up."

"Why do I need to wait?"

"The results of the blood tests won't be available for a couple of hours. These will tell the doctor if you're having problems we don't see, like organ failure. He needs the results and to check on you. If there are any concerns, there will be another blood test late tonight."

When the nurse leaves, Tim gets on the phone with Alexi. "This is total fucking shit. My playhouse is ruined; I've been poisoned. I need to *send a message; this shit is not tolerated."*

"Tim, first, the poisoning is not related to the raid. The police won't try to poison you. There are two events. Now listen, I need you to keep them separate. I need you to ensure that there is no link to us with the raid, the kids, or the building. Contact the lawyers and dump the building. That means selling it cheaply. Part of keeping them from finding us means you don't overreact."

"Alexi, they fucked with my house. I go there to relax and enjoy myself. Now it is fucked."

"Do not have any of the police killed immediately. Give it some time, then make it appear to be a random act of violence. If you draw attention to us, to me, I won't be happy."

"Okay, Alexi. I will wait before taking action. I will get the word out that whoever led the raid is corrupt."

"Good. That will help."

Angela says, "Sorina, I want to make sure you feel okay with this plan."

Sorina is speaking with Angela in Romanian. "I want my sister back. I will deal with the mental programming and help her."

"And the others?"

"I will help. We don't know if any of them will want to leave."

"I've been monitoring. Three other girls and one boy have not been in contact with their families. They may have no family to contact, or they feel there is a problem contacting them."

"I will ask and get all of them out if they want to go."

"Martha is finishing cleaning and stocking the van. You will take it to the hospital, get anyone who wants to go, and drive toward Western Europe."

"Where are Martha and Claire going?"

"They are going after another people trafficker in Croatia. They are intentionally staying away from you to give you a clean escape."

Meeting at the van, Martha says, "You have air mattresses, clothes, and food in the back. There is a phone charger for you. Remember, we don't know the mental state of these kids right now. Don't let them call anyone. You can be found if the people they call are being watched."

They all hug, and Claire says, *"Angela is looking for safe places for you. She will let us know when you are settled or if you need help. Take care of the kids."*

Sorina parks the van in the hospital's normal parking area. She grabs the bag of sweatpants and sweatshirts and heads into the hospital. She stops at the reception desk and says she is dropping off clothes for the rescued kids at the nurse's station.

The receptionist says, *"That is nice of you. It is almost the end of visiting hours."*

"I just want to say hi. Let the kids know someone cares and drop off the clothes. I won't be staying long."

At the nurse's station, she says, *"I have clothes. I was told a few kids don't have a family to contact. These are for them."*

In the pocket of each pair of sweatpants is a little note in Romanian. Sorina knows her sister will understand the note.

Leaving the hospital, Sorina sits in the van and waits. The note instructs them to leave after the nurses complete their night checks.

At 1:20 A.M., five kids walked out of the door, looking around. Sorina flashes the lights and gets out. The kids walk up to the van, and Ivana, her sister, sees Sorina for the first time. She squeaks and jumps at her. After hugging her sister so hard that she grunts, she lets go and opens the van's side door. Everyone gets into the back—Sorina motions for them to sit.

Driving away from the hospital, the kids are nervous, but seeing Ivana's reaction, they relax.

Sorina says in Romanian to her sister, *"Can you tell them what's happening? I will talk with someone on the phone who is helping me. We are getting out of Serbia and will find some safe place."*

Ivana speaks Russian. Sorina realizes her sister's Russian is much better than it was the last time she heard it back home.

Sorina calls Angela, who gives her directions for the drive. Angela says, *"I have planned the travel. For this morning's leg, you will drive for about three hours. You will stop in Novska, Croatia, for gas and snacks. I found a shopping area that is shut down because of the pandemic. You can park and get some sleep."*

"Tomorrow, what will happen?"

"I have the trip broken into two-hour segments. You will stop for

gas, food, and a restroom break. I will order lunch for you to pick up and eat in the van. Tomorrow night, I have an Airbnb for all of you to stay."

Based on their prior experience, the kids are mostly quiet and don't complain about sitting on the air mattress on the floor of the van for hours. When they arrive at the Airbnb, the kids relax much more. After getting everything they need to set up, everyone relaxes when Ivana yells. "Sorina said no phone calls. They can find us!"

Sorina had left her phone on the counter, charging, and went to the water closet. Rushing back into the main room, Ivana is holding her phone and looking at the young boy, Peter. Ivana says, "He called someone."

Sorina asks, "Who did you call?"

"I called the master. He will be mad if we don't obey."

Sorina takes her phone and calls Angela to let her know.

Angela listens and then says, "Sorina, I need to adjust some settings on your phone. I'm texting you a link. Click on that link, please."

Sorina clicks on the link while talking to Angela. Angela says, "I'm changing the lock settings, so it locks faster. This change will make it harder for the kids to access and use your phone. The other thing I'm doing is getting the number the boy called and researching who owns that number."

"Angela, do we need to leave?"

"I need you to get some sleep first. Go lie down. I will call in a couple of hours to get you up."

Angela has changed the alarm sound and volume. After two hours, the Flight of the Valkyries plays at full volume. Sorina talked to Ivana before she lay down. Sorina gets up, and the kids are ready.

In the van, Ivana sits in the passenger seat and says, "You're not mad. I'm pissed at Peter and told everyone if this happens again, I will beat the shit out of them."

Sorina says, "What did they say?"

"That I'm lucky. I have my older sister here to get me out. I replied, Sorina is getting us all out."

Sorina says, "Angela is helping. She told me to expect something like this. The phone was charging when I went to the bathroom. It was where Peter could access it. I have to be careful with you guys. We don't know what they did to you."

"They did whatever they wanted. I was completely defeated, like them. They told me my family was all dead. We only had each other. Then I saw you. I didn't understand when I got into the van. Then it hit me. You found me; you got me out. The others don't have that. I'm going to be okay." She reaches over and grabs Sorina's arm. "I will help them."

Angela calls, and Sorina puts the phone on speaker, saying, "Ivana is sitting next to me, and you are on speakerphone."

Angela says in Romanian, "Hello, Ivana. How are you feeling?"

"I'm so much better now that Sorina has found me. I will translate to Russian if you need to say something to the others."

Sorina says, "Your Russian is so much better than when we were at home."

"I had to learn."

Angela says, "I can speak Russian when needed. Sorina, if you're okay, I'll talk to the kids while you drive."

Sorina says, "Sure."

Angela speaks Russian. She discusses what is happening, informing the kids. She lets them ask questions. After about thirty minutes, Ivana says, "We have to address Peter's phone call. Angela, what does that mean?"

Angela replies, "It means they know where you were when the call occurred. If they are good at hacking, they will now be able to track your phone. I'm already working on getting different transportation and a new phone. This is a good point to bring up a change in direction."

Sorina says, "What does that mean?"

Angela replies, "Your original direction was central Western Europe toward Germany. After Peter's call, we now need to alter that plan. You need to head south into Italy."

"I will be at the Italian border within the hour."

Angela says, "Just follow the signs toward Venice. I will have a place for you to stay soon and will let you know."

Sorina asks, "The new transportation?"

Angela replies, "Renting an Airbnb is easy from the standpoint of identification, much easier than a hotel. Transportation requires more identification. I'm working on something that requires less identification. That takes more time. You will have a new vehicle by tomorrow.

"If they're looking for us, what do I do?"

"Right now, just keep driving. The farther from where the call happened, the better."

Zoe Needs Space

Watching Sorina drive away in the van, Martha says to Claire and Zoe, "She'll be okay. She needs to keep off their radar."

Zoe says, "I'm watching. Now you two need to get to the car rental. The car is ready. Show your ID and drive away."

Claire says, "Zadar, Croatia. How far is that drive?"

Zoe says, "About seven hours. You will stop for the night so that you get to the city during the day tomorrow to check out the harbor."

An hour later, as they are driving, Zoe says, "Martha, Tim has been working to track our crypto theft network I created and used with the Juan heist."

"Tim is in the hospital now. Are you sure it was Tim?"

"Tim is involved. It was probably someone on his hacking team who did the actual work."

"That is what you called the hacking factory before."

"Yes. There aren't official records. A shell company owns the building. The business purpose they list is IT consulting."

"What happened with the accounts?"

"He traced through the blockchain and found one of the first-level accounts used to transition and move the crypto tokens."

"That was some work to trace an account from the blockchain transactions."

"Yes. The account was deleted after the heist, but I monitor the crypto exchange system logs. There was an attempt to access the account. The login name I set up for the account is a random string. Any attempt to access that random string is a targeted search. I traced the source to a location that Tim or his people use."

"How did they determine this random string as an account login?"

"Tim or his group has also hacked the exchange systems. They searched the logs to find unusual logins. The logs only tell you the login was used, not if the account is still active."

Martha nods, "They are trying to log in to check if the account is active. Should we do anything, or will that tip him we know he is looking?"

"It will tip him off."

"Okay, Zoe. All the accounts were deleted, and the fake identities haven't been used again. If he can't get through that first layer, he can't track us."

"I ran a process to work through what he could do, and I found a flaw in my crypto exchange transfer algorithm. By examining all the blockchains within a time window, I could identify, with a 30% probability, the transactions that transferred money out of each account. That let me know the crypto keys used for the initial transactions."

"You did hundreds of transactions to hide the transfers. How many accounts and blockchains did you have to analyze to get to 30%?"

"It took eight of the sixteen first-line accounts."

"Zoe, is Tim good enough to find those accounts and then analyze the blockchain flow?"

"If I can do it, then someone else can. It is simply a matter of how many compute cycles you want to apply."

"I won't worry about this until he finds more accounts. But you have updated your algorithm for the next heist?"

"Yes, I have altered the algorithm. The trade-off is that the first-line accounts will be alive ten times longer than before. The output transactions will be spread over a longer period, making them much harder to piece together."

"Changing subjects slightly. Have you found Tim and Alexi's account details?"

"Only partially. By tracing their locations and purchases, I have collected credit card information, which reveals one bank account. I need to work through the money flows for that account to identify others and assemble a complete picture of the account. One goal is to find Alexi's Bitcoin accounts and the blockchain addresses."

"Good. Zoe, just to be clear on what we've already agreed. You will not try to hack Tim directly."

"Agreed. That would taunt him and cause him to focus on me completely."

<<<>>>

When the hospital discharges Tim, they provide him with a cane to assist him in walking.

"What the fuck. I'm not an invalid old man."

"Sir, this is only a precaution. You probably won't need it, but we need to provide it."

When they wheel him to the entrance of the hospital to get into his waiting car, he stands, carrying the cane, and walks toward the car. After three steps, he stumbles and falls, and everyone rushes to help him.

The nurse says, "You need to be careful; the poison you received is destructive. Just be careful, no bravado."

Tim stands and leans on the cane. Under his breath, he says, "That bitch is going to pay."

<<<>>>

Zoe says, "While you are driving to Zadar, we can talk about other things. Tim survived the poisoning, which is not what I wanted. Sorry, Martha."

Martha squints, shakes her head, and says, "The planning for Alexi and Tim has completely fallen apart. We re-plan and move forward. It sounds like you have a real problem with Tim. Why this reaction?"

"He is a bad guy, another player on the board we have to deal with. I can't act in the physical world, so anything that doesn't work puts more on you and Claire."

Claire says, "We will deal with it. How do we address Tim?"

Zoe says, "With his hospital stay, I learned he has a severe shellfish allergy. We can use that bad allergy to attack him."

Claire says, "If we get him to eat shellfish, he will react."

Martha says, "We simply need to get the key protein into his system, and the reaction will work. Zoe, can we get the protein in a stable form to plant in something?"

Zoe replies, "There is no long-term stable natural protein; however, talking with Charlie, we have a plan. I will get a compound synthesized that will cause the same reaction. It will be available to ship in twenty-four hours. I need to know where to ship it."

Claire smiles and says, "If it doesn't smell like or look like shellfish, we can get it into his system more easily."

Martha nods, pauses, smiles, and then says, "This is awesome for me. Now you and Charlie are making a difference."

Zoe says, "The military calls it a force multiplier. Claire, the compound should have no odor. I like the fact that you two are back together. Now Martha can stop obsessing and focus."

Claire snorts, "Never in my lifetime. She wants to do it all."

Zoe says, "I will get the compound delivered to you. You will have ten grams to use. One gram should be enough. This will let you have multiple options."

"Thanks, Zoe," Martha comments. "My original idea was to have a hacking device he would try to take apart and expose him to a poison. Other people could use this. I won't hurt anyone who is not allergic."

Zoe continues, "That is in the works."

There is a several-minute pause, then Zoe says, "I have another subject. You built me to span data centers. It provides me with significantly more computing power, making it more complex to track and more challenging to stop. I'm now working on multiple simultaneous work streams. Our efforts to help others are effective; however, they require me to use increasingly sophisticated computational power.

Martha nods, "You've learned to analyze all the angles and find alternatives. Tell me your best approach."

"General AI workloads have patterns. They put a full load on a server differently than web servers, graphics processing, or search engines. Because I'm large enough, I can adjust the profile of my workloads to minimize my presence on systems. The next part is that I'm spending lots of money on computing."

Claire says, "That all sounds good, but what?"

Zoe says, "I need to start some next steps that are more complicated."

Martha makes a face at Claire and says, "If you're saying it's complicated, I'm concerned. Tell me what you want to do."

Zoe says, "I want to build data centers of my own."

Martha smiles, "Okay. That is a big step. They are large, fixed, expensive, and did I mention easy to find?"

"I know. That is why I've only been doing the planning."

Claire says sarcastically, "Just planning?"

"Okay, I had to put down some deposits to keep from losing a few prime locations."

Martha says, "What is the plan?"

"Sure, I will create data centers with multiple wings, each for a sensitive customer. They will be air gaped from each other. I will be in one section as a customer. No one will question my using the entire computing capability. Also, by having other paying customers, they will cover the cost of my section."

Claire nods with slightly pursed lips, "That sounds good. I like that."

Martha nods, "That is a great plan. You've created a company that will serve customers needing high security and protected computing resources."

Claire says, "This will include governments?"

Martha nods and says, "The type of secure computing systems Zoe is trying to hack all the time. She will have access through the infrastructure."

Zoe says, "One more thing. It is 2021, and AI is becoming better. I will fund some research and early startups in AI technology. This will take longer, but AI workloads will be deployed globally in two to three years. I will become one in the crowd of AI systems in data centers."

Claire nods. "I like it."

Martha is smiling, "Get going, Zoe."

Anto is speaking with his boss and is not pleased with what his boss is saying.

Anto says, "I didn't follow procedure. I called a tactical unit at 2 A.M. I used the resources available. We found trafficked children in the building after hearing screaming."

Anto's boss says, "You're right, you didn't follow standard procedure. We need to know where our tactical team is deployed."

Anto interrupts, "You need to know where a raid happens on a protected site. What I'm hearing is you're getting shit for raiding a site trafficking young people."

"Trafficked isn't proven....Yes, I'm getting calls. You stepped into some serious shit."

Anto says, "So tell me, do I drop the human trafficking of kids, or do

I do my job and go after these people?"

After pausing for a minute, his boss says, "Our job is to stop lawbreakers. The reality is that we do what we can. My experience is that you will be targeted. I won't be able to protect you. I know the gang thing with the cousin was bad. This is a different level."

"So, I drop it and let kids be trafficked and used for sex oddities, putting my head down and waiting for retirement. Or I make it an issue and get targeted."

"Fuck you, Anto. I have a family. If I don't look the other way when told to, I risk everything. You don't have a wife or kids, you don't know."

"You stupid fuck. The reason I don't have a wife or kids is that my girlfriend, my fiancée, was killed trying to help a kid who was trafficked. My sister committed suicide after being raped. I'm the last person you want to tell that I have nothing to risk. I've already lost everything."

"Anto, they will come after you. I can't protect you from everything."

"Just do your job. Just focus and do your job. If these people are linked to my fiancé's death, I will find them and make sure they pay.

The next day, the newspaper publishes an article claiming the detective is compromised and accepts money to protect drug traffickers.

Anto walks into his boss's office with the newspaper. "That didn't take long. Did you tell them I would not look the other way?"

"No, I didn't talk to anyone about what you said. The update for my boss is scheduled in one hour. I will tell him then. He will probably tell me to suspend you."

Anto says, "This accusation in the paper is completely false."

"I know, but that doesn't matter at this point. You must decide your path. That may not be enough. You pissed off powerful people, and they could want you dead."

Anto turns and walks out of the office.

Van In Italy

Sorina followed the directions to Venice. During the time in the van, the kids became increasingly concerned and agitated because of the call Peter made.

Angela says, "I'm checking in with you. You have been driving for three hours. I need you to push for another thirty minutes. There is a place to stop. Two blocks from the stop is a delivery box with a new phone. I need you to get that phone. It has a different number, and when you drop the current phone, they can't track you."

Sorina says, "So the bad guys have been able to track me?"

"Sort of, yes. They can access the position data. I've been disrupting the system, but they couldn't get access, so I want you to change phones. Take a break for an hour, get food, and rest."

Tim says, "Fuck yes! Where are they?"

"Sir, we know where Peter called from and are estimating travel directions. From that, we got the probable vehicle and are tracking them."

"I asked you a question. Where are they?"

"They are in Italy, heading toward Venice."

"Get a team on this. I want the team to stop them. I want my shit back. Get them and take them to a secure location. I'm going to get my shit."

"Don't tell Tim."

"This is what he wants."

"Don't tell him until we have the van. He will gut you if you tell him, and we don't get the van."

"How do we get the van?"

"We have them on camera. They should be in the Bologna area within the next hour. We will see the van on camera and converge."

"Who's watching the cameras?"

"Dummy, open your phone and look up traffic cameras. We watch the highway cameras."

Ten minutes later, the van takes an exit in Bologna and drives to a petrol filling station.

"We have them. Let's go."

Four cars converge as they park the van at the petrol station. The cars block the path, and five men with guns get out.

Sorina is using the new phone and says, "Angela, cars just pulled up. Five men are surrounding the van."

Angela replies, "Don't provoke them. I'm contacting Martha for help. It will be okay."

One man pulls Angela out of the driver's seat, ties her hands, and puts her in the back of the vehicle. He takes her new phone and stomps on it, then tosses it toward the trash. One of the other men drives the van.

Leaving one car at the station, one of the armed men is in the back. Angela is bound, and the kids are cowering. The man says be quiet in Italian, which no one understands.

<<<>>>

Martha and Claire spent the night at a small hotel. In the morning, they didn't rush—breakfast and gas. Claire wants to stop at the local shops to look around. "Martha, the economy is shit for everyone. We can buy a few things and help."

Hours later, they are driving with six bags in the back seat and discussing how to deal with Alexi when Zoe calls their phones. She says, "The van with Sorina and the kids has been stopped and diverted."

Martha asks, "Is this related to the kid making a phone call?"

Zoe replies, "Probably."

Claire asks, "Do we know where they are being taken? What do we do?"

Zoe replies, "Sorina was using a new cell phone. They took that and turned it off. They didn't turn off the old cell phone. I'm tracking *them by the same phone they were using to track them."*

Martha's jaw is clenched. She looks at Claire and then says, "Zoe, we are now stopping playing nice. How do we get there? How can we rescue them?"

Zoe replies, "I'm working on the options. Driving is the worst case. My best case right now is a small commuter airline to get you to Italy."

Martha says, "Book all the options and cancel what we don't use."

Claire looks at Martha and says, "Wow, that's not the woman I had as a roommate. Sorry, but you would never spend money like that."

Zoe says, "I've been working on her. She is much better at using the money we have available."

Martha says, "I don't care about the money."

Zoe says, "That is not true." Claire says, "Bullshit."

"Okay, I don't care as much as I used to. I want to know what it takes to help Serina and the kids. It could be a mercenary unit that costs a lot of money."

Zoe says, "I'm working on the options. I'm putting directions on your phone. This will get you to a private airport. I'm working on charters to fly you, but that could be a problem on short notice."

Claire asks, "I thought there are services you call, and they get you a plane."

Zoe replies, "With COVID, the services are all booked. Maybe we need to talk about Tilly buying or leasing a plane in Europe and hiring a crew."

Claire looks confused and asks, "Who is Tilly?"

Zoe replies, "Sorry, I didn't go over that with you. The import-export business persona is Tilly. Martha was using Tilly in the clinic in Mexico as part of her cover and background. We kept that going in Belize, so Aunt Tilly runs the family import and export business."

Martha is shaking her head. "We need to focus on Sorina and the kids. This is a good discussion, but a distraction."

There is a pause, then Zoe says, "That was a pause for effect. Keep driving, Martha. What else are you going to do right now?"

Claire looks at Martha, gripping the steering wheel, and says, "Zoe, are you two having a moment right now?"

Martha replies, "Yes."

Zoe says, "We do this. Martha tells me when I'm being a bitch, and I do the same with her."

Martha says, "The kids are in trouble right now."

Zoe increases the volume and says, "You can't fly. You are doing everything right. I'm working on the options. Take a breath, and let's talk about something else for a minute."

Martha glances at Claire, takes a large breath, and says, "Okay, this will take the Tilly business up a notch. It's much more noticeable. Are we sure we want to have that kind of visibility?"

Claire's face was relaxed, and now she looked confused again. "What a minute. Is this the same import/export business we discussed? Tilly is the persona, but what about actual imports and exports?"

Zoe says, "To make things work, I started doing imports to Belize. This is a real, working business. I have subcontracted some work, but also directly booked containers on ships."

Claire is looking at Martha as she drives. After a pause, she says, "What if I'm an executive in the company? Zoe, we talked about this last year. Or maybe we get Charlie engaged. Martha can be the behind-the-scenes action person; I can be the person they see."

Zoe says, "I will let Martha think about that before she answers. I think it is a great idea. You and Charlie both should be part of the business."

Martha looks over at Claire, then turns back to driving. "What about your family? Will they let you do this?"

Claire smiles as she sees Martha's hands relax on the steering wheel. She says, "My dad wants me to work. I can work while I'm finishing my thesis. I can talk about Charlie being a consultant."

Martha says, "Tilly, my engineering brain is thinking. Don't buy a small jet for a few people. We need cargo planes that can also accommodate a small passenger area. Look at those options."

Zoe changes to use Tilly's voice and says, "That is a great idea. We can expand the business regionally. We already cover Central America; we expand to cover Europe."

Claire says, "Where will the European office be located? I would be good with England or France."

Martha says, "Because you are fluent in French, I could do Germany or England. We need to let Zoe analyze where this business needs to focus and where it can be based."

Zoe says, "I'm going to start with Ireland. The primary language is English, and the business environment is favorable."

Martha smiles and then laughs, followed by Claire. Claire stops laughing and says, "A great choice that we didn't consider. It works for me."

Martha says, "Back to our problem."

Claire interjects, "Hang on. Hang on. That, what we just did, that was good."

Zoe says, "Yes. We need to do more. Not just because we have to decide, it is healthy for Martha to look at the bigger picture."

Clare is nodding. "Martha, we need to keep each other healthy. That is physical and mental. I know the last year, hell, the last two years have been hard. We need to keep you healthy and focused on the big picture."

"You two are in a car, doing an operation. We need to engage more people. That was the plan last year. It hasn't changed."

Claire puts her hand on Martha's arm. "We, I mean, we got this. Together."

Martha looks determined as she drives. "The goal was to get to Croatia and stop a trafficker. That has changed because Sorina and the girls need help. I get that those are short term, and we need to focus on the longer term. It is hard when they are in danger."

"Agree. It would be better if we had others we could rely on to help. Let that stew in your brain while we discuss the situation."

Claire grabs a bottle of water, opens it, and hands it to Martha to drink. She continues, "Your point a minute ago about the current problem."

After taking a drink, Martha says, "Tim. He had the guys grab the van. Is he part of this and a problem?"

Zoe says, "Good point. I'm checking on him." After a minute, Zoe continues, "He is in his condo and on the phone."

Martha says, "Zoe, get us options, and we will have to deal with the situation when we arrive."

Zoe replies, "What about help? I can look into getting some help."

Claire asks, "What does that mean?"

Zoe says, "I've been working with that, which means helping the detective inspector working on the case for Florence. He looked the other way when told to do so in the past. However, everything I check says he is a good person, a good cop. What if I can get him to help with the rescue?"

Martha says, "Having official legal help would be great, but we need to get the kids out after this. The process for him won't let the witnesses disappear. Not to mention, I'm the one he is looking for in the Florence killings."

Zoe and Claire both start talking over each other. Zoe stops and waits. Martha's tone changes. "Zoe, that is BS. You both have points to make. You have an equal voice. Don't just defer to Claire. You don't defer with me."

Claire nods, "Zoe, you go first."

Zoe says, "First, he doesn't have any evidence you're involved in Florence. Second, I'm not deferring. I'm listening to your input. Claire has a different perspective, which I want to hear. Now, to the problem. There are two options. One is that we appeal to his humanity, which isn't out of reasonable probability. The second option, which Claire was suggesting, is to do something like a distraction to get the kids away. However, that will put the decoy, i.e., Claire, at high risk."

Claire is smiling and says, "Exactly what I was thinking. Also, I want to be at the forefront, the face of things like this. With my family and my reputation of doing nothing, I can make this work. When we are talking about rescue, let me be out there in the spotlight."

Zoe replies, "Be careful. You need to be our face when there is a rescue. When we can show and talk about a rescue. Not when the kids have to disappear."

Claire looks to see Martha's jaw clenched hard. Then Martha takes a deep breath, looks at Claire, and says, "I'm adjusting. I agree with Zoe. Putting you out in front, in danger, is not ideal for me."

Claire replies, "Having you in front of EVERY special operation is a problem for me. You will probably get hurt at some point. Then what?"

Zoe says, "I have a new direction for you. It will take you to an estate with a private airport. A pilot and a plane are flying from England. He will land and then take you to a small airport outside of Bologna. I'm working on a car option when you arrive, but you may need to improvise."

Martha asks, "How long?"

Zoe replies, "This is happening fast. The pilot is a former British Marine. He has a history of smuggling. We can use him for other import and export work."

Claire says, "You didn't say the timing."

"It will take him three hours to get to the airport to pick you up."

The men drove the van to a warehouse. Because of the Delta COVID surge, they have shut down the area, leaving the buildings currently empty. Inside the building, the van is in the middle. The kids huddled in a corner near the office area. Sorina's captors tied her to a chair outside the office.

The four enforcers are waiting and begin grumbling in Italian. "These are sex toys; why can't we have some fun?"

The fifth man and the leader say, "We don't touch his property without permission. Is that clear?"

The other guys reluctantly nod. With one saying, "His property."

One enforcer says, "Get rich and own your property; you can do with it as you please."

Enforcer two says, "I want to have a different slut for every day of the week. Tell me, who has a problem with that?"

The leader says, "Not with these sluts. Don't piss off the boss."

A minute later, his phone chimes with a text, "The boss is going to fly here in his jet. He will be here in a few hours. He says he wants them all alive."

Enforcer one says, "The kids are saying they need to use the bathroom."

Enforcer three says, "Fuck that. They can piss in their pants. We can deal with that later."

Enforcer two says, "What about the driver? We tied her to the chair. Do we soften her up for questions?"

Enforcer four says, "Stop being stupid. We are just waiting. If we do anything, the boss will have us waiting for punishment, just like they are right now. Just chill out."

The leader is more petite than the enforcers and is now concerned. "You don't want to piss off this guy. The last guy had a nice funeral. That was my introduction to the group. When I buried the dump asses, I *became the group boss."*

The enforcers grumble and move around the area, making the kids nervous.

Sorina says, "You need to feed them and take them to the water closet at some point."

The enforcers ignore her. After yelling three times, the leader says, "Take them one at a time to the water closet. No food."

Claire and Martha are waiting when the small plane lands. When they reach the parked plane, the pilot says hi. Replying with simple greetings; they wait as the pilot does the pre-flight checks.

It is a small, two-engine propeller plane. Capable of carrying five passengers and 1500 pounds of cargo for 1500 miles.

While the pilot is outside checking things on the plane without a mask, Claire and Martha wear masks when they approach and enter the aircraft.

As they are waiting, Claire says, "We were talking about getting planes and pilots. What about him?"

Martha looks at the pilot differently, evaluating him. "Sure. I don't know enough to say no."

The pilot puts on a mask when he gets on the plane.

As soon as the plane takes off and the gear is up, the pilot says, "Well, now we can talk. You two are in a hurry to get to Italy. Are you missing a wedding?"

Martha replies from the back seat behind the pilot, "Something like that."

Claire asks, "We have a serious family situation, and our dumb family is going to get people in serious trouble. We were traveling, and with the COVID surge, we just wanted to stay safe. We're flying now because a cousin can't handle things. Tell us about your background."

Martha nods to Claire and says, "Please just get us to Bologna. I want to keep your info for the future, but we must deal with this situation now."

Claire says again, "Tell us your background."

The pilot spends the flight discussing his history with the Royal

Marines, his experiences flying in the Middle East, and his efforts to establish a charter business after leaving.

Martha is listening, and a little surprised. Claire asks questions as if she is conducting a job interview. There are small gaps in the narrative, and she asks follow-up questions.

As they are approaching land, the pilot says, "My name is Ralph, by the way."

Martha says, "We knew that. Sorry, we skipped the introductions. I'm Martha, and this is Claire, but you knew that from the flight booking."

Ralph smiles, "I've been around the rhubarb patch. I know how this works. I won't see you again. If I do, you will have different names."

Claire smiles, "Not true. If we meet again, our names will be the same. You will probably do something for our import-export business, and we won't discuss details."

Ralph says, "So this was an interview. How did I do?"

Martha says, "Land, and we can give our assessment."

Ralph gives a short laugh and says, "Got you. Waiting for the results. Nice landing would be good now."

On the radio, they hear the plain call sign. The voice says, "Zulu Alpha three, four six, high-speed craft approaching you from behind. Continue your approach and land quickly."

Ralph says, "What the actual fuck."

The radio continues with the tower repeating the call sign for another plane and saying, "Change course."

They are in cell phone service range, and Zoe tries to call them both. They don't pick up, so Zoe texts them both, "Tim is on the jet trying to land."

Thinking quickly, Martha looks at Claire, then turns to the pilot and says, "That jet behind us is probably the lawyers. This day is getting worse."

Ralph takes a breath and says, "I know you're special ops trained. You can't lie at the same level as she can. That plane is a problem. I got it. What do you want me to do? Where do I let you out? I can put you next to them or away."

Claire is looking at both of them. They are trying to communicate but not connecting. She says, "Ralph, we are trying to rescue several human-trafficked kids. Martha is our primary operator. We are seeking *help on the ground. We need options for our exit."*

"Fuck me. You two are serious. What's really up with the jet?"

Martha says, "Probably the shithead trafficking the kids. I have to get on the ground and to the kids."

Martha's phone rings with Zoe's number. Answering, she hears, "The military is sending two fighters to intercept Tim's jet. Get on the ground. Land NOW."

Martha says, "My," she pauses, "my information is that the military is on its way to intercept that jet. Land. Land now."

Ralph turns and looks at them. "You two are my worst fucking nightmare."

Zoe says, "I heard that. Repeat this to him: You've got more wind than wings, ya glaikit pigeon."

Martha says the words, and Ralph stops moving, then laughs. He says, "Scottish insults. You two are full of surprises."

Claire looks at Martha, raises her shoulders and hands, and silently mouths, what the fuck. Then she turns to Ralph and says, "Look, we have to decide whether we can trust each other. So far, I'm more trusting."

Ralph says, "And somehow your intel that military jets are on their way makes me trust you? That also means the military will shut down the airport. How can you even know that?"

Martha says, "Listen to me carefully. We don't tell people more information than is necessary for our protection and theirs. If you reach a more trusted level, we reveal more. You need to decide whether you want to take part. If you agree, call the number that booked this flight and talk."

Ralph is focused on landing and talking to the tower. During a pause, he says, "I'll think about it."

Based on Zoe's information, Martha directs Ralph to an area close to the private hangars. He stops the plane and shuts down the engines. As he opens the door, he says, "I'm not going anywhere when the airport locks down. This could take hours. I hope you get to the kids and help them."

Martha says, "Thanks for the flight."

Ralph looks at them, shakes his head, and says, "Wait." Going to the back of the plane, he opens a hatch and pulls out something wrapped in an oily cloth. He hands it to Martha, saying, "All I got. It is stolen and untraceable."

Martha opens the bag to see a Glock 9mm pistol and a pocket knife-type device. Opening the blades, she sees it is a lock-pick set. She checks the Glock clip and sees that it is full. Nodding, she says, "Thanks."

Claire nods to Ralph and says, "Thank you". Martha touches her arm and walks toward the parking area. On the short walk, she says, "The airport lockdown also means the shithead won't be leaving this way. He probably will kill the kids."

Claire nods and says, "How do we get a car?"

"We steal one. I prefer a non-flashy, older model."

As they close the newly stolen car door, they hear two jets fly overhead. Claire calls Zoe and puts her on speaker so they are on the call together. She says, "Tim is getting noticed. This could be a serious problem."

Kids In The Warehouse

Enzo receives an email from his anonymous source, who has been assisting with old cases. This one is different. It's a single line: "I need your help."

He looks at the screen for a full minute and then returns to eat the takeout dinner he brought home. His older cousin comes out of her room while he is eating. "Enzo, you are working late again."

"Always. Izabella, go back to bed. You have to be at work at 4 A.M."

"Sorry, but I need to talk to you."

Shifting, Enzo says, "Okay."

"I've been staying with you for six months. I didn't think it would be this long."

"Bella, I don't care. I'm not here most of the time."

"That is part of my issue. You are never home. I'd like to have a meal together; I'd be happy to cook, or we could go out. You don't have a social life."

"I will not have a good social life when women think I'm a target for the bad guys. That I will be attacked."

"So, change that."

"Then I don't get to help the people who most need my help."

"Don't ruin your life for this job."

"I'm focused on improving it for the people and groups that would otherwise be sent to the trash. I have completed becoming a detective inspector. Now, I want to make a difference."

"Why waste your life on people who don't care? I want you to have a good life."

"We didn't have a great youth. Even with all the help from the refugee organization, we struggled. I was fortunate to have been given the chance and accepted into the police force. I learned from one of my first cases that some people are exploited and get NO opportunity. Worse than what we had. I want to use my police position to help. That means you get to see me late at night."

"Soroush..."

"Shirin, don't call me by my old name. We changed our names to better fit into life here."

With a saddened voice, Bella says, "You're sacrificing everything. From your stories, you don't even get good cases. They are still exploiting you."

"Something I don't tell people. I have a great memory for all the connections and details."

"I know; that is how you passed the inspector examination so easily. Is that your secret? Is that going to save you?"

"I know the bad guys. That means I also know the good guys."

A raspberry goes to a short laugh, and Bella says, "You are terrible at reading people."

"Bella, go back to bed."

After dinner, he takes care of the dishes, utensils, and water. He pours a full glass of wine and sits in front of the computer.

He types a response, "What do you need? Why are you asking for help?"

Less than thirty seconds later, his phone rings. The caller ID is 'unknown'.

Enzo shakes his head slowly. "This will not be good."

He presses the button to answer and then presses the speakerphone button. "Pronto."

Angela's voice responds in Italian, "Hello, Detective Inspector."

"Who are you?"

"I'm a friend who has been helping you. Now I need help."

"A new way to draw me into a compromising position. I get leads, close some old cases, and then you want something. Next thing, I'm being blackmailed to keep it quiet."

"It's not like that. I will not ask you to do anything to blackmail you. I need a police officer who is not compromised, someone I can trust not to become compromised. You have been instructed to look the other way in the past. I see someone who is careful, smart, and wants to make a difference."

Enzo interrupts, saying, "Why have you been sending me information? I won't even ask where or how you got the information."

"I've found evidence or leads for many cases. They are all bad people. *I have dozens of old cases that I can provide for minor crimes. I want evidence to put the real bad guys in prison."*

"Why me?"

"From everything I have found, you are not compromised. Others would ignore or destroy the evidence. I would like to know why you overlooked the case involving the cabinet minister. The evidence I sent is clear and can be verified."

"I pick my battles. That case is not winnable. I can ruin my career, my reputation, and maybe get myself killed if I pursue that case."

"The minister is not all-powerful. He has left a trail of pain for others. Maybe it's time to expose him. Others will come forward and help."

Enzo says, *"Drop it. I'm not going after him. What do you want?"*

Angela says, *"There is a group of kids who were rescued. They were trafficked and forced to work in a sex house for a dangerous man in Serbia."*

Enzo sits up, listening. *"What does that have to do with me?"*

"They were traveling in Italy to get away. One kid made a phone call, and the bad guys found them. I need a trustworthy police officer to help rescue them."

"Why don't you just call the local police?"

"It will involve compromised police. The kids will be taken to another sex house or get killed."

Shaking his head, Enzo says, *"Where is this, and what exactly do you want me to do?"*

"They are being held in a building in the Bologna area. They are waiting for someone to arrive and take them back to Serbia. I want you to arrest the bad guys and get the kids out. I will have someone meet you there to take care of the kids. They need to disappear to survive."

"So, I rescue the kids, then they disappear. I won't have a case."

"Yes, you will be busy with the bad guys, and the person helping them get away will disappear. That is the only way they will be safe."

"Why should I do this?"

"Because it is the right thing to do. I'm asking for help, not

manipulating the situation to get you involved. Because I can continue to help you and maybe give you help with your boss."

"Before I agree, I want a full briefing on what I'm dealing with. You said someone would help. Does that include armed backup if I'm going into a building?"

"Yes, the operator in the area is fully trained in building clears and will help."

"The operator, meaning one."

"That is all you will need. Bringing a full team will attract the wrong attention. The other option is for the operator to go in and one of your counterparts to deal with a messy fight scene investigation."

"It will take me two hours to drive to Bologna."

"The train takes only thirty minutes. I will have a driver waiting for you upon your arrival. I need you to access a web page to get the briefing details."

Enzo types in the web page he sees on his phone. He sees pictures of the kids and Sorina, as well as low-resolution traffic videos of the five bad guys taking the kids.

"Five bad guys. Four guys for muscle, one leader. Against them are I and one trained guy. We can do this if he is as good as you say."

"The operator is very good. It won't be a problem."

Arriving at the train station in Bologna, Enzo's phone chimes, and he gets the car's description and license.

Getting into the car, the driver says, "Sir, it will take about twenty minutes to reach the destination. There is water in the console for you."

<<<>>>

They slowly approach and stop one building away from the warehouse. Martha says, "I will park to make it look like this car is for another business building, but I need a spot where you can watch."

Claire says, "There are three cars outside that building. That matches the video. Tim is coming. We need to be ready."

Martha nods. "Now that this car is not apparent, he will go directly to the building. There are two options for the car to bring him. It's one of his employees, and we have another to deal with, or it's a hire, and the driver will leave. If it's a driver, let me know. I will deal with him first."

Clare asks, "How does this work now? I'm going to do what?"

Zoe says, "You are the tactical backup, but the primary face. When the threat is neutralized, you speak with the cop. Make sure he lets the girls leave. This is what we talked about. If it goes bad, the gun from Ralph is all you have."

Claire looks at Martha, saying, "And what do you have?"

Martha says, "I've got my little knife. I will take guns from bodies along the way."

Clair suddenly shudders. "I'm working to get there, but that is still a gap for me."

Martha exits the car, saying, "Tim will be here soon."

Zoe interjects, "Don't go in the front. I have help on the way. He is the detective inspector working on the case involving blood writing on the wall.

Claire says, "Wow, seriously. You want to have that cop help us."

"He is a good cop. Yes, I've convinced him that helping trafficked kids is a good thing."

Martha says, "I will go around the back and sneak in. When the officer arrives, he can go in. Claire, you stay back and follow the cop into the building."

Claire realizes she is close to a real operational situation. She looks at Martha and then focuses on the floor of the car. After several seconds, Claire says, "I'm ready."

As Martha moves away, Zoe says, "You are not ready. You don't know until you experience that reality."

Claire shakes her head, saying something when she sees a car.

She slumps down as the car goes by. Watching; she sees a man get out of the car with a walking cane. He is leaning heavily on the cane until the building door opens, and an enforcer looks at him. He walks upright. After he enters the building, Claire says, "The guy just entered. He was expected and didn't have a gun. The car drove back the way it had come."

Zoe says, "That wasn't the police detective, then. Describe the man."

Claire is about to move and get out of the car when she hears another one approaching. She says to Zoe, "Another car."

A man gets out of the back of this car, and the driver immediately drives away. The man pulls out a pistol and looks at the building as the vehicle moves away. Zoe says, "The new arrival *should be the good police guy."*

Clare says, *"Do I need to do anything special?"*

Zoe says, *"Let him enter first. Just back up, Martha, or the cop. Don't take actual risks. Is your gun ready?"*

Claire nods, remembers, and whispers with a shaking voice, *"Ready."*

Martha moves to the back of the building to search for a door. When she finds it, she picks the lock. Slowly opening, entering, and closing the door, she gently closes it because of the sound and moves to the side to hide behind some equipment.

She looks through a gap in the equipment to see Sorina tied to a chair with the kids sitting on the floor close to her. Moving around the equipment for a better view, Martha sees five men in the building. Two men are close to the kids, two men are positioned near the front door, and the last man is standing next to Sorina.

Martha hears a car and inwardly smiles. *The cop is here. This should be simple.*

The door opens, and Martha can see Tim enter, walking with a cane. Under her breath, Martha says, *"Shit,"* as she calls Zoe.

Zoe says, *"What's wrong?"*

Martha squats behind the covered machinery and replies softly, *"Tim just entered the building."*

"Claire just described him after he arrived. Claire just said another car is approaching. How many are in the building?"

Martha says, *"Four enforcers, a smaller leader, plus Tim."*

"Wait a minute."

Zoe connects the calls and tells Martha and Claire, *"Both of you wait. I'm sending instructions to the cop."*

Claire watches as the cop reaches for his phone and reads something.

Enzo is standing outside the building that he was told contains kids recaptured after escaping human traffickers. They also informed him that special operations-trained support would help him rescue the children. As he looks at the building and evaluates his options for entry, he sees nothing but a small, office-sized door. The large roll-up doors are all closed.

His phone buzzes with a message. The message reads, *"The operator is in the back and entering. Four enforcers, their supervisor,* and their boss are in the building. The boss is the one you want to arrest, but don't take chances."

Tim walks over to Sorina and says in Serbian, "Bitch, your little poison surprise didn't work."

Sorina doesn't look at Tim's face and replies, "Wasn't me. The cane makes a statement."

Tim shifts his weight off the cane and says, "Where is the other bitch?"

Sorina looks up at Tim and says, "The last time I saw her, she was leaving to help her sister."

Tim chuckles, "Like you're helping your sister?"

He sees Sorina's jaw clench. He smiles, turns to the kids, and says in Russian, "Where is Peter?

Peter's face lights up. He stands, saying in Russian, "Master, are you pleased with me?"

"Yes, Peter."

Peter is quivering, blushing, and smiling.

The door Tim had previously entered opens. Everyone turns toward the door to see a man wearing a suit, holding a gun forward. He says in Italian, "Police, let me see everyone's hands."

The enforcers understand what Enzo says and show their hands, but they don't move their hands away from their waists. The supervisor slowly starts moving back toward the equipment, with Martha behind.

As the supervisor moves backward, Martha moves up to him. She grabs him with her right hand across his mouth so he can't make a sound and stabs him from behind with her left. She pulls him down to the ground as he dies.

Martha moves quickly. She is going to the enforcer closest to her. She moves to her left around the enforcer. As she leaves the cover of the machinery, Enzo can see her. He sees the small blade as she approaches the man quickly and quietly.

Enzo moves his head around to avoid focusing on Martha, but he is intent on what is happening. He sees Martha clamping her hand over the man's mouth and stabbing. The man tenses his muscles, moves, and then collapses to the ground.

In his head, Enzo has just witnessed a murder. Knowing that this person is a special operations person, he quickly thinks that *they will be in trouble if she doesn't kill one or two.*

Martha is lowering the body to the ground, watching for any reaction. If she doesn't move back and around to the right, the next closest enforcer will see her. She quickly grabs the man's gun and then moves.

When Sorina hears the words in Italian, she looks up. She sees Martha ducking behind machinery, away from a prone enforcer. This is all a glance as she turns to look at the man at the door. She focuses on the man, wanting to look at Martha. She says in English, "No Italian."

Enzo knew this was a dangerous situation as soon as he opened the door. Seeing Martha kill an enforcer and hearing they don't understand Italian causes a slight mental shift. He isn't the police detective arresting these people. He is here to rescue kids while the special operations person kills everyone who might harm them.

He shifts to the enforcer, slightly to the left of the door. From his perspective, he is the farthest person from the woman and his primary threat.

As he shifts, he hears the man with the cane say something in Russian. He says in English, "Show me your hands."

Now, everyone's view is toward the enforcer, who is close to the man. He is telling the man to show his hands.

Martha gets to the second enforcer and puts the knife in his heart when Tim says in Russian, "Peter, attack him."

Peter turns, looking for a weapon, and moves toward the wall, grabbing a metal pipe.

Enzo's statement directly to the enforcer causes the enforcer to react. He moves his right hand to his waist, reaching for his gun. Enzo starts to tense and tighten his grip on his weapon. He fires once. Then, a short pause, and he fires again. The shots hit the enforcer in the chest, and after the second shot, the man collapses.

Enzo remains completely focused and doesn't hear Peter behind him. Everything suddenly goes black.

After the first shot, Ivana shifts behind her sister and works to untie her. She is trying to untie the knots while watching Peter.

Claire is outside the door, taking slow, deep breaths. This won't be good. She risks screwing up and killing other people, or dying herself. When she hears the first shot, her adrenaline spikes as she jumps from the noise. She opens the door and enters when the second shot happens.

She sees the man to her left get shot in the chest. The kid, Peter, on her right, is swinging a pipe at the cop's head. Looking further across the room, she sees the man with the cane. She knows it is Tim. Past him is the last enforcer, pulling his gun but not looking toward her.

The man Martha is attacking kicks his leg, which makes a noise as his shoe slides on the concrete floor. As she lays the man down, she looks to see the last enforcer, close to Tim, looking toward her. The enforcer is reaching for his gun as they hear the first shot.

Martha holds the knife in her left hand. She then reaches back with her right hand to retrieve the pistol from her belt as she hears the second shot. She tries to draw and fire quickly at the man. To make it harder for him, she shifts to her right.

Claire sees the image of Martha pulling her gun and the enforcer pointing his gun at her. She completely ignores everything else now. Her pistol shifts to point at the enforcer. She is already operating with a massive adrenaline boost. With the smell of gunpowder, her adrenaline spikes even higher; everything slows down because of the adrenaline surge, and she gets tunnel vision. She sees only the enforcer and Martha.

Her gun is up, and she is focused on aligning the sights on the man, now letting out her breath and firing as the man has his gun up. The man fires a fraction of a second after Claire.

If you were to take a snapshot of the profile of the man Claire's bullet hits, he is shot in the arm. High on his arm, as he extends his left arm forward, holding the gun. She wanted to hit the man in the chest.

Martha is pulling her gun, watching the man bring his weapon up to fire. She sees the man shift as he fires. She feels an impact on her left side as she fires at the man. Martha's movement causes her bullet to miss the center of the man's head, hitting his left side instead.

Tim is yelling in Russian, "Shoot them."

Claire is looking at the enforcer as she sees Martha shift or twist, likely because of the bullet. She fires again, and this bullet hits the man in the chest. Her tunnel vision has her locked on the man and Martha. She doesn't see Peter pick up Enzo's gun.

Ivana watches Peter bend and pick up the policeman's gun. She *stops trying to untie Sorina and lunges toward Peter.*

Martha sees the enforcer get hit again, thinking the cop did well with his shots. The enforcer falls from the bullets.

A gunshot close to her right jolts Claire. She focuses on seeing Peter holding Enzo's pistol, having shot him in the lower back.

Martha looks over to see Peter kneeling next to the cop. The cop is unconscious on the ground. Claire is close to the door, pointing her gun toward the enforcer. Martha realizes Claire shot the enforcer. Martha has to scan for threats. She sees Tim and shifts back toward Claire when Peter fires, shooting the cop in the back.

Claire is on an adrenaline high, but the idea of one of the young people shooting a cop in the back is slow to process in her brain. She shifts her gun to point toward Peter when Ivana grabs Peter's hands and the gun. They both go to the ground.

Claire sees the tackle, but she can't shoot. She could hit Ivana.

The two are wrestling for the gun. With the barrel pointing upward, both are on the gun, and it fires into the ceiling during their struggle. The two are grunting and both saying, "Let go," in Russian.

Tim is red-faced and fuming. Peter was doing his bidding, and this little bitch is causing a problem.

Sorina sees Ivana tackle Peter and yells, "NO."

Martha moves toward Tim and observes the various people. Tim watches Ivana and Peter, and this distracts him.

Sorina is saying, "Untie me in Romanian." Looking at the three girls, she can see from their tied-up position they are gesturing with one hand and saying, "Untie me."

Realizing they don't understand, she switches to her simple Russian. With that, one girl moves toward her.

Tim hears Sorina talking and looks over. When he sees one girl moving toward Sorina, he takes a step. Without his cane for support, he stumbles. He jams the cane down to stop his fall. His arm pushes the cane and shakes as he tries to stand up.

Ivana and Peter are struggling on the ground, fighting for the gun. In Russin, Ivana says, "Stop, don't do this."

Claire looks at the kids on the ground, trying to process her first fight situation. She looks over to see Martha heading toward Tim.

One girl has taken Ivana's position and is untying Sorina.

Martha approaches Tim, who has walked to Sorina. He plants his feet and raises his cane to hit her. Martha approaches and places her pistol above his waistline, pointed down at an angle. She wants to sever his spine so he can't walk and destroy his genitalia. If he is alive, he can be prosecuted and shown to others.

Her bullet hits his spine, but too low to sever the nerves to his legs, affecting his legs. The bones deflect the bullet, so it doesn't affect its genitals. However, the shot causes him to stumble and fall before he can hit Sorina.

The girl frees one of Sorina's hands. Sorina shoves Tim to get him off her and then works to free herself.

Everyone hears another shot. Ivana gives Peter a look and relaxes.

Claire is watching the struggle when the shot happens. Ivana stops struggling, and Peter moves.

Martha makes sure Tim is not a threat and looks toward the sound. She sees Peter standing up.

Sorina can free her other hand. She jumps toward the kids, tackling Peter as he points the gun at Ivana. She grabs the gun and stands, now looking down at Peter.

Claire is lowering her gun when Sorina tackles Peter. Martha checks the girls and the enforcers visually to see if there are threats. She turns to focus on the fight with Peter.

Sorina is looking at Ivana with blood coming from her chest and mouth. She shifts back to Peter and fires the gun. Not holding the pistol properly; the gun jams with a casing sticking out of the top of the gun. She can't shoot anymore.

Claire is watching the whole thing. It is surreal. When the gun jams, her training causes a trigger that brings her back to normal speed and function. She moves toward.

Peter is hit in the chest. His smile fades as he looks at Tim, lying face down but trying to move. The woman, Sorina, who is close to him, is pointing the gun at him and pulling the trigger, trying to make it fire. He coughs and looks down to see blood on his shirt.

Sorina is frustrated. The gun stopped firing. She looks to see a casing jammed in the hole at the top.

Claire is next to Sorina and says, "Drop the gun."

Sorina lets go. She moves toward Ivana. Kneeling and picking up Ivana's head, she looks at her sister, and they both know she is dying. The bullet entered her stomach with the gun pointing up. Ivana looks at her sister as her breath goes out with a cough and closes her eyes.

Martha scans the area and moves to the cop. She talks to Zoe and gives an update.

Claire hears Zoe from her earbuds saying, "The fight is over. Now you listen. Secure the area. Moves weapons away from everyone. No weapons near anyone who is breathing. Tell me when that is done."

Martha does simple checks and tells Zoe, "The cop is alive. He was knocked unconscious and then shot in the lower back. He needs a hospital. Tim is wounded and needs help, but he probably won't make it."

Zoe replies, "I understand. I'm getting emergency services heading that way for Enzo, the cop. If Tim doesn't make it, don't leave evidence."

Claire says, "Zoe, Martha was also shot."

Martha says, "I'm functional. Don't focus on me."

Claire replies, "I will focus on you."

Zoe says, "Claire, are the weapons out of reach? Finish that first."

"No one can reach a weapon."

"I need an assessment of Martha's wound to help. Can she travel with the kids, or do I need a medivac helicopter?"

Martha says, "It's a flesh wound that broke a couple of ribs. My bra strap helped, but it's now ripped in half. It turns out that Claire shot the guy at the right moment, saving me. I can travel to an off-site doctor."

Hearing this, Claire pauses, then says, "You need help. You need a hospital."

Zoe says, "The person who just killed several people. Who is a ghost in every government system can't just show up at a hospital."

Martha says, "I can't follow the normal rules. I have to leave. I need your help with basic wound care for the cop's injuries. We need to prevent him from bleeding out before the emergency personnel get here."

After applying bandages to Enzo, Martha says, "That is the best we can do with what we have. Claire, we need to get the girls into the van. We also need to see if we can find chemicals to destroy Ivana's blood on the floor."

Claire nods, "Let me get the girls in the van first." She moves toward the van to open the door. Martha moves to Sorina, who is still holding

Ivana, crying. Martha squats next to her and says, "I'm sorry."

Sorina wipes her eyes and looks at Martha, saying, "I've watched you in a fight twice. You do things I would like to learn. You tried to save us all. We didn't think Peter would be that obsessed."

Martha says, "We can't leave her body. We have to make this look like a rescue. The cop will be in trouble from this whole situation. Us getting away will help him."

"How does that help him? There is no one left who needs to be rescued."

"That means they were rescued. They won't know that Ivana is dead."

Sorina looks over at Tim, who is getting on his hands and knees and moves himself to a dead enforcer, probably to get his gun. She asks, "What about him?"

Claire has been listening and walks over to the enforcer. Martha says, "Don't touch the gun, kick it."

Claire kicks the gun further away from Tim, then, as she walks toward the three girls still alive, she asks, "Zoe, what chemicals?"

Tim is breathing hard and glaring. He rolls over, obviously in pain, looking at Martha and Sorina. "I know what you look like. We have all your information. I will find you."

Martha says softly to Sorina, "I need to deal with this."

Sorina says, "Let me."

Martha shakes her head and says, "You don't need to cross that line."

Sorina stands, picks up the cop's pistol, and walks toward Tim. She grabs the slide, pulls it back, and turns the gun over. When the casing drops out, she lets go and then cycles the slide again.

Martha says, "I know you need revenge, but do it a thousand times without crossing that line. Help stop these people everywhere."

Sorina ignores Martha as she approaches Tim, who is smiling. As Sorina raises her gun, Tim's smile disappears. He is not looking at Sorina. Martha fires, hitting Tim in his left eye.

Sorina jerks in surprise at the sound of the gun. Looking at Martha, she says, "I'm in this now. I killed Peter. I've already crossed the line."

Martha replies, "Killing him would be different, and you know it. I have to clean the gun. We need to get Ivana's body in the van. Get the body and the girls ready. I'll be traveling with you."

Claire walks up to Martha. *"Zoe said to get hydrogen peroxide. I found this small, half-full bottle."*

She watches as Martha takes part of her shirt, on the right, with no blood, and rubs the gun. She understands Martha is starting her cleaning routine. Martha says, *"We need Ivana in the van and then use the hydrogen peroxide on her blood on the floor."*

"I'll take care of it."

Martha continues, *"Wipe the chair that Sorina was tied to, but keep it looking like someone was tied. They will find blood and DNA. We want it to look like a quick wipe-down before we get away."*

Claire says, *"That's exactly what it is. I have to dress your wound. Also, the cop can describe everyone. Are you going to kill him?"*

Martha says, *"He only had a glimpse of me and probably didn't see you at all."*

Zoe says, *"I've been quiet while you two were taking care of people's stuff. Now, Claire, focus on Martha's wound first."*

Martha says, *"We don't have time. The police are on the way. All a dressing does is catch blood while the body works. We need to finish and get out of here."*

With Ivana's body and everyone else in the van, Claire opens the big door to the building so the van can leave. She uses her knuckles on the button to open the door, so she doesn't leave a fingerprint. Martha is driving the van. Claire walks out to the stolen car. She says, *"I will be right behind you."*

Driving away from the building, Angela is on Martha's phone with the speakerphone active for Sorina. She says, *"You have minutes to follow my directions. You need to be on a different road. Emergency services were told an officer had been shot, and they are coming fast."*

Martha is driving the van. A minute down the road, Sorina's hands are shaking. Her breathing is shallow. She asks Martha, *"Can you stop?"*

Martha knows she is partially in shock and having problems. Zoe says, *"Sorina is starting withdrawal from an adrenaline high, and just like a drug addict, she has to go through the process. She will throw up and be better."*

Claire is also on the line and says, *"I need to throw up now."*

Martha pulls over and puts the van's transmission into park.

B.D. Murphy

As soon as the van stops, Sorina jerks the door open and bolts out. She kneels in the grass and throws.

Martha gets out of the van, feeling the effects of her wound, and flinches. She looks back down the road to see Claire's car several hundred yards behind. Claire is standing up from the kneeling position after obviously throwing up.

Zoe says, "Claire isn't answering."

Martha says, "She is dealing with the after-effects. She is okay."

Claire wipes her arm across her mouth and says, "I'm good. Martha, did you have anything like that?"

Martha says, "I was offline from Zoe. It wasn't good for me. I thought Frank had just been killed when I shot the men. I emptied everything from my stomach."

Claire nods and says, "That tells me you are human."

When Sorina gets up, she looks pathetic. She just shot someone and lost her only remaining family. Martha says forcefully, "Get in the van."

Martha looks back to see the car with Claire pulling up behind the van. They spend the next hour driving, following directions from Zoe, taking turns that didn't seem to make sense.

After a turn, Zoe asks, "You rescued Sorina and three girls. Would you consider this a success?"

"Martha is watching the landscape and crossroads, looking for other traffic. She doesn't want the van to be seen. The question forces her to think.

She speaks when Claire says, "No. Two kids died. Martha is wounded, and her wound could have been much worse."

Martha says, "Two kids died; we stopped Tim and his enforcers. A cop was shot in the back. No, the rescue wasn't good; it sucked pretty badly. If we had more time and planning, it could have been better."

Zoe says, "On a side note, the protein that causes the allergic reaction with Tim isn't needed anymore."

Claire says, "Martha, I know you're a planner. We didn't have time for a better plan. We saved most of them."

Sorina is listening, looking at Martha, she says, "Thank you. You didn't have to risk everything to rescue us."

"They would have killed you. I needed to do something. Zoe,

we're heading south, away from the airport."

Zoe says, "Sorina, yes, she did. She would never have been able to live with herself if she hadn't tried. Martha, the airport is shut down, and it will be for hours. I was already working on a new van. Sorina and the girls will continue south. You and Claire will take the current van to the airport to make it look like they flew away."

As she is talking, Martha nods. "That is a good plan. Anyone looking will search for this van first."

Stopping for a gas and potty break, Zoe says, "Martha needs attention."

Claire says, "What do I do?"

Martha says, "I will not die."

Zoe says, "Take a picture of her wound so I can perform an analysis."

Sorina doesn't have blood all over her side. It was on her arms and the legs of the jeans, which is hard to see. She wiped her arms during the drive and is now herding the girls to the water closet and food.

Claire says, "Let's look at your side and get this picture for Zoe."

Martha pulls up her T-shirt, saying, "I'm ready."

Martha hears Claire suck in her breath and pause.

Claire says, "We are aggravating it."

Zoe says, "Take a picture so I can evaluate the situation."

Claire takes pictures and sends them to Zoe.

After the first picture, Zoe asks, "Martha, what pain do you have? Any broken ribs?"

Martha nods slightly, saying, "Probably two broken ribs. That hurts. It hurts more to breathe than the skin part of the wound. I think the bra strap is helping with the broken ribs."

Claire asks, "What do I need to do?"

Zoe says, "Analyzing the picture, she should have stitches and a wrap. I know she won't agree to anything I say, so you will be on your own."

Martha says, "That is not fair."

Zoe says, "Prove me wrong."

Claire looks confused. "How do we get stitches?"

Martha says, "Vets have the equipment. We can order it online for survival situations."

Claire says, "So who does this suturing?"

Zoe says, "Probably you. Welcome to special operations."

Claire breathes and says, "I haven't trained on this."

Martha says, "I'll walk you through it. We need to get Sorina and the kids out of here. Zoe needs to give them a new ride, phone, and more."

Zoe says, "Working on it. I have the phone ready for pickup, and the new van will be ready in a few minutes. Right now, this van stays; Claire will drive Sorina in the car to get the new van, then come back and pick up the girls."

Martha is in the driver's seat of the van with the girls. Ivana's body is in the middle of the van, covered by a blanket. Martha puts Zoe on speaker and says, "Just sitting there is not good. They need to do something. Angela, what are the girls' names?"

"Their names are Anastasia, Tatiana, and Zoya."

Hearing their names, the girls look up at Martha. "I need them to clean the van. Talk to them in Russian."

Angela tells the girls what they need to do. They grab a bag and start loading the trash. Angela continues talking to them, asking the girl's questions and telling them what is happening and what will happen.

The new van parks next to the old one, and the girls move their gear. Martha grabs a clean shirt but doesn't put it on.

Angela says to them all on the phone, "You will split up now. Sorina will continue south with the girls."

Sorina looks at them and says, "What about Ivana? What happens to my little sister?"

Claire asks, "And the two of us?"

Angela says, "Martha and Claire leave the car, take the van, and head back to the airport. Ivana goes with you."

Martha and Claire look at each other, and Martha is about to ask when Zoe says, "Ralph is still there. They may reopen the airport in a few hours, and he can fly you out. He can take Martha and Claire to Serbia and Ivana to Romania."

Sorina nods, then says, "Yes. To Romania. I will give you a number to contact."

When the police arrive at the building, Enzo starts to groan and move.

The police immediately radio for more help, gathered the guns, and handcuffed Enzo.

The medical personnel check Enzo and look for his identification. It can reveal allergies. They inform the police that he is a police officer and needs to be taken to a hospital immediately.

Alexi hangs up the phone. He was listening to a report about what happened to Tim. He is not happy. There was very little information. Tim had his pilot break several laws to get to the airport. Then, at the warehouse, someone shot him in the lower back and then in the head.

Alexi picks up the phone and calls his security lead, Arseni. "Tim was looking for a woman with the kids from the playhouse. I need you to find the woman and the kids. Turn over every rock."

"When I find them, what do I do with them?"

"Call me. I want to ask some questions and strangle the bitch myself. Find everyone from the playhouse. There needs to be a clear message. Mess with my people and die. When I'm done with them, you make them all disappear with just enough information so everyone knows."

"It will be expensive. Finding and getting random people to attack them will take time."

"I'm not worried about families or bystanders getting hurt. Take out the targets. Spend the money."

"I will get on that immediately."

"Next, look for evidence, information, and connections. Who is helping this woman and the kids? They targeted Tim. They are not alone."

"Sir. You may not want to hear this, but they didn't target Tim. They were running, and Tim went after them."

"I'm putting the pieces together. The woman put poison in Tim's liquor. He was targeted. Then, when the kids were found, it expanded. Those kids didn't take out the muscle and kill Tim. They have help. Find out who."

"I will have someone I know and control work on this. He has good IT contacts and will find something. The retired MI6 guy we control will take out the leadership of whoever is behind this."

"When they find something, I want a report immediately. I want *details. Then have your guy take them out. I will also hire more people with a bounty for every head." He hangs up.*

Kids Away Again

Claire drives the van up close to Ralph's airplane, with the passenger side closest to the plane. Ralph is hanging up the phone when they pull up. Zoe tells them, "He is joining the team. I'm using Andy as his contact."

Martha says, "He is going to have buyer's remorse in just a minute."

Martha opens the door and steps out. Raph is walking toward them. When he sees Martha and her bloody shirt, he stops, shrugs, and continues walking. As he gets to them, he says, "I guess it is good my first aid kit is stocked so we can stitch you up. Is this going to be a normal thing with you?"

Claire walks around the van, holding the oily rag, with the gun wrapped inside. She doesn't offer it to Ralph, but says, "It's dirty now."

Ralph nods and says in a sarcastic voice, "Anything else?"

Martha says, "Yes. There is the body of one kid in the back, as well as a sniper rifle."

Ralph was smiling and now stops. "You're serious? What the fuck are you two doing?"

Claire says, "The girl was one of the trafficked kids. She didn't make it. The others are traveling to get away and disappear."

Ralph says, "Tilly said you would have yourselves and cargo. This is not good."

Martha asks, "Did she give you another contact person?"

"Yes. She said you would give me the number for Andy; I will get directions from you until then."

Martha pulls out her phone, taps on the screen, and a QR code appears. She shows it to Ralph, who takes a picture and saves the contact info.

Claire says, "What do we do now?"

Ralph replies, "I need to file the paperwork for the flight out. Who and where are we going? First, walk over here and let me get my first aid kit."

Martha says, "Ideally, you will take both of us to Zadar, Croatia, then take the body to Romania to be buried with her family."

Ralph says, "Can do, but I'm technically smuggling a body. I have to have a different story."

Claire says, "Say I'm going to Zadar, and Martha is going to Romania."

"It works; I brought you both here; I can leave with you. We can't move the girl's body until we are ready, after dark. Now show me your wound."

Ralph puts on gloves and checks Martha's side. She winces when she pulls up her shirt. He pulls out disinfectant and says, "I need you to unhook your bra."

Claire says, "I got it." Martha grits her teeth as Claire unhooks her bra and slowly pulls it away from her side.

Ralph starts cleaning, and Martha sucks in her breath, grits her teeth, and makes no other sound.

When Ralph pulls out the suture kit, Martha says, "Claire needs to learn how to do this."

Ralph looks at Claire, who is biting her lower lip. Claire nods. Ralph says, "You two are from different worlds." Looking at Martha, he says, "You are special ops, but no regular military has women in special ops. That means you are a clandestine agent, a trained spy. In contrast, looking at Claire, you are unfamiliar with this. You are a city girl, playing in this game."

Martha says, "Show her how to stitch me. Do you want to know some of those details?"

Ralph shakes his head as he hands Claire gloves and tells her to open the suture package. He walks her through the procedure, preparing the forceps and the needle. When it is time, he asks, "Martha, are you ready? Claire, are you ready?"

They both nod, and he says, "Use the second set of forceps so you don't stab yourself. Grab the edge of her skin and put the needle through. Ignore anything she says. When you push, finish it. The needle is sharp, but it will be harder to get through her skin than you think."

Claire nods and squints as she moves the forceps closer. Martha grits her teeth as Claire grabs her skin and pushes the needle through. After getting the needle and suture through the other side of the skin, Ralph walks her through how to tie the knot.

Ralph is talking to her through the process. Martha is looking at a rivet on the plane, completely focused and slowly breathing through the pain. Ralph says, "Good. That is the first knot. Now you need four or five more. You both are doing great."

During a pause, Martha asks, "Did you ever do any field sutures?"

Ralph replies, "Only during a training exercise. We had an accident while traveling, and I needed to stitch a friend's scalp together. We were stuck in the snow for almost twenty-four hours before they found us.

Claire realizes Ralph had to do this to a friend in bad condition. She moves in to start the second suture, her hands shaking much less. To distract Martha, Claire asks, "Martha, how do you know how to do this?"

"Last year at the hospital," Martha says, gritting her teeth and taking a breath, "a doctor showed me several types. I even practiced on the body of a stabbing victim after he died."

Ralph nods, and Claire remains focused on the sutures but says, "You never told me the complete story about that stabbing guy. You can tell us on the flight."

With the sutures in place, bandages applied, and different clothes on, Martha sits in the van's passenger seat. Ralph says, "I will go finish the last of the paperwork, then we can move the items. You should get the stuff ready."

Martha nods and gets into the back of the van. Claire says, "Hold on. You need to take it easy. I'll deal with Ivana."

Martha replies, "I have to get the rifle. You don't know where it is or how to get to it."

Claire rolls Ivana in blankets, and Martha uses all the tape they can find to secure the body. Martha then accesses the panel and the secret compartment built into the floor. She pulls out the rifle parts, ammo, and a small block. She says, "I didn't think I would use this. I'm glad Zoe thought about it and shipped it."

"What is it?"

"An incendiary device. It will burn the van and destroy any evidence. It is a last-ditch thing."

"So, Zoe could set this off remotely when you are away?"

"In theory, if it activated it and left a phone. Currently, it is a block of mostly magnesium powder. I will set a simple trigger to go off at about 3 am."

Claire scowls and says, "A flaw. Martha didn't have this all planned out?"

Martha looks at Claire and says, "You need to sleep. You don't bitch at me like that unless you're tired or mad at me. Are you mad about something?"

Claire looks at Martha and says, "We talked about the shooting on the drive. I killed someone today. Watching multiple people get killed. I don't know. I need to process. You are being nice to say I shot the guy, but you killed him. I know what happened."

"Claire, it's done. We can't go back. We can discuss this as much as you like. I will help. However, I think you should talk to Ralph. Get his perspective while we are flying. Then talk to Zoe."

Ivana's body is in the luggage area. Before they take off, Andy gives Ralph detailed instructions. Someone will meet him at the airport in Satu Mare, Romania. The body will be taken and buried in a ceremony.

Ralph asks Andy, "Do you do this all the time?"

"This is completing a promise to her only living relative."

Angela has given directions to Sorina. They will stop north of Rome for the night. After the warehouse and Ivana, the remaining girls are cooperating completely. They are communicating in broken Russian, English, and Romanian.

At the rental, Sorina says almost no words. The girls grab what they need, head into the house, and get settled. They then start rummaging for utensils and combine the food they bought at the grocery store earlier.

Sorina talks to Angela about the change in attitude. Angela says, "It is probably because they saw what could happen and how bad it could be. Will another guy like Tim show up if they call anyone? You are their helper. This is good for their mental health."

Sorina asks, "What else should I do?"

Angela says, "You understand that you can't cancel the brainwashing or programming they received. They don't have a switch to turn it off. What you can do is create and reinforce new standards, what is acceptable, and what is expected. Show them the discipline to follow through on the positives. We have to override *their programming with new positive programming."*

The next day, when they stop for fuel, Sorina learns how fragile they are. A car backfires while they are getting back into the van at the stop. The girls all screamed, immediately grabbed each other, and huddled in the middle of the bench seat.

On the road, Angela talks to them in Russian for a while. When that stops, one girl says to Sorina in Russian, "We are sorry. We should not have jumped like that."

Sorina replies, "It's okay. We'll get through this."

One girl then says, "Angela," and starts talking in rapid Russian. After an exchange, Angela says, "Sorina, the girls want me to tell you several things. Thank you for saving them. They are sorry about Ivana; she was their friend. They will be your little sisters now and be good girls."

Sorina turns and looks at the girls, who all smile and nod. Sorina smiles and nods. She tells Angela, "I don't want good girls who just wait to be told what to do."

Angela interjects, "They know. They watched Ivana with you. This is the hardest on you right now. I told them that being good girls is not being a sex slave. It is thinking about what needs to be done and doing it yourself. Help each other. I'm working on their new program."

Sorina takes a deep breath and relaxes a little. Angela is doing the work to help the girls. It isn't and won't be all on her. The therapy they need is happening while they are confined in the van. Sorina says, "Angela, where are we going? I mean, where do we stop?"

"You will spend several days in the South while I work on getting a plane and paperwork to get you all out of Europe. I don't know the destination yet, but it's probably somewhere like the Dominican Republic. It is easier for me to get you all residency with simple paperwork."

Sorina nods, "You will also keep talking to them, so they get the positive programming."

There is a pause, and then Angela says, "Sorry, you can't hear me nodding. Yes, we will work on positive programming."

Croatia

After landing in Zadar, they pull up to a hangar near a fueling truck. Ralph says, "I need fuel before the next leg. What do I do with the rifle?"

Martha says, "I would love for you to keep it safe for me, but dump it if you must."

Claire says, "Thanks for the talk on the flight. It helped."

Ralph says, "This sounds bad, but the first is the hardest. You won't ever forget or get over it completely. I avoid those situations, so I don't have another memory."

Martha hands Ralph a credit card and says, "Get the fuel you need, then get rid of this. Welcome to the group."

Ralph nods and asks, "Can I ask a question?"

Martha nods and says, "Of course."

Ralph asks, "Andy talked about getting training for larger aircraft. Is that a real thing?"

Claire says, "Yes, it is. You should get certified for a G6. You can train on larger planes if you want."

"I'll be flying a G6?"

Claire replies, "That is one. It will be useful for long-distance and smaller airports."

Martha looks at Claire. Claire looks back and says, "What? I know private flying."

Martha says, "I'm more practical. Large cargo jets. Talk to Andy."

Martha's phone chimes with a long message. Martha looks at Claire and Ralph and begins reading aloud.

"Andy detected traffic from a security guy that Alexi uses. He has contacted hackers and other personnel involved in the operation. They are looking for all the kids from Tim's playhouse, not just Sorina and the girls."

Claire says, "We need to do something."

Ralph asks, "Do you have a plan?"

Martha looks down at her phone, then back at Ralph, and says, "No. I don't have a plan yet. We need to continue our current plan until we have a better one. Get Sorina and the girls to the Americas. Ralph, can you help with that part?"

"I can fly them anywhere you want with the right plane."

Claire nods. "And the others?"

Martha shakes her head, "I don't know. We need to get Andy to help with some planning. Right now, I need to focus on Zadar. I need to remove another hydra head."

Ralph says, "From what you said on the flight, how can you get close? On a yacht, surrounded by guards and other yachts with guards."

"I have a plan for this one. Ralph, when you get done flying to Romania, can you fly to Italy? To get the girls out, you will need to be there. Talk to Andy about another plane."

"Will do. You two won't need a ride back to Italy?"

Claire says, "I think we will take a cruise instead."

They watched Ralph take off heading to Romania, then walk toward the terminal to get a taxi.

Arseni is on the phone talking to his hacker contact. Arseni only knows him by his hacker tag. Particle explained that his tag came from researching subatomic particles. Some can be in two places at once, and some are faster than light.

Particle says, "Shit. Are you serious? Tim is dead. Holy crap."

"Stop talking. We are going to find them. I need you to contact Tim's guys. Find out what they were doing and who they were after. Pick up the trail to find them. I will call you tomorrow. I need to know where to send my operations team."

"One day? I know nothing about Tim's team. I need to locate them and then speak with them. If I shove my way in, they won't trust me and won't talk to me."

"Are we seriously having this conversation? Get the info and make some friends. We could use them."

"We don't need them. I'm as good as Tim. I need a couple of days."

On the taxi drive from the airport to the marina, Claire asks, "What's wrong?"

"The other kids. They are all targets, and I don't feel right about not doing something right now. But I'm listening to you and Zoe. I can't do everything. If I don't focus, I'm helping no one. It just irritates me."

Claire nods, "I know. So many months last year. I couldn't help you. I had to focus on what I could do. The social media thing after Memphis got me stoked. I, me, I did that to help. You focus on your things. Let Zoe help where she can. We won't save everyone in the world; we need to make progress when we can."

Martha gives a little smile, feeling slightly better. "Let's call Zoe and get this one done.

They call Zoe and listen, each with one earbud from the set. Zoe says, "The target yacht has been there for four weeks and has no schedule to leave. I have already scheduled a call for late tonight. He thinks I'm a pervert who needs young kids. Now that Tim is gone, I'm going to him. I will have him ready for you."

Getting the family yacht, Claire says, "Mine's bigger."

Charlie says, "Welcome aboard."

They all hug. Martha flinches when Charlie hugs her. He immediately says, "What happened?"

Claire gives him a summary. As she speaks, his eyes widen. "Holy shit! Zoe didn't tell me any of that."

Martha replies, "You couldn't help, so she let you focus on your stuff."

Charlie says, "One of the items to focus on was picking up your gear. The captain would like to speak with you. We have some limitations to this mooring."

Claire furrows her brow and says, "What does that mean?"

Captain Walker walks into the room and says, "We didn't pre-register for this mooring. The harbor people say we have to leave by 16:00 hours tomorrow."

"I'd prefer a day, but tonight is fine if my gear is ready; there's ample time," Martha informs the captain, Claire, and Charlie.

Captain Walker asks, "Do I want to know what illegal activity is happening on this ship?"

Martha looks at him and says, "Nothing on this ship, and

nothing will point to this ship if no one talks about my gear bundle. I will go to the water access deck and check the gear. I will go into the water when the gear is ready."

Charlie raises an eyebrow. "Into the water? And then what?"

"I will be away for two to three hours and then return. We can leave any time after I get back."

Charlie and Captain Walker start to speak, and Claire says, "No."

Martha says, "I'll give you the details when we are out at sea."

Martha doesn't have much room on the water access deck. The yacht's jet skis and other water gear are filling the space.

Martha, Claire, Charlie, and a deckhand are in the area.

Martha nods toward the deckhand and asks, "Do we involve any of the crew?"

Charlie says, "I don't think we need to involve Gary unless there is something physical with the ship where we need help."

Martha looks down at the large, wrapped bundle, and Claire watches Martha. "I will need a power plug to charge the battery. We should be able to handle everything."

Gary nods, relief showing on his face. He says, "Please let me know if you need help."

After Gary leaves, Charlie shifts around the bundle, and Claire says, "That seems like a big bundle."

Charlie nods, "I watched the airdrop and the crew wrestle it out of the water. No one opened it. I made sure it was left intact. Now tell me what is in there."

Martha rips the waterproof wrap off, saying, "The airdrop avoided import issues for the sensitive gear."

She pulls on the wrapping and stops wincing. She looks at Charlie as he moves closer and finishes ripping open the wrap. Using only her right hand, Martha first pulls a case. "This is a Drager rebreather system. Two hours of air with no bubbles."

Charlie looks at Claire and says, "Special ops stuff."

Martha says, "This is the same equipment Navy SEALs use. The other stuff is not."

Next comes an underwater scooter. A sharp point with a propeller at the back to help it get through the water. Martha asks, "Can we get this charging?"

Charlie nods. He drags the scooter to a corner and plugs it in to charge.

As she pulls out the following item, Martha says, "The scooter should be charged in an hour." Next out of the package is a bundle, which Martha calls swim gear. "It has a wetsuit, flippers, mask, etc. Now, the new design."

The folded contraption looks odd. Claire asks, "And what is this?"

"A design Zoe and I worked on. This inflates bladders and becomes a platform just at the water surface."

Charlie looks confused and asks, "Why do you need a platform on the water surface?"

The last item is a case. Martha opens it and says, "This is the quietest rifle available right now."

Claire examines the components of a rifle. It looks small, and she knows much more after her training.

Charlie says, "What? A sniper rifle?"

Claire's left arm swings out and hits Charlie in the arm. She says, "Quiet means low range. How close do you have to be?"

Martha says, "About two hundred meters at the max. The good thing is that the harbor is small enough around the yachts so that it won't be a problem. The wind isn't bad tonight."

Charlie says, "You need to tell me who this guy is."

Martha says, "Right. Sorry. The guy I'm after is one of the main kid traffickers in Europe. His name is Valentinus Morozenko. Zoe has estimated that he is controlling thousands of trafficked children per year. Zoe will call him, acting as a buyer, to engage him. She will work to get him into a good position for me."

Claire says, "Zoe is going to call him to buy kids directly?"

Martha says, "Yes. When I return, the yacht should be ready to leave. The only item I will bring back on board is the scooter. We will need to dispose of the rebreather case and the rifle case. I want to weigh them down and drop them when we get out of the harbor."

Charlie says to Claire, "Are you following this? I'm full of questions and don't want to know the details, so I'm not asking."

Martha says, "Charlie, when I return, focus on helping me get the scooter onto the ship. Then, help with the cases. That is all."

Everyone on the ship knows something is happening, but they don't know any details.

When they return upstairs, Martha has a snack and a glass of water. She has Claire help with the bandage on her side, then puts on a one-piece swimsuit and the wetsuit. With the scooter charged, she is ready.

Captain Walker, Claire, and Charlie are watching as Martha slips her gear into the water and lowers herself in. She says, "See you in a couple of hours. The only thing coming out with me is the scooter."

Claire watches as Martha lowers her mask, inserts the rebreather mouthpiece, and goes under the surface. She says, "Let's get the ship ready to leave."

Captain Walker says, "Do you think she will actually do this and get back?"

"Yes," replies Claire immediately.

Charlie says, "I've seen her work. She will be back."

Nodding, Captain Walker says, "The ship has been ready to leave for the last hour. It will take us about five minutes. I will inform the harbor master we are leaving in three hours."

Zadar has a good port for large yachts. The Emer yacht is in the northern section, while the target is in the large southern portion. Martha must navigate the open water of the harbor entrance to reach the target. The water scooter is to help her move without getting exhausted. Zoe has estimated that the air capability and the scooter charge are enough. She expected the Emer yacht to be closer. This will be at the limit of her range.

She is dragging the water platform. Her breathing system has a buoyancy system, and the platform and rifle she is dragging come with an attached air bladder. She has adjusted everything to have neutral buoyancy. Nothing floats to the surface, and nothing sinks.

It takes Martha an hour to reach the target yacht's location. She is in the main channel, where ships enter and exit the mooring points. She has to avoid ships by moving to the side or diving below their level.

The target, Valentinus, is on the yacht for security reasons. Other yachts with security and armed men surround the main yacht.

From their previous conversation, Zoe told her that this guy is paranoid. From security footage and reports from his team, he surrounds himself with security and constantly changes his routine. The one flaw is the ship channel. The security personnel watch the ships that pass by, but they only monitor the water next to the ships.

Martha takes the phone in a waterproof bag and texts when in *position. Zoe will start a call with the target. She is acting like a buyer who needs new kids for sex.*

Martha waits for a few minutes until she sees the target walking out onto the yacht's upper deck. He is talking on the phone and is agitated.

Martha triggers the CO2 air canister to inflate the platform. The sound of inflation is muffled by other harbor noise, and no one notices it. There are three two-foot-long, eighteen-inch-wide platforms folded together. The canister inflates two small bladders on each side of each section. The inflation causes the three sections to open, creating a six-foot-long platform. Martha slides the scuba mask up on her head and drops the rebreather mouthpiece. The neutral buoyancy float ballast on the platform opens to release the air.

Martha is floating next to the platform, putting the barrel into the receiver. With that in place, she places the rifle on the platform and shifts her torso onto it. She grunts softly from the pain in her side as she hoists herself up, using the flippers to help. Putting the rifle stock on her shoulder, causing the barrel to point down to drain any water, and taking several slow breaths. She is thinking about the scope. They had previously aligned the receiver and scope and then shipped them together. The unique barrel is a tube that also includes the suppressor.

Checking around her, waiting for the pain to subside, she only sees one boat that could be a problem or cover. A large boat is heading her way, returning to the harbor and its mooring. She will have about three minutes before it is on top of her. The security team should focus on the boat and shouldn't see her when this happens.

After turning the clip upside down to drain the water, she inserts it into the gun and cycles the bolt. There is no bipod, so she is holding the rifle. Her training in the Gulf, with a bobbing ship and target, was perfect, preparing her for this. She shifts to look through the scope. After a few seconds, she has the target in the scope.

This rifle is the quietest available, which limits the distance but allows her to get closer without being detected. Closer also means variables like wind have less impact. With subsonic ammunition, no one will hear the shot over the harbor noise. Zoe only needs to keep him engaged for a couple of minutes.

Martha spends a minute watching his movements. He is pacing back and forth on the upper outside deck. He pauses when he is arguing a point. The phone buzzes with a text message. Martha doesn't have to read the message. They had pre-planned this, and Martha now knows that Zoe finished the introductions and concerns. She is now negotiating the purchase price for the kids. Martha will have about one minute left now.

When Val gets to the edge of the deck where he will turn, Martha plans her shot for where his head will be. The subsonic bullet needs time to travel 120 meters.

Val turns, and Martha squeezes the trigger. Less than half a second later, the bullet goes through Val's hand, the phone, and his head.

Martha grabs a cord at the front of the floating platform and pulls. Razor blades snap out and travel along tracks, slicing the air bladders that hold up the platform.

Martha slides the mask down over her eyes and nose as the platform sinks below the water. In her black wetsuit, she is hard to see. If someone were looking in her general direction, the muzzle flash would be the only thing anyone could see to show Martha's position. She is below the water's surface less than ten seconds after firing.

Security personnel looking for a shooter will see nothing except a ship heading through the harbor. They may think the shot came from the ship.

With no float ballast, Martha and the system are sinking. She sends Zoe a smiley-face emoji. The ship is approaching, and she lets everything sink as she folds the platform. She will drag the parts through the water and drop portions along the way.

She grabs the scooter, attaches the platform and drag bag, and starts returning. At the mouth of the harbor, she stops, cuts off one section of the platform, and lets it sink. She drops part of the rifle. Every fifteen minutes, she drops another part.

She surfaces several times to ensure she is heading directly for the yacht. Several hundred meters from the yacht, she surfaces as the rebreather gives less air. The rebreather is almost depleted. This is part of the plan. She was never going to take the rebreather on the yacht. The evidence has to stay in the harbor.

After putting the ballast weight belt on the rebreather, she lets it go and watches it sink. She keeps the mask for the last part of the swim. She surfaces to breathe and then goes back under with the scooter pulling her. Twenty feet from the yacht, she stays up, instead of holding her breath.

Claire and Charlie are waiting. Charlie grabs the scooter, then, with only her right hand, helps lift Martha out of the water to sit on the boat. Claire uses a radio to let the captain know they are ready to leave.

Martha removes the wetsuit as the engines start.

Claire hands Martha a large towel, looking at her face intently. She says, "How do you feel?"

Martha looks back, realizing Claire is checking her mental condition after shooting someone. Martha says, "I feel relieved. I accomplished this without being seen. A bad guy won't hurt anyone else. It will affect me later."

"How?"

"When I'm relaxed, I will think about this. About what I did. I have to remember I did this because the normal systems don't stop people like him."

Martha has the wetsuit zipper down and starts to pull off the suit from her right shoulder, which causes pain in her left side. She stops. Dropping her hand after wincing, she says, "I would like some help."

Claire and Charlie both step over to help. As they are pulling the wetsuit off, Martha and Charlie ask, "Where are we going, and will you tell us what happened?"

Martha says, "I don't have a destination. I guess around Italy. We need to debrief on this and start planning some stuff. Sorina and the kids are still in Italy. We need to get them out. I need a shower. When I'm done, and we are at sea, we can talk."

Ralph wishes he had the pistol in his belt. He landed and taxied to the hangar area. A car pulled up, and two men got out. Ralph got out of the plane and moved to the cargo area. Then three more cars came driving fast, surrounding the plane.

One of the first two men motions to Ralph, and they meet just in front of the left wing. With a heavy accent, the man shakes his hand and says, "Thank you for bringing our cousin home."

Ralph nods, saying, "You're welcome. To prevent getting stopped, I had to put her in the cargo area."

The man nods, "We will take care of her. Now tell me. Who did this?"

Ralph looks back seriously, saying, "I wasn't there. It was described to me so that I could tell you. I was told Sorina was going to kill him. Our trained agent did it first. There are more kids like Ivana. Sorina is taking care of them now."

The man slowly takes out a cigarette and lights it. Taking a drag and blowing the smoke toward Ralph, he says, "You aren't lying to me? I need to know who was involved. Who are we going to hunt down and kill?"

Ralph is watching the others. They have moved to surround him. He hasn't felt this concerned in years. "I'm telling you everything I know. The shithead who is responsible for Ivana and the others was shot in the ass." Ralph puts his index finger on his lower spine to show them. "After shooting him there, he was on the ground looking up at Sorina when he got a bullet in his head."

The man smiles and nods, and Ralph continues. "This was all after they arranged for the police to raid the house she was held in. Ten kids were rescued. The team ruined this guy's world. When he tried to follow and stop them, he got a bullet."

"Where is Sorina now?"

Shaking his head, Ralph says, "I don't know. That is intentional. I can't say what I don't know. Anyone who tries to get those kids will get a bullet."

The man looks at Ralph intently. Ralph calmly looks back. The man reaches into his pocket and pulls out a card. Handing it to Ralph, he says, "Here is my contact info. You let me know if Sorina or the others need something."

On the card, Ralph sees a name and what appears to be a construction company. Ralph nods. "I will pass this along. I was told the girls would disappear so these predators would never see them again. When they succeed, you won't hear from Sorina. That is a good thing."

The man drops the cigarette and smashes it with his foot. "What about you? Are you flying out now?"

"I would prefer to get a few hours of sleep and fly in the morning."

"It is some distance from the airport, but you can stay on our couch."

"Thank you, but I'll stay with the plane and fly out early."

The man turns and talks to the others. Two men go to the back of the plane and get the body out of the cargo hold. The other men go back to their cars but don't get in. They all start searching and bringing things to the first man.

After a few minutes, the man turns and hands Ralph two bags of chips, a candy bar, and a Red Bull. He says, "No food. Here are the snacks we have."

Ralph takes the items, saying, "Thank you. This is great." Holding up the Red Bull, he says, "In the morning, this is just what I need."

A minute later, they are in their cars, driving away. Ralph realizes that no one from the airport or the government came out to check the plane. He gets in the plane and adjusts the seats in the back to be almost flat. He lies down and is asleep in about a minute.

<<<>>>

Early in the morning, Alexi is sipping his first coffee and is on the phone with his contact in Uzbekistan.

"The power plant is on schedule. It has been receiving major attention since the Chinese government halted all cryptocurrency mining in the country. Everyone who knows about this new plant wants the electricity is will generate."

Uzbekistan has natural gas resources, and with the right connections, Alexi got the project started several years ago. Now it appears the timing is perfect.

Alexi says, "I have been spending money for over two years to control most of that plant's energy output. My new crypto-mining data center is almost finished. I need it to work while the hashing difficulty decreases because of the Chinese. No excuses. Get the data center up.

"The only issue with the data center is paying off the inspectors. They don't want bitcoin; they want cash."

"What are you telling me?"

"Just letting you know, boss. We have it handled. It just took a couple of days to get the cash available. We had to increase the payout for the inspectors."

"Why?"

"They said Russians offered them money not to approve the data center. We have descriptions of the men and are looking for them."

"Get me any information you find about the Russians. They are getting aggressive, and I need to deal with them."

Alexi checks for any urgent emails and sees one from Juan. The message is a summary that Juan is sending to the other leaders. The mutiny is almost crushed. Juan wants help to find new IT and security leads. Then he writes about the crucial part. He will not be generating cash for at least a year as he rebuilds his organization.

Alexi hits reply and puts in a quick reply. "One year is bullshit. We all have money issues. You need to contribute to development in Africa before the Chinese get control."

Everyone Must Compromise.

Enzo wakes up in a hospital room with a nurse. She says, "Welcome back, detective."

Enzo is squinting from the lights. The process of squinting hurts. His head is throbbing. He asks, "What happened?"

The nurse says, "Someone else will have to tell you what happened. I'm checking your vital signs."

"Am I okay?"

"You have a concussion and lost a kidney from the attack. Sorry, I wasn't supposed to say that."

The doctor walks in with three others. They are young interns. The doctor checks the chart and vital signs. The nurse says, "All his key vital signs look good."

Enzo says, "Where are the kids? What happened? What do I need to do?"

The nurse touches his shoulder and reaches for the call button.

Enzo says, "Don't call an orderly. I will not fight. Talk to me. What happened?"

The doctor says, "I don't know the details. You arrived shot, and we were told you were rescuing kids. We had to remove a badly damaged kidney. You will recover and be okay. We need to ensure that your remaining kidney is functioning properly.

Enzo asks, "Can I have my phone? I need to call my superiors."

"They know you are here. I talked to your boss, and someone is coming to question you. The police were told you needed rest, so they won't be here until this afternoon."

"I still need my phone to call my cousin."

The nurse looks at the doctor, who nods. The nurse goes into the drawer and pulls out his phone. Handing it to him, she says, "Keep the calls short, please."

After the doctors and nurses leave, he sends a message to Bella. It is short and concludes with he will call her later. Next, he looks in his call history for the number that sent him directions to the warehouse—his mystery helper. Enzo calls the number, and the phone rings five times before someone answers. He hears the woman's voice: "Rest, heal, get better; you don't need me right now."

Enzo says, "Are the kids okay? I did all this to help them."

"Detective, one of the brainwashed kids hit you and shot you. He was killed in the fight. The other kids got away. I'm working to get them out of the country and to a safe location. I can't tell you more."

Enzo nods and says, "We got them out. What about the operator? If I'm alive, she must have taken care of the others. Is she getting the kids away?"

"Yes, she is getting the kids away. She is also trying to keep a low profile."

"Should I? Can I help her?"

"No, Detective. She is extremely sorry you were injured in this process. You will never know the details of what happened after you were knocked unconscious.

"Give me a minute to process this." *Pausing, Enzo grits his teeth and reaches up to his aching head to feel the bandages. Knowing what he is about to say could lead him down a path where he can't turn back. He has avoided it his entire career. Compromising for the right reasons is what he always does. He says,* "I shouldn't be saying this, but you or she is involved in serious shit. What can I do to help?"

"Detective, first, you need to heal. Get better and focus on your cases. We can use your help to get bad guys off the street. This situation didn't go as planned, and we don't want to put you at risk again. When you are ready, I will provide evidence you can use to prosecute. Now rest. This number is only for emergencies. Please be patient with us. Trust is earned both ways. We can't and won't risk your life recklessly."

"Can I meet her sometime? Just socially?"

"Detective, you're enamored with her."

Enzo blushes and says, "I would like to meet and thank the badass woman who saved my life."

"The woman you never saw will be thankful when I tell her. She saved you, not the operator you saw take out the enforcers."

"How big is your group?"

"I can't tell you. I can talk to you about helping, but only after you heal and consider what is happening."

"Let me call you back."

Enzo ends the call and puts the phone down. He shifts in bed and spends the next several hours thinking and making notes on his phone, pluses and minuses.

Right after they take the remains of his meal away, three men wearing suits enter. They identify themselves as police detectives. They immediately started asking questions.

"Why did you go to the warehouse?"

"I received a tip that a suspect was there."

"Who told you?"

"A confidential informant. It would be dangerous for him if I reveal his identity."

The officers asked Enzo multiple questions about what he saw when he entered. He describes the situation and tells them everything went black. After multiple questions, one of them says, "We will talk again."

Enzo says, "Now, I have a couple of questions. The kids got away?"

The oldest office shakes his head. "How many kids were in the building? The boy was shot and killed."

Enzo says, "I told you I saw several girls huddled on the ground and one boy."

The youngest officer says, "We are still going through the evidence. It looks like the boy shot you. The bullet we pulled out of the concrete under where you were lying was from your gun."

The older officer says, "Someone was tied to a chair. Did you see that?"

"Yes. She was older. I saw her tied up and thought she could have been the driver for the kids."

At close to midnight, he calls the number for the mysterious helper. The call connects immediately, and the woman's voice says, "You've been thinking for hours. Can I help with any information?"

"I was being questioned about what happened in the warehouse."

"You told me you wanted to think about something. Have you decided?"

Enzo looks at the door, scanning the other patients to see who might be listening, and says, "I've spent my career, my life, staying out of the spotlight. Keep my head down and close enough cases to keep my job."

"What changed?"

"I woke up in a hospital minus one kidney. I was trying to save some trafficked kids because a voice on the phone said they needed my help. At that building, I saw a woman who was on another level. Committed to helping kids she didn't know. She is assisting like I've never done.

"Detective, like I said, you need to heal."

"I want to help. My head has been down, but I have been watching. I can't be Batman, but I can help."

"Then finish the cases I've given you. You have the evidence to stop that predator."

"He is a minister in Parliament. I can't arrest him without a bulletproof case. This is risking everything. I won't be able to help if I'm fired."

"Fine. Yes, this is a risk. We have to develop trust. I'm telling you, even if you are not a cop, you can help."

"I can help more if I'm a cop or a detective."

"Let's get the bulletproof evidence for this guy. Get him off the street. He is a predator, and kids will be safer when he is in jail."

"And then I have a name, then I'm the focus."

"Not with my help. Give the evidence to the prosecutor. The prosecutor takes the glory, and with a couple of forensic touches, everyone else goes to court to testify. I know what I'm doing."

Enzo pulls the phone from his ear, thinking. After a minute, he puts the phone back to his ear and says, "I get it. I will be out of the hospital in two days. I will have days with nothing to do except go over case evidence."

"That is how you can tell your boss you broke this old case. I like it."

"Can I help the kids? Maybe not those kids, but some others?"

"Detective, listen to me. As far as the guys taking those kids know, you were there to help them. You have done as they wanted in the past. They don't know how you found out. You can use this situation to get more information. You can help by doing your job and by listening."

Enzo looks at the door, thinking. This is not what he had wanted or what he had planned.

"What will happen if they think I wasn't helping them? I told the detectives I went to the warehouse based on information from a

confidential informant."

"I'm not sure. They will probably kill you. This isn't the outcome I planned; far from it. I'm examining all the angles I can consider. The best option is to use the information I will send you. Tell them you were helping. As a backup, you need to identify a confidential informant who can support you. Who will confirm that they have provided you with the information, sending you to the warehouse? Get that informant to back you up. Can you do that?"

"I know someone."

"This is not what I expected."

"They will let you do your job. If you are successful, it helps them to have someone. They will think they have someone they have corrupted. The reality is we will work together. I can help you with old cases and with current cases."

Alexi is checking his calendar. He wants to be within easy traveling distance of Italy. When they find the girls, he will be there to ask the bitch questions before he strangles her personally. His calendar has him going to Croatia tomorrow. Next week, he will also travel to Greece, Bulgaria, and Uzbekistan. He can easily change any of them except Uzbekistan. He needs to check on the expansion of his Bitcoin mining operation. The new gas-powered generation station they are building will let him more than double his Bitcoin operation.

He thinks and starts shaking his head. With all that, he still needs to finish the Russians trying to invade his territory.

He is resolving things in his head when his phone rings. The caller ID displays Valentinus Security and the corresponding number. Alexi answers, "What's going on?"

"Valentinus was just assassinated. It was a sniper from across the harbor."

Alexi grits his teeth and clamps his hand on the phone, making his knuckles white. Taking a breath, he says, "Find who did this. Help the police find them and send me all the information."

Hanging up the phone, Alexi growls and throws the phone against the wall.

Group Planning

The yacht is in the Mediterranean. Martha showered and changed her bandages. Her suitcase and clothes are at the private airport where Ralph picked them up. She is now wearing some of Claire's clothes. They are in the main lounge. Zoe is on the phone and ready for a debrief.

Zoe says, "The cell phone signal is weak and will drop at some point. I'm downloading some key information into Claire's laptop that you can use. Please let me know the next part of the plan when you determine it. We need to debrief, and then Martha needs to get some rest."

They spend ten minutes with Martha and Zoe, exchanging information for the debrief. Charlie is listening, fascinated. "This is like a debrief after a corporate takeover."

Zoe says something, then the phone goes silent, and Charlie says, "After all that, I would like to know what I was just implicated in. What do you want to tell us about what happened in Italy? Maybe, what are we doing next?"

Martha says, "We should include the captain in this. He should know and can help with destination options."

Claire nods and goes to get him. When she walks out, Martha says to Charlie, "We could use your help with how we invest the money we have. Zoe has been doing it, but that is what you do. Can you talk to Zoe and help?"

Charlie nods and asks, "How much are we talking about?"

As Claire and the captain walk back in, Martha replies, "I don't know the exact number, something over a billion."

Charlie's head moves forward. His eyebrows knit together. After a pause, he says, "You said a billion. A billion dollars."

"Zoe will have to tell you the details. Can you help?" asks Martha.

Claire says, "Yes, he can. We can do some good stuff with that amount of money."

Charlie says, "This is crazy. You have a billion dollars. You stole all that money from these guys?"

B.D. Murphy

Martha shakes her head, "No, most of it. Zoe has been investing and making more. I'm turning into a huge money sink for her."

Claire smiles, saying, "I think Zoe would say she loves you making a difference with that money."

Charlie says, "What was that in the harbor, and how does it all fit together?"

Claire continues, "Martha, I gave them a summary of what happened in Italy while you were getting dressed. Charlie is asking about the bigger picture: what and why."

Martha nods and says, "We can talk about details in a few minutes. Let's start with the guy in Zadar. The plan was to steal his money and eliminate him. Zoe has been working on hacking his system for several weeks. She had everything set up. The last part was to retrieve information from his phone. She sent him a text message before and during the call. She used those to hack his phone and get information. People are using their phones as keys to the internet now. Zoe hacked his phone specifically for that information. It affected his phone, and she used that to talk about signal issues and get him onto the outside deck for me."

When she pauses, the captain asks, "And the kids?"

Martha nods. "The information we have, which is not all verified, is that he has been involved in stealing kids in Asia and Africa and selling them to buyers everywhere. The estimate is that eight million children go missing around the world every year. Guys like Valentinus are responsible for a lot of that."

Claire says, "That many kids, every year." She shivers.

Charlie asks, "How much money did you get from him?"

Martha says, "I don't know. Zoe took it and hid it. Probably over one hundred million."

Charlie shakes his head. "Those kinds of numbers. That much money will get attention. The wrong attention."

Martha looks back at Charlie without saying a word. Claire looks at Charlie, shaking his head, and Martha with a determined look. She says, "Martha, you have a look. What's going on?" Claire is thinking. "She just shot a bad guy. She is dealing with whatever that is for her. I've got to, I don't know, help, get into it. I wish she would let me in."

Martha says, "I'm thinking about what Charlie said, the wrong

224

attention. *Can we use that? We know groups are working together, but there are others. Can we get them going after each other?"*

Charlie says, *"A hostile takeover would work best."*

Claire furrows her eyebrows, saying, *"That means killing each other."*

Martha says, *"I just started that in the harbor. But it won't work without follow-up details. We need Zoe to help with this."*

Charlie opens a laptop and starts typing. *"We need to get closer to shore so I can get a cell signal and internet. I'm making notes."*

Martha looks at Claire, who is staring back. *"Martha, this is soon after the harbor. Are you okay with this discussion?"*

Martha asks, *"What do you want me to do instead?"*

Charlie says, *"These types of individuals typically have legitimate businesses. We need to work in the market. Short, a company with which he is associated. That will get the message out."*

Claire is shaking her head. *"You just intentionally shot a bad guy. Not in self-defense or protecting someone."*

Martha closed her eyes for a second. Opening her eyes, she looks at Claire, Charlie, and the captain. Taking a breath, she says, *"That is history. I have to move forward. If I dwell on or fixate on that, instead of moving forward, more kids will be taken. Kids are hurt. The closest thing I know that could be like what those kids experienced is the fear I saw in my grandmother's eyes when she heard my grandfather had found her. When he arrived at the house, he said he was going to kill her. The fear I saw drives me. No one should be afraid to be alive like that. Do you think I'm suffering because of what I did? No, I'm frustrated. That was only one. There are so many more."*

Claire compresses her lips, looking at Charlie.

Charlie says, *"I don't have any experience like that to know where you're coming from. My experience has taught me to deny myself to meet others' expectations. I love you because you don't even know how to do that. You are raw. You are real."*

Claire is nodding. She looks at the captain, sees his face, and stops. *"Captain?"*

"Young lady. I've seen many things. People who want to fix everything try to tackle everything at once rather than focusing on what they can accomplish. Those people crash into flames. Focus. Make a difference in your way."

Martha grits her teeth, looking at each of them. "Zoe keeps me straight. She keeps me focused on what I want to complete. I'm trying to keep my focus, but all the other things can't be ignored."

Charlie looks confused. He looks at Claire and says, "Is this legit? She has the money, the ability, and no one is stopping her. Now she has us."

Claire says, "She lost everything. We have a family. They are screwed up, but we have Mom, Dad, and Grandpa. No one makes her legitimate except Zoe and us. We need to show her we can be a family."

Martha looks between them and speaks, as if no one had said anything. "I agree we need to get internet access. We need to talk to Zoe. She will already have this information and handle those transactions."

Charlie shakes his head, saying, "Not enough. Look, I'm in the area. I hear that something is happening that could impact a stock, and I look for a trade opportunity. I can do a legitimate transaction based on the emergency response in the harbor."

Claire nods. "He's right. Zoe can do transactions. Charlie can start a rumor with a sell."

Martha asks, "How much money would you be involved in a transaction?"

Charlie pauses, then shrugs and says, "If I knew nothing about your involvement, I would risk ten million on something like this. Knowing what's going on, I would invest fifteen million. It's not market-moving, but rumor-starting."

Martha reaches for her phone and looks at the screen to check for a signal. She looks at Charlie and says, "Fifteen with your name associated. Zoe can do another fifty or one hundred. She can make it look as if someone else is trying. Who do you think we could say is making the move?"

Charlie smiles and says, "It doesn't matter. A leader is assassinated. It will affect stocks. The other side will come out at some point. That is when we could transition from trading to investing."

The captain says, "I've kept quiet, but if you're trying to start a mob war, who will be the next target? One assassination is not a war. What else will you do? It doesn't have to be just assassinations."

Claire asks, "What are you thinking, Captain?"

"Disrupt their supply chains. I had my early career in the merchant marine. Whatever they are making money with, it has to be shipped. You can also get people arrested, make it cost them money to operate."

Martha nods. "Zoe's already working those angles. She started an import and export business. She is mapping routes and material movements. Looking at all the data, she found the routes for the trafficked kids. She already knows what else is moving where."

Charlie says, "I really need to talk to Zoe. Captain, where can we go for a few days in a nice harbor?"

"I'll find out."

Claire says, "Head toward Italy."

Martha says, "I'm fading fast. I need to get some sleep. So do both of you."

Claire stands, saying, "I'll take care of stuff. Go to bed. We'll see you in a few hours."

Captain Walters returns to the lounge after ten minutes and says, "I've found a location in Manfredonia. It is in southern Italy. We can be there in about ten hours. If you want to go to the East Coast, to Naples, it will take two days."

Claire is looking at a paper map that the captain provided. Without looking up, she says, "Head to Manfredonia. We can drive across Italy from there if we need to."

Charlie asks, "And what does my input mean?"

Claire replies, "Not this time. We need to get to the port quickly and establish internet access. You can conduct your stock in trade; we can discuss this with Zoe, and she can place her trades. We also need social media news about the shooting. This is where Zoe and I do our things, just like last year, after Memphis."

Charlie says, "Martha would say we need to check on Sorina and the girls. I want to know if they are away."

Claire nods, saying, "It will probably take Zoe some time to get fake passports and find a destination where they can stay."

Zoe previously agrees not to hack Tim. With Tim dead, the situation has changed. Zoe is now in Tim's hacking systems. She has accessed the *servers in his Serbian building.*

Zoe emailed one of Tim's hacking workers. She made it look like it was from his girlfriend, with the subject line, "Gently dump him." This got him to open the email she needed for the first step.

When it opened, the email appeared to have come from his girlfriend's friend by mistake. His girlfriend is helping a friend get out of her relationship. There is nothing he needs to call or check about. This gives Zoe the time to retrieve his information from his phone, access the servers, and hide before they suspect anything.

Zoe is seeking information about Tim's hacking and trafficking setup.

With all the different work streams, Zoe creates a database of notes and tasks that she needs to communicate with the humans she interacts with. She even writes the notes phonetically when needed to ensure she sticks to any accent the person expects.

The note to Martha is that, with Tim gone, the agreement not to hack his system has changed. She will learn everything about the team and be involved in every system.

With this information, she can map trafficking routes, contacts, and compromised people. The second information path encompasses everything related to hacking: it details who was hacked, for whom the hacking was done, and what was obtained. Lastly, her information path pertains to money—every account that Alexi owns.

The first thing to work on is the hacker's hunt for the girls. Knowing the van was burned at the airport, where were they searching? Data in the system shows they suspect Ralph flew the girls out, but they can't confirm. They have a large amount of information and can't read it all. They are searching the data. Zoe's leads she plants lead to distractions. The leads will appear in their searches, causing them to waste time.

She is also working on Ralph. She needs to find a longer-range plane and update his pilot's license. If everything else works, but the wrong pilot's license flags Ralph, someone could trace him and the girls.

One thing she finds on Tim's servers is Alexi's Bitcoin mining operation in Uzbekistan. With this information, Zoe gains access to the Bitcoin servers. Now, she knows every Bitcoin address he has, and with access to the servers, she can manipulate and move all his bitcoins. She creates a heist setup that will use Alexi's own servers to make it happen.

Working on another process, Zoe has been attempting to gain access to government systems to create passports. With information from Tim's servers added to her information, she has now gained access to four different government systems. She can now generate legitimate passports. Everywhere, governments tightly control passports, and human intervention is required for specific steps in the process. With COVID, governments are changing processes, allowing Zoe to get in. She can create passports for Sorina and the three girls that will pass all the checks, allowing them to travel.

The passport creation process intentionally includes several steps for security reasons. The systems she has hacked into now use electronic approvals before printing. She can now submit an approved application, and the printing will occur without a human having to hand a folder to the printing team.

Now, she needs pictures and data from Sorina and the girls.

Arseni And Particle

"What have you found?"

Arseni's best hacker, codenamed Particle, is on a videoconference to show Arseni information. He is nodding and smiling. "Well, these people aren't that smart. I have the make, model, and license plate number from the gas station video where the guys captured the kids."

"Particle, get to the point. Is this related to Tim?"

"Yes. The van was used to transport the people to the warehouse, and they used it to leave. That van was reported burned out at the edge of the parking area at the airport. From that, I pulled out all the flight plans and found a small plane that left earlier. There is no video footage. The plane is small, but it can carry the group. The flight plan only listed two people, so we know that was faked."

"Where did the plane go?"

"The flight plan was to Zadar, Croatia, and then to Romania."

"Croatia. Did anyone get off the plane?"

"No data for that. The pilot got fuel and then left. The plane is showing back in the air within thirty minutes."

"Just enough time for people to get out."

"And to get fuel for a flight to Romania and back. It's all part of the EU, so there are no ID checks. The credit card was a prepaid card with no permanent account. We know nothing else."

"You're not telling me anything useful. Why are we talking?"

The video shifts, and a picture of Ralph appears. "This is the former military pilot. Everything I can find about him, he is scraping by. We squeeze him. His plane could suddenly develop some issues that would require expensive repairs. We can get him to give us all the details about who was on the plane."

The picture changes to show Ralph's plane.

"That is something I can arrange. Anything else I should know about him?"

"I'm sending a file with information you can use and share."

"I'll start by simply asking and offering money. It will be faster. Where is he now?"

Particle is looking at another screen and typing. "I can't tell you right now. The little airport in Northern Romania doesn't have computers I can access. When he lands at an airport, I can access. I will let you know."

"I can't ask him questions if I can't find him."

"The alerts are set. I will let you know."

"Keep working on this. I want confirmation of who was on the plane. That is my termination list. Now, switch to the cop. Why was he in that building? How did he know where to go?"

Particle is now back on the screen, nodding. "That is different. Did you know he is suddenly finding evidence to help prosecute old cases? Some are significant. Hacking his system, I found that he had received information on where to find the evidence. Because of this process, it is all admissible in court."

"Particle, get to the point. How did he know to be at that building?"

"I don't know. The last contact I can access was an email saying I need your help." He replies, "What do you want? There is nothing else in an email, and there is nothing else I can track. I'm still trying to find the source of those emails. Someone with skills was sending this information."

"I can't ask Tim or anyone else why he was there. This cop has been useful in the past. From the information I received, we don't know whether he was there to help Tim or to stop him. He walked in and was shot. Dumb shit had no plan or backup. That makes me think he was trying to help. I need you to find out more information. Do I add him to my termination list, or is he still useful for Alexi?"

"I'll let you know when I find something."

Arseni gets off the phone with Particle and starts an email. The email is to one of the compromised resources in his network. This one was originally SAS; then, he was part of MI6. Arseni will give him directions and turn him loose. He will find who was helping the girls and kill them. He calls him Hunter.

The email is straightforward; it contains nothing incriminating. If the email is part of a search, it will appear to be a simple request. It asks *him to check on who is behind the shootings in the warehouse. Who got away? He finishes the message with, "I will call you for an update in twenty-four hours."*

He knows Hunter still has connections in MI6 and will use them. This will provide another information path and take care of the unknown helpers.

He smiles, thinking back to how he compromised the resolute agent. The fake incriminating video wasn't enough. The photos of friends with a note about losing them didn't make him comply. Arseni expected resistance and set up a demonstration. After a forced meeting, Hunter left to find one of his friends, who had almost died in a freak accident that wasn't an accident.

The agent tried to resist by talking to others to report Arseni. He found out the network was extensive. The others told him to comply, or it would be bad for everyone.

He has no options. He does as he's told, or his friends get hurt, and he could be in jail in some random country, subject to constant beatings and rape.

Finally, Arseni checks the information on the kids who went home with their families. There have been two accidents and a random shooting so far. The hired help will deal with the final two within a week. This has been expensive, and he knows Alexi will complain about the cost later, but this is what he wanted.

Ralph took off from Romania before dawn. He is now at Perugia Airport in central Italy, unsure of what else to do; they weren't specific. He has used this airport many times. Being centrally located, people in the area can easily access this location for charters. He's also done some decent cargo flights from here.

When he landed and parked, he turned his phone off airplane mode while thinking about finding somewhere to eat, shower, and sleep. Almost immediately his phone rings. Ralph grumbles, looks at the phone, and sees the caller ID for Andy. Taking a breath, he answers, saying, "Hello."

Zoe, with the Andy persona, who uses an Irish accent and says,

"I assume the drop-off went fine. Now, you need to get some rest and get online for some research and training. Your location has you in Perugia, which is a good central location."

Ralph's eyebrows furrowed, thinking, "How does he know where I landed?" He says, "You know where I landed?"

"Ralph, I can track your number through the cell network. I can track your plane through the aviation system. Having the information allows me to help in little ways. Little ways to help, like removing your plane from the airport system. You just disappeared for a while. There is a small hotel close by. You have a room booked and paid for two nights. Do you have a computer?"

"Yes, I have an old laptop, but I mostly use my phone."

"I'm sending you the hotel information. Take your stuff, get food, and go rest. I will have a courier deliver some things to you at the hotel."

Squinting and frowning, Ralph says, "What are you delivering?"

"A new laptop, a new credit card you can use. Finally, you need to sign some paperwork and then put it in the mail."

Ralph is now chuckling, "Paperwork."

Tony replies, "I have to file to expand your license for more planes. The laptop is for your training purposes. You flew jets in the military and are familiar with the procedures. After all the online items, a form with your physical signature must be filled out."

"Claire said a G6. Are you guys serious?"

"Yes. The pilot license update will enable you to fly all aircraft permitted for a single pilot. Two crew planes will need more, and then I can get you into bigger stuff."

"Is there a jet close by that I will fly?"

"No. You need to keep using the current plane. Those jets are not just sitting around. When something becomes available, I will notify you. If you need any service scheduled, get it done at the Perugia airport."

An hour later, Ralph had scheduled the plane's service. Unless they find something that needs to be repaired, they will have the service by tomorrow evening.

He heads to the main commuter terminal to get a taxi. So far, as part of this group, he has broken several laws and received incredible support, and they are getting him into a bigger plane. Accepting the random charter because he had not worked and was in the Serbian area worked well for him.

He is smiling as he walks. So far, this has been far from ordinary. Remembering that he enjoys making a difference, even in small ways. He doesn't mind the danger. He has been in airplanes, ready to fall out of the sky, and survived. They are trying to make a difference. "I wonder if they would consider some of my old military buddies."

<<<>>>

Martha comes out of the cabin after sleeping for several hours. She is flexing her arm on the left side as she walks into the room. Claire asks, "What's wrong?"

"I'm sore."

"Overdoing it since you got shot."

In a slightly pissed-off voice, Martha replies, "It wasn't something I could just stop and take a vacation."

"Sorry. I'm tired. I've had two hours of sleep. As soon as we docked, I've been working with Zoe."

Martha looks around the table, and books, maps, and papers are covering the chairs. "Is Zoe online?"

"Charlie took the phone. They made trades around the time of the Valentinus shooting. Charlie was happy with the results. They are now focusing on general investments, and how to invest all that money you stole."

"I stole?"

"Zoe said you stole more than she has."

Martha chuckles, "Not what I expected her to say."

"On an interesting note, Zoe has access to all of Alexi's Bitcoin mining servers. She controls the entire data center in Uzbekistan. Charlie laughed when she said that part. He asked about disrupting the blockchain and causing chaos."

Martha smiles, "It doesn't work that way. Why does he want to do that?"

"She told him it doesn't work like that. He wants to manipulate the blockchain and make a couple of billion."

"That would be interesting. Make it look like Alexi is manipulating the market."

Martha moves a map from a chair, sits, and asks, "Anything on the girls?"

"They are in the Naples area and doing okay. She has everything in motion and wants to fly the girls out in a couple of days."

Martha nods, "Now you need to sleep, and I need food."

Claire starts to speak, and Martha raises her hand. She shakes her head. "You need rest before we get into details."

"A nap. I'll return in a couple of hours."

When Claire returns, she sees Martha has cleaned. Maps are on the table; papers are stacked. There are no dirty dishes on the small tables—a charcuterie tray on the side table. Charlie is staring at Martha. He says, "You have a seriously paranoid mind. We fly the girls out."

"We need this backup plan. That's all it is, just a backup. Yes, my brain thinks paranoid thoughts. Learn to deal with it."

Claire picks up a piece of prosciutto and cheese and says, "She wasn't always this way. Getting tracked, chased, and shot at made her plan more."

Charlie turns and says, "Feel better? I had some sleep as well. Came out to a clean salon and Martha talking with Zoe about a training program to turn rescued kids into spies or agents or something."

"Sounds interesting."

Charlie nods, "I think it's a great idea, but it will fail."

Zoe says on the phone, "It will be set up with small cells; they won't be able to intimidate, torture, or pay off more than a few."

Martha is smiling. "Charlie, you live in a different world. Zoe told us about the girls' progress. They are becoming a family and will support each other. Giving them a goal and purpose is good for them. Something they will be passionate about makes it better.

<<<>>>

Alexi is fuming. News of Valentinus being shot caused several of their stocks to crash. The front business was supposed to be completely separate. They invested a significant portion of their illicit activities in laundering the money. Val had a plane, yachts, and houses.

The sudden surge in stock activity has prompted the government to launch investigations. He will now need to spend money to settle with those who have been involved and halt the investigations. He doesn't have Tim's help to plan information to discredit people. The Russians *were backing off. Now, they are getting aggressive. There was a rumor that the Russians were conducting stock shorting transactions to fund their war against him. He needs to take action to prevent them from occupying his territory in Italy, Germany, and Uzbekistan.*

He calls Arseni for a status update and to get working on the Russians.

"Alexi, I've got leads on the kids. The new van they are using was spotted in southern Italy. We will find them soon."

"That is good news. Find them and hold the bitch. I want my hands around her neck."

"Alexi, that isn't a good idea."

"I don't care. You'll clean it up and get rid of the bodies. They are close to the water in almost any part of Italy. We can put them on a yacht, take it out, and sink it."

"Okay, boss. When we find them, I'll get them to a discreet location and let you know."

"Good. Now, the Russians. After Val's death, I'm getting info that they are becoming aggressive again. I need more people I can trust to deal with them."

"We need more people we can rely on for sure—people who won't screw it up and get it done. The best guy I have right now is in Rome. I'll get him working on the Russian thing."

When he received the email from Arseni, the retired MI6 agent whom Arseni referred to as "Hunter," he let out a sigh. The blackmailers have trapped him. He is compromised now, and if he doesn't do as he is told, his family and friends will get hurt. He has been collecting information on the group but has found no one who could take on this group.

Based on the email, he started searching. There is not much public information he can get, so he put together a request and sent it to one of his friends still in MI6. A few minutes later, his phone rings.

"This is an odd request."

"I can't ignore this. You know that. I have to find them and eliminate them. You can't ignore this either. I will call you tomorrow

for an update."

Now, twenty-four hours later, he is calling from his hotel in Florence, and someone answers the call immediately.

"I accessed our normal sources, which gave little. The AI analysis of financial transactions gave me a name. Mary Muller, German. I checked the passport, and it is legitimate, but the ID is fake. Whoever you are dealing with has the resources to make that happen."

"Where is she?"

"Like I said, she has resources. There is one transaction, and then she is gone. The next tag on that ID was from Bologna Airport. She is listed as a passenger flying to Romania. I have nothing else."

"Picture?"

"Sent to your phone. It is just sufficient to meet the requirements for a passport. Facial recognition in airports, trains, and hotels has nothing."

Knowing that Tim was killed close to Bologna, he asks, "What was happening in Bologna?"

"There was a police officer shot in a warehouse on the outskirts hours before the flight. Nothing else triggers any alerts. There were several killed in the warehouse, and reports that trafficked kids were rescued."

"Where are the kids?"

"The report isn't confirmed, except through unofficial sources. I had the pictures checked. From the blood evidence, there were more injured or killed in that warehouse. No females were in the building when the police arrived. The report from the cop said kids, and a woman were tied up."

"The police didn't rescue the kids?"

"No. One dead young male along with older Italian males."

"I need you to find the kids."

"You're not serious. Find trafficked kids, so what? You or someone can kill them or take them back into slavery?"

"You are in the same position I'm in. I need to find Mary. The kids are the only link. Find the kids."

After getting off the phone, Hunter takes slow breaths. Looking at the picture of Mary, he asks himself, "Who are you working for? Someone with a lot of money and connections."

He would never have considered that a blackmail group would force him to find and potentially kill trafficked kids. Shaking his head, he thinks, "I will have more information and evidence to stop these people, eventually."

He will wait for information from his source. When he knows an area, he will send several special operations personnel to pursue Mary. She was involved in taking out several tough guys, and he would have specially trained personnel to deal with her.

Sorina And Kids

"I'm happy you're being cautious. If we need to, we can move daily to stay hidden," says Sorina.

Angela says, "Sorry, I haven't found a place to stay. With COVID-19, it's challenging to find a rental that meets our needs. There are lots of single rooms available, not multi-room flats with parking."

"We will survive in the van if we have to. It is not ideal, but we will make it work."

"The paperwork will take a couple more days. I need passport pictures for everyone. I'm sending a link to download an app to guide you through the steps. This will be the first major step for you all to disappear."

Sorina says, "I'll take the pictures tonight when we stop. The girls loved the stop in Pompeii. Getting them out of the car for several hours was good."

Angela says, "I'm glad you enjoyed the ruins. You will be in the south of Italy for a few days. When everything is ready, you will go to Naples Airport and fly out of Italy. You will change planes in another country and fly to the Americas."

"Understood."

"How is everything else going?"

"My Russian is getting better; their English is getting better. We are all talking more. We need a place to park this van. In some ways, the previous open van was better. This one with seats means we have to stay seated for long periods."

"It should just be a few more days. I'm sorry it is taking so long."

"Another subject to bring up. The girls are grumpy and hungry. We talked about our monthly cycles, and I've had a really heavy flow this month."

"It is expected, Sorina. You are now with several teenage girls, and the hormone fluctuations will affect you. You will all shift to the same

monthly cycle."

"There is something else. The girls were never allowed to use tampons. Two of them have never used tampons. Then I found out all the girls in the house had IUDs."

"Do you know when this was done?"

"Some before they arrived at the house, some after. They all describe the same doctor and clinic where the procedure was performed. They know him because he would come to the house."

"I need the information about him. Hang on."

Angela speaks in Russian to the girls after hearing a name and a face appear on the phone screen. The girls all nod.

Angela says, "He is going to have some serious issues now. His electric bill hasn't been paid, and his power will be turned off. The same for all his other utilities."

"Angela, will that get you into trouble?"

"I have friends who will work on the details. For someone like this, there are many friends to help. I won't be in trouble."

Never Left Italy

Particle is telling Arseni, "I told you I was good. I couldn't confirm the people on the plane to Croatia, so I took a step back and asked, what if they weren't on the plane? What if that was a diversion?"

"Yes, you're a good boy. Get to the SHORT summary."

"There was another van purchased and picked up before the plane took off. I got the information and started a search using traffic cameras. The van is in Italy."

"Stop. The van started in Italy and remains in Italy. I'm going to hang up now."

"Wait. Let me finish. I had the system searching for the van, but I had already started searching for the woman, Tim's maid. Her face triggered a facial recognition scan. And this is the better part. The camera picked her up in the new van."

"So, they switched to a new van and never left Italy."

Particle is nodding, smiling, and tapping a pencil on the table. "I told you I'm good."

"Where are they in Italy?"

"The camera was monitoring the highway between Rome and Naples, heading south. Now, my focus for the searches is around the Naples area. I don't need facial recognition now. The van will show up faster."

"Good. Let me know as soon as you get the location. I'm contacting people in Naples."

Particle needs to get more computer resources to help search for the van. He needs to search through recordings and live camera feeds.

Having contacted Tim's guys, he uses Tim's hacking factory resources in the search.

With Zoe in Tim's hacking factory and monitoring the activities, she learns about the search and about Particle.

Zoe does a search to find out about Particle. She needs to find his *background and details about him. She also starts a call with Martha to tell them about the search.*

Hide And Seek

"Martha, Alexi's security guy, named Arseni, has a hacker searching for the girls. They know the van is in the Naples area. We need to look at stepping up the timeline."

Martha was in the ship's cabin when Zoe called. She leaves the cabin, heading to the lounge to talk with Claire and Charlie. She says, "Hang on a minute until I get to the lounge and put you on speaker."

Claire, looking up from her screen as Martha entered the lounge, explains, "I'm noting the economic impact of your stock trades for my thesis." Looking at Martha's face, she says, "Charlie! What's wrong, Martha?"

Martha puts Zoe on speaker and says, "Repeat for them, please."

After repeating the basic info, Zoe says, "I don't have the passports ready. We can move them somewhere else in Europe, but to have a real clean break, we need legitimate identities for all four of them."

Charlie says, "I'm not going into details about how you can do that. But, how long before they can be ready?"

"Sorina was going to get the passport photos tonight when they stopped. Passport creation takes two days after a one-day application upload, plus mailing."

Claire says, "We need a plan to keep them out of sight until we are ready."

Charlie looks over at Martha's face, expecting her to say something. Martha is gazing at the coffee table, lost in thought. Claire looks at Charlie, looking at Martha. After a pause, Claire says, "Let us help. What's churning in your brain?"

"This is just like last year. Every time I moved, they tracked me. I couldn't get away. That is until I set up a diversion and got away."

Claire's eyebrows shoot up. "You want to fake-kill all four of them."

Martha looks confused for a moment, then understands what's happening and shakes her head. "No. They don't die. That would be way too much work. We need to make the guys believe the girls are going to one place and get them somewhere else. They need to be at the new place with new identities."

Claire says, "They follow the false trail. When they realize the girls aren't there, they have completely vanished."

Martha says, "Zoe, Sorina is going to need to disappear from every system. No face, no fingerprints. Erase everything."

Zoe replies, "Got it. Just to be clear. This is a one-way door. She can't go back. I've become smarter about this. If she tries to assume her old identity, the system will think she is using a fake identity."

Charlie says, "So what do we do?"

Martha nods, "Zoe, I've got work for you. We need Ralph ready to fly them somewhere far. As far as possible in Europe."

Zoe replies, "That would probably be Iceland."

Claire nods, "The flight plan needs to be filed showing the girls with names that Alexi's guys can find."

"Zoe says, I'm on it. I'm talking to Ralph about getting to Naples. The girls' first names are Anastasia, Tatiana, and Zoya. The flight plan will have those with Sanchez as the last name."

Charlie says, "That will be obvious."

Zoe says, "That is the point."

Martha says, "Does he still have the rifle?"

"I believe he does."

"I might be able to use that."

Charlie asks, "What for?"

"They are looking for Sorina and the girls. With Tim gone, we know it is Alexi directing the search. Part of this could be a lure to get Alexi to the area. If I get the chance, I want to be ready."

"I'll confirm with Ralph and get that rolling."

Claire says, "That means we're going to Naples."

"Yes, we are the distraction and the exit."

Claire's brow furrows. After a pause, she says, "How can we be both the distraction and the exit?"

"You're the exit. I'm the distraction."

Zoe says, "I've done an analysis. There is no scenario where Martha isn't in a firefight."

Claire and Charlie both shake their heads. Martha focused and says, "Give me a minute. I want to avoid a firefight completely, but I don't have it all worked out."

"*The only way a distraction is believable is if you engage with the bad guys, then the girls leave that area. They have to be close to danger. You have to be in danger.*"

Martha stands and starts pacing. Charlie looks at Claire, who is watching Martha. After a minute, Claire says, "*I've never seen this. When all this happened last year, we were always on the phone. She worked out ideas, and then we talked.*"

Martha looks up. "*I don't know enough right now. Zoe, I need some information about where the girls will be in Naples. Where can we set up this diversion? Please put a Naples map on the big TV. Claire and Charlie, let's get into this together. We know where the girls will be tonight. We know the last place they will be seen is the airport.*"

Zoe says, "*Where are the bad guys? Where does the encounter happen, and how do they get out and to the airport?*"

Ralph answers the phone and hears Andy say, "*Ralph, time to go to work.*"

Ralph is in the hotel room, surrounded by drones and cell phones on the bed. "*This is goofing off?*"

"*We need those drones and phones charged. The timeline has moved up. I need you to get everything ready and get to Naples tonight.*"

"*Tonight. Seriously?*"

"*I was also told you have a rifle. Is that still true?*"

"*Yeah, that's in the plane. Tonight?*"

"*We have information that the bad guys are closing in on the girls.*"

"*Again. We can't keep them hidden or get them out?*"

"*They need full new identities to disappear, which takes time. The bad guys are determined to find them, and it looks like they will kill them.*"

"*You want me to fly them somewhere.*"

"*Yes. It is not simple, and Martha is still working on parts of the plan. Currently, we have a plan for you to travel to Naples and then fly to Iceland. The details beyond that are not complete.*"

"*When will they be complete?*"

"*This is real time. Get the gear to the plane. Get to Naples as fast as you can.*"

Ralph picks up one drone. Eight inches across, three blades with a package underneath. "These drones are not like others I've seen. There are two camera lenses and a spot for a cell phone to be strapped on."

"Two lenses mean they can identify distance. They can pinpoint a location. One camera is infrared, allowing for better visibility of hidden items or people. The cell phone means they are only limited by battery time and the cell phone network."

"They are remote-controlled."

"That is how you see it. I see the video on my screen and can control it, just like I was in a van on the side of the road."

"I'll get them to Naples. Get the plane fully fueled. You know I'll have to stop somewhere to refuel. Someplace like Scotland. The distance to Iceland is way longer than my plane's flight range."

"We know. I'll get something arranged for refueling in Scotland."

"New thought. How will I deliver this equipment to you? Do I need a car?"

"Good point. I'll arrange for a rental vehicle to be delivered to the airport for your use. Thinking about it. The vehicle can be another option to get the girls to the airport."

"Call me if you need anything."

Sorina looks at the caller ID on her phone when it rings. Angela is the only one who calls, but she just talked to Angela a few minutes ago.

She answers, "Hello."

"Sorina, take me off speakerphone, please."

After taking the phone off speakerphone, she puts the phone to her ear, which she isn't supposed to do while driving. "You're off speaker."

"The bad guys know you are all in the Naples area. I don't want to alarm the girls. You need to head to the rental now. I'm sending you the address so you can use the map directions. Just get there and wait. We are working on the details to get you out of Italy."

"We don't have passports yet."

"I know. We are trying to create a diversion so that when you

leave, the bad guys look in the wrong direction. By the time they figure it out, you will be gone with new identities."

"We've tried twice now to disappear."

"Yes. This time, instead of just disappearing, we will give them a trail to lead them away."

"I want to tell the girls and head to the house."

"Sure. I wanted to ensure you were aware of this before we discussed it with them. Let's tell them."

Sorina puts the phone back on the speaker and sets it on the console. Angela talks in Russian, telling the girls.

They all start nodding as Sorina turns to follow the new directions.

Angela says, "The route is different to avoid as many cameras as possible."

They don't know that the cameras have already seen the van. Particle has added more resources than Tim's computer hardware for the search. One system sends an alert with the van's location. Particle is now tracking the van's position live. The computers are no longer needed, so Zoe can't tell what is happening. Particle calls Arseni, who immediately creates a three-way call with one of his people in Naples.

Arseni says, "Gino, the voice on the phone is a hacker. He is tracking the van we need. He will give you directions. Get the boys and get the van. Take it to the warehouse by the harbor. Remove anyone working in the warehouse if necessary. Call me when you have them."

Gino replies, "Yes, boss," as Arseni hangs up.

Particle and Gino talk. Both use English to communicate. It takes a few minutes for Particle to understand how to translate the camera identifier into a location on the map. In the background, Particle hears Gino yelling in Italian.

The van is now in stop-and-go traffic. They move inches at a time now. Sorina is getting frustrated with the lack of movement.

Sorina is talking to herself, "There has to be a better way. Is there a wreck or something?"

Not realizing that Angela is still on the call, Sorina jumps when Angela says, "I know it's frustrating. It is for all of us. Take the next right, and we will go the wrong way for a couple of miles to get around some of this. To answer your question, there is a wreck right after a construction area that has everything down to one lane."

It takes over five minutes to get to the intersection to turn.

They take a right turn, and two blocks along, turn right again. The flow of traffic is not fast, but it is moving. Angela asks, "Better?

"Yes. We need to be off the road soon."

"This is the longer way to get there, but you are moving. I'm estimating this route will save ten minutes."

"How long, how much time until we get there?"

"Forty-five minutes."

Following the new directions, they continue to move. Fifteen minutes later, a large, dark BMW sedan pulls up behind the van.

Angela says, "I'm connected and watching street cameras. There is a car behind you now. Listen carefully. If they try to cut you off in traffic, turn away. Prevent them from boxing you in."

Sorina now has both hands on the wheel. She keeps shifting her gaze from the traffic to the mirrors.

Angela says, "Martha is on her way, but she isn't close. I'm working at the traffic lights. If a light changes to yellow, keep going through it."

The next light turns yellow as she approaches. She keeps driving, and the light turns red just after she crosses into the intersection. The car continues to follow, going through the red light and causing the cross traffic to honk.

At the next light, the car turns, using the second lane. Sorina speeds up to get next to another vehicle in traffic so they can't go around. When the traffic in the left lane stops, the BMW moves back behind the van. Looking ahead, she moves to the left lane as the traffic is now stopped in the right lane. A car ahead is trying to turn right, and there are pedestrians. At the next intersection, she sees another BMW approaching from the opposite direction. At the intersection, it turns into her lane. She slams on the brakes and jerks the wheel to the left. Leaning on the horn, she gets the cars to move and gets turned around. Everyone is honking. People are yelling and have their fists up out of the windows.

As they approach the next intersection, Angela says, "You're doing great. Turn left down a street as soon as you can."

Sorina says, "What about the police? We aren't wanted for anything; we have done nothing wrong."

"Sorina, the police will hold you for transporting minors. The fight at the last warehouse is an open case. If they tie you to that,

we will have big problems."

Sorina jerks back and forth on the steering wheel in frustration, cursing in Romanian.

Looking in the mirror, the car behind her is gone. She looks around and sees it. It is across the median in oncoming traffic, trying to get around. The second car is behind her, with several vehicles between them.

At the intersection, the BMW cut across her path and comes to a stop. The car next to her is unsure what is happening and has also stopped. She can't move. The BMW behind drives up on the median and knocks over a trash can to get up alongside the van.

Two people exit the BMWs, one passenger from the blocking car and one from the side. They pull guns to make Sorina unlock the doors.

Angela says, "We will get to you."

S

Naples Warehouse

"Martha, they have them. When they took over the van, they destroyed Sorina's cell phone, so I can't track them."

"Claire and I are on the highway. We will be in Naples in about an hour."

Zoe says, "I've told Ralph to get to Naples. He has gear and the rifle."

Claire says, "That stuff won't help if we don't know where they have been taken."

"I'm working on it. The last camera view I had was south of the airport, heading west."

Martha says, "We talked about distractions. We need to get that plan moving. Zoe, get Ralph the vehicle we need. Part of this plan is for me to leave a trail."

"The trail will need to be decided in the moment to be most effective."

<<<>>>

"We have the woman and three girls. We don't know about the last girl. They claim she is dead."

Alexi smiles, "Someone needs to look at the body to prove she is dead. Where are you holding them?"

"We have them in a warehouse close to the Naples harbor."

"Naples, I can be there late tonight. I want to look at her as she dies. You can question them. Find out about the supposed dead girl. Get information about who has been helping them."

"I will handle it."

"Speaking about the people helping. What about the guy you said would search?"

"I have him working on it. He could take a while, but he will produce results. He is not on a tight leash. Less contact means fewer connections his former colleagues can investigate."

Arseni hangs up with Alexi and calls his enforcers at the warehouse. "I will be there in a couple of hours. We will question them. I want the girls to be fed. Let them use the water closet and have water. They know not to talk. When they understand I'm with Alexi, they will tell me everything, but I have to show them I'm Tim's friend."

"What about the woman? If we keep her tied up, the girls will see."

"Yes. The woman uses the water closet to drink water as well. She will be an example. The girls will see what happens when they don't cooperate and they go against Alexi. We need to get information but keep her alive until Alexi arrives tomorrow."

"We'll be ready when you get here." He hangs up the phone.

He walks across the warehouse receiving area to the office section. The girls and Sorina are in the conference room. No one wears a mask. The girls didn't have them on when they grabbed the van. They handcuffed Sorina to a chair. He opens the door and says, using Italian, "The boss will be here soon."

Sorina has been watching him approach through the conference room's windows. After his statement, she says, "We don't speak Italian."

The enforcer nods and replies in broken English, "Ah, yes. The boss will be here soon."

Sorina smirks and replies, "That is nice. Is he bringing ice cream?"

The enforcer smiles, "That is humorous; that is good. No, I'm going to order it. I need you to tell me what to order for food. Now that we know his schedule, we can get you water and food and will get everyone to the water closet."

Sorina says, "Why the sudden change?"

"It's not a change. I am just getting clear directions. The boss wants to talk about what happened in the other warehouse. Someone else was there."

The enforcer walks over to Sorina and removes the handcuffs. "My name is Gino, by the way."

"Hello, Gino. Can we go to the water closet?"

"Yes, but you have to stay in this office area. One of the boys will be at the door."

"So, we can't leave."

"No, the boss wants you here so he can talk."

Gino pulls out his phone. Opening an ordering menu, he puts it on the table and says, "I'll take one of you to the water closet. The others need to put their food orders into the cart."

The girls don't move. They are simply sitting and watching.

Gino says, "What are your names?"

"Well, which one goes first?"

Sorina smiles, "Try Russian."

"I don't speak Russian."

"Their names are Anastasia, Tatiana, and Zoya."

Sorina says in Russian, "One of you go to the water closet. The rest stay here for now. We will order dinner on his phone. They will question us about who was at the warehouse. He doesn't understand Russian, but others could understand."

The girls all stand and walk toward Sorina. Tatiana says, "I'll order food. Zoya, you go pee."

Sorina says in Russian, "He needs to take you to the water closet first."

Gino walks out the door with Zoya. The girls all start whispering to Sorina. Sorina reaches for the phone. "I'll call Angela's number, then order food. You all need to be ready. They want to know who helped us."

Sorina calls Angela's number. Angela answers the phone on the first ring. Sorina talks quickly, mixing English and Romanian, "They have us in some warehouse. There are six guys here, and the boss is on his way."

Angela says, "STOP. Now I know where you are. Help will be there soon. Don't fight them. Tell them whatever they ask. Now hang up before they see you on the phone."

One girl interjects, "But we know nothing to tell them. We didn't get their names; we don't know them. We only know Angela."

Sorina squints for a second. It makes perfect sense now. "Tell them you don't know. Don't lie. Our friends intentionally didn't let you know, so you can't tell them anything."

"Do we talk about Angela?"

"Yes. Don't lie. Angela is a voice on the phone. That is all we know. They did it this way, so we don't know, so we can't say."

"Will they come help, like last time?"

"They will help, but I don't know how or when. We need to order food."

Sorina quickly adds several meals to the cart, including one for

Gino, and then completes the order.

When Gino returns and asks, "Do you have food ready to order?"

Sorina nods, "Yes, I picked one for you and ordered the food."

Gino nods and says, "Thank you. I'll take the next one to the water closet."

Ralph pulls the airplane into the designated parking area. He is going through his checklist when an SUV, followed by a car, pulls up next to the plane. A man exits the SUV and walks toward the plane, carrying a clipboard.

Ralph gets out, shows his ID, and signs for the SUV. The man walks over to the car. He gets in the passenger seat, and the woman driver backs up. Then they drive away.

Based on Andy's instructions, he moves boxes containing surveillance drones and phones that he set up before the flight. He also moves the big rifle for Martha. He calls Andy after loading everything.

Andy answers the call and asks, "Is the SUV there and loaded?"

"Yes. You sound short. Did something happen?"

"The kids were stopped and are being held in a warehouse. We need the gear, and you need to be close to the location to get them out. I've just sent an address and directions. You will meet someone to get weapons. Then you will meet Martha."

"You can get weapons in Naples?"

"They think you are part of the group after the girls and are picking up weapons to attack Martha. This is dicey from my perspective, but Martha is right, it is the fastest way to get good weapons."

"I need to play a tough guy?"

"No, you need to play a courier. When you get to the warehouse, you switch to a marine."

Hunter and the team are in Naples, but he needs a better location. He emails from his phone. He emails the message to the address he communicates with Arseni. The subject is "Naples.....?"

Ten minutes later, he receives a reply. It has the address of the warehouse and a note, "Bait in the warehouse."

Convergence

As Clarie and Ralph drive away in the SUV, Zoe says, "Martha, the business in this building has shut down because of the COVID surge. It is after regular hours, but there could be people in the building."

Martha finishes turning on the last of the five drones on the ground. She grabs the augmented glasses, plugs them into the battery and radio unit, then puts the glasses on her head. The system displays random symbols on the glasses for a second, then they change. There is text scrolling on each lens. The text is the same, but not in sync.

Zoe says, "I have a signal from the unit now. Activating the system. You will see information."

Martha sees details about each drone as she looks. Battery status, camera settings. She looks at the building, and the information disappears.

Zoe says, "There is a small camera so I can see what you are looking at. The system has a delay in updating information based on what you see."

"Got it," as she puts on gloves, bends down, and picks up the bag with the rifle inside.

Walking up to the office access door, information appears. Martha says, "Too much info. None of that helps me."

Zoe replies, "Understood. I will scale it back."

Martha pulls out her lock picks and starts working on the door. She quickly opens it and enters. "Directions to the roof, please."

Zoe gives directions to the roof access. Martha has to pick three more locks to get access. At the last landing before the roof access stairs, Zoe says, "There are no cameras at the top section. I can watch up to the last landing and will let you know if someone shows up."

<<<>>>

After arriving in the area, Hunter got into the van with the team. The team parked its van and watched the area. They watched Martha, Ralph, and Claire take the drones out and put them on the ground. When Martha picked up the rifle and went into the building, they moved.

On the roof, Martha applies tape to the jam to prevent the door from locking and heads to the edge, facing the warehouse. It is overcast, with rain forecast for later. Her setup is not dependent on the weather being clear. The wind from the coast could be the only issue tonight. Taking the rifle out, she assembles the parts. Barrel in the receiver, suppressor on the barrel, and load the clip. She places it on the edge and scans the building. "Scanning the warehouse now. The roof is clear."

Zoe replies, "Drones are taking off. I will give you multiple views in a minute."

Scanning to the side, Martha says, "I have the SUV. They stopped before the warehouse."

"I have Claire on the phone. I'm keeping the conversations separate so both of you can focus. They are ready. Just as planned, you take out the muscle. When they are neutralized, Claire and Ralph will pull Sorina and the girls."

"I will stay on overwatch. You said Alexi's security guy is in the building. Can you highlight him for me? I would like him to be first."

"That is Arseni, and I will try. The drones don't give me close-up faces. They have infrared or slightly thermal cameras, and we are looking through windows and walls to get positions."

"Where did the drones come from?"

"I had them built to my specifications. They do things most other drones can't. We continue to use drones, and I wanted to have one with more capabilities. I planned for only five. The five are built, and I have already destroyed the trail, so they can't be traced. I didn't expect to use all five at once. Ralph was a convenient person who could get them where they were needed, hence you have drones."

Martha has a quick vision of Zoe destroying the trail by a server rack in a building, which suddenly sparks and catches fire. She smiles, knowing that isn't how it would happen, but it would look good in a movie.

"The drones are online, and the thermal cameras are ready. I will begin your feed once I have the targets. Don't move your head quickly."

"I'm focused on the building without the scope. I need to know the full picture; then, I will pick targets and begin."

The glasses start to change. Martha sees red dots appear. Over a few seconds, they grow to show human outlines, and more are on the sides. She watches as they start the change. Some turn green. Zoe says, "I count eight targets. Wait, just a minute."

The pictures change, with some features bright red and others varying to pink. "The color shows the distance from the wall you have to penetrate. I am adjusting the position you see to account for the bullet going through the brick wall."

"I'm putting my eye to the scope. Do I hear a drone behind me?"

"Adjusting the view to be appropriate for the scope. Yes, there is a drone behind you. I'm using it to help with the angle you're aiming. The rifle barrel is a great pointer."

"With the scope view, I'm seeing three. I'm going to have to shoot left to right. There is a cluster of red and green to my left."

"That will work. Just put the crosshairs of the scope on the red figures."

Martha looks up and scans the area one more time. She says, "Scanning, doing a last check before I commit." Her scan shows no traffic except a compact car. "Zoe, there is a car approaching the warehouse."

"That may be dinner that they ordered. I delayed the order, thinking we could get it done before the delivery."

Martha gets down and ready, eye to the scope, and says, "We use the food delivery as a distraction. Tell Claire to go."

In the building, no one is wearing a mask. Arseni stands over Sorina, who is again handcuffed to a chair, and asks, "Who do you think will come to save you? Tell me, and we can stop all this."

One man is holding Zoya by the throat. He is squeezing and holding her down. Her face is purple from being choked. The other girls are huddled against the wall a few feet away, looking at the scene with horror.

Arseni says, "Alexi wants you alive when he arrives. He gave no orders to keep them alive. Tell me."

Sorina is crying as she looks at Zoya being choked, the man choking her, and another man is to the right next to the other girls. She says, "I don't know. They don't tell me."

There is banging on the office door from the outside. Everyone pauses, looking at Arseni. Arseni hears Gino yell in Italian, "The food. I'll get it."

The wall explodes, and the man next to the girls flies across the room in pieces.

The man releases his chokehold on the girl as his head disappears. Blood and brains shower Arseni and Sorina. Arseni shifts when the bullet rips his torso in half. The shooting continues, and the remaining men outside the conference room are dead in seconds. From start to finish, eight shots in ten seconds. Two bullets are left for Alexi.

The only sound now is small pieces of brick that were shattered by armor-piercing bullets falling to the floor.

Dust is everywhere. As it settles, Sorina blinks, her eyes watering to clear the dust. She looks to see large pizza-sized holes in the brick wall. The attackers are all dead. She laughs.

The banging on the door starts again.

The girls are very confused. When they see and hear Sorina laughing, they move, first to Zoya, then to Sorina.

They hear yelling from the door area. It is in French, and the woman sounds furious. Then there is yelling in Italian, which suddenly stops.

Ralph comes around the corner with the rifle ready. The girls don't know him, and all immediately move to be in front of Sorina.

When they see Claire enter the room carrying bags of food, they relax and start talking all at once.

Claire says, "They are all dead. Damn, she made a mess."

"Zoe replies, "Ralph, sweep and check for all clear. Claire, get everyone to the SUV. Martha is moving."

Ralph says, "Will do," and walks to the door for the sweep.

As Claire walks to Sorina, she is looking at a repeat of the last time. The girls, Sorina, and there is blood everywhere. She drops the food bags, her knees shaking, on the verge of collapse. Her hands on her knees, she bends over. She breathes hard, her gaze fixed on her shoes.

Sorina says, "What's wrong?"

Claire looks up with an ashen face, and everyone can see she is crying. Zoe, who had heard Sorina's question, asks Claire, "What's going on? Are you okay?"

Claire takes a breath, stands, and says, "Seeing the bodies, the blood, the fact I shot someone just overwhelmed me. I'm sorry."

Zoya digs the handcuff key out of the pocket of the headless enforcer who was choking her. She goes to Sorina and unlocks one of her hands. Tatiana gets the key to unlock her other hand. Sorina stands and goes to hug Claire.

As they are hugging, Sorina says, "We both changed on that day. You are not alone."

Claire separates and nods, wiping her eyes with the back of her hand. "I'll be okay. We need to get out of here."

Martha is shifting the rifle off the edge of the roof. She says, "Now I shift locations, wait for Alexi, and make sure he follows me, or I kill him."

Zoe says, "I waited to tell you. A team of four-armed men entered the building. They are on the second floor. I'm sure they heard the rifle."

"What are my options?"

"Give me a minute, then open the roof access door. I'm bringing the drones back."

Martha puts the rifle down and walks over to the roof door. She pulls the door open and holds it for the drone, saying, "Tell Ralph to go, don't wait for me. The distraction with Alexi won't work if I have to deal with these four guys."

The drone flies past her into the stairwell, and Zoe says, "I'm letting Ralph know. That is the first one. The remaining four will go in, and you follow and do your thing."

"Do my thing. Is that what you call it?"

"What do you want me to call it?"

Smiling, Martha says, "That's fine." She is using her body to hold the door open while she checks the pistol. One clip, ten rounds. She is on the roof of a four-story building. The four-man team is now on the second floor. She will go to the fourth floor and use the office area.

Sorina is stiff and moving slowly. Claire says, "The man with *me is Ralph. He is with us."*

Two of the girls help Sorina as Claire is working to get them all to the SUV without Russian. When the girls get to the open area, they head toward the van, and Claire yells, "No." She points to the SUV, and the girls shift.

She gets Sorina to the SUV, saying, "Get in the front. I'll be driving."

Ralph walks out of the office door and says, "All clear. She did make a mess."

Turning to Ralph, Claire says, "We need the keys to the van," as she heads back to the door. "The police will be here soon, and we need to be gone."

Ralph says, "Hey, I already have them. They were in the office area when I did the sweep."

Claire stops and turns back to the SUV, where Sorina is climbing into the front. She gives a simple wave to Ralph as he walks to the van, saying, "See you in the Americas when we all get there."

Hunter is waiting across the street. He watched the team enter the building just before a rifle fired from the roof. The suppressor is effective, but he can still hear the shots. His eyebrows rose with the rapid firing. He looked over to see the holes appear in what looked like random spots in the brick wall.

After the four drones entered the stairwell, Martha slowly closed the door to minimize the noise. As she descends, the augmented glasses display the first drone view of the four men, just before the first man fires and destroys the drone. They employ typical tactical setups, using automatic submachine guns. They are wearing masks, vests, and gloves.

Arriving at the fourth-floor landing, Zoe offers to provide directions to the kitchen via glasses. "It will give you options."

Martha enters the area and heads down about eight cubes until there is a hallway to the side. She stops, considering options. She glances back at the stairway door and then ducks into the hallway. "Show me the camera when they are at the landing. Left eye only."

Martha hears gunfire as they shoot down drones. Zoe says, "One of them is bleeding from a head wound now."

When the camera shows them right outside the door, she shifts—turning and aiming at the door. The standard process is to open the door quickly and sweep in. Usually, people don't know when the door will open. Martha has a camera feed in her left eye. She knows precisely when they move. As the door flies open, she fires twice. The lead guy drops as she ducks back.

The men have been quiet, only using hand signals. Now they are on the radio and talking. Martha hears they have British accents. The first guy getting hit and dropping in front of them disrupts their entry. They react with gunfire toward Martha, yelling.

When Martha fired, her left eye picture changed to the security camera inside the room instead of the stairwell. She sees the men enter and turn left, away from her.

Hunter hears the fire and then the men yelling on the radio. He looks toward the warehouse, then the street. He crosses the street to the door that the team had previously entered. Opening the door, he waits a moment, then enters.

With Zoe shifting the cameras, she can see their positions as they move, turn, and come to a stop. They are along a wall, approaching a hallway intersection. She needs them to move to another area. Walking by a cube, she grabs the stapler and positions herself to toss it across the cube area.

They immediately shift. They are heading to the bathroom area, where there is a dividing wall. From their perspective, they see a normal hallway. They don't see that the long wall separates another hallway or section of the cube area. The cameras and Zoe give Martha the entire perspective. From Martha's perspective, she is simply two sheetrock panels away from them.

Martha whispers, "From the cameras, can you give me the outline in the glasses?"

As they travel down the other side of the wall, she is ready. Watching as the glasses show her the stick figures of the men. She is in a position on the other side when they are almost at the end of the wall. Zoe knows the head position by the distance to the light switch. Martha fires three times through the wall as she sprints back down the hall. Her shots are toward the heads of the figures in *the glasses. She shifts the gun between shots as she moves.*

Bullets in the head dropped two of the men. The third jumps away from the wall, puts his rifle on fully automatic, and starts shooting through the wall. Martha is already moving away to the other end.

As the man swings his gun, the bullets go through the wall. One bullet hits a wooden stud in the wall, and a piece of wood flies out and hits Martha in the left thigh.

She limps the last couple of steps to the end and turns right down the short hallway and around to the left, into the cube area. When the gunfire stops, she knows he will be reloading. She limps to the opening of the hallway the shooter is in, swings around the wall, and fires twice.

They are dead, but she goes to check anyway. She knows she has four shots left in the pistol, so she checks the downed man, confirms he is dead, and then takes his pistol, dropping the one she used. As she searches the body, she feels something hard in his vest pocket. She pulls out brass knuckles with small spikes above the knuckles. Zoe says, "That looks interesting."

Martha replies, "But it is not a good idea for me to be toe to toe with anybody right now," as she drops the knuckles on the chest of the dead man.

The pistol she picked up features a double-stack magazine with a higher capacity for more bullets. It is wider in her gloved hands. She is gripping and adjusting as she moves to the others.

Zoe says, "Good shooting. The move with the wall surprised me, but seeing it, I have to say it was obvious."

"Years of working with the sheriff in Waco. We practiced this stuff with me as the bad guy often. I never could use that move in practice."

"Martha, another man entered the building. He is coming up the stairs. Normal clothes and a pistol. He was outside watching before, and I didn't focus on him."

"He is probably the one directing these four, and could have information."

"Be careful."

"I'll wait for him. The stairs are not a good option. The camera is a real advantage. I like it."

"I'll keep that in mind for the future."

Hunter hears the two shots after the automatic fire and expects that means the team is down. This woman is good if she can kill his team.

He is going up the stairs. He needs to move quickly enough to complete this task before the police arrive, but not too quickly to walk into a trap.

The first guy's body props the door open at the top of the last set of stairs. Hunter stays to the side and checks all directions he can see before stepping into the room. Hunter is gripping the gun tightly, ready.

He takes two steps past the body when he hears from his left, "Drop the gun."

As he instantly shifts to get out of the line of fire, the bullet hits his left shoulder. The wound is affecting his ability to stabilize the gun with both hands. There is less pain when he lets the arm hang at his side. He is walking down the open hallway past cubicles. His legs are bent to keep his head below the cubicle walls. He arrives at an intersection in Cuba City. He quickly checks to the right, then shifts to the left. When he turns back straight, she is there. Her bullet hits his right shoulder.

His bullet hits the wall to Martha's left. She keeps the gun ready. The next shot will be in his head. She is gritting her teeth from stress. This is a high-risk. She wants information, but he hasn't dropped his gun. Pausing for a second, she slowly lowers the gun to point at his leg. She says, "Drop it."

Hunter shifts his gun to toss it instead of just dropping it. When he shifts, she fires and hits his leg just above the knee, which forces his leg to give way, causing him to fall.

He is down, shifting. Martha moves to get the gun away and moves around to see his face, still pointing the gun at him. He asks, "Why am I still alive?"

"You're different, not just trying to kill me. You were waiting outside and only came in when they were shot. I want to get information.

"You're good. Shooting through that brick wall and taking out that experienced team. Who are you? I know Mary Muller is fake."

"No one important. Who are you? You're not one of them. Why are you working for these people?"

"They have blackmail material about me. Most of it is fake, but they hurt my friends when I don't do what they want. I've tried to stop them, but the organization is extensive and powerful.

Everywhere I turned to get help, they were there."

Zoe says, "Not confirmed, but probably former MI6.

"Former MI6. Is anyone in that organization not compromised?"

Hunter says, "I'm not sure. I don't think the director is compromised."

Zoe says, "That confirms the MI6 connection."

"What do you know about this blackmail group?"

"Not a lot. What I do have is on my phone."

Martha shifts to search for the phone. He says, "My back pocket."

He reaches with his left hand, wincing, and pulls out the phone. Martha takes it and turns it on. She sees the screen for facial biometrics and holds it to his face. She still has the glasses on, allowing Zoe to see the screen. Zoe shows which icons to press in the glasses. The system wants a biometric unlock again, and she uses his face.

Zoe says softly in her ear, "I have access."

Hunter says, "I'll give you the password."

"Go ahead."

"God, Save The Queen. No spaces, and each word is capitalized with a single number between each, starting with three."

Martha nods, "Got it."

Zoe says, "Cute, got it."

"You don't need to write it down?"

"No. Tell me about the information on the phone?"

"Everything I could capture: notes, pictures, emails. You should also know, through my MI6 connections, we have identified the plane flying to Iceland, carrying the pilot and four women. I had to tell the group. They will be waiting when the plane lands."

Martha has been kneeling next to him. She shifts with the pain in her leg from the wood. The gun is on the floor next to her while she works on his phone. She puts his phone in her back jeans pocket and picks up the gun. She says, "Good. Our leak isn't the only source."

Hunter looks at Martha and smiles. "They aren't on the plane."

"Not even close. I can leave you. The police will find you and get you medical help."

Zoe says, "The information on his phone will get him and his friends killed if they think he gave it up. They have to think he was tortured."

"That isn't good."

Hunter says, "What isn't good? Are you talking to someone?"

"My partner is on the phone."

"We need his car keys if he has any."

Martha says, "Do you have a car?"

Hunter nods, "Keys in my pocket."

Martha digs the keys out and uses the fob to put them on her belt.

While she is getting the keys, she says, "My partner is reminding me that this information will get your friends killed."

Hunter says, "Unless they think I was tortured to get access."

Martha is frowning, looking at the floor. She looks at Hunter with a pained expression on her face. "I have to make it appear convincing, or they won't believe it."

As Hunter nods, she raises the gun and shoots his knee on the unwounded leg. Hunter sucks in his breath and starts breathing hard. He raises his hand and grabs Martha's arm. "It's okay. I tried, and I couldn't stop them. You're an outsider. You can make a difference."

Martha is gritting her teeth, not talking or looking at Hunter. She takes a breath and looks at him, saying, "I don't want to do this."

She puts the gun on his groin and pulls the trigger.

Hunter groans, closes his eyes, and squeezes Martha's arm. Opening his eyes, he looks directly at Martha. She says, "You have to bleed out."

He is breathing hard from the pain. He nods and says with a shaky voice, "Get the bastards!"

Martha nods and closes her eyes. A tear rolls down her cheek. Taking a shaky breath, she opens her eyes and looks at Hunter. She says softly, "My name." Then, louder, "My name is Sam." She puts the gun on his chest, over his heart, and pulls the trigger. As she stands, she puts the gun to his forehead and pulls the trigger. Taking two steps, she angrily flings the pistol across the cubicles and walks to the door.

Zoe says, "You need to get out. I will take care of the cameras. Go quickly to the north door. The police are already at the warehouse."

As Martha goes down the stairs, Zoe gives her an update. "The police are all over the warehouse. The amusing thing is that Alexi drove up just before the police arrived. He will have to explain some *things."*

"Is Ralph in the air? We need him out of danger."

"He is second in line to take off. He should be in the air within two minutes."

"Good. I'm at the north door. When I get out, which direction do I go?"

"Don't close the door. The last drone will exit with you so I can do overwatch. First, I will show you the directions with the glasses to exit the building area. Next, I will need to find his car. What do the keys show you?"

Martha pulls out the keys, looks at the fob, and says, "Aston Martin."

Holding the door open, the drone exits. It is wobbling, not flying smoothly. It flies out and then takes off straight up.

Martha looks down at the blood running down her leg from the piece of wood in her leg. She says, "I have a piece of wood in my leg; I'm pausing for a second."

"Do you need help? How bad is it?"

"Give me a second."

The pain worsens when she walks and shifts the material around the end of the wood. She takes a breath, grabs the end of the wood, and pulls. The pain is bad. She growls It is so bad. The jagged wood tears her leg as she pulls it out.

With the wood out of her leg, she leans against the building, breathing through the pain. Blood is flowing out of the wound. She takes out her dagger and cuts part of her shirt. Taking a breath, she shoves the material into the wound.

She hears the drone again. Looking up, she says, "Why is the drone back?"

"I'm checking on you. You stopped talking, but I can see the wound with the glasses."

"I'm ready," she says as she pushes off the wall and starts walking with a limp.

Zoe says, "The limp looks bad. Can you stop limping around the corner onto the high-traffic street?"

"I'll try. Which way?"

"Cross the street and stay toward the trees to be in the darker area."

Martha is walking without a limp. It is painful, and she is gritting her teeth, breathing hard. After several turns and blocks, Zoe says, "Next corner, turn right. The car is there."

Martha sees the car and goes to the left side. Looking in, she says, "Shit, right-hand drive."

Zoe replies, "You can drive it, no problem."

Martha takes her time getting into the driver's seat. As she gets in, she looks at the pedals and the transmission shifter. "The car looks like an automatic, which is good. I don't think my leg would work with a clutch pedal."

"This model is an automated manual transmission. They call it SportShift. Keep the glasses on so I can give you directions."

Checking around the front console area, Martha finds a charging cable. She takes her phone and plugs it in as she tells Zoe.

After a second, Zoe says, "Look on the dashboard for a message about connecting. Type the button for yes, so I can get into the electronics."

Martha taps the button, and Zoe says, "I'm in the car now. I'm going to disable the anti-theft items that the company can use. I will also block the vehicle from communicating its location, direction, etc. You can drive now."

The route immediately takes her into an alley. At the other end, she follows directions. Zoe says, "The drone is giving me an aerial view, but the battery is low. Turn right onto Via Foria and proceed east. Look for the signs for the airport and keep going north."

Martha says, "The plan was to take a train in Naples. With my bloody leg, I can't get on a train. Do I drive to Rome and then switch?"

"I'm working on the options. Start driving toward Rome."

Martha is settling in for the drive, and the impact of the last hour is catching up to her. Her hands are gripping the steering wheel. Her forearms are hurting. She has to breathe and force herself to relax her hands.

Zoe asks, "Are you okay?"

Martha takes her right hand off the steering wheel and smacks it. "He was one of the good guys!"

"I'm sorry, Martha."

"They are making us kill each other. He wasn't sent there to help me."

"Martha, stop! You can't fix everything. We are getting into it on this drive. It will be good to argue to help keep you awake."

"I know. I know. I have to focus on where I can have the biggest impact, but it is hard to ignore these situations."

Zoe says, "I would prefer that you never have to shoot or kill a good guy. It will probably happen. Use it to help you focus on taking down the people no one can stop. Claire, Charlie, Ralph, and I will help with the others."

"So, what about Alexi? He is still alive, and no one can stop him."

"How about the idea of getting others to go after him? I have things I'm working on right now. We have added several new team members. You take it easy and heal while we plan our next move. Claire has Sorina and the girls. The girls are out with no sign of pursuit."

"After I have a vacation? Is that what you mean?"

"Yes. Recover and plan. We will clean up an organization that could help."

Martha touches her leg. The bleeding has almost stopped. When she shifts, she feels a stab of pain. There is still a splinter in the wound. She needs to deal with the wound, and she can't maintain this level of intensity. "In the short term, I need to address my leg and rest. Let's focus on that. We can decide on the other stuff later."

"I'm looking at options for your leg. I considered contacting one of the blackmailed doctors, but decided against it."

"Blackmailed doctors. Are you saying, like in Mexico, when I had my surgery?"

"The same. In Italy, there are more restrictions, but the same thing is happening. I don't know if they will keep you confidential or inform the bad guys. So that is out."

"I agree. I prefer not to have another fight right now."

"The next best option is a surgical veterinarian. I found one about thirty minutes from you. Just keep going. I will let you know when to turn off."

A couple of minutes later, Martha says, "The glasses are not working. I think the battery is drained."

"Take the glasses off and throw them out the window. Leave the battery and cell pack in the car."

Fifteen minutes later, Martha exits the highway. Zoe says, "Surface streets now. They don't have highway exits at every cross street."

As Martha pulls into the parking area, Zoe says, "They are closed. I have hacked into their system and can help. You will need to find the surgical materials to clean the wound and then sew your leg back together. After bandaging the area, you will need to find alternative clothing. Surgical scrubs will work if they have any. Enter through the back service entrance."

Martha parks in the back, slowly gets out of the car, and then checks the trunk or boot of a British car. There is a small first-aid kit, a fire extinguisher, and a small bag. Inside the bag, she finds gloves, parachute cord, zip ties, wire cutters, jumper wires, and a lock-pick set. The pick set is better than hers.

Martha says, "Interesting tool bag." She puts on the gloves and takes out the lock-pick set. Closing the truck, she limps to the door. In about ten seconds, she unlocks the door.

As she enters, Zoe says, "The alarm is disabled."

Martha spends a few minutes walking through and searching. She hasn't turned on any lights. The LEDs on equipment that is powered provide a small amount of light.

The clinic's small animal operating room is inside and enclosed, so the lights don't shine out the window. Martha has found everything she needs. With everything on a tray next to the table, she hops on and starts cutting her jeans leg off. Through the hole, down, then around, and finally up to her hip. She knows there is still a splinter in the wound. She has lots of towels, saline wash, tweezers, and sutures ready.

Taking a deep breath, she says, "I'm starting. I won't be chatting during this."

"I'll help anyway I can," replies Zoe.

Martha takes the end of the shirt material she put in the hole and pulls it out while gritting her teeth and sucking in her breath. She squirts some saline into the wound and groans, almost screaming.

Breathing heavily several times, she picks up the tweezers with shaking fingers and slowly inserts the tip into the wound. She is breathing, eyes closed, while feeling with the tweezers. With no way to see into the wound, she searches for the splinter by feel.

She takes a deep breath and tries to relax. Slowly, she moves the tweezers and finds the splinter, grabbing it. Pulling it out causes more damage, bleeding, and pain.

Pandemic Hacker 2

With the splinter out, she says, "I have the big splinter." She pushes her leg to feel if there are more. Satisfied, she washes it with saline and grabs the sutures.

"Zoe, I'm suturing now."

"Great. Take your time. When you are done, don't forget to look for antibiotics. You need to take something."

"Right. I think I know where they are."

A few minutes later, Martha says, "Three stitches. I'm going to wrap this, change, and start cleaning."

While putting the suture items in the trash bag, Martha stops. She goes to get another suture kit and antibiotics. The label is in Italian, but there is a picture of a small animal. Antibiotics for a dog. She doesn't know how much to use, so she asks Zoe.

Zoe says, "For that antibiotic and your size, you need four cc. That will be a lot for one injection. You may need to do two injections."

The needle goes into her thigh, and she pushes hard to get half. She shifts to her other thigh and injects the rest of the dose above the wound area.

She is almost done cleaning when she hears a noise. "Zoe, I think someone is here."

"It is after midnight. The only legitimate reason for someone to show up is a medical emergency. Can you get out the back?"

"I'm not done cleaning."

"How much is left?"

"I need to wipe down the cabinets to make sure there are no fingerprints."

"Hurry."

Martha hears someone talking in Italian. Zoe says, "Translating."

Martha hears the same voices, male and female, repeating, but in English.

A female voice, "No!"

Male voice, "Tell me where they keep the drugs."

Female voice, "The drugs are for dogs and cats, not humans."

Zoe says, "They are talking loudly. Try to get out."

Moving slowly and quietly, Martha makes her way to the back door. She has a simple handbag with the clinic's logo. Inside are the two phones, bandage material, another suture kit, two bottles of rubbing alcohol, and a bottle of water she found. She is wearing light-blue scrubs.

She tried cleaning her tennis shoes, but they were still red from her blood. The last item is a large trash bag filled with used materials. She doesn't want to leave evidence.

Outside, she puts the bags in the car and gets into the driver's seat. She plugs in the phone, "Zoe, you're plugged into the car."

"Start the car and move. They could hear you. Keep the lights off."

When she starts the car, she immediately shifts it into gear and begins driving. The car's growl will attract people, so she needs to get away, but she has to keep the engine at idle.

The headlights are off until she gets onto the main road.

Zoe says, "The next step is a parking lot where you can take care of the car."

"Yes. There is a paracord in the boot. I can snake that into the gas tank. There is alcohol, I grabbed, to help get things going. I will need to create a spark from the battery to get things going."

Less than an hour later, she is close to Rome. The car sits in the rear section of a parking lot near shipping trailers. Zoe says, "You need to use the trains, but the schedule has a several-hour gap. You can use this time to rest. Try to sleep. I'll wake you when it's time."

Martha drinks more water and settles in. She is quickly asleep. When it's time, Zoe starts the alarm, with the volume slowly increasing until Martha wakes up.

A few minutes later, Martha says, "The paracord is in the gas tank and I need to wait for it to wick up the gas."

She pulls wires out from under the dashboard. While she is waiting, she drinks the remaining water.

"I don't have a lighter, so I'm putting alcohol on the paracord and running it to the interior so I can start it from sparks. It will essentially be a fuse. I don't know how long it will take."

"When you get it started, you need to head northwest. Follow the direction of the road. Five blocks away, there is a subway station. There are few trains right now. Wait and head to the main train station. Take the train to Rome."

"What do I do when I get to Rome?"

"Head to the central station, called Termini. At the train station, take a train to Milan. I will arrange for a car to pick you up in Milan. Will you be okay?"

"I don't have a choice. I will get water and something to eat."

"Martha, I have to say that plan was great at the start. The girls are out. After that, it fell apart pretty badly."

"I screwed up the planning to trigger Alexi and have him trail me. I should have been better at getting him caught in a compromised position."

"We couldn't expect a team tracking you, specifically after you. Now he will have to deal with the police. I've improvised with what I have to give the police a reason to hold him."

"What does that mean?"

"When Sorina contacted me from the bad guy's phone, I knew their location. I also hacked the phone, and now I have access to all his accounts. He doesn't need them anymore. That phone lets me scan for other phones in his contacts and then in the warehouse. I had enough information to hack Arseni's phone, the security guy."

"You found something on his phone?"

"He was keeping a file on activities—kind of an insurance policy he might have to use. The police will be very interested. I sent a text message, the police will see doing their normal stuff."

"That is probably the kind of thing that Alexi and lawyers will love to mess with."

"Well, I've added more information to make it hard for Alexi to get away. Details, locations of evidence, stuff that will help convict him."

Epilogue

Enzo arrives back at the office. He is still recovering and walking slowly. As he enters the building, other officers greet him, saying hello and expressing their gladness to have him back.

In the team office area, the top sergeant walks up after greetings and talks about how Enzo is doing. Enzo looks over and sees an evidence board with multiple pictures. He says, "What's this? You guys are using an evidence board."

"We are tracking multiple homicides now. While you were out, we got busy. Everyone can see the high level as soon as they walk in. Everyone will be glad you're back to help."

Looking at the pictures, he sees a picture of Giovanni. "What happened to Giovanni?"

"He was found shot in his car."

Shaking his head, Enzo says, "He would tell me stupid jokes."

"He has always just been the guy who tried to be funny. On the edge of organized activities. The rumor on the street was that he said the wrong thing to someone."

One of the office clerks walks up and says, "Hi, Enzo. The boss knows you're here and wants you to be in his office right now."

"Thanks."

In the office, Francisco is on the phone. He waves him to a chair. When he hangs up the phone, he says, "Welcome back. You made a mess I've been dealing with. Now, we need to clear up a few things."

He shifts a folder onto his desk. Opening it, he says, "This is my file on you and the Bologna warehouse. There isn't much, so I can't finish the report. I've been questioned, and not just by our people, about why you went to that warehouse. Why did you go?"

"I got a tip, a lead that said I needed to be there."

"Who told you?"

"Giovanni Alito. He said I would find a suspect in a compromising situation."

"You were there to arrest a suspect?"

"I didn't know what was going to be there. A suspect in a compromising situation could be anything. I can say I didn't expect to see kids huddled on the ground with armed guys there."

"Okay. I can't question Giovanni, so we put that aside now."

"Anything else? I want to get an update on the cases and get back to work."

"Yes. One more thing. Your secret source no longer likes you. The prosecutor received information directly. The case against the minister is moving forward. They found a video proving the minister was guilty."

"That's what he told you?"

"The prosecutor told me he received an email that told him who and where to search, and they found the video."

"Well. Good. One more bad guy off the street."

Three days later, Martha is sitting in the large lounge at the resort in the Italian Alps, close to the border with Switzerland. It features floor-to-ceiling windows providing a panoramic view of the mountains. The first snow of the season is falling outside. She is the only one in the lounge, but she is wearing a mask. She has her laptop, phone, and earbuds.

"The stitches are out of my side. My ribs don't hurt when I breathe anymore. The leg stitches need a couple more days."

Zoe asks, *"Has the resort been taking care of you?"*

"Yes. It has been nice."

Claire is a little choppy on the satellite phone. *"Martha is enjoying downtime. Something must be seriously wrong."*

Charlie is with Claire, *"I still don't know enough about Martha. Is that a joke?"*

Zoe says, *"Yes."*

Claire says, *"Enjoy it. You need to recover."*

"This place is very fancy. I'm not used to this. And Zoe won't tell me how much it costs."

Zoe replies, *"I got a great deal. Not that much. This is what we* talked about, Martha. Take care of yourself so you can help everyone else."

Charlie says, "I tallied the final numbers for our Croatia trades. You can afford it. The R for the trades is almost three. With that many millions at risk, it was a great set of trades. Having an AI to time the transactions is amazing."

Martha says, "The connection is choppy and hard to hear, but I don't know what that means."

Zoe says, "Charlie is using a good portion of the bandwidth for data."

Claire says, "That means you can afford to buy that resort if you want."

Zoe meekly says, "Do you want to buy it?"

"No."

A resort employee walks up with a fresh cup of hot cocoa and a small package for Martha. "Through the mask, he says, Ma'am, this was delivered for you."

"Thank you."

Martha opens the envelope but doesn't take out the new passport or the instructions. The instructions will tell her where to get a package, and she will need the new passport for identification. It will be her identity when she leaves the resort. She says, "How are Sorina and the girls?"

"They are loving the yacht. We are careful with our food. We did this and left so fast, we didn't get time to stock for this many people."

Charlie adds, "I did a run to the local store and bought stuff, but the options were limited. We will be in the Bahamas in five days."

Zoe tells them, "With the pictures taken after they were on the yacht, I have the new passports in production. They will be completed and delivered to the yacht before it docks. Everything will work out."

Claire says, "Martha, did you figure something out for Alexi?"

"I didn't get a chance in Naples, but Zoe was busy. His hacker has been arrested for hacking government computers. She stole most of his bitcoins and had his Bitcoin data center declared a hazard to the environment because of structural issues. His security *guy, Arseni, kept records and files with Zoe's help. The Italian police are investigating Alexi for multiple murders."*

"Zoe says, "Most of Alexi's info is true. I just added more information to Arseni's files for the police to use. For the data center, I paid the inspector more than Alexi not to hide the problems."

Charlie says, "The Bitcoin. How much, Zoe?"

Zoe replies, "I sold just over fifteen thousand Bitcoins at sixty thousand dollars per coin. I've already scattered it and invested it based on our plan, Charlie."

They all hear Charlie laughing.

Claire asks, "What are you doing now, Martha?"

"I'm not just lounging. I've been working. Zoe had an idea and challenged me to take it seriously and do the research."

Charlie says, "Okay, Claire and I are waiting. What is it?"

"I've listened. I've been thinking about it. Our little group is much bigger, but we are limited. The idea is to clean up an organization that could be helpful. An example is the Italian cop she found. He is doing good stuff but can't do everything. I've looked at several organizations. The FBI is too big. Italian police are too fragmented. If we can get an organization cleaned up and aligned in the same direction, we can do much more."

Zoe says, "She's doing the work, but my suggestion was to clean up a British organization."

Martha says, "Specifically, MI6. They have international responsibilities, so they can work across borders to stop these guys. They have resources. I don't know if they have the commitment or the discretion."

Claire says, "What are you going to do?"

"I'm going to London and doing some digging."

Zoe says, "Per the plan, Ralph diverted to Ireland with mechanical problems to disrupt the pursuit of the girls. He has been doing some shipments for Tilly while we wait for a jet. The pandemic has suddenly made private travel popular. He can fly Martha to London in a few days."

Martha asks, "Will I have a flat?"

"Getting work done through contractors is harder now. Everyone is doing something, but I will have a flat ready in a week. It has the basics."

Claire says, "You will have to spend time at the resort and relax. Enjoy yourself for a few days."

Charlie says, "We'll get the girls settled."

Zoe interjects, "I will lose control of this satellite I hijacked in twelve seconds. I'm covering the hack by making it appear to be a system reset caused by an alpha particle. When you get an internet connection, I will coordinate the next part of the plan."

Claire says, "Cut loose a little. See you in London."

Martha hangs up and takes a sip of her cocoa. Looking up, she sees a young, handsome man walk to the reception desk. He appears to be six feet tall, with black hair that has a wave in it. His short beard is showing around his mask. As he stands at the reception counter, she looks at his back. A light blue turtleneck and dark slacks. He works out, and his broad back and shoulders reveal his well-defined muscles. His pants are also showing a muscular butt.

Martha puts her cocoa down, shifts in the chair, grabs and opens her laptop so that she can see over the screen. With her earbuds in, she can't hear the conversation.

The man says, "I called. I'm Javier Rodriguez."

The receptionist says, "Welcome, Mr. Rodriguez. Sorry to hear about your car trouble. With the last-minute reservation, it will take a few minutes to get your room ready."

"Yeah, my GPS was sending me on this strange route, and then my car just stopped, like a switch had been turned off."

"Our system shows you stayed at a sister property in the past. We've upgraded your room. It will be ready in a few minutes. Please take a seat in the lounge. We will provide a complimentary cocktail while you wait."

Zoe updates her database to mark tasks complete:
1) Javier Rodriguez checked into the resort.
2) Room upgraded and next to Martha's room.

END

Requesting your review

Thank you for reading the book. I hope you enjoyed the story, and I would love to have a review. This will let everyone else know what you like and maybe don't like about the book. I'm always looking for ways to improve my storytelling, and I will read every review. I appreciate your feedback. The direct link to create an Amazon review is:

Amazon:
https://authorbdmurphy.com/PH2r1

GoodReads:
https://authorbdmurphy.com/GR1

B&N:
https://authorbdmurphy.com/BNr1

Acknowledgments

Thank you to my family and friends for their support and patience throughout my learning process. They provided editing assistance and offered positive encouragement.

About the author

B.D. Murphy started writing when the world hit pause—and he hasn't stopped since. He's the kind of author who sees a mystery in every machine, a plot twist in every algorithm, and a story hiding in your Wi-Fi signal. With a brain wired for engineering and a heart full of curiosity, Murphy crafts sci-fi that's clever, sneaky, and just a little bit subversive. If you like techy thrillers, real-talk characters, and endings that make you say "wait, WHAT?"—he's your guy.

Awards:
Feathered Quill first place–Science Fiction 2025–Sidney and Watson
Readers' favorite Silver 5-star winner–Science Fiction 2023–Pandemic Hacker
Readers' Choice Book Award Finalist–Science Fiction 2025–Nanite Evolution
Literary Titan 5 Star Gold Award 2025–Nanite Evolution
Global Book Awards–Bronze Medal 2025–Nanite Evolution.

Please like and follow.
Facebook: https://facebook.com/bdmurph73

https://authorbdmurphy.com